A Courtship on Huckleberry Hill

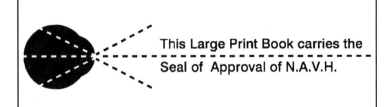

This Large Print Book carries the
Seal of Approval of N.A.V.H.

THE MATCHMAKERS OF
HUCKLEBERRY HILL

A COURTSHIP ON HUCKLEBERRY HILL

JENNIFER BECKSTRAND

KENNEBEC LARGE PRINT
A part of Gale, a Cengage Company

GALE
A Cengage Company

Farmington Hills, Mich • San Francisco • New York • Waterville, Maine
Meriden, Conn • Mason, Ohio • Chicago

Copyright © 2018 by Jennifer Beckstrand.
The Matchmakers of Huckleberry Hill.
Kennebec Large Print, a part of Gale, a Cengage Company.

LIBRARY OF CONGRESS CIP DATA ON FILE.
CATALOGUING IN PUBLICATION FOR THIS BOOK
IS AVAILABLE FROM THE LIBRARY OF CONGRESS

ISBN-13: 978-1-4328-4781-4 (softcover)

Published in 2018 by arrangement with Zebra Books, an imprint of Kensington Publishing Corp.

Printed in Mexico
1 2 3 4 5 6 7 22 21 20 19 18

A Courtship on Huckleberry Hill

CHAPTER ONE

Elsie Stutzman forced a smile and took the last bite of asparagus potato raisin casserole on her plate. She swallowed decisively, and it slid down her throat like a cup of wet cement.

Ach. She'd been so excited to come to Huckleberry Hill to live with her grandparents that she'd forgotten about Mammi's little cooking disorder. Elsie loved asparagus. She adored potatoes and even liked raisins. But when all three of them swam around together in a lumpy cheese sauce made especially for her, Elsie found it difficult to be enthusiastic.

"How did you like the casserole, dear?" Mammi said, her eyes twinkling with all the affection of a seasoned Amish *fraa*.

Elsie didn't know what to say. She would never do anything to hurt Mammi's feelings, but if she praised the casserole too eagerly, Mammi would insist on scooping her another helping. She shuddered at the thought. "It was *appeditlich,* Mammi," Elsie said, leaning back and patting her stomach. "I couldn't eat another bite."

Dawdi — Grandpa — spooned another large helping of casserole onto his plate. Elsie was astounded. Dawdi had eaten Mammi's cooking for more than sixty years. How had he survived? "This is one of the best meals you've ever cooked, Annie-banannie. The king of Canada doesn't eat this *gute.*"

Mammi giggled like a six-year-old. "Now, Felty. The king of Canada probably has two or three chefs to cook for him. I've never even been to cooking school."

Elsie caught her bottom lip between her teeth. Had anybody ever suggested cooking school to Mammi? If the whole family pooled their money, they might be able to send her away for a whole month. Elsie squinted in Mammi's direction. Asparagus potato raisin casserole with sides of creamed cabbage and banana cornbread muffins. *Nae.* Mammi was the dearest, most lovable soul in the world, but a month of Sundays at cooking school wouldn't make a dent in her odd culinary imagination.

"It's a very good thing the king doesn't know about you," Dawdi said. "He'd ask you to go to Canada to cook for him."

Mammi went to the fridge. "Now why would I want to do that when all I've ever wanted is to cook for my family? Everyone is always so appreciative."

"Of course they are," Dawdi said.

Well, at least they were appreciative in front of Mammi, but Elsie could think of no one but cousin Reuben of all the grand-children who actually enjoyed their grand-mother's cooking. Still, it gave Mammi so much happiness to bring joy to her family through food. She never needed to know that there was a lot more indigestion than joy going around.

Mammi clapped her hands. "Who wants cake?"

Ach, du lieva. If Elsie fell into the bathtub tonight, the lump in her stomach would pull her to the bottom. She'd drown for sure and certain. "I couldn't eat another bite, Mammi."

"Now, Elsie," Mammi scolded cheerfully, "this is your Welcome-to-Huckleberry-Hill-and-Happy-First-Day-of-School party. We had Welcome-to-Huckleberry-Hill punch, and now you need the Happy-First-Day-of-School cake. It won't be a party unless you eat some."

Elsie sighed. She would do anything to

9

make Mammi happy, even brave a daily stomachache — which was probably her lot in life for the next year. "Of course I must have some Happy-First-Day-of-School cake." The first day of school was still a week away, but Elsie didn't think they should let anything Mammi had baked sit that long. It might sprout feet and crawl away.

Mammi reached into the fridge and pulled out a beautiful layer cake with creamy dark chocolate frosting. The frosting swirled around the cake like a sky full of wispy clouds. It was truly a work of art.

Elsie glanced behind her. Was someone she hadn't met living in the house or had Mammi made that cake herself? "It's beautiful."

Mammi's eyes lit up like a propane lantern. "*Denki,* dear. I'm very *gute* with pastries." She set the cake on the table. "It's my mother's German chocolate cake recipe."

Elsie's mouth watered. She adored German chocolate cake. Maybe Mammi didn't need cooking school after all.

"I made some changes to make it low fat," Mammi said. She furrowed her brow. "Which, when you come to think of it, makes no sense at all. I gave up losing weight when my *mamm* passed on forty years ago, and you, Elsie, are thin enough to fit through a keyhole."

Elsie was almost afraid to ask. "What changes did you make to the recipe?"

"I used white beans instead of oil. Esther told me not to, but she is always trying to give me advice about my cooking, as if I didn't teach her everything she knows."

Aendi Esther, Mammi's oldest daughter, was famous for her cinnamon rolls. Elsie had a feeling Esther had learned to cook in spite of Mammi.

Elsie watched with trepidation as Mammi cut the cake and served her a generous slice. It looked like regular chocolate cake, except for the small bits of beans that dotted the inside layers. Elsie swallowed hard. She liked beans, and everything tasted better mixed with a *gute* dose of chocolate.

Mammi served Felty and herself a slice and sat down next to Elsie at the table. "Now, Elsie, dear, your *dawdi* and I invited you here because our school needed a new teacher. We are overjoyed you got the job."

Elsie nodded. She was overjoyed too. Considering how the Amish gossip mill operated, it was a miracle she had been hired anywhere, and she wouldn't mess it up this time. She'd hold her tongue, no matter how much the parents or the stodgy old school board provoked her. Elsie scooted a piece of the bean-and-chocolate cake around with her fork. The children would like her — at least, she hoped so — and she had no doubt she would love the children. It was the adults Elsie had a harder time with. She firmly believed that school was for the children, not the parents, and had unfortunately shared that opinion on one too many occasions. The school board didn't especially appreciate a schoolteacher who spoke her mind.

"I am wonderful grateful to you for helping me to a job, Mammi." She'd been living in Charm with Onkel Peter and Aendi Clara for three years teaching school. Without a job, she probably would be forced back home to Greenwood, which was even smaller than Bonduel, Wisconsin, where Mammi and Dawdi lived.

Mammi waved her hand in the air. "Never mind about that. The teaching position wasn't the real reason we wanted you to come, but for sure and certain, it came at a convenient time."

Elsie nibbled on her bottom lip. "You didn't want me to come here to teach?"

"*Jah,*" Mammi said. "I mean, *nae.* We know how badly you want to be married.

We asked you to come to Huckleberry Hill so that we could get you a husband." Mammi practically glowed. "Felty and I have just the boy for you."

Elsie's mouthful of thick, gooey, beany chocolate cake got stuck halfway down her throat. Mammi thought she wanted a husband?

So did Wyman Wagler. Despite her blunt refusal, Wyman had persisted in pursuing her all over Charm. He had chased her clear out of Ohio. She had hoped that if she left town, Wyman would take the hint that she wasn't interested. Her declaration "I refuse to marry you" hadn't stopped him. Surely her moving to another state would cool his passion. She could only hope.

Elsie cringed at the very idea of hurting Mammi's feelings, but the thought of being matched to some pale-faced, eager, sniveling young man was even more unbearable. She set her fork decisively on her plate, signaling to her grandparents that she had something wonderful important to say. She tempered her words with an affectionate smile. "Mammi and Dawdi, I came to Bonduel to teach school. I'm only twenty-two. I don't want a husband."

The wrinkles on Mammi's forehead bunched tighter together. "Ever?"

Of course she wanted to marry.

Someday.

But if she gave her *mammi* even the slightest hope that she might budge, Mammi would not rest until she'd introduced her to every boy in the county. "The whole family knows how *gute* you are at matchmaking, but Aaron needs your help more than I ever could. He's almost twenty-nine and thinks girls are silly and stupid." Her brother would be annoyed if he knew that Elsie had stabbed him in the back, but she was desperate, and Aaron was the perfect distraction.

Mammi nodded, and her wrinkles grew wrinkles. "Aaron is a hard case. But I haven't found a girl yet who can put him in his place." She tilted her head to one side and drummed her fingers on her cheek. "It wonders me if Carolyn Yutzy might suit. She used to be in my knitting club."

"She's a wonderful-*gute* girl," Dawdi said, between hearty bites of cake.

Elsie nodded her encouragement. "Carolyn Yutzy? What kind of girl is she?"

Mammi smiled and patted Elsie's hand. "You're so unselfish, thinking of Aaron's needs before your own, but Carolyn can wait. You're here, and Aaron is trapped in Greenwood. He's not going anywhere. There will be plenty of time to work on him once you're engaged."

Elsie sighed, much louder than she intended, but at least she had Mammi and Dawdi's attention. Her resolve to hold her tongue died like a frog on the interstate. "Mammi and Dawdi, you are the best grandparents a girl could ever ask for. I love you to the moon and back, but I don't want you to match me with anyone. I want to concentrate on being the best teacher I can be. Boys are nothing but a distraction, and I'd rather not have to fend off any romantic notions while I'm here. There are plenty of boys back in Charm, or even Greenwood." Not that she'd consider dating any of them — especially Wyman Wagler — but it might make Mammi feel better about Elsie's marriage prospects.

"The boy I have in mind is truly your perfect match," Mammi said, cheerfully unmoved by Elsie's pleading.

"It wonders me if he isn't too tall," Dawdi said, obviously trying to throw Elsie a bone.

Elsie took it. "*Jah.* I'm only five foot one. I don't like tall boys."

Mammi frowned. "How tall is too tall?"

Elsie pulled a number from the air and hoped Mammi's intended boy was a giant. "Five foot four." Wyman Wagler was five-five.

Unfortunately, this didn't seem to deter Mammi in the least. Her laughter sounded like a bubbly brook tripping over the rocks. "Felty is six-three."

"I used to be six-three," Dawdi said. "I'm shrinking all the time."

"Well, dear, you used to be six-three, and I'm only five feet, and look what a *gute* match we are."

Dawdi scooped another piece of cake onto his plate, making sure to catch the errant beans. "The best match I ever could have asked for, Annie."

"It doesn't matter," Elsie said, trying not to lose her temper. How could she be cross about her *mammi*'s stubbornness when Mammi had probably passed that trait on to Elsie? She stood and stacked the dishes.

"No need, Elsie, dear. You are the guest."

"I'm going to do the dishes every morning and every night while I stay here. It's the least I can do."

Mammi smiled, and the lines around her eyes congregated closer together. "But you'll be busy with your boyfriend."

Elsie started filling the sink with hot water. "Please don't match me up with anyone, Mammi. I don't think I could stand it."

"But, dear, you can't see how unhappy you are. Only a *mammi* truly knows, and I

16

hate seeing my grandchildren miserable."

Elsie sighed again, even louder than before. She should have known better than to try to discourage Mammi. It was like trying to hold back the Ohio River with her arm. "Would you agree to a compromise?"

Mammi squinted in Elsie's direction. "What kind of compromise?"

"Let me be for four months. I need the time to improve my teaching. Then, in January, you can match me up with whomever you want." Elsie nibbled on her bottom lip. January was a long way away. Maybe Mammi would forget about the whole scheme by then.

Mammi brightened considerably. "Let's hang a big calendar by the door and mark off the days until January. That will give you something to look forward to during the long winter." She practically leaped from her chair and pulled the small calendar from the wall above her sofa. "This will never do. I'll have to go buy a bigger one." She took a sheet of paper from the drawer and did some counting in her head. She wrote on the paper, rolled some tape behind it, and stuck it on the wall. It said *134 days to January 1.*

Felty nodded. "A countdown. You're wonderful clever, Banannie."

17

Elsie gave Mammi what passed for a smile. Her grandparents were both in their eighties — a time when old people started forgetting things. They'd probably forget the whole thing before Thanksgiving.

Unfortunately, Elsie had a creeping dread that when it came to love, Mammi's memory was as sharp as a tack. Elsie would be foolish to hold out even a sliver of hope.

CHAPTER TWO

Sam Sensenig was so mad, his hat would have caught fire had it been a hotter day. He didn't have time for this. He barely had time for the work he needed to do on the farm. He certainly didn't have time to put a teacher in her place. Wasn't it the school board's job to learn everything about a new teacher before they hired her? How hard would it have been to find out that the new teacher had a mean streak, that she liked to pick on little crippled boys who couldn't fight back? How dare she? How could the school board have been so negligent? And how would Sam ever make things right for Wally?

One thing was for sure. That new teacher was going to get a talking-to she would never, ever forget. If he reduced her to a quivering blob of tears, all the better. She'd get a taste of what she'd done to his *bruder* — and it was mighty bitter.

Sam jumped off his horse, Rowdy, and stormed toward the schoolhouse. He hadn't taken the time to hitch up the buggy, because his wrath needed to be swift and severe. He opened the schoolhouse door and stomped up the stairs, making sure the smack of his boots against the steps was loud and intimidating. The teacher would know someone was here who wouldn't be bullied or belittled.

At first he didn't see her amid the bright posters and stacks of books. Nearly every inch of wall space was covered with pictures and words, as if a children's book had exploded and its contents had stuck to the walls. A hand-drawn picture of a cowboy hung on the wall above one of the bookshelves. The cowboy played a guitar, and notes floated around him like gnats in the air. "Sing Unto the Lord a New Song, Psalms 96:1," it read, and at the cowboy's feet were empty hooks and block letters that said, "Perfect Attendance."

An overflowing basket of bright red paper apples graced the opposite wall with a sign that read, "Welcome." Each of the apples had a child's name written on it, Wally's included. Too bad Wally wasn't truly welcome in this classroom. The teacher had made that very clear.

The decorations were surprisingly bright and cheery for someone rotten to the core.

A head popped up from the other side of the teacher's desk. She must have been kneeling behind it when he came in. She stood, and he took an involuntary step back. The new teacher wasn't old or broad-shouldered or severe-looking, like Sam had pictured her when Wally had come home crying. She looked young, definitely younger than he, with shiny mahogany hair and shocking green eyes. And she couldn't have been much taller than five feet — just a slip of a thing. She didn't look capable of bullying anyone.

Sam squared his shoulders. He knew better than to judge someone by the way they looked. This new teacher might well be the prettiest girl in five counties, but if her heart was black as coal, her beauty was an illusion.

Her smile lit up the entire room, and Sam caught his breath and nearly forgot why he had come. *"Hallo,"* she said.

Sam shook his head a couple of times to clear it. No pretty face would distract him from his brother's pain or from the fact that she had caused it. "Are you the teacher?" he said. He meant it to sound like an accusation.

She stiffened. "I am," she said, as if daring him to attack.

He didn't like that little show of defiance, as if she hadn't done anything wrong. He stepped around the desk and got closer so he could loom over her, glaring down at her like she was a bug he was about to squish. She tilted her head way back to look him in the eye, but didn't back away, didn't grab the desk behind her for support, didn't even flinch. Her composure irritated him to no end. "What gives you the right to pick on my little brother?"

She matched his glare with an icy one of her own. The room got twenty degrees colder. "May I ask what little *bruder* we are referring to?"

"Wally Sensenig — my little *bruder*. He came home crying. You should be ashamed of yourself."

"Wally — the boy who is taller than me and outweighs me by about forty pounds? That *little* brother?"

Sam spat the words out of his mouth. "*Jah.* Wally, the boy who only has one leg. The boy who can barely walk. The cripple who you made stay after school to wipe desks. He got a blister. On his one *gute* hand."

"Hmm." The teacher narrowed her eyes

and angled her head as if to get a better look at him, as if he were the one who had to justify himself. "I believe I underestimated your *little* brother. He threatened to send you over here to tell me what was what, but I was skeptical. Wally really does have you wrapped around his finger, doesn't he? I'm impressed at his cleverness."

"His cleverness? Wally isn't clever. He's a cripple, and you embarrassed and shamed him in front of the class today. You're unfit to be a teacher, and I'm going to call you up before the school board."

She cocked an eyebrow and pursed her lips, seemingly unimpressed with his threat. "Maybe you should sit down before you pop a blood vessel in your neck. And don't call Wally a cripple. He's better than that."

Sam crossed his arms over his chest and tried to look as immovable as a boulder. "I demand you apologize for embarrassing my brother."

She still seemed completely unconcerned, as if she hadn't done one thing wrong in her whole life. "What do you want me to apologize for? For the part where your brother flipped Toby Byler's math assignment into the mud? Or maybe the part where Wally put his foot on the desk and refused to do his letters?"

"*Jah,* go ahead and poke fun at the fact that Wally only has one foot."

The teacher shook her head in disgust, which made Sam seethe. Who did she think she was? "You want me to apologize?" she said. "Well, I suppose I am sorry. Sorry that you have let your *bruder* get away with this nonsense for so long."

"What do you know about me or my family?" Sam growled. "I won't let a mean, petty bully like you think she can judge me." He pointed in the direction of his house, as if she'd be able to see Wally from here. "Our *dat* is dead. Did you bother finding that out before you decided to pick on him? Our *mater* is sick, and I have three younger *bruders* and a *schwester* to take care of."

The teacher pressed her lips together. Oy, anyhow, she was stubborn. "I'm sorry about your *dat,* but that's no excuse for bad behavior."

"And a little boy's deformity is?"

"You keep calling Wally little. Why? Is it how you think of him, or how he acts?"

Sam had had just about enough of this nonsense. "Don't you dare try to pin the fault on me. You're the one who ridiculed my *bruder* in front of his friends."

She sighed a great sigh, in case he hadn't already gotten the message that she was

24

barely putting up with him. "What exactly am I supposed to have done to your brother?"

"You know full well what you did."

"I'd like to hear what your *bruder* told *you* that I did."

Sam drew his brows together. "Are you accusing my *bruder* of lying?"

"I'd like to know what you think I said to him. If your *bruder* really told you the truth about what happened, then I can't imagine why you're so mad, unless you're naturally unreasonable and short-tempered."

Sam caught her words with resentment. He only lost his temper when he had good cause. He wasn't anything like the teacher, who took her anger out on helpless cripples. How dare she admonish him? "You're the one who's unreasonable and short-tempered, and my little *bruder* suffered for it today."

The teacher expelled a deep breath, laced her fingers together, and pinned him with a sober gaze, as if she'd made her mind up about something. "It does not give me pleasure to tell you this, Mr. Sensenig, but your *little bruder* is a selfish, careless boy who is bent on making every child in the school as miserable as he is."

"And you've decided this after only five

days? That says more about your character than it does about my brother's behavior."

Sam's throat burned. This teacher was beyond belief. How had the school board missed her mean streak?

"Does your brother have a prosthetic leg?"

The sudden change of subject made Sam's head spin. "What?"

"A fake leg. Does your brother have one?" she said.

"*Jah.* We fitted him for a new one only a month ago, but it hurts his stump, so he doesn't wear it."

She studied his face, and he thought he caught a hint of compassion. He was obviously imagining things. "I would think that hobbling around on those crutches would be even more painful, don't you?"

"I don't know. Who are you to judge?"

"I'm not judging. Just curious. I want to help."

Sam threw back his head. "Hah. Wally doesn't need your help. Stick to teaching him reading and arithmetic, and show some kindness and pity, if you're capable of such emotions."

She quietly sucked in a breath and bit her bottom lip. It was a cruel thing to say, but he wasn't going to quit telling the truth just because it was painful. And this teacher needed to hear it plain. "Wally does not need my pity," she said softly, as if trying to rally her composure.

Guilt niggled at the back of his skull like a mosquito buzzing near the ceiling. He'd nearly done what he come to do — which was make the new teacher cry — and now that she looked on the verge of tears, he didn't have the heart to push her over the edge. He took a step back and shoved his hands into his pockets to make himself seem less threatening. "You need to examine your hard heart, Miss . . ." His voice trailed off. He didn't even know her name. She didn't offer it. "The *kinner* need affection, not cruelty."

The fire leaped into her eyes again. "I don't need instruction from some presumptuous busybody on how to do my job."

Sam had no idea what *presumptuous* meant, but it couldn't have been a compliment.

Apparently finished with the conversation, she pulled the chair out from under her desk, sat down, and started shuffling through some arithmetic papers. "Stick to farming or belittling people or whatever it is you do for a living," she said, not even looking at him, "and I will concentrate on my students, thank you very much."

Sam wouldn't let her get away with dismissing him so easily. He went around to the other side of the desk and pressed his hand over those math papers. She was forced to look up. "I'm keeping my eye on you, so don't think you'll be able to get away with anything like this again. If you so much as sneeze in Wally's direction I'll see to it that you are dismissed. Is that clear?"

She narrowed her eyes and glared at him as if he were manure on her boots, but she didn't reply. She probably realized she'd already said too much. He turned on his heels and clomped down the stairs. He'd told her off but good. Wally was safe.

Her voice caught his ear just as he reached the outer door. "What about allergy season? Can I sneeze during allergy season?" Then she laughed, a light, airy laugh that caught him off guard and made his blood boil over.

He slammed the door behind him and made the whole school rattle.

Chapter Three

Sam walked in the back door and tried to leave his bad mood outside. He had too much on his plate to spend one more second stewing about Wally's teacher. Lord willing, she'd mend her ways. If not, he could take his complaint to the school board.

Sixteen-year-old Magdalena stood at the sink scrubbing her hands with a small brush. Maggie worked at the egg factory, and she always came home with filthy hands. Nothing less than five minutes of scrubbing would do for a girl as fastidious as Maggie. She couldn't stand dirt under her nails.

Mamm sat at the table refilling the salt shaker and the sugar bowl. She'd been better these past few weeks. The thought of the *kinner* back to school always perked her up.

Sam went to the sink and gave Maggie a kiss on the forehead and to the table to give his *mamm* a kiss on the cheek. "How was work today, Maggie?"

"*Ach,* the sorter broke twice, and we ended up cleaning eggs by hand."

"The Yutzys should have Noah Mischler rebuild it," Sam said.

Maggie snorted. "They need a new one, that's what. That thing is forty years old, at least. Amos thinks it can hold together with duct tape and baling wire forever."

"Where were you off to?" Mamm said. "I saw you ride the horse out of the yard like his tail was on fire."

Sam frowned. He didn't want to trouble Mamm with the details. "I went to see the new teacher."

Maggie's ears perked up. "*Ach.* Danny says she's wonderful nice."

"Danny said that?"

"*Jah.* And Perry thinks she's pretty." Maggie's eyes sparkled with a tease. "Did you go to see if the rumors are true?"

Perry and Danny were Sam's two youngest brothers. Wally was thirteen, Perry ten, and Danny had just turned eight. Perry and Danny were both in school with Wally at the one-room schoolhouse, but Sam hadn't heard any complaints from either of his youngest brothers about the teacher. That was probably because Perry and Danny had both of their legs and all of their fingers. The teacher probably only picked on cripples.

Sam pressed his lips together. Was that pretty little uppity pip-squeak of a girl really that mean?

"Well?" Maggie prodded. "Is she as pretty as they all say?"

Sam barely heard the question. "Pretty is as pretty does."

Maggie stopped scrubbing and eyed him suspiciously. "What happened? You're not already on the teacher's bad side, are you?"

"She was harsh with Wally today. I made sure she knew I wouldn't stand for that."

Maggie's eyes got rounder. "Sam, how could you? It's only the first week of school. You can't be mean to the teacher. Our three *bruders* have to live with the consequences the rest of the year."

"I wasn't mean," he said, only half telling the truth. He'd gone with the express purpose of browbeating that teacher into submission, and though he hated to admit it, he had let his temper get the better of him. It was *deerich,* foolish, of him to think he could persuade the teacher to treat his *bruder* kindly by offering her nothing but anger. Righteous indignation was one thing, but losing his temper had made him appear weak and unreasonable instead of in control and dead serious.

That teacher had done something inexcusable, but Sam hadn't been much better when he'd confronted her.

But, *ach, du lieva,* mistreatment of his *bruder* always made Sam irrational. Did no one have compassion anymore? Didn't anyone follow the commandment to love thy neighbor as thyself?

"Is Wally all right?" Mamm said, the familiar lines of worry appearing in rows along her forehead.

Sam patted his *mater*'s arm. "He was wonderful upset when he came home."

"Will you check on him?"

"I was just about to go down. With a cookie." He grabbed three cookies from the jar and ambled down the stairs.

Sam heard the ominous music and the screams of death before he got halfway down the steps. Wally must really be upset. He was playing *Medal of Honor*.

The basement in their house wasn't much more than a cellar with cement walls and floor, some food storage shelves, a sofa, and a TV. After Wally's accident, the bishop had given permission to have the basement wired for electricity so Wally could have something to take his mind off his pain and the amputation. Sam had bought him an Xbox and a couple of harmless games. That was four years ago, and Wally spent hours down here when he wasn't in school. He always seemed to have a stack of games. Sam had no idea where Wally got the money to buy them, but he figured Wally had some kindhearted friends who gave him a few extra dollars when they could.

Even though the bishop had given permission, Sam wasn't thrilled with the video games. They were so glaringly *Englisch,* some of them so violent that even Sam couldn't watch. But Wally loved them, and there was little in his life that brought him any sort of pleasure or comfort anymore. Sam didn't have the heart to put a stop to it, or even limit Wally's playing time. The poor kid could barely walk. It seemed cruel to take away his one source of happiness.

Wally had gotten really *gute* with the controller, even though he was missing three fingers on his left hand. Sam got to the bottom of the stairs and glanced at Wally's hand, feeling that familiar ache right at the base of his throat. No kid should have to go through life with only one foot and half a hand. It wasn't fair. Little boys were meant to run and play. Little boys' *faters* shouldn't die of heart attacks. *Gotte* had asked too much of this one little boy.

The kid who half an hour ago had hobbled into the barn with tears streaming down his face was nowhere to be found. With the game controller grasped firmly in his fists, Wally sat on the sofa and stared at the screen as if all his hopes and dreams lived there. He rocked his body back and forth with the motion of the action on the screen, occasionally groaning or growling, depending on how he was doing.

"I brought cookies," Sam said, plopping himself next to Wally on the sofa.

There was a few seconds' delay before Wally glanced in Sam's direction. "Cookies? Great." He took his hand off the controller long enough to grab a cookie from Sam and take a bite.

"What are you playing?"

"*Medal of Honor.* I'm on the fifth level — almost done."

Wally's soldier shot his gun, and digital blood splattered across the screen. "I thought I told you to turn off the blood." No boy's happiness depended on seeing gore and dismembered bodies.

Wally grunted as if he were very put out. "It's funner with the blood."

"I doubt it. Maybe you should play *FIFA.*" There was no blood in *FIFA,* even when a player got injured.

"Just let me finish this level."

Sam didn't like it, but he let Wally keep playing. He'd found out a long time ago that finishing a level was almost the most important thing in any video game. It was better to interrupt after the level was over. Sam sat for another five minutes, blankly staring at the screen, letting his conversation with Wally's teacher play over in his head. Something hadn't seemed quite right. "Wally, did you throw somebody's arithmetic papers in the mud?"

"Huh?"

"Did you throw a kid's math work in the mud?"

No answer. Wally's tongue stuck out of his mouth. He must have been at a challenging part of the game. Sam's irritation bubbled up like milk on the stove. He didn't want to ruin all the fun, but didn't he have a right to expect Wally to listen when they needed to have a serious conversation?

After the day he'd had, Sam was in no mood to take a back seat to the video game. He got up from the sofa and switched off the TV.

That got Wally's full, resentful attention. "*Ach,* what did you do that for? I was almost done with the level. Turn it back on."

"I need to talk to you, and you don't listen when you're playing your games."

"Turn it back on, Sam. I can listen and play. I just need to finish this level."

Sam shook his head. "If you can listen and play, what was the question I just asked you?"

Wally took the drastic measure of pushing himself up on his one leg and hopping toward the TV. "You can't just turn it off while I'm in the middle of a level."

For the second time today, Sam thought he might explode with anger. But he never yelled at Wally. Wally had enough hard things in his life. Sam went behind the TV and unplugged both the TV and the Xbox. "Don't hop. You'll hurt your knee."

"Ach!" Wally growled. "Now it won't even save. I'll have to start all over again."

Sam swallowed the guilt that rose like bile in his throat. Wally had so few things that made him happy. "I'm sorry, Wally. You can turn it right back on, but I need to talk to you." He put his arm around his *bruder* and helped him back to the sofa.

Wally clamped his arms across his chest and turned his face away. "It doesn't matter now. My game is ruined."

Sam sat down next to his brother and pushed a cookie in his direction. Wally didn't even glance at it. "Did you throw someone's math paper in the mud at school today?"

"You stopped my game to ask me that?"

"*Jah.* How you treat others is more important than any *Medal of Honor* game."

Wally still refused to look in Sam's direction. "I wasn't looking where I was going, okay? You're not going to get mad at me for accidentally bumping into someone, are you? Reuben made a joke, and I turned around and laughed and knocked into some goofy second grader. The kid dropped his stupid number paper and cried like I'd shot him with a rifle. Teacher got mad at me for something I didn't even do."

That seemed reasonable. The teacher had overreacted, just as Sam had suspected. "I'm glad to know you weren't purposefully being mean. But you should try to be more careful. You're tall, and the little kids don't always have time to get out of your way."

Wally scowled. "I'm not very stable on my crutches — but you wouldn't know how that feels."

Sam swallowed the lump in his throat. "*Nae,* I wouldn't. I'm sorry for that." Sam couldn't begin to imagine how hard it must be for Wally, so he tried to make things as easy as possible for the poor kid. That's why he'd dropped everything and ridden to the school. He'd be hanged before he let some snooty teacher mistreat Wally. She'd show Wally the respect and understanding he deserved, or Sam would see that the school board hired someone who did. "I'm sorry more people don't show compassion."

Wally suddenly seemed very interested in having a conversation with Sam. "Did you talk to the teacher?"

"I talked to her."

Wally leaned closer as if eager to hear some juicy gossip. "Did you tell her what was what?"

Sam pressed his lips together. Wally shouldn't take so much pleasure in the teacher's comeuppance. Sam had tried to put her in her place, but he wasn't so certain she'd listened. It annoyed him to no end that she didn't seem intimidated or persuaded. "She won't give you any trouble again, and if she does, you let me know, and I'll go to the school board."

"I warned her not to cross me," Wally said. "I bet she's sorry now."

"She said you put your foot on the desk."

"So? My stump hurts when I sit for a long time. It helps relieve the pain on that side to prop my foot up."

It made perfect sense to anyone with a

reasonable bone in her body — which didn't seem to include Wally's teacher. How could Wally be expected to sit at his desk like a normal child? Sam frowned. Wally seemed to be able to sit quite comfortably for hours in the basement playing Xbox. Of course, the sofa was much softer than a school desk chair. Maybe Sam should send Wally to school with a pillow.

"Reuben put his feet on the desk too. Teacher didn't like that, because Reuben had mud on his shoes. She got mad about the mud, but then she let Reuben go home and made me stay after and clean all the desks. She made me do it twice because she said the first time wasn't *gute* enough. I got a blister."

"You already told me."

"I probably won't be able to hold the pencil tomorrow. Not that Teacher will care. Like as not, she'll make me do my work anyway."

Sam's gaze flicked to Wally's right hand. There was a little blood blister on the tip of his ring finger, but it didn't seem to get in the way of Wally's video game. Could it really hurt that bad? Sam got blisters and scratches all the time. He'd learned to work past them. If he let every little injury put him down, he'd never get anything done on the farm.

Sam pressed his lips together. Why was he second-guessing this? Wally had been through something terrible. He already had enough pain in his life. The teacher had made things worse, and now she knew that Sam wouldn't stand for anyone hurting his little *bruder.*

Sam messed up Wally's already unruly hair, jumped from the sofa, and plugged in the TV and the Xbox. "I'm going out for chores. Let me know if you need anything."

Wally didn't answer. He was already pressing buttons on the remote, turning everything back on, looking for his game. Sam hoped Wally would be able to finish his level without having to start all over again.

Sam bounded up the stairs and back into the kitchen. Maggie had finished washing her hands and was holding a pink envelope with a heart stamp. "This came for you in the mail."

Who would be sending him a pink envelope? There was no return address, but the handwriting was definitely a woman's. A small knitted clump of yarn fell out of the envelope when he opened it. The stationery inside was also pink.

Dear Sam,

My granddaughter has just come to town, and I would very much appreciate it if you would come to our house and meet her. She is from Greenwood and needs a husband something wonderful, and I think you will do the trick. It has to be a secret because she wants to wait until January, but I say, the early bird gets the worm. Would you and your family come to dinner at our house on Friday night? You can meet my granddaughter, and I will make my famous Indonesian beef stew. It's a vegetarian dish.

Much love,
Anna Helmuth and Felty —
but he didn't write this letter.

P.S. If you need more convincing, I have enclosed a small dishrag.

Sam drew his brows together. Anna and Felty Helmuth were a very kind old couple who lived on the other side of town on a rise of ground they'd named Huckleberry Hill. Anna had a reputation as a very *gute* matchmaker and a very bad cook. They didn't live in Sam's district, but he took a load of hay to Felty every summer and

41

helped him get it into the haymow. Anna always told him what a nice boy he was. Sam probably should have been pleased. When someone wanted to match you up with one of their relatives, it was usually a compliment.

But he had no time for a wife, and a girl who needed her *mammi* to find her a husband was probably thirty-seven years old with no teeth. Sam preferred teeth. He folded the letter and handed it to Maggie. "What should I do about this?"

Maggie quickly read over the letter and giggled. "We should go, Sam. At least I wouldn't have to cook dinner."

"Anna wants me to meet her granddaughter. I'd rather get a cavity filled."

"But what will you tell her?"

Sam fingered the whiskers on his chin. "I'll think on it while I do chores. It will have to be an honest excuse that discourages her from ever asking again."

Maggie smiled. "From what I hear, nothing discourages Anna Helmuth."

"That's what I'm afraid of." Sam gave his sister a wink and walked out the back door. He didn't have time to waste on bad teachers or toothless girls. The corn would be ready soon. He had to make sure everything was prepared before his uncle and cousins came to help bring it in.

Perry and Danny were in the barn milking the cows. They only had two cows, so Sam couldn't justify buying a milking machine, but he wanted to expand. He had plenty of *gute* pastureland and enough acreage to grow more feed corn. He'd need a silo, but those weren't expensive. With a dozen heifers, he could justify putting in milking machines and a storage tank, and he'd almost saved enough money to do it. The trick was convincing Mamm that a small dairy would be a wise use of their money.

Sam helped Perry muck out, then tended to the animals and cleaned his tools. Then he and Danny walked the fence line looking for repairs that needed to be made before it got dark.

Sam nudged Danny and pointed to an errant wire sticking out from the fence. "Here's one." Danny held the strand of wire steady while Sam wrapped it back around itself.

Sam's next-door neighbor, Rose Mast, wandered toward them from her side of the fence. "*Hallo,* Sam. *Hallo,* Danny. Do you want to see our new goat?"

"A new goat?" Danny said, showing the

excitement only an eight-year-old could muster.

Rose smirked in Sam's direction. "Mamm wants to try making goat cheese."

Sam raised an eyebrow. "Who doesn't like goat cheese?" Rose's *mamm* was always elbow-deep in one project or another. She never finished anything, so her house was cluttered with half-done quilts and needle-work, exotic spices and strange kitchen gadgets that never got used. *Ach, vell.* The good news about goats was that they didn't require much care. The new goat could live quite happily for many years, running loose in the Masts' pasture without any attention at all.

Danny looked up at Sam. "Can I go see it?"

"Hurry. Maggie wants us in for supper at five o'clock."

Danny gingerly slid between the barbed wires of the fence to Rose's side of the pasture. He secured his hat on top of his head and peered at Rose. "Will you show me?"

Rose glanced at Sam and fingered one of her *kapp* strings. "Dat built a little pen behind the barn. Go and see. Prissy and Lydia Ruth are out there."

Danny took off across the pasture toward

the three-story barn that loomed over the Masts' farm.

Rose leaned her hand on a fence post as her gaze darted back and forth between Danny and Sam. "Did you like the cookies?"

Sam furrowed his brow. What cookies was she talking about? "They were *appeditlich.*" That was true enough, even if he couldn't remember eating them.

She stuck out her bottom lip. "You never got them, did you?"

He grimaced. How could she see through him like that? "I'm sorry, Rose. It's been a hard day. I don't remember any cookies. I'm sure they were delicious. Everything you make is *gute.*"

Her face fell. "I found a recipe especially because you said you liked coconut."

Coconut. Okay. He vaguely remembered coconut. Last week some sort of lumpy, roundish coconut cookies had appeared at his house on a paper plate. Sam and Wally had eaten them without even bothering to find out where they had come from. "*Ach.* I remember. The coconut haystacks. Wally and I ate every last one in about half an hour. I'm a *dumkoff* for forgetting."

Rose brightened considerably. "I forgive you, but I'm writing my name on the plate next time. I don't want you to forget. A girl gets worried."

Rose and Sam's families had been neighbors for years. The Mast children and the Sensenig children had grown up together, practically like siblings. When Sam and Rose were younger, they and their brothers and sisters had spent most of their summers playing together. They ran around the pastures and explored the woods for hours at a time. They hid in the haymow and waded in the creek a mile from the house, sneaking frogs and pollywogs home in Mamm's canning jars. Mark and Mose, Rose's older *bruders,* built a secret hideout in a big old tree in the forest, and they all took turns guarding it from intruders.

Of course, once they got older, they had naturally grown apart, except for Rose's brother Mark and Sam's sister Naomi. They had married each other four years ago.

Sam and Rose were still friends, even though they didn't spend nearly as much time together as they had when they were children — mostly by Sam's choice. After Sam's *fater* had died, Sam had even less time to spare. Rose was now at the age to think about marriage. When a girl and boy spent a lot of time together, people just assumed they were a couple, and Sam didn't want anyone to think he and Rose were a couple — especially Rose herself. She'd had a little crush on him when he was twelve and she was the ripe old age of eight, but her infatuation had petered out years ago.

Rose had always been the tagalong kid sister — whiny and prone to pout. Just because her brother had married his sister was no reason for the gossips to expect a romance between the two of them.

Rose had sandy brown hair, full lips, thick eyebrows, and eyelashes that touched her cheeks when she blinked — they were that long. She was pretty, in her own way, and lots of boys were interested. Rose stuck out her bottom lip altogether too often, but Sam couldn't imagine it would be long before she had a steady boyfriend.

Sam knelt down and snipped an errant wire with his cutters. "Did you go to the gathering last night?" Maybe she'd already met her future husband.

"*Jah,* but it wasn't any fun. You didn't show up."

He shrugged. "Gatherings are for *die youngie.* I'm too old yet."

Rose harrumphed. "You're only twenty-four. No one would call you a bachelor until at least thirty."

"It's good for you to go to the gatherings.

47

You're younger."

"The new teacher was there, and she's your age."

Sam clenched his teeth. The new teacher? How dare she show her face when she couldn't even show kindness to one little boy in her class?

Rose frowned. "*Nae,* that's not right. She said she is Davie Bontreger's age, and Davie is twenty-two." She sighed. "*Ach, vell,* it doesn't matter. You should have come."

"What did you think of the new teacher?" Sam said, trying not to sound hostile.

"She's short. If you visited during school, you'd probably think she was one of the scholars. She played volleyball almost the whole time until the singing. My sisters like her. Prissy says she wrote a song about the times tables so the *kinner* could learn them, and she sings and smiles all day long."

Sam slid his wire cutters into his pocket. "She was mean to Wally today."

Rose's mouth fell open. "What did she do?"

"She got after him for accidentally bumping into someone on the playground, and then he put his foot on the desk, so she made him stay after school and clean up." Sam pressed his lips together. When he said it out loud, it didn't seem all that serious.

But it was Wally she'd mistreated, a kid who deserved compassion, not contempt.

Rose nodded. "He does put his foot on the desk."

"How do you know that?"

"Prissy says he does it all the time."

Of course he did it all the time, but the teacher hadn't taken the time to find out why. "His stump feels better if he rests his foot on the desk."

"Oh." Rose blinked rapidly and fanned up a breeze with those eyelashes. "Come to think of it, Lizzy complained that the teacher wouldn't let her braid Mary Lynn's hair during singing time. That seems a little petty, doesn't it? Do you think I should mention it to my *dat*?"

Rose's *dat* was on the school board. "He should know that we're concerned. It would be *gute* for them to keep a close eye on her."

"Okay. I will tell him. We must protect Wally. Things are hard enough for him already."

"*Jah*," Sam said. Rose understood about Wally, and Sam was grateful for the sympathy.

Rose seemed to forget what they had just been talking about. "What's Wally's favorite kind of cake?"

"What?"

"I'm going to make Wally a cake for being such a brave boy. What is his favorite kind?"

"I don't know. He likes chocolate, I guess."

Rose clapped her hands. "*Wunderbarr.* I will make him a chocolate cake and you a coconut pineapple cake."

"*Denki.* Wally will be very happy."

Rose was only nineteen, yet she had more kindness and sympathy in her little finger than that new teacher would have in her whole lifetime.

Too bad the school board hadn't hired Rose.

Chapter Four

Elsie blew a frustrated puff of air between her lips.

Toilet paper.

Who would steal the toilet paper?

She had her suspicions, but it would be unfair to make assumptions when school had only been in session for two weeks and she was just getting to know the children. Children needed the concern and care and trust of their teacher, even when they didn't deserve it, or maybe especially when they didn't. Elsie's expectations were high for all her students, but some of them resisted her guidance. Those were the ones who needed her most of all — children like Wally Sensenig, who had been coddled and babied for so long, he was incapable of behaving any other way.

With two rolls tucked under her arm, Elsie trudged to the porta-potty that served as a bathroom for the school. She wrinkled her nose as she opened the door. At least it wasn't as unbearably stinky as the outhouse at the school in Charm. But still a porta-potty. The thought was repulsive enough.

She caught a glimpse of the children play-ing in the yard for recess. It was strange that they never played any organized games, like volleyball or softball. Those were Elsie's favorites. She might have to get a game go-ing.

Wally Sensenig stood off to the side with his friend Reuben Schmucker. Wally leaned heavily on his crutches, never joining the other children in their play. The crutches couldn't have been comfortable to run with, but Elsie sensed his leg was more of an excuse than a reason. Instead of being someone on the outside looking in, it seemed that Wally was overseeing the chil-dren rather than wishing he could join in.

Wally Sensenig was unlike any child she'd ever taught before. He was missing his leg just below his knee and three fingers on his left hand. He limped around on crutches and acted as if he were the most picked-on, unfortunate boy in the whole world. Yet Wally was used to getting everything he wanted. Elsie had overheard him tell his friend Reuben about his video games. He had a TV and a video game player in his house, which his brother had specially wired for electricity.

Wally had already defied her several times, and they'd only been in school two weeks. His schoolwork was shoddy, at best, and his attitude was worse. After three days of cleaning up after school, he'd finally stopped propping his foot on his desk, but now he used it to trip the little kids when they had the misfortune of passing his desk. Elsie prided herself on keeping her temper firmly in control, but Wally had tempted her resolve many times.

She couldn't help but be impressed with how cleverly he had manipulated everyone and everything around him. The children catered to him, and not because they felt sorry for the one-legged boy. For sure and certain, they were afraid of him. Wally Sensenig was a bully pretending to be a victim, and Elsie had no idea what to do about him or how to help.

One thing she could not do was appeal to his family. Wally's *bruder* was the most foul-tempered, unreasonable person Elsie had ever had the misfortune of meeting, no matter how breathtakingly good-looking he was.

When she had looked up that day and seen him standing in her classroom, her heart had tripped all over itself, and she was thoroughly disgusted with herself for reacting that way. Wally's *bruder* was sinfully handsome, with a mop of curly, light-brown hair and a day's growth of stubble that made him seem mysterious and discontented. Even his scowl was attractive, like some tortured hero from a romance novel. That was, until he opened his mouth. She'd never met anyone quite so rude, and as a teacher, that was saying something.

She probably shouldn't be so hard on him. Wally had manipulated his *bruder* just as he had every other person in his life.

He was clever that way.

But that didn't mean Sam Sensenig had a right to storm into her school and yell at her. *Ach!*

Wally had come to school the next day gloating like the king of the hill. He'd marched right up to her desk first thing. "My *bruder* said he told you what was what."

She had pretended to look puzzled for half a second. "Your *bruder*? Which one was he? I've had so many parents visit in the last few days."

Wally had frowned in confusion. "My brother Sam. He said you'd better not pick on me or he'll tell the school board."

She had tapped her finger to her cheek.

54

"*Ach,* yes, Sam. He seems like a very nice person. He wanted to make sure you're learning all you can. We had a very nice visit."

That was not the reaction Wally had been looking for, and he had crept back to his seat and kept his mouth shut for a good half hour.

He had no doubt expected Elsie to turn into a little mouse and let Wally have free rein of the whole classroom. He was quite put out when Elsie had made him stay after school and wash desks again. *And* empty all the garbage cans — not an easy task on crutches. Elsie had fully expected to see Wally's *bruder* a second time in as many days, but Wally must have felt unsure enough that he hadn't mentioned it to his *bruder.*

Gute. Elsie would have been perfectly content never to lay eyes on Sam Sensenig again.

She stuck a new roll of toilet paper in the dispenser and put the two extras on the shelf next to the toilet. She'd ask the children to keep a close eye on the porta-potty. Maybe the toilet paper thief wouldn't dare a second time.

"You were making fun of me because I'm crippled," she heard from a voice just

55

outside the porta-potty. It was Wally. No one else could manage to sound threatening and whiny in the same breath.

"We were not. Max and me just wanted to play catch, that's all."

"You looked at me the whole time you were throwing it," Wally said. "You know I can't play softball because I only have one leg. Do you think I'm a freak?"

"*Nae,* Wally. No one thinks you're a freak. We're all sorry about your leg."

Elsie held her breath. Not only did the porta-potty stink to high heaven, but she was listening carefully for any sign of physical contact. If Wally started hitting Johnny Wengerd — at least that's who it sounded like — she would throw that door open and make sure that boy got all five-foot-one inches of her wrath.

"Softball is not allowed at this school," Wally said. "If I can't play, no one can play."

"You think he's a freak, Johnny. Admit it." Reuben Schmucker was there too. It made sense that Wally would have someone to back him up.

"I do not."

Despite her misgivings about how sanitary the porta-potty was, Elsie pressed her ear to the door. She didn't think they'd moved away, but she heard nothing but silence.

Just as she was about to emerge from Smelly City, Wally spoke. "Bring me a quarter every day for the rest of the year, and I'll forget you laughed at me."

"I've only got five whole dollars."

"Then bring me five dollars, and I'll forgive you. But I'm warning you, never play softball again, or I'll tell Teacher you make fun of cripples. She'll give you the ruler."

Elsie bit down hard on her tongue. How dare Wally use her to scare poor Johnny Wengerd. She'd never, ever used the ruler on a child in her life, even though she was sorely tempted to show it to Wally Sensenig. Apparently Wally liked to invoke a higher authority when he made his threats. He'd done it with his brother. But Wally would soon learn that those tricks wouldn't work on her.

"Okay, Wally. I'll bring the money tomorrow," Johnny said, and even from inside the porta-potty, it was plain he was close to tears.

Their footsteps faded, and Elsie finally felt safe to come out. Just in time too. She had almost given in to the urge to pass out from the fumes.

Elsie had heard the expression *hopping mad* before, but she had never actually known what it meant until now. She stomped back to the classroom, too angry to think about ringing the bell. The scholars would get a few extra minutes of recess while her blood cooled to a simmer.

Elsie would not put up with that type of behavior in her school, no matter how big of a tantrum Wally's brother threw — no matter if the school board fired her tomorrow.

She paced back and forth between two rows of desks, thinking of all sorts of appropriate consequences for Wally Sensenig. She wouldn't use the ruler or any other form of corporal punishment. The Amish taught nonviolence, and Elsie believed that applied to the classroom too. Children learned best in an atmosphere of love, not one of fear or shame. But that didn't mean she wasn't demanding. She expected the very best her scholars could give her, and they loved her for it — or at least, she hoped they did.

Wally was a special case. He was manipulative and clever, pitiful and unlovable all at the same time. And his brother had let him get away with bad behavior for too long. Elsie heaved a sigh. Wally was thirteen years old, almost fourteen — big for his age, which was why he thought he could bully the other *kinner* — but he was also just a boy. Adolescent boys were full of spice and energy, and they could be mean and stupid. Wonderful stupid.

But that wasn't a reason to give up on them.

Elsie had never given up on one of her students, even when they gave up on themselves, like Wally had. Wally wasn't a lost cause, by any means. All anyone had to do was look at his leg to see he'd been through something horrible. No one, no matter how old, would have been able to handle all that pain and all those emotions and come out undamaged — that included Wally and his entire family.

Wally's *fater* was deceased. According to one of the boys she'd met at the last gathering, Wally's *bruder* Sam had responsibility for the farm and for the family. He was just as confused and lost as Wally was. Maybe she shouldn't have been so harsh with him.

She shook her head. Sam had been rude and abrasive. He got everything he deserved. But she could at least understand why he had reacted the way he did. It was probably all he could do to keep things together at home.

Unfortunately, all this insight didn't solve the problem of what to do about Wally right now. She couldn't allow him to bully his classmates, but she couldn't force him to be nice either. If she wanted a real change of heart, it would have to come from Wally himself.

Elsie sat at her desk and pulled open the bottom drawer. It was time to give Wally a lesson he'd never forget, and she would do it at second recess today. Wally would make a wonderful fuss, and Sam Sensenig would be at the school so often, he'd probably have to set up a tent on the front steps. He'd do a lot of yelling and scowling and gnashing of teeth.

Elsie squared her shoulders. She could handle Wally's big brother, and maybe teach him some manners in the process. Unfortunately, she couldn't snub her nose at the school board. Wally needed her, and somehow she would make Sam understand. But would she have a job long enough to see it through?

Elsie was so antsy, she could barely sit through the arithmetic lessons, and she was the teacher. She finally gave in five minutes before she was supposed to dismiss them for recess. "Students," she said, rising from her desk and lifting her softball mitt into the air. "For recess this afternoon, we are going to play a big softball game with the whole school."

An audible gasp spread throughout the room like a leak from a bicycle tire. Elsie stole a look in Wally's direction. He pressed his lips together and stared down at his math paper as if he were suddenly very interested in his times tables. He wasn't happy about this. Not happy at all.

Gute. The more she could ruffle his feathers, the better. Wally was about to get thrown twenty feet outside of his comfort zone.

Some of the children glanced doubtfully at Wally as if wondering if they needed his permission to play. Elsie clapped her hands to divert their attention. "Grab your mitts," she called, smiling as if the greatest adventure awaited them just outside. Some of the children jumped to their feet. Others tentatively put their papers in their desks and dawdled, as if expecting Elsie to tell them she was only joking about a softball game.

"I left my mitt home," Lizzy Mast said, her gaze flicking to Wally's face.

"You can borrow someone else's when they go up to bat," Elsie said.

Little Mary Zook, a new first grader, stood beside her desk with her finger in her mouth. "But what about Wally? It's not nice to leave him out."

Reuben Schmucker folded his arms across his chest as if daring Elsie to try to make him budge from the desk. "*Jah.* We don't play softball. It hurts Wally's feelings."

Elsie smiled as if she had some very *gute* news to tell. "It is so thoughtful of you to think of Wally, but we're not going to leave him out. He is going to play with us." She gave Wally the most pitiful, most sympathetic look she could muster. "Unless you're afraid to play."

Wally frowned. "I'm not afraid."

"*Gute.* Then let's go."

The children trickled down the stairs, the ones who even bothered to bring their mitts to school anymore picking them up on the way out the door.

Wally's frown turned into a scowl. "I'm not afraid," he said, plunking his good leg on the desk. "Are you blind or just plain stupid? I'm missing a leg. I can't play."

She decided to ignore the "stupid" remark. Softball was the battle she needed to win. "You can play. You've got one *gute* hand and another pretty *gute* hand. It's not that hard to hold a bat and hit the ball."

Wally grew more and more surly. "I'm not playing."

Elsie shrugged. "Suit yourself. If you don't play, you have to be one of the bases."

His eyes widened to twice their size. "I'll get stepped on."

"Then come and play — or are you afraid you can't even hit as well as the first graders?"

"I can't hit better than anybody. I'm crippled."

Elsie cocked an eyebrow. "I don't think you're a cripple. You're missing a leg. So what. I'm a girl, but I can still hit better than you or Reuben."

Reuben finally stood up. "You can't hit better than me."

"I'll bet I can," Elsie said. Her smug smile was sure to irritate both of them.

Reuben swatted Wally in the shoulder. "I want to play. Come on. We're better than her."

Wally narrowed his eyes in Reuben's direction. "Go play. What do I care? You're not my true friend anyway."

Reuben slumped his shoulders. "Okay. I won't play."

Elsie pretended not to care either way. "You both still have to come out. And you each have to be a base." She had to work very hard to keep from laughing at the looks on both their faces. They obviously were astounded by the thought that Miss Stutzman would actually make them be bases for reals.

They were slow, but she was insistent. She found them each a mitt — even though they protested they weren't playing — and shooed them out the door. Outside, Jethro Glick and Tobias Raber were tossing a tennis ball with each other. There were also three softballs getting passed around. Wally and Reuben stood with their backs to the backstop, no doubt trying to decide if they should defy the teacher and sit on the steps or join a team so they wouldn't get stepped on.

Elsie had two eighth grade girls, Ida Mae Burkholder and Ellen Zook, pick teams. Reuben and Wally were the only eighth grade boys. Was it any wonder they thought they ruled the roost?

Ida Mae, a bright, mature, very sweet girl, cleared her throat and chose Wally Sensenig first thing. Elsie could have hugged her. Wally almost gave himself whiplash, he turned so fast. The surprise on his face was priceless. Someone had actually picked him. He immediately wiped all emotion from his face and shrugged as if he couldn't care less, but he slowly ambled around the backstop on his crutches and stood next to Ida Mae, who gave him a shy smile and a nod.

Reuben got chosen second, and since he didn't have to prove his friendship anymore by not playing, he pumped his fist in the air and ran to Ellen's side.

Elsie had twenty-three children in her class. They divided into teams of twelve. She put herself on Reuben's team because she wanted to pitch to Wally. The goal was to make him very, very angry.

Elsie's team was up to bat first. Wally limped all the way out to the edge of the field where it was unlikely he'd get a ball hit to him. He was on the team, but it was obvious he didn't want to make a fool of himself trying to field a ball. That was fine with Elsie. Wally was on the team. That's all she could hope for. Yet.

They let the younger children bat first, so it was a short inning, but *die kinner* laughed and squealed and jumped for joy even when they got out. Elsie's heart swelled three sizes. No child should go through a school day without the chance to play softball. Wally had gotten his way for far too long.

Elsie insisted on pitching for her team. She lobbed easy ones in for the little kids to hit and faster and harder ones for the older students. Johnny Wengerd was her first baseman and a crackerjack catch. He never missed a ball if it came within five feet of

65

him. After three innings, everybody on the other team had batted but Wally.

Elsie bit her bottom lip as Ida Mae handed him the bat and said, "It's your turn, Wally." It sounded like a question.

Wally stared at the bat in Ida Mae's hand. He narrowed his eyes and scanned the faces of his teammates, almost as if he were daring them to laugh at him. Almost as if he *wanted* them to laugh at him.

Of course he wanted them to make fun of him. Their laughter would give him a reason to make them feel guilty about ever playing softball again and to feel even worse about poor one-legged Wally Sensenig. But Elsie hoped that there was some small part of him that wanted to play for the fun of it, wanted to hit and run just like the other kids. That was the part of Wally she had to help him capture. Hopefully, he hadn't buried it so deep that it couldn't be found.

Everyone on the ball field seemed to be holding their breath. Surely Wally was disappointed that no one was inclined to laugh or even snicker. Did he not realize how frightened they were of him? Toby Byler, a brave second grader, dared to give Wally an encouraging smile. Wally ignored him.

Tossing one of his crutches aside, Wally took the bat from Ida Mae. He half limped, half hopped to home plate, clutched his crutch handle with his left hand, and lifted the bat in his right hand. He wasn't going to be able to hit much of anything like that, and he certainly wasn't going to hit anything very far. What he really needed was another leg to stand on. A prosthetic leg would do the trick.

Elsie tossed a nice, easy ball over the plate. She wanted Wally to hit it. The lesson would come afterward. He swung the bat wildly and missed, throwing himself off balance and nearly toppling over. He righted himself, turned around, and glared at his teammates. Surely now they would give him a reason to throw a tantrum. With eyes wide, his teammates held deathly still, as if even the slightest movement would cause an explosion. Even Wally's brother Danny seemed to understand the importance of this moment. He didn't budge. Elsie wanted to cheer. What *gute,* kind, smart children they were.

Wally raised his bat again, and Elsie did her best to lob one right in the path of Wally's swing. He chopped awkwardly at the ball and managed to make contact. The ball pinged off the bat and bounced three feet behind home plate.

"Foul ball!" Johnny called.

With that small bit of success, Wally grew more determined. He tapped the bat on home plate then pointed it at Elsie. "I'm hitting it over your head this time, Miss Stutzman."

Elsie arched an eyebrow and smiled. "Oh no, you won't."

With singular concentration, Elsie tossed the ball right over the plate where Wally would have the best chance of hitting it. It was a wonderful-hard swing, especially considering he had one hand around his crutch. The ball glanced off the bat with just enough power to make its way back to the pitcher's mound. Elsie couldn't have asked for a more perfect hit — almost as if *Gotte* was directing where that ball landed.

For a split second, Wally didn't seem to know what to do.

"Run, Wally!" Ida Mae yelled.

Wally dropped his crutch and furiously started hopping toward first base. He hadn't a prayer of making it unless Elsie "accidentally" dropped the ball or purposefully overthrew Johnny at first. One of the children might not have been brave enough to field the ball and do what had to be done, but Elsie was, and she did.

She scooped up the ball and threw a bullet to Johnny. Johnny was almost surprised as the ball landed in his mitt. Without mercy, the teacher had just thrown Wally Sensenig out.

Wally wasn't just out. He was decisively out — out before he'd made it five feet from home plate.

At the sound of the ball striking Johnny Wengerd's mitt, Wally seemed to lose all sense of balance. He tripped over his own foot and hit the ground hard, sending a cloud of dirt into the air. Some of the children gasped; others cried out. Wally had fallen. The boy with one leg had hurt himself trying to play softball. It was the most terrible day in the history of the school.

Dust swirled around Wally like a swarm of angry mosquitoes. He glanced up at Elsie, and a look of deep hurt flashed in his eyes — as if he'd trusted her and she'd somehow betrayed him. The hurt disappeared as quickly as it had come, to be replaced with frustration, pain, anger, and despair. He buried his face in his elbow and growled like a bear in a steel trap.

Elsie's heart fell, and she very nearly ran to his side to help him up. Wally was helpless and lost, like a puppy abandoned on the side of the road. But she bit her lip and stood her ground. He was also a manipulative, spoiled bully, and people had been making excuses for him for far too long. This was for Wally's own good. He'd been handed the easier way out for years.

Wally swiped his arm across his eyes as if to banish any thought of tears. "Stop laughing," he yelled, even though no one was making a peep. "Quit staring at me."

Ida Mae grabbed Wally's crutches and ran to him. She knelt down, hooked her elbow with his, and tried to help him up. "It's okay. Come on, Wally."

Wally untangled his elbow from Ida Mae's and nudged her away from him. "Leave me alone. Everybody just leave me alone." He snatched his crutches from Ida Mae's hand and stood up. "You all hate me, and I hate you. Just leave me alone."

That was what Elsie was looking for. Wally needed to get good and mad. Down deep, Wally was a fighter. He just needed a reason to fight.

He leaned heavily on his crutches, as if he'd die without them, and hobbled as fast as he could toward the little pony cart that he drove to school every morning. Was he going to leave? She couldn't allow him to retreat to the safety of his basement and his video games. His brother had insulated Wally from his feelings, any feelings, and it was time for Wally to feel more than just the dull ache of loss and the numbness of a wasted life. Even pain was better than nothingness.

Elsie slapped her hand against her mitt as if nothing were amiss. "*Gute* game. *Gute* game. You all played hard. Please gather up your mitts and bats and return to the classroom. Ida Mae will supervise singing time until I get back."

Elsie handed her mitt to Johnny and ran toward the far side of the school. Wally had already fetched his pony and was leading it toward his cart. Despite what he wanted people to think, Wally could move very well with those crutches, and he had almost made it to his pony cart and freedom. "Wally Sensenig," she said, in her most rigid teacher voice. She hated to use it, but Wally needed to know that at least one person felt neither pity nor contempt for him. He needed to be reassured of her determination and her strength. And her faithfulness. She was on his side, even if right now he considered her an enemy.

He didn't even pause when she called his name.

She raced past him and planted herself on the seat of his pony cart. "Wally Sensenig, where do you think you are going?"

"Home to tell my *bruder* what you did."

If he hoped to scare her, he'd have to do a lot better than that. "And what did I do?"

"You embarrassed me in front of the whole school."

"You embarrassed yourself," she said, with a mildness to her voice she hoped he recognized.

His eyes nearly popped out of his head. "*I* embarrassed *myself*? I'm a cripple, and I can't run. I can't help it."

"You're not a cripple, and your embarrassment had nothing to do with how you run. You embarrassed yourself because you threw a temper tantrum."

Wally glared at her. "You got me out."

She folded her arms and raised her eyebrows. "I treated you just like all the other children."

"I'm not like the others," he snapped. "I'm a cripple. You're supposed to let me get on base."

"You're not a cripple," Elsie snapped.

With one hand holding the reins of the pony, Wally jabbed a finger in her direction. "You dropped Linda Sue's ball so she could get to first base."

Elsie laced her fingers together. "Linda Sue is six years old, and this is the first time she's played softball at school. Of course I let her get on base. You're a big boy, Wally. I'm not going to treat you like a baby — and I don't think you want me to."

"I only have one leg. You should be nicer to me."

"I'm nice to all my scholars."

"Everyone except me," he said.

Elsie stood and hopped off the pony cart. "I don't have favorites, Wally. You will always get a fair shake from me." She turned and walked back toward the schoolhouse. "Come back to class, or even the little kids are going to say you're a baby. I don't think you'd like that." She kept up a brisk pace, hoping against hope that he'd follow.

"You'll be sorry," he mumbled under his breath.

She glanced behind her to see Wally lead the pony back to the little corral and then head toward the school. Elsie smiled. It took guts to come back to class after he'd stormed off that way. He'd passed his first test.

CHAPTER FIVE

Rose Mast had an uncanny sense for when Sam was out in the pasture. He'd only just got out here to inspect the cows' hooves, and there was Rose, skipping toward him as if she were on her way to a picnic. "*Hallo,* Sam," she said, waving and carrying on as if she hadn't seen him for months.

He set his bucket of tools on the ground. *"Hallo,* Rose. *Wie bischt du heit?"*

"How am I?" She stuck out her bottom lip in a pout. "You didn't come to the *singeon* last night."

"Mamm wasn't feeling well."

Rose hopped up the steps of the nearby stile then down to Sam's side of the pasture. "You should come to the *singeons,* Sam. The bishop doesn't like it when people miss."

Sam scrunched his lips to one side of his face. "I don't think the bishop cares if I'm there or not."

Rose ran her finger along the top of the fence until a barbed wire stopped her progress. "The new teacher was there. She acted nice, but I saw right through her. You and I know what she's really like. And then she . . . well, she's a snob, that's what she is."

Of course she was a snob. She spoke her mind as if she was smarter than everyone in the county. Just another reason to dislike her. Sam glanced at Rose. "What did she do?"

Rose stuck the tip of her ring finger in her mouth and chewed on the nail. "The boys gathered around her like cows to a shade tree. I couldn't get a word in."

Sam could well believe it. The new teacher was as pretty as a field of daisies. Prettier. Every unattached boy in Bonduel was probably circling. Too bad they didn't know how unpleasant she was.

"I don't like her," Rose said. "What she did to Wally was shameful."

Sam's heart swelled. Rose was loyal to a fault. "*Denki* for sticking up for my *bruder*. But don't worry yet. The boys will find out what she's really like, then they'll avoid her."

"She said about four words to me all night, even though she sat two people down from me during the singing." Rose scrunched her lips together. "She said it was nice to meet me, and she hoped to get to know me better. Then we talked about my sisters. She says Lizzy is growing into a fine young woman."

That sounded like a little more than four words, but Sam wasn't inclined to argue. Rose was on his side. That was all that mattered.

"Davie Bontreger heard that she got fired from her last school."

Sam's ears perked up. "Does he know why?"

"*Nae,* but he said it was a big secret, and she left Charm, Ohio, the very next day and came straight up here to teach at our school."

Not only was the new teacher unkind to students, but she had more than a few secrets. The school board would want to know. He pressed his lips together. He'd never been one to spread gossip. The school board would hear nothing from him but what he knew of himself. "Did you tell your *dat* about what happened with Wally?"

"Of course," Rose said, nodding like a scholar who hoped to win her teacher's favor.

"What did he say?"

Rose leaned in and pumped her eyebrows

up and down. "He says he is concerned."

Concerned? He should be more than *concerned.* At least Rose's *dat* was aware that there could be a problem with the new teacher. Lord willing, the teacher had taken Sam seriously and wouldn't cause any more trouble. If she was willing to repent, Sam was willing to give her another chance.

"Are you coming to the barn raising on Friday?" Rose asked.

The barn raising. He'd completely forgotten about the barn raising. This was *gute* news indeed. He had reluctantly agreed to bring his family to Anna Helmuth's for dinner on Friday so he could meet her granddaughter, but now he'd have to cancel because of the barn raising. What a wonderful-*gute* excuse. He bloomed into a smile. "Of course I'm coming."

Rose returned his smile with an even wider one of her own. "I'm bringing sticky buns."

Even better. No toothless granddaughters and Rose Mast's sticky buns. "I really like sticky buns."

"You do?" She looked down at her hands and played with one of her apron strings. "My *mamm* says I'll make a *gute fraa* someday because all men want a wife who can cook."

Sam smiled. "I know you will. He'll be fat and happy, whoever he is. I saw Vernon Schmucker making eyes at you at *gmay* last week."

She groaned. "He's already fat, and he's almost forty."

"He's not that old," Sam protested with a tease in his voice. "He can't be more than thirty." He rubbed the stubble on his chin as if deep in thought. "But Vernon isn't good enough for you. You could have your pick of any boy in either district."

Her eyes sparkled even though she tried to frown in mock dismay. "*Nae,* I'll be an old maid for sure and certain."

"Of course you won't. All the boys think you're pretty. All you have to do is pick one and give him some encouragement. What boy is even going to try to resist those brown eyes?"

Rose's whole face seemed to light up. "You really think so?"

Sam turned around at the sound of thudding footsteps to see Danny and Perry tearing across the pasture. The younger boys always walked home from school, while Wally drove the little pony cart. "Sam! Sam! Wally is in the basement yelling and throwing bottles," Perry said.

Danny bent over to catch his breath. "He

put a hole in the wall with his crutches."

Sam froze, afraid of what he would hear. "What happened?"

"Teacher made him play softball, and he fell."

The teacher made a one-legged kid play softball? What kind of a monster was she?

"He thinks all the kids laughed at him, but we didn't. Nobody laughed, but he's still mad."

Sam glanced at Rose. "I need to go."

Rose laid a gentle hand on his arm. "*Jah.* Wally needs you."

Sam ran across the field and into the house. Even from upstairs he could hear glass breaking and the sound of Wally's pitiful wailing. He bounded down the stairs. Three bottles of canned peaches lay in broken pieces on the floor, the peach juice oozing across the cement toward the floor drain. Wally stood with his face against the wall, slapping the cement with his open hand. He was howling and hollering, even though Sam didn't see any tears.

"Wally! What's the matter?"

Wally seemed to notice Sam for the first time. He moaned and threw himself into Sam's arms. "The teacher made me play softball. She said if I didn't play I'd have to be one of the bases."

Sam couldn't believe what he was hearing. "She said you had to be one of the bases?"

"She made fun of me because I couldn't hit the ball, and then when I did, I tripped when I was trying to hop to first base. The kids laughed at me because I'm crippled." Sam pulled Wally closer, and Wally buried his face in Sam's chest. "Please, Sam, don't make me go back there. I never want to go back."

Sam was so angry he thought his skin might fall off. No one should have to suffer the humiliation that teacher had inflicted on one little boy.

"You're suffocating me," Wally said.

Sam let out a tortured breath and relaxed his grip around his brother. "I'm sorry. I'll go over there right now."

Wally pulled from Sam's grasp and wiped at his eyes. "*Denki.* I want her to get what's coming to her."

Sam placed his hands on Wally's shoulders. "I'll do everything to make sure that teacher is gone by the end of the week. I warned her to be nice to you. Now she's going to see that I don't make idle threats."

"Okay," Wally said, cheering up considerably. His brother would always protect him. He could be sure of that. He looked down at the broken bottles of peaches. "I'm sorry I made a mess."

"Don't worry about it. You were upset. I'll send Maggie and the boys down to clean it up. I'm glad you didn't get carried away and break the TV."

"Me too. Can I play *Halo* until you get back?"

"What is *Halo*?"

Wally shrugged. "Just a new game I got."

"Okay, but it has to go off as soon as I get home."

Wally pumped his fist in the air. "Woo-hoo! This is the best day ever."

Sam nodded gravely. A *gute* day for Wally. The worst day for his teacher.

CHAPTER SIX

Elsie's heart betrayed her, even though she was determined to be calm. It felt as if an *Englisch* teenager with a drum set had taken to practicing on her ribs. When school got out, she had been tempted to lock the doors and drive the buggy home as fast as she could, but that was the coward's way out, and she knew it. Sam Sensenig would eventually catch up to her, and she'd rather face him head-on than hide in the shadows. She refused to appear weak.

She *was* weak. Weak and timid and prone to getting her feelings hurt — but as long as nobody knew that, she would be okay.

There was no doubt in her mind that Sam Sensenig would be stomping up her stairs as soon as his horse could get him there. Wally had endured the rest of the school day in silence, shooting daggers with his eyes whenever she looked his way. When she'd dismissed the children, he had sauntered up to her desk as best as he could on crutches and told her that he was going to have his revenge.

She huffed out a breath. Wally was determined to make it hard for her to love him.

Elsie took off her *kapp,* smoothed her hair into place, and re-pinned the *kapp* on her head. She splashed some cold water on her face, which she was sure was bright red, and sprayed a little lavender oil on her neck. Lavender was supposed to be calming to the nerves, but short of spraying the whole bottle in Sam Sensenig's face, she didn't see how it was going to help much.

She sat at her desk and willed her heart to beat normally. Sam Sensenig was going to come in shooting fire out of his mouth, hoping to intimidate her with his size and brute strength, but she had a few tricks of her own. He would underestimate her, and that might keep him off balance long enough for her to try to reason with him. She could only hope. Either that or she'd be back in Ohio before she had a chance to eat the jalapeño banana bread Mammi had made for dinner.

Elsie smiled in spite of herself. All things considered, going back to Ohio, or even Greenwood, had its advantages.

She was wound so tightly that she jumped

out of her skin at the sound of the door at the bottom of the stairs. *Ach, vell,* Sam had slammed the door, so it wasn't altogether unreasonable to think she would have jumped.

He clomped up the stairs in those heavy boots he'd worn last time. He meant to intimidate her. Well, it was working. She was scared out of her mind, but she wouldn't back down. For Wally's sake, she couldn't back down.

He reached the top of the stairs, and Elsie caught her breath at the sight of him. So handsome . . . so unpleasant. She didn't think it was possible, but Sam Sensenig was scowling with his whole body.

She made a check mark on the paper in front of her and gave Sam the most dazzling smile she could muster. It would make him doubt his power to intimidate her. "I see Wally told you I wanted to speak with you. *Denki* for coming so quickly."

That pulled him up short, but not for long. He strode toward her like a cougar stalking its prey. "You wanted to speak to me? *Gute,* because I would have words with you." He came around the desk and stood above her, no doubt hoping to make her a nervous wreck. He'd stood over her the last time he'd come. This time, she was ready.

She stayed put, so that if he insisted on standing there, he'd have to look way down and talk to the top of her head. It made him seem ridiculous, and gave her a little more power. Many Amish men were used to having the final say, being the law in their homes, and weren't accustomed to being contradicted by a woman. Sam was not going to enjoy this conversation.

Elsie was determined to stay calm — even though she didn't have much hope for it. If she didn't go on the offensive, she'd end up cowering in the corner. She looked up and widened her smile until it hurt her face. "You first," she said, giving her voice a little lilt. Another sign to Sam Sensenig that she wasn't afraid in the least, even if she was. "Why don't you sit down?"

He hesitated for a moment, but must have decided he'd like to have the conversation face-to-face instead of mouth to head. He went around to the other side of her desk and pulled one desk forward from the front row to sit on top of. He had to brace his feet on the floor to keep the small child's desk from toppling over. Once he was situated, he leaned forward and glared at her with those icy blue eyes.

The raw anger she saw took her breath away. "I am disgusted by your cruel, inhumane treatment of my *bruder.*" He chewed on every word and spit it out like poison. "I only came to tell you that I went to Menno Kiem's house before I came here." Menno Kiem. One of the members of the school board. "I will be meeting with the entire school board tonight to demand they fire you immediately. You are the most heartless girl I have ever met, and you will burn in the fires of hell for what you've done to my *bruder.*"

Well. She hadn't expected him to mince words, but *burn in the fires of hell*? Elsie knew she was provoking him, but she couldn't help herself. "So much for Christian forgiveness."

He seemed to erupt. "Christian forgiveness? What about Christian charity and love for your fellow men? If you had even a spark of goodness in you, you'd be on your knees begging my forgiveness. But I don't expect it. That's why I'm going to the school board."

Elsie wanted this job. She wanted it badly, if only to help Wally — if only to heal the harmful environment he had created here. But she couldn't do what she had to do if she was forever worried about keeping her job. "If you want to have me fired, have me fired. I am not so desperate for a job that I must bow to your wishes or be punished. The only person you'll be hurting is Wally. He needs me."

Sam nearly lost his balance on the desk he sat on. "Needs you? You are the last person Wally needs. You have done more harm to him in two weeks than every cruel word that has ever been spoken to him."

She drew a deep breath and paused for a long moment. "Why are you so convinced that people are cruel to Wally?"

"Because they are. He tells me about it almost every day."

Elsie leaned back and studied Sam's face. "What do you do when he comes home so upset?"

Sam narrowed his eyes. "I give him my love and comfort. He doesn't get it from anywhere else."

"And then you try to make him feel better by letting him play video games."

"It's the only thing that makes him happy."

Elsie shook her head. "To you, he'll always only be a poor little crippled boy. You've given up on him, just like everybody else except me."

The fire in his eyes flared hot. "How dare you say that? You treat him with cruelty. I would do anything for Wally."

"Except for what he truly needs, Sam."

"You don't know anything." Sam might have burst into flames he was so upset. He ran his fingers through his hair, and he looked terrible and fierce and breathtaking all at the same time. In that instant, Elsie's heart broke. Sam's love for his brother tortured and paralyzed him.

Elsie didn't want to be his adversary. She cared about Wally too. It was probably the one and only thing she and Sam had in common.

She stood up and walked around the desk, dragging her chair with her. Even at the risk of getting it bitten off, she reached out her hand and took his as if she were going to shake it. He was probably too shocked to fight back. She pulled Sam and her chair to the reading corner, where another chair waited for them. "I'd like to talk with you face-to-face, without a desk between us and without the danger of your falling over every time I say something offensive."

Sam furrowed his brow, obviously suspicious that she might have put superglue on his chair, but he nodded curtly and sat down. His back was ramrod straight, and he was no doubt getting ready to unleash more wrath upon her. "I'm going to the school board, even if you apologize."

"I wouldn't dream of apologizing." She shouldn't have said it. It only heightened Sam's hostility. She took a deep breath and sat down, pulling her chair closer to him. A dangerous move, but if she wanted to prove her sincerity, she had to offer a little concession in return. "Sam," she said, trying to sound reasonable and ignore his glare at the same time, "what did Wally tell you happened today?"

"He said you made him play softball and then laughed at him when he tripped." He leaned forward. "He said you threatened to make him a base if he didn't play. Don't you know how humiliating sports are for him? Or maybe you do know and you don't care."

Elsie swallowed the reply that was on the tip of her tongue, reminding herself yet again that Sam was not her adversary. "Did you know that Wally won't allow anyone to play softball at recess?"

"What do you mean *won't allow?*"

"He tells the other children that if they play softball, it's the same as making fun of him, then he bullies them into giving him money for being so unkind. He scares them and makes them feel guilty at the same time."

Sam shifted in his chair. "You're making

that up. Wally is a cripple. He can't make anyone do anything."

"Don't call him a cripple. Wally might only have one leg, but he's a big boy. His friend Reuben is even bigger. They threaten the younger kids and scare them into bringing money to school."

Sam propped his elbow on his knee and swiped his hand across his mouth. "I don't believe it," he said, as if trying to convince himself.

Elsie didn't want to rub it in, but Sam needed the plain truth. "How else could he afford all those new video games?"

Sam studied Elsie intently, and something seemed to shift on his face. "I . . . don't know if I believe it."

She had a long list of Wally's sins, but maybe that was enough for one day. Sam didn't need the burden of everything, and he probably wouldn't believe it if she gave it to him all at once.

She reached out and patted Sam's arm. He stiffened at her touch. "Wally doesn't need another video game. I know you think you're protecting him, but what Wally needs is a kick in the seat of the pants."

"Making him play softball is more like a kick in the teeth."

"If we treat Wally like a helpless cripple,

he will never believe he can be anything more than that. He needs someone who will challenge him, someone who doesn't think that the only thing he's good for is playing video games."

"But everything else is too hard for him. Playing video games *is* all he can do."

It was Elsie's turn to be angry. "Don't say that. Don't ever say that."

Sam pressed his lips together, either resenting what Elsie had said or considering it. "I'm not here to talk about what you think of Wally. I'm here to tell you that I think it's disgraceful to force him to play softball and then make fun of him when he can't hit. All the kids laughed at him, and he was only trying to make it to first base."

She wanted to growl. Instead she looked him straight in the eye. "Sam, I know what you think of me, but I would never make fun of a student."

"Wally says you did."

Elsie longed to point out that Wally was a bully and a liar and that he would say anything to get his way, but it was quite too soon for that. Sam would probably stand up and try to talk to the top of her head again. So instead she shrugged as if she hadn't a clue why Wally would say such a thing. "Maybe Wally thought I was making fun of him when I wasn't. He's very sensitive about his leg."

"Wouldn't you be?"

Elsie sighed. Sam was too stubborn to give an inch. "I suppose I would. But just so you know, no one laughed when Wally tripped. That is his imagination talking. He was sure that the children would laugh, so in his mind, they did."

"Why should I believe you when you say you didn't make fun of him?"

Elsie was done trying to reason with him. "You don't have to believe a word I say, Sam Sensenig. Go have your meeting with the school board, but be sure that you don't say anything against me that you can't take back later. It's a sin to bear false witness. Maybe you should ask Perry and Danny what happened, if you're really concerned for the truth."

Sam bolted to his feet. "Don't think I won't."

"I can only hope you will."

He tapped his hat back on his head and gave her one more glare for *gute* measure. "Don't make Wally play softball again. It upsets him."

She wouldn't agree to that in a million years, so she just smiled as if he were her favorite person. "Goodbye, Sam. It was wonderful-*gute* to see you again." She'd never told a bigger lie in her life.

After dinner, Sam put on his church clothes and tried to tame his hair with his fingers. His curly hair didn't ever behave, but at least he'd made the effort. Danny, Perry, and Maggie were doing the dishes, and Wally was firmly ensconced downstairs playing *Halo.* Sam drew his eyebrows together. Where *did* Wally get the money to buy his video games? Sam didn't believe for one minute what the teacher had told him about Wally making other children give him money. Wally couldn't even walk without crutches. He was too helpless to bully people.

And what about the softball game today? For sure and certain, Wally's teacher had made up her own version to protect herself. Sam pressed his lips together. He didn't want to believe her, but neither did he want to bear false witness. There was one way to find out the truth before he went to the school board. He strolled into the kitchen. "Danny and Perry, I need to talk to you in the living room."

Danny grinned, elbow-deep in soapy water. "Does that mean we don't have to do the dishes?"

Maggie let out a good-natured groan. "Don't take my helpers."

Sam winked at his sister. "They'll be right back. Don't finish the dishes without them."

Danny wiped his hands on the towel. "Aww, why can't Maggie do the dishes herself? She's a girl."

Sam cocked an eyebrow. "With an attitude like that, you'll never get a girl to marry you."

Danny and Perry followed him into the living room, and he motioned for them to sit on the love seat. He sat on the ottoman next to it. "Do you remember when you came running to the pasture and told me that Wally was crying and throwing things?"

Perry nearly rolled his eyes. "It happened today yet. Of course we remember."

"I want to know what happened at school that made Wally cry."

"I told you," Perry said. "He fell when he was running to first base."

Sam rested his elbows on his knees. "Did the teacher make fun of him?"

Perry thought about that for a second. "Wally hit the ball right at her and she threw him out, but she got everybody out, except for the little kids."

"She didn't get me out," Danny said.

Perry eyed Danny as if it should be obvious. "That's because you're one of the little kids."

"I am not. I got a *gute* hit."

Perry looked at Sam. "She's a wonderful-*gute* pitcher. And she hits farther than any of the other girls." He frowned. "Maybe she should have let Wally get on base. He can't run good."

"But he's not one of the little kids," Danny said.

Sam placed a hand on each of his brothers' knees. "She didn't make fun of Wally?"

"*Nae.* She wanted him to play like all the other kids, but Wally was mad that he had to play. He doesn't let anyone play softball."

Sam tried not to let the surprise show on his face. The teacher had said as much, and Sam had dismissed such talk as ridiculous. "What do you mean?"

"He can't play, so he tells everyone else they can't play either," Perry said, as if it were the most natural and just thing in the world. "I think Miss Stutzman hoped he would have fun."

Sam couldn't, wouldn't believe what he was hearing. Danny and Perry must have been mistaken, that was all. "Wally says the other kids laughed at him when he fell."

Danny shook his head. "Nobody laughed at him. Ida Mae tried to help him up, but he got mad and pushed her away. Then he wanted to go home, but Miss Stutzman wouldn't let him."

Perry nodded, just as adamantly. "She made him come inside and quit pouting."

Quit pouting? Was that what Wally did?

Sam's chest felt as if it were full of lead. Of course Wally pouted. It was how he got his way. "*Ach.* Okay. *Denki.* That is what I wanted to know."

Perry stood and shuffled his feet. "It wonders me if she shouldn't have got him out."

"But he's not a little kid," Danny said.

They argued about it all the way back to the kitchen. Sam covered his mouth with his hand and sat in silence, listening to his brothers and Maggie finish the dishes. He hadn't been wrong about the teacher — she was mean and contrary and proud. But maybe she hadn't purposefully tried to embarrass Wally by making him play soft-ball. Maybe it was like Perry said. Maybe she wanted Wally to have fun. Maybe she wanted all the children to have fun. Sam had played softball almost every warm day when he was in school. *Die kinner* should have the chance to play.

Sam frowned. He didn't like being wrong and seldom admitted it when he was, but he couldn't go to the school board with a story that hadn't happened, or at least that had several different versions. He would not bear false witness.

He heard the thud of Wally's crutches against the kitchen floor. He always came up halfway through a game to get a cookie and a glass of milk.

"Wally," Sam called.

Wally poked his head into the living room. He was as cheerful as a redbird. "You going to see the school board yet?"

Sam nodded slowly. He had asked them to meet him. He couldn't *not* show up. "*Jah,* but I am not going to ask them to fire your teacher."

A line appeared between Wally's eyebrows. "But you told me she'd get what was coming to her."

"And she will. She will." He laid a reassuring hand on Wally's shoulder. "I think we should give your teacher another chance. Maybe she just really likes softball."

More lines congregated around Wally's mouth. "But you said you were going to get her fired. She laughed at me because I'm a cripple and told all the other kids to laugh at me."

Sam kept his temper. Wally was very sensitive. Because he felt things so deeply, he believed bad things had actually happened even though they were only in his head. Hadn't the teacher said as much? "I think you were so upset about falling that you thought maybe the children laughed at you."

"They did," Wally whined. "They did laugh at me."

Sam tightened his grip on Wally's shoulder. "Okay. Okay. Whatever you say, but you need to give the teacher another chance."

"Another chance to embarrass me?" Wally's pitch rose with every word.

"*Nae.* Another chance to get to know you. You're a fine young man."

Wally pressed his fists to his eyes. "I am not. I'm a cripple."

Only a few hours ago, Sam had said that very same thing about his *bruder.* Now he didn't like that word so much. "You are not a cripple. Don't say that about yourself."

Wally snapped his head up and scowled in Sam's direction. "That's what Teacher always says." He narrowed his eyes. "What did she do to you?"

"She didn't do anything to me, but she's right about that. You are not a cripple."

Wally pursed his lips and, with the crutches tucked firmly under his arms, folded his hands across his chest. "I'm not going back to school. If she makes me play softball again, I'll die of shame."

Sam's heart hurt just thinking of the burdens Wally already had to bear. He nearly gave in. What would it hurt to let Wally stay home from school? They could do his lessons here.

Nae. Wally needed other children. He stayed home too much as it was.

"It could be fun," Sam said.

"To die of shame?"

"To play softball."

"I hate softball."

Poor Wally. He truly was miserable. The most important thing was that he didn't dread going to school. No child should dread going to school. Sam mussed Wally's hair. "You don't have to play softball if you don't want to, and you can tell the teacher I said so."

Wally studied Sam's face and nodded. "I'll tell the teacher you said I don't have to play."

"Jah."

Wally smiled. "Okay. She thinks she's so smart. I'm going to tell her first thing tomorrow."

Sam expelled a quiet, frustrated breath. He wished Wally wouldn't look so smug. It made Sam feel like a fool. But Sam's feelings didn't really matter. Wally had something to look forward to. Sam had to be happy about that.

CHAPTER SEVEN

"Oh, dear, Elsie. Bad news!"

Elsie sat up with a start and tried to get her bearings. She was on the sofa at Mammi and Dawdi's house, and Sparky the dog lay on the rug at her feet. Elsie had thought to do some reading and had ambled to the sofa after a dinner of some strange concoction called *couscous.*

"Bad news?"

Mammi held a piece of paper in her fist and studied it as if it were written in code. "I invited a nice family to dinner tomorrow night. They had to cancel."

Elsie shook her head to clear it. Mammi had invited whom? She must have fallen asleep. It was the life of a teacher. If she sat down after school hours, she immediately fell asleep. So much energy was expended on the scholars.

Especially this week. It had taken every bit of gumption and resolve to keep Wally

Sensenig from dragging the classroom into complete chaos. He was back to putting his foot on the desk, and she was back to making him stay after school. The day after their first softball game, he had asked to use the bathroom and spent an hour in the portapotty during math lessons, so she'd banned him from using the toilet except during recess. It seemed heartless, but she was determined to teach him that privileges came with trust, and she didn't trust him as far as she could throw him.

Almost daily he and Reuben Schmucker collected money from the other children when they thought she wasn't paying attention. Wally didn't realize that she was always paying attention. When she saw him taking money, she would secretly repay the children and reassure them that Wally wouldn't be bullying them much longer. That was all she could offer them. Unfortunately, the money and bullying problem would have to wait. Elsie was slowly but surely unraveling Wally's well-ordered, comfortable life, and it couldn't be rushed. She wanted to help him, not break him, even though he was determined to break her. What he didn't know was that Elsie had a backbone of iron. She would not break.

The only thing that could ruin her plans

was the school board, and to her surprise, she hadn't heard one peep from them all week. After Sam Sensenig's threats, she had half expected to be back in Ohio by now. Maybe he had actually discovered the truth. Or maybe he was keeping a list of all the bad things she was doing to his brother, waiting to go to the school board when he had a notebook full of sins they couldn't possibly ignore.

The teacher won't let Wally go to the bathroom. The teacher threw Wally out at first seven times. The teacher makes Wally clean desks. The teacher wants to take away Wally's income.

Elsie pressed her fingers to her forehead. Reuben was another headache. His problems were born of a pain and loneliness Elsie couldn't begin to imagine. But something told her that if she got Wally, Reuben would follow along. Reuben was loyal and eager. All he needed was a *gute,* strong friend to point him in the right direction.

The good news was that, despite his resistance, Wally was making progress. On Tuesday he had strutted into the school and announced that he didn't have to play softball ever again because his *bruder* had given him permission. Even though she'd been expecting that, Elsie had wanted to give Sam Sensenig a large piece of her mind — even if it meant having to be in the same room with him. Instead, she'd organized another softball game at recess and told Wally he'd have to be a base if he didn't play. Wally had looked sufficiently shocked that his teacher could be so cruel. She had seen the wheels turning in his head. He would tattle to Sam the minute school was out. But then Jethro Glick, bless his heart, mocked Wally for being a fraidy cat. Jethro was a seventh grader and one of the few boys Wally and Reuben didn't bully. Maybe because Jethro was as big as both of them. Or maybe because Jethro was just one of those kids who simply refused to be picked on.

For some reason, Jethro's taunts worked. A dare had been thrown down. Wally had joined their game and hit the ball three times. They'd all been piddly little hits, and Elsie had thrown him out every time, but Wally hadn't fallen once on the way to first, and he hadn't thrown any sort of a tantrum. They'd played four straight days of softball, and Wally had been getting a little better every time. Today, he'd hit the ball far enough that he almost made it to first before Tobias threw him out.

Now Wally needed to realize that he could

be a better hitter if he tried. Too bad she couldn't plant the idea in his head. He'd have to figure it out for himself.

Mammi stared at Elsie as if she was expecting an answer to a question Elsie hadn't heard. Elsie was going to have to pay better attention. "Who is coming over, Mammi?"

"He's not," Mammi said. "And neither is his family. It seems there is a barn raising tomorrow and he . . . and the family . . . are going."

Elsie knew her *mammi* well enough to be suspicious. "Who is *he*?"

Mammi waved the paper in Elsie's direction. "*Ach.* Nobody. Just a nice young man and his *bruders* and *schwester.* I was going to make my famous mushroom lasagna."

A nice young man. *Ach.* Would it do any good to scold Mammi for being persistent? Seeing as how the nice young man had canceled, Elsie didn't see any reason to make a fuss about it. Of course, there was bound to be a next time. Soon it would be too cold for barn raisings, and the nice Amish boy would run out of excuses. Elsie stood and wrapped her arms around Mammi's waist. Mammi was one of the few people Elsie could look in the eye when they stood next to each other. "Mammi, I know you mean well, but we agreed that you wouldn't try to match me with anyone until January. I'm too busy to have a boyfriend."

Mammi laughed nervously. "Now what gives you the idea that this nice young man is meant for you? He's too tall. Don't you think he's too tall, Felty?"

"He's as tall as me, and I'm not too tall for you, Banannie."

The little wrinkles bunched up around Mammi's eyes. "*Vell,* I suppose he's not too tall, but that doesn't mean you're a *gute* match. I can't imagine that you like muscles or nice straight teeth. This young man has both. And he's so very handsome. The girls keep an eye on him. I don't suppose you'd like someone like that, would you?"

Elsie shook her head and tried to push back the smile forming on her lips. Mammi was persistent and clever, and she had a little bit of a sneaky streak. "I'm sure that if so many girls are interested, it won't take him long to find one to fall in love with. He doesn't need me at all."

Mammi threw up her hands. "*Ach,* Elsie. You are the only one he needs. What am I going to do with you? How are you ever going to find a husband if you avoid perfectly nice young men with *gute* teeth?"

Elsie grinned at her *mammi.* "He's the one

who canceled. Not me. He's avoiding me. Did you make the mistake of telling him what I look like?"

Mammi scolded Elsie with her eyes. "Stuff and nonsense. He never would have canceled if he knew what you look like. You are as fresh as a daisy and twice as pretty. But you're right. If I want him to come over, I'm going to have to do more than crochet him a dishrag. He's got to know how pretty you are."

Elsie shook her finger in her *mammi*'s direction. "Don't you dare, Mammi. Leave the poor boy be."

Mammi sighed and made a big show of tearing up the note in her hand. "All right. I will do my best to wait patiently until January." She threw the paper scraps in the garbage, but she wasn't fooling anybody. Mammi wouldn't rest until Elsie had met that nice young man months before January. Elsie would have to be extra vigilant.

The only thing more horrible than the thought of a nice young man picked out especially by Mammi was the thought of Wally Sensenig's awful brother Sam stomping up her steps at school.

Elsie shuddered. *Please, dear Lord, keep nice young men and Sam Sensenig far away.*

But especially Sam. He was worse than a

three-year stomachache.

Sam spread fresh straw for the horse while Perry milked the cows. He and his brothers hurried through the chores so they could return to the barn raising by five. Sam had been at Hoover's place for most of the day helping with the barn and had only come home to do the afternoon chores and fetch his *bruders* back. The barn had gone up fast, as it always did when thirty Amish neighbors got together to build something. They'd work until it got dark tonight, and then come back on Saturday morning to finish up.

A barn raising was the best kind of community project. Amish and *Englisch* alike came together to help each other, each man working hard to build as sturdy a barn as possible. The women worked just as hard, fixing large amounts of food for a herd of hungry men, washing dishes, wiping tables, and doing it all over again at the next meal.

Rose Mast had been at the Hoovers' all day, making a point to serve Sam extra-large helpings. It was nice to have a friend who watched out for him like that, especially one who made such *appeditlich* sticky buns.

Sam ran some fresh water into the trough and hung up his pitchfork. "Are you done,

Perry?" he said.

Perry stopped singing long enough to answer. "Almost. Three more minutes."

Sam strolled out of the barn and toward the house to check on Wally and Mamm before he left. Wally hobbled toward him on his crutches with a baseball bat and a ball in his hand. "Will you pitch to me?"

"Pitch to you?"

"I want to practice hitting."

Sam didn't change his expression, even though firecrackers were going off inside his head. Wally wanted to practice hitting? He hadn't willingly gone outside for three years. What had happened? Surely this wasn't the new teacher's doing.

Nae, she was mean and uppity and a puny little thing. The last time they'd talked, Sam was certain she'd killed any excitement for the sport that Wally might have had.

Sam resisted the urge to look at his pocket watch. They'd be late getting back to the barn raising, for sure and certain, but if Wally wanted to play ball, they'd play ball until they couldn't stand it anymore. He nodded. "Let me get my mitt."

There was an extra spring to Sam's step as he jogged into the house. He wasn't going to question Wally's sudden interest in softball. If Sam acted like anything was amiss, Wally might decide he didn't want to practice after all. Sam grabbed his mitt, and Perry's as well. They'd need a catcher, and Perry wouldn't mind. Perry was easy that way.

Sam came back outside and directed Wally to a wide expanse of lawn behind the house. He found a good-sized rock in the flower bed and positioned it on the ground as home plate. He whistled to get Perry's attention. Perry emerged from the barn, and Sam motioned for him to join them.

"You wanna play ball with us?" Sam said.

"Okay." Perry turned his back on Wally, widened his eyes at Sam, and took his mitt. Even Perry recognized that something out of the ordinary was taking place in their backyard.

"Okay, Wally," Sam said, pointing to a spot near the house. "You stand here, and I'll pitch from here."

"You've got to go farther back," Wally said. "You're too close." Sam took a step back, and Wally shook his head. "Go back three giant steps. She stands right even with first base."

Sam backed up until Wally nodded. He was far away. Too far. Wally would never be able to hit the ball.

Perry squatted behind Wally as Wally

dropped his right crutch. With his other crutch tucked under his left arm, he raised the bat with his right hand and wrapped his left thumb and index finger around it. A shard of glass stabbed Sam right through the heart. Wally couldn't hit the ball. He could barely stand and hold the bat at the same time. No wonder he had come home so upset on Monday. The teacher never should have expected this of him.

Sam turned to stone as he gazed at his brother. Better to let him play video games for the rest of his life than to make him suffer this indignity. He couldn't do it. He *wouldn't* do it. "Maybe we should do this another day, Wally. I've got to get to the barn raising."

Wally made a face. "You were at the barn raising all day. *Cum.* I want to learn how to hit a home run and make Miss Stutzman mad."

Sam's throat was so dry he couldn't swallow. As gently as he could, he lobbed the ball in Wally's direction, hoping the poor kid wouldn't fall on his face when he swung the bat. Wally took an awkward swing, chopping down on the ball in order to keep his balance, but he managed to make contact. The ball traveled about four feet forward, but it was four more feet than Sam had expected. He let out a breath he hadn't realized he'd been holding. "*Gute* job, Wally. You hit it."

Wally sneered. "That wasn't nothing. That was a little-kid hit. I want a home run. Teach me how to hit a home run."

It was no use. Wally would never get any power on that swing while trying to balance himself on a crutch, but it broke Sam's heart to have to tell him that. "I . . . I don't know, Wally. Just swing harder, I guess."

"I'm swinging as hard as I can."

Sam trudged to home plate. "Raise your bat. Let me see how you hold it." Wally had less control of the bat because he was missing the last three fingers on his left hand, but his thumb and index finger gave him enough stability to hold the bat correctly. "Keep your finger and thumb on your left hand tight around the bat. That's what gives you control. Now swing level instead of down. Try it."

Wally adjusted his swing by putting more weight on his leg. Sam pitched at least two dozen balls to him, and once he got the hang of the new swing, Wally hit a good portion of them. They went farther, but according to Wally, they were still "little-kid hits."

After the seventh hit that barely dribbled past Sam's feet, Wally chucked the bat on the ground. "This is *dumm.* I can't do it." Sam wasn't surprised when he saw the tantrum brewing. He was only surprised that it had taken so long.

"It's too hard with your crutch," Perry said.

"If you haven't noticed, *dumkoff,* I only have one leg."

"Wally," Sam barked. "That's no way to talk to your *bruder.*"

Perry shrugged. "You have a fake leg. You're supposed to wear it so you don't have to use the crutches."

"You know I can't wear that."

A year after the accident, the doctors had fitted Wally with a prosthetic leg, but he had hated it from the very beginning because it hurt his stump. He'd only given the leg about three weeks before he gave up on it, but Sam had never insisted that Wally wear it. Things were hard enough for the kid. Sam hated seeing him in that much pain. The crutches were easier for Wally, and Sam didn't have the heart to make Wally use the leg. During the summer, Sam had taken Wally to the doctor to have him fitted for a new, bigger leg, even though he hadn't held out much hope that Wally would wear it. He had thought maybe Wally would try it now that he was bigger.

"Why don't you put your leg on?" Perry said, as if what he was suggesting was no big thing. "It wouldn't hurt to see if you hit better."

"Yes, it would hurt." Wally fell silent, leaned more heavily on his crutch, and stared at the bat in his hand. "I don't know how to walk on it," he murmured.

Sam wasn't quite sure what to say, but Perry persisted. "You don't have to walk on it. Just use it to give you some balance."

Wally didn't say anything for a full minute. "Okay."

Perry smiled. "Okay. I'll go get it." He tossed his mitt in the grass and ran into the house.

It felt as if Sam was standing in the middle of a perfectly balanced seesaw, and he didn't dare breathe for fear of sending the whole thing crashing to one side or the other. Were they really in the backyard playing softball together? Did Wally truly believe he could learn to hit the ball? Had he really agreed to put on his leg?

Sam pretended to study a patch of lawn directly at his feet until Perry came running back carrying Wally's leg and the sleeve that fit over his stump. Wally had refused to go to physical therapy to learn how to use it, but it might work well enough to give him some balance. And a little more power.

Wally sat down on the ground, rolled up his pant leg, and spent several minutes trying to figure out how to put everything on correctly. The doctor had walked him through the steps in July, but Wally hadn't planned on wearing it, so he had barely paid attention.

Sam and Perry stood frozen in place, watching him intently while trying to pretend they weren't paying attention to anything in particular.

Wally slid the stretchy fabric sleeve over his stump, then picked up the prosthetic leg and slid the hard silicon sleeve over the stump. They had gotten Wally the leg with a normal-looking foot. Sam thought maybe he'd be more apt to wear it if it looked like a real leg.

There was a locking pin at the bottom of the fabric sleeve that fit into the sleeve of the artificial leg. It took Wally several tries before the pin clicked into place, anchoring the leg to Wally's stump.

Wally finally finished and let Perry help him to his feet. He limped into position, and Sam was sure he'd fall on his face. But he stayed upright and held out his hand. "Give me the bat, Perry."

Perry handed Wally the bat and got out of

the way. Wally took five very tentative practice swings and nearly lost his balance each time.

Sam risked calling out a little advice. "Try putting more weight on it. Plant your feet." Your *feet.* That had a nice sound to it.

Wally adjusted his stance and grimaced. "It hurts."

"Just takes a little getting used to, and it will give your armpits a break."

Wally cracked a smile. "My armpits have calluses."

"Try a few more swings," Sam said.

Wally planted his feet and swung the bat, first in an easy, slow motion, and then harder and with more force as he felt more stable on his feet.

"Keep your swing level. You're not chopping wood."

"Throw it to me," Wally said. He adjusted the position of his fake foot, swung the bat, and toppled onto his backside. Sam fully expected him to make a face, maybe pound his bat on the ground or toss it into the bushes. Instead, he acted as if he didn't mind falling down and held out his bat to Perry. "Pull me up." Perry nodded, grabbed the end of the bat, and pulled Wally to his feet. Wally planted his feet again and raised his bat. "Pitch it, Sam."

Sam tried not to let his hopes gallop away from him. Wally was standing on his own, eagerly waiting to hit a softball. He'd probably miss. He'd very likely fall over, but that didn't seem to matter to him at the moment. He wanted to hit the ball.

Sam's first pitch was outside, and Wally didn't even try to swing. Perry caught the ball and threw it back to Sam. "Strike one!" he yelled.

Wally gave Perry a dirty look. "That was way outside. You need glasses."

Sam threw it again, and Wally swung hard and fast. He finished his swing before the ball even crossed home plate.

"Watch the ball hit your bat," Sam said.

The third pitch did the trick. Wally concentrated hard on the ball and took a little desperation out of his swing. There was a satisfying crack when the ball met the bat and sailed a few feet over Sam's head. It was an infield hit but the hardest one Wally had made yet.

Wally dropped his bat and raised his hands into the air. "Woo-hoo!" he yelled. He fell on his seat again but kept cheering for himself while sitting on the ground.

Perry slapped his hand against his mitt. "You hit it, Wally!"

Wally reached out his hand to Perry.

"Help me up. I want to hit again."

Sam grinned and jogged back to retrieve the ball. They might not make it back to the barn raising, but the look on Wally's face was worth missing it for.

Sam kept pitching, and Wally got better at hitting. Perry went into the house and recruited Maggie and Danny to field balls. After half an hour, Wally was consistently hitting it past what would have been second base, but Sam could tell he was getting tired. Sweat poured off his brow, and he panted hard to catch his breath.

"Maybe it's time to stop," Sam said, after Maggie had made a diving catch of one of Wally's fly balls. "You're getting tired."

One thing Wally did well was pout. He pursed his lips and fixed his jaw in an unmovable line. "I'm not tired. I want to keep hitting."

Perry stood up from his catcher's position and tapped his mitt against his leg. "You can't just hit, Wally. Miss Stutzman says you have to get on base."

Wally's frown etched itself into his face. "I hate Miss Stutzman."

For a second, Sam did too. Couldn't she be satisfied that Wally could hit the ball? He wrapped his fingers around the back of his neck. *Gotte*'s way was not hate, and it would do Sam well to remember who was responsible for Wally's sudden interest in softball.

"Maybe you can run on the new leg." Perry was wise beyond his years. Wally wouldn't be pushed, but he could handle a little nudge.

Wally stared at his fake foot as if he'd forgotten it was there. "Not fast enough," he mumbled.

Perry picked up the bat and handed it to Wally. "But you could practice. Just like you practice hitting."

"Okay," Wally said, pressing his lips into a determined line. "Throw me another ball, Sam."

Sam was convinced that they should quit and save the running practice for another day, but it was hard to say no to Wally when he had his heart set on something. Sam ambled back to his invisible pitcher's mound and threw a pitch. Wally swung with every ounce of power he had left and sent the ball flying over Maggie's head.

"Ach," Maggie said as she turned and ran for the ball.

"Go, Wally. Go!" Perry shouted.

Wally dropped the bat and seemed to catapult himself in the direction of first base. He took three astoundingly strong steps before coming down hard on his prosthetic leg. The leg buckled under him and snapped at the knee joint. Wally screamed as he fell. The pin must have detached from the leg. His artificial leg jutted out from his real leg at a right angle.

Sam dropped his mitt and sprinted to Wally's side. Wally grasped his knee and screamed in agony. Sam pushed back his pant leg and gasped. The fabric sleeve had come off and the metal joint had grazed Wally's stump, leaving a big gash and a stream of blood. Maggie, Danny, and Perry stood over him, watching with horror-stricken faces at the sight of Wally's bleeding stump.

Sam lifted Wally into his arms and carried him to the house. "Maggie, get some water and towels. Perry, bring the leg."

Wally clamped his hands around Sam's back and buried his face in the crook of Sam's neck. "I'm never using that leg again," he wailed. "I hate it. I hate softball. I hate Miss Stutzman."

Hate was not *Gotte*'s way, but Sam was still going to have words with the teacher. It was time to put a stop to this nonsense once and for all.

CHAPTER EIGHT

Dear Sam,

I am wonderful sorry that you and your family couldn't make it to dinner last night. We had mushroom-ricotta lasagna, and it was delicious. My granddaughter was especially downhearted that you could not come. She puts on a brave face, but I know she is truly longing for a husband. If you could please go to the singing tomorrow night at Eicher's house, I would be forever grateful. I have talked her into going, but she doesn't suspect that I have arranged it so you two can meet. Please don't tell her that I set the whole thing up. I'll do my best to be sure she's wearing her pink dress.

Felty will deliver this letter on his way to the market. I hope he finds you home.

Much love,
Anna Helmuth

P.S. I have enclosed three pot holders and a dishrag.

Sam folded Anna Helmuth's letter and put it in his pocket. His problems were piling up like Mamm's mending. Mamm had taken to her bed again, Anna Helmuth wanted him to marry her granddaughter, and Wally's leg was bruised all the way up his thigh.

He couldn't do much about Mamm when she got like this. Naomi and Rosemary, his married sisters, often came over during the day to sit with Mamm and try to make her feel better.

The singing tonight was a more pressing problem. He needed to find Anna's grand-daughter and tell her — nicely — that he wasn't interested and that Anna shouldn't waste any more pot holders on him. Then he needed to corner the new teacher and try to have a reasonable conversation with her about Wally. Wally would not be playing softball ever again, and she would stop insisting that he did.

Sam scrubbed his hand down the side of his face. He'd have to soften his demands if he wanted a reasonable conversation instead of one where she got defensive and he got angry. He'd treated her unfairly the last time they'd met, and Sam was man enough to admit it. Danny and Perry had both confirmed her story, and even though Wally's feelings had been hurt, it seemed Miss Stutzman hadn't done it intentionally. He probably should apologize for making some assumptions.

He clenched his teeth. Why should he be the one to apologize? The teacher had made Wally play softball. It wasn't Sam's fault that Wally had hurt himself.

The Eichers had swept out their barn until it looked like *die youngie* could have eaten off the cement floor. It was the middle of September, and the weather was perfect for a singing. Sam stood beside the open barn door, scanning the arriving people for any sign of a girl in a pink dress. He was concentrating so hard, he didn't even see Rose Mast until she was right beside him.

"Sam," Rose said, beaming like a pair of headlights. "You came! I almost made myself sick, I was that afraid you wouldn't come."

"I have to . . . uh . . . *jah.* I came."

Rose stuck her bottom lip out in a pout. "But you didn't come back to the barn raising on Friday. I waited for an hour."

Sam expelled a long breath. "I know. I'm sorry. Wally wanted to practice hitting, and then he fell and cut his stump."

"Cut his stump? Oh, no! Is he okay?"

"He's bruised, but I think he's going to be okay."

Rose leaned closer. "Lizzy says the new teacher makes them play softball every day, and Wally gets out every time."

Sam nodded. "He wanted to practice hitting. He says he wants to hit one over the teacher's head and make her mad."

Rose frowned. "She shouldn't make them play. Wally must feel so humiliated."

"*Jah,*" Sam said. "It's time to put a stop to it. I don't want to see Wally get hurt worse than he already is."

"Of course not. Doesn't that teacher have any compassion?"

Speaking of that teacher, Sam did a double take when Miss Stutzman came strolling down the lane wearing a wonderful-pretty soft lavender dress. The color accented her green eyes, like a lilac bush at the height of its glory. Her beauty almost made Sam forget how unpleasant she could be.

Sam recognized the moment she caught sight of him. Her smile disappeared, and she lowered her head and veered to her left, no doubt hoping to pass through the barn door without being seen. He had come specifically to talk to her. He wasn't going to let her get away. "Here comes the teacher."

Rose made a face. "She's so stuck up."

"*Denki* for being on my side."

"I'm always on your side, Sam."

"I need to talk to the teacher. Go in without me. I'll come find you."

Rose's mouth relaxed into a smile. "You will? Okay. Put that teacher in her place. For Wally's sake." She turned up her nose and flounced into the barn.

The teacher kept drifting to her left in hopes of avoiding him altogether. Sam quickly stepped in front of her, blocking her path to the door. She had no excuse but to at least acknowledge him.

She flinched as if expecting him to smack her or something. He frowned. Did she truly think he was that horrible? "*Guten owed,* Sam." It sounded like a challenge. He'd already put her on her guard, and he hadn't said a word. But this time he wasn't on the attack. He wanted to reason with her. Wally had been hurt, and Sam no longer believed that the teacher purposefully wanted to harm his *bruder.* She may be stern and unfeeling, but she would want what was best for Wally.

He hoped.

He shouldn't have been so hostile the first

two times they had met. She probably didn't think he was capable of a calm discussion. Unfortunately, he got a little irrational when it came to Wally's well-being.

The teacher tried to step around him, but Sam blocked her way. "Miss Stutzman, I need to talk to you," he said. His tone would have soothed a newborn *buplie.*

She looked as if she'd just eaten a whole plate of dandelion greens. "You have completely ruined two perfectly *gute* days in just two weeks, Sam Sensenig. Are you bent on ruining the *singeon* too? Because if you are, I think I'll go home."

Sam wanted to kick himself. He had made himself unpleasant, when he had only been trying to make the teacher see reason. Didn't she understand that? Hadn't she ever dealt with protective parents before? "I don't want to ruin anything. I just want to talk to you."

The teacher looked past Sam, and her expression brightened considerably. Sam turned as Carolyn Yutzy and Matthew Eicher came up behind him. Matthew was younger than Sam, and single. The girls liked him because he had golden-blond hair and a *gute* face. Carolyn was a pretty, sturdy brunette who had a twin sister. Carolyn was smart and sensible, and Sam liked her a lot, but he wasn't keen on socializing with anyone right now. He had to talk to the teacher.

Matthew held out his hand to shake. "*Hallo,* Sam. We don't see you at many singings."

"Carolyn!" the teacher said, grabbing Carolyn's hand as if they had been best friends since first grade. "*Denki* for inviting me. Did you save me a place?"

"Wait," Sam said, and all three of his companions stared at him as if expecting some big announcement. "I need to talk to the teacher before the singing starts. In private."

The teacher squared her shoulders. "Can't you be satisfied with harassing me on school days?"

Carolyn narrowed her eyes in Sam's direction and put her arm around the teacher. "Don't be rude, Sam. You can talk later."

Sam wasn't one to be put off. "I'm not going to yell or get mad."

Carolyn's eyes became barely visible slits on her face. "You yelled at Elsie?"

The teacher linked elbows with Carolyn. "We had a disagreement. That's all. Can you show me where to sit?"

Sam folded his arms across his chest and shuffled to the right to keep the teacher from passing him again. It felt like they were doing a dance. "I just want to talk, Miss Stutzman, and I promise I'm going to be wonderful nice. Won't you feel better to hear what I have to say now instead of wondering through the whole singing?"

She arched an eyebrow. "Not really."

"Not if you're going to yell at her," Carolyn said.

Sam growled softly. "I'm not going to yell."

"You're snarling," Carolyn said. "And your nostrils are flaring."

Matthew chuckled. "Maybe you should talk to him, Elsie. We don't want him to have a stroke."

"I'm not going to have a stroke." Sam stuffed his hands in his pockets in an attempt to appear less threatening. "Miss Stutzman, there's been an accident, and Wally's been hurt." It wasn't the whole truth, but it might convince her to listen.

The teacher caught her breath. "*Ach, du lieva!* What happened? How bad is it?"

It did Sam's heart *gute* to see that the teacher was concerned for Wally. "Can we talk?"

"Is Wally all right?" Carolyn said.

Sam had to backpedal a little or there'd be four Amish *fraas* and three elders at his house by morning. "He's going to be fine. It's a small injury, but something the teacher needs to be aware of before tomorrow."

Carolyn eyed him with suspicion. "Okay then. But only if Elsie agrees."

Elsie nodded reluctantly. "Save me a spot."

Carolyn and Matthew strolled back into the barn. Sam glanced inside. Rose sat on a bale of hay, her eyes following every move he made. At least one person cared about how *he* was feeling. He turned back to the teacher, who looked doubtful and concerned at the same time. "Do you mind if we sit at the table over there?" He pointed to a picnic table that sat under a tree in the Eichers' yard, out of sight of the barn.

The teacher nodded and trudged to the picnic table as if she wanted to get this over with. She sat on one side, and Sam sat on the other. "Tell me what happened to Wally."

Sam laced his fingers together. "On Friday he asked me to help him practice hitting the softball."

The teacher raised her eyebrows. "He wanted to practice hitting? Has that ever happened before?"

"Nae."

She burst into a smile. "He wanted to practice," she said, almost to herself. "He wanted to practice." She turned her smile in his direction and nearly blinded him. "This is very *gute* news."

"*Nae,* it isn't. He got hurt."

"Go on then. What happened?"

"He couldn't hit with his crutch, so Perry convinced him to put on his fake leg."

Her smile got wider. "He put on his prosthetic leg? This truly is the best news."

Sam deepened his frown so that she knew this was nothing to smile about. "The leg helped him hit better, but when he tried to run, he fell and got a big cut on his knee."

The teacher winced. "*Ach.* That's too bad. The leg will take some getting used to."

"He's not going to get used to it. He's never going to wear it again."

She tilted her head as if to get a better look at him. "Why not?"

"He's got a bruise the size of a soup bowl."

"So?"

"It hurts too much to wear, and it hurts too much to play softball. I'm sure you can understand why he shouldn't play softball anymore."

"*Nae,* I don't understand."

"I told you. It hurts him. But I don't mind if the other children play. Wally under-stands."

She shook her head. "He hurt his leg, but

that's no reason to quit softball."

"He hates it. He only plays because you make him."

She rested her palms on the table and leaned in. "He asked you to help him practice hitting. It doesn't sound to me like he hates it."

Sam pressed his lips together. The teacher needed the truth, whether she liked it or not. "He told me he wants to hit one over your head because he hates you."

To his surprise, the teacher giggled. "Of course he does. That's as good a reason to play as any."

"Haven't you heard a word I said? Wally hurt his leg. I watched him fall and then had to listen to his screams as we bandaged up his leg. I'm never letting him go through that again. I don't care what the other kids do, but I must insist that Wally not play softball."

The teacher caught her bottom lip between her teeth and studied Sam's face for so long, he wondered if she was memorizing his eyebrows. "Sam," she said, in a low, husky voice that he found quite unsettling, "Wally is a born leader, and he could be an inspiration to these children — an example of someone who never gives up. But all he's good at is making people feel sorry for him.

You want Wally to be comfortable and free from pain. You treat him as you see him — like a poor little boy who can't do anything because he will get hurt — but that won't make him happy, and that certainly won't make a man out of him."

"Wally is missing a leg. It's cruel to expect too much of him. Wally thinks you're mean."

"Of course he thinks I'm mean. I'm the only person who has demanded anything of him for years."

"No one should demand anything of Wally."

"Why not? He's not a baby."

Sam opened his mouth to argue but snapped it shut again. What . . . what was she talking about? He demanded things of Wally. Wally didn't have chores on the farm, but Sam made him keep his video games straight and made sure he took a bath every day and never let him leave the house without combing his hair.

Nausea crept up on him like a raccoon on the roof. He pressed his palm to his forehead and leaned his elbow on the table. Wally wasn't a baby, but he hadn't washed a dish, milked a cow, or mended a fence in four years. Sam rarely said no to Wally. He got cookies and milk every day after school, courtesy of Maggie. He got food brought to him on a tray because it was too hard to walk up the stairs for dinner. When Wally had a problem at school, he snapped his fingers and Sam was right there to solve it with the teacher. If Wally wanted revenge, all he had to do was show enough tears and his *bruder* Sam would jump to his defense. He'd been so pitiful that he'd even convinced Sam to have their home wired for electricity so he could play video games all day. The only thing Sam had demanded of him was that he go to school, and even then, Sam hadn't expected much. School was enough. Wally hadn't been required to learn anything.

Sam's world came crashing down around him right there at the picnic table. He had turned Wally into a spoiled, lazy, selfish little boy who got everything he wanted because Sam felt sorry for him. It was no one's fault but his own.

Sam covered his eyes with one hand. "Tell me about the money."

"The money?"

"You said Wally takes money from the other children."

The teacher shifted on the bench. "That is a story for another day."

He locked his gaze with hers. "Please tell me."

133

She stared into the cornfield. "Wally and Reuben Schmucker make the other children give them money — usually during recess. When I know of it, I replace the money that gets taken."

The bile rose in Sam's throat. He didn't want to believe it, but now that he considered it, it could be the only explanation for Wally's impressive collection of video games. "Why don't you make him stop?"

"It's not that easy."

"It's very easy. You should have told me. I'll make him stop."

She actually reached across the table and grabbed his wrist. Her touch tingled all the way up his arm. "Please don't."

"But he's bullying the other children."

"I've had a serious talk with the children. I told them that if Wally takes their money, they are to come to me and I will pay them back. I told them that Wally needs their help to learn something very important, and I asked them to be patient for a few more weeks and turn the other cheek with Wally and Reuben. I want Wally to understand how wicked it is to threaten someone and take their money, but he must come to it himself. We can force him to behave, but that doesn't change who he is inside. I want to see a change of heart, and I know Wally has it in him."

Sam found it nearly impossible to breathe. "You . . . you want to help him."

She nodded.

"You like him in spite of everything?"

She twitched her lips wryly. "Of course I don't like him. He puts his foot on the desk, he bullies the first graders, and he tattles to his *bruder.*" She tightened her fingers around his wrist that she was still inappropriately touching. "I don't like him much, but I do love him, and I want to help him."

"Denki," he managed to squeeze out past the lump in his throat. "I've been blind, and Wally knows my weakness. You didn't really tell him he had to be the base, did you?"

The teacher's smile was quite the most beautiful thing he'd seen all day. "Wally likes to exaggerate, but that part is true. I wanted him to play, and I needed to give him a *gute* reason."

Sam chuckled before growing serious almost immediately. "I . . . I feel paralyzed. How do I know when Wally is pretending and when he's really upset? The first day you played softball he came home and cried and threw things. It didn't seem like he was making it up."

"He wasn't making it up, and I feel bad

for how upset he was. I am trying to destroy his comfortable life, and he isn't going to give in quietly. I don't want him to. I want him to fight his way out of this corner he's painted himself into."

Sam slumped his shoulders. "The corner I've painted him into."

"This isn't anybody's fault, Sam. You can't blame yourself."

He shook his head. "My *dat* died five years ago, and a year after that Wally lost his leg and fingers in a threshing accident. I feel so sorry for the poor kid. I've done everything I can to make him happy, but I've done everything wrong."

"*Nae,* you haven't. How old were you when your *dat* died? Nineteen? Twenty? Barely a man yourself. You did the best you knew how. You're still doing the best you know how. There's no use regretting the past. Learn from it and move forward. Right now, it's more important for Wally to be uncomfortable than to be happy."

"But what can I do? I'm not strong enough to withstand Wally's tears, but I can't stand by knowing that he's bullying other children or getting away with being lazy and selfish."

"I don't want Wally to hate you. You are his big *bruder.* He depends on your strength and understanding."

"But I've been doing it wrong for four years. I'm a failure."

"Don't say that. Don't ever say that."

He cracked a smile. "You used that same voice when you told me to stop calling Wally a cripple."

Miss Stutzman's lips curled upward. "It's my teacher voice. The children know I mean business with the teacher voice." She fingered one of her bonnet strings. "Give Wally a chore or two, and that's all. Don't preach to him and don't let on that you know about anything that goes on at school. That is the plan for now."

"Okay," Sam said. "I can do that."

The teacher stood up. "I'm giving you fair warning. I will have Wally playing softball tomorrow and every day until it gets too cold. It's going to save him."

Sam nodded. He didn't like the thought of Wally in pain, but this was for his own good. Sam would do well to remember that. He reached out and snatched the teacher's hand before she walked away. "*Denki,* Miss Stutzman."

Her smile made him forget his own name. "You're welcome. And call me Elsie. I feel like an old woman when someone your age calls me Miss Stutzman."

Miss Stutzman was definitely not an old woman. A girl as pretty as she should not be allowed to teach school. Like as not, all the little boys were in love with her. How would they concentrate on their lessons?

Dear Sam,

I have to apologize for my grand-daughter's bad behavior. I couldn't talk her into wearing her pink dress to the singing. I hope you didn't spend all night searching for her. Please do not be upset. I am determined to get you two together one way or another. I am planning a secret picnic in which we will invite my granddaughter and a dozen families. You will be able to meet her there, but remember it's a secret. What day next week would be good for you?

Anna Helmuth

P.S. Here is a scarf and a pot holder for the cold months ahead. Well, the scarf is for the cold months ahead. The pot holder is for cold and warm months.

CHAPTER NINE

Elsie cupped her hands protectively around Maizy's tiny shoulders as they both faced the class. "Scholars, we have a new student here at Mapleview School. Her name is Maizy Mischler, and she is a first grader."

Jethro Glick raised his hand. "Miss Stutzman, Maizy isn't new. Her family is in our district."

"That is true, Jethro, but some of the children don't know her because they live in the other district. Maizy's parents have agreed to let her come to school, but they want to be sure that everyone treats Maizy kindly. I told Maizy's *mamm* that this is the nicest group of children they would ever meet and that we would take very *gute* care of her."

Maizy couldn't have weighed more than forty pounds, and she looked like she barely cleared three feet. She had a button nose and bright, expressive eyes that seemed to take in everything around her as if she were trying to memorize it. Her *mamm* had fashioned her hair into a bob and tied a bright green scarf around her hair.

It had taken three visits to the Mischlers before they would even consider sending Maizy to school. Maizy was their oldest, and she had Down syndrome. The Amish called her a "special" child, and Maizy's parents couldn't see any reason to send her to school. She couldn't string more than two words together, and she wasn't going to be able to learn much. But Elsie felt strongly that every child should have the benefit of an education, whether their capacity was great or limited. She'd finally talked Maizy's parents into at least letting her come to school for a week. It would be *gute* for Maizy and especially *gute* for the other children.

Elsie took Maizy's hand and led her to a first grader desk. "Will you all be good helpers with Maizy?"

"Yes, Miss Stutzman," some of the children said.

Elsie watched Wally out of the corner of her eye. He seemed mostly uninterested in the new student. He had a mean streak, but she didn't think he'd pick on Maizy. He wasn't *that* mean, and Maizy probably wasn't worth the trouble.

Wally had limped into school this morning on his crutches, which shouldn't have disappointed Elsie, but it did. Sam said he'd tried the prosthetic leg for the first time on Friday. This was only Monday. The leg idea was going to have to marinate in Wally's brain for a while. She didn't know how bad his leg hurt from falling on Friday, but if the bruises were as bad as Sam said they were, Wally probably couldn't bear to put any weight on the prosthetic leg. Elsie would swallow her disappointment and be patient.

Like Sam had said, it had taken Wally four years to get into this state. It would take some time to pull out of it.

She bit her bottom lip. It felt like a wall of warm water washed over her whenever she thought of Sam Sensenig. This was a great improvement over nausea. He had actually been civil to her last night, and surprisingly humble for someone she didn't think had a meek bone in his body. She really liked his smile and his light brown, curly hair. She imagined her fingers getting stuck in it. What would that feel like?

The scholars were staring at her as if they expected something . . . maybe a lesson? She felt her face get hot as she cleared her throat and went back to her desk. The children couldn't possibly know what she was thinking. No need to be embarrassed.

Morning lessons went as usual. After lunch, she organized their recess softball game. Reuben Schmucker was always picked first, but Wally kept going down farther in the order. He couldn't hit, and he couldn't run. The team captains had started to see him as a liability. Wally sat on the schoolhouse steps apart from the other children, moping like a hound dog, until Jethro Glick finally picked Wally on his team. Wally scowled. "I'm not playing."

It seemed that today was the day he was going to test Elsie's resolve. "You know the rule," Elsie said. "If you don't play, you have to be a base."

Wally narrowed his eyes and slowly rolled his pant leg up over his knee. Some of the little kids gasped. Sam hadn't been exaggerating. Wally had a fine cut right at the knee and an impressive bruise that went partway up his thigh. "I got this playing softball on Friday."

"Oy, anyhow," Toby said under his breath.

"I'm not playing today, and you can't make me."

"Nice," Elsie said, nodding her approval. "It looks like you were playing hard. Makes you look tough."

Wally might not have even been aware he was doing it, but he sat up straighter and pulled his shoulders back — probably realizing that he was pretty tough. But he'd drawn his line in the sand. Elsie wasn't going to get him to play today.

Maybe it was a *gute* thing. Wally would soon figure out that it was no fun playing a base.

"Okay, Wally," Elsie said. "You will play first base." Everybody knew that she meant he had to be the base, not the baseman.

Wally gave her a toothy, nasty smile and hobbled to where first base should have been. He was probably looking forward to being the base. He liked to think he was a victim, the one everybody picked on. Maybe he hoped it was one more thing he could go home and tell Sam about. Elsie didn't mind the thought of that so much. She didn't think Sam would come storming into her classroom anytime soon. But if he did, Elsie wouldn't mind seeing Wally's handsome *bruder* again.

Wally sat in the dirt and set his crutches right in front of him where runners would be most likely to trip on them. Maybe he wouldn't be so smug on a wet day.

Elsie and the rest of the children did their best to ignore their very surly first base. The children tried not to step on him, but he would frequently stick out his hand when someone ran by him to try to trip them up. The children were good-natured about it, even as Wally got grumpier and grumpier. It truly was no fun being a base.

When it was Maizy Mischler's turn to hit, Ida Mae stood behind her and cupped her hands around Maizy's as she gripped the bat. Elsie pitched a slow and easy one over the plate and Maizy — or actually Ida Mae — hit a little blooper toward third.

"Run, Maizy, run," Ida Mae yelled. Maizy turned around in a circle unsure of where to go.

"Over here," Wally yelled, waving his arms over his head. "Come to me."

Stunned by Wally's sudden show of — what? kindness? humanity? — Elsie stood motionless as every child squealed for Maizy to run to Wally. Even Martha Raber, the third baseman, ignored the ball and yelled for Maizy to run.

Maizy smiled and pumped her little legs in the direction of Wally's outstretched arms. Maizy was by no means nimble on her feet. Elsie caught her breath as Maizy snagged her foot on a rock jutting up from the ground and fell with a thud into the dirt.

Elsie, Ida Mae, and some of the older kids

ran to Maizy's side, but Wally, really fast on those crutches when he had to be, beat them all. Three pairs of arms reached out to help Maizy up at once.

"Maizy, are you okay?" Elsie said, brushing the dust from Maizy's dress.

"Did you hurt yourself?" Wally asked.

Maizy's breathing came in stops and starts as if she was going to cry at any minute but was somehow able to hold it in. She pressed her fists to her eyes and rubbed away any tears that might have tried to escape. Her eyes were red-rimmed and watery, but not a tear fell.

"Do you want to go sit down on the steps?" Elsie said, feeling very guilty that Maizy had gotten hurt on her first day of school.

Maizy shook her head. "Play."

Elsie pressed her lips together. "Okay. You are on first base."

Wally frowned. "Miss Stutzman, she fell. She shouldn't play anymore."

Maizy shook her head more adamantly. "Play. I play."

Elsie glanced at Wally. "She wants to play."

Wally didn't argue, but he didn't look too happy about it either. He hobbled back to his place on his crutches and sat down. "*Cum,* Maizy," he said.

Maizy sat next to him in the dirt.

"Nae," Wally said. "You have to run to second when somebody hits."

Maizy understood him. She smiled, stood up, and turned her face toward second. Martha threw Elsie the ball, and Elsie called for the next batter up. To her left, she could hear Maizy sniffling. She pitched a ball, and the catcher threw it back to her. The sniffling got harder. Elsie glanced at first base. Maizy was standing steadfastly next to Wally with tears streaming down her face.

Wally laid a hand on her shoulder. "Are you okay?"

Maizy nodded, knelt down on one knee, and laid a hand on Wally's bad leg. "Ouch," she said.

Wally blinked rapidly and nodded. "Ouch."

Maizy placed a little hand on either side of Wally's face. Wally froze like a pond on New Year's Day. "Ouch," Maizy said. "Ouch." She patted Wally's cheeks three times and kissed him on the forehead.

When she pulled back, Wally awkwardly patted her shoulder. "It's okay."

Elsie couldn't see to pitch. She pretended she had something in her eye and dabbed at the tears before any of her students suspected. It was no good for the teacher to cry. Ever.

Maizy made it all the way to home before the inning was over. Her grin got wider with every base she got to. At third base, she took Martha Raber's hand. "Help," was all she said. The next batter hit the ball into the outfield, and Martha, the third baseman, walked Maizy home.

Wally sat on first base with his chin propped in his hand and watched the other children hit. Elsie had a feeling that no matter how bad his leg hurt tomorrow, he'd be playing softball. Being the victim wasn't all that fun.

When it was Maizy's turn to hit again, she eagerly picked up the bat and held it out for Ida Mae to help her. She hit the ball again, this time right at Elsie. All the children yelled for Maizy to run. She grimaced and took off toward Wally. Her steps got slower and slower the closer she got, and it was obvious something was wrong. Since Elsie didn't move, Tobias, the catcher, ran onto the field and picked up the ball. Seeing that Maizy was in trouble, Wally grabbed his crutches, jumped from the ground, and ran toward Maizy. Tobias threw the ball in the direction of first base, but first base wasn't there anymore. Wally reached out for Maizy's hand and plopped himself on the ground between home and first. "She's safe," he called.

The children on Maizy's team screamed as if they had just won the World Series. Ida Mae and Linda Sue hugged each other. Johnny Wengerd and Toby Byler stomped their feet and kicked up a cloud of dust.

"Teacher!" Wally yelled, pulling Maizy onto his lap as if snatching her from the edge of a cliff. "She's bleeding all down her leg."

Elsie dropped her mitt and ball a second time and ran to first base — which was Wally. Wally pulled Maizy's stocking down to her ankle. There was a cut on her shin oozing blood.

Wally furrowed his brow. "You're a brave little girl."

"Okay, then," Elsie said, making her voice loud enough so all the children could hear. "Ten more minutes of recess. I'll take Maizy in and take care of her leg."

Ida Mae was never far away when someone needed help. "Is she okay?"

Elsie nodded. "She'll be okay." She bent down and lifted Maizy into her arms. "Let's go get this cleaned up, Maizy girl."

Wally pulled himself up. "Can I come?"

"*Jah,* Wally. *Denki.* I wouldn't have known if it hadn't been for you."

Wally lowered his head as if she'd awarded him Scholar of the Year. "You're welcome."

They took Maizy into the school, and Wally sat next to Maizy while Elsie washed out her cut and put three Band-Aids on it. Maizy didn't make a peep, and even Wally seemed impressed with her bravery. Once her leg was bandaged up, Maizy wanted to go outside for the last part of recess. Elsie told her she could.

Leaving his crutches propped against a desk, Wally helped her down the stairs by holding the railing in one hand and Maizy's arm in the other. He hopped. She limped. Elsie's heart swelled as big as the sky. Wally hadn't seemed to have a second thought that he wasn't capable of helping Maizy. If he forgot himself more often, Elsie would soon have nothing to worry about.

Wally came hopping back up the stairs, retrieved his crutches, and hobbled to Elsie's desk. "Miss Stutzman, there's a problem between home plate and first base. That's why I think Maizy tripped." He bowed his head. "And why I tripped too."

"It's nothing to be ashamed of, Wally."

He glanced up at Elsie as the corners of his mouth sagged. "I'm not ashamed about tripping. I ashamed for making such a fuss. Maizy didn't barely make a sound, and she was bleeding."

Elsie nodded. "I see."

"But I'm not talking about that. There is a big rock buried under the softball diamond, and it sticks up right between the bases. It's easy to trip on, and it needs to come out."

Elsie sat on her desk and folded her arms. "Do you want to try to dig it out?"

"I think I could get Reuben and maybe Jethro and Tobias to help me."

Elsie tried to keep her face expressionless, even though she thought she might burst into tears. "That's very kind of you to think of it."

Wally pushed his arms from his crutches so he stood taller. "I just don't want Maizy to trip again."

"You'd have to do it after school."

"Do you have some shovels?"

"Nae," Elsie said. "You'd all have to bring your own."

"Okay. Maybe Sam will help us."

Elsie had a feeling Sam would jump at the chance. "You should ask him."

For the first time since she'd known him, she saw Wally's real smile — not the smile of revenge or power or manipulation — but a genuine, thirteen-year-old-boy smile. A thirteen-year-old boy who wanted to do something nice for someone else. "I will. Sam does nice things for people all the time." He turned around as if he was headed down the stairs, then stopped and turned back. "Miss Stutzman, I think . . . I mean . . . some people have it worse than I do. Like Maizy. I'm wonderful sorry for her."

Elsie curled her lips. "You don't have to feel sorry for Maizy. She doesn't feel sorry for herself." Elsie crinkled the Band-Aid wrappers in her hand. "Maybe *Gotte* sent her to our school to teach us all something."

Wally thought about that for a second. "Maybe He did."

"It is a wonderful-*gute* idea to dig up that rock in our field. We've got to be able to run to first base. But don't think that this gets you out of being the base next time."

Wally smiled with his whole face. "I'm not going to be the base for long. I'm going to hit, and you're going to be so mad."

She was looking forward to it. She really was.

CHAPTER TEN

For some strange reason, Sam's breath caught in his throat as soon as he mounted his horse. It made no sense. He was making a visit to the school, not riding a roller coaster.

The teacher's eyes were the color of new maple leaves in the spring, and her skin was as smooth as butter cream, but that didn't have anything to do with the pounding of his heart or the sweaty palms or the dry throat. And it certainly wasn't her smell — like a field of lavender on a warm summer day. Sam had a fondness for lavender, but that didn't mean it had the power to turn him into a quivering blob of nerves.

All he could determine was that the teacher had smiled at him the last time they'd met, and she had grabbed on to his wrist like he was an old friend. Girls shouldn't grab on to people's wrists like that. It made them nervous.

Sam secured Rowdy's reins to one of the hooks on the outside wall of the school near the water spigot and washtub that served as a trough. He turned on the water and filled the trough halfway before trudging up the school steps and opening the door. "Hello?"

"Hello?" came the answer. Her voice made his heart gallop like a racehorse.

Two rows of softball mitts lined the railings on either side of the stairs. The children were playing again. Sam smiled. The teacher had performed a small miracle. At least at the Sensenig house.

Sam went up the stairs. The teacher was writing on the board. *Wait on the Lord. Be of good courage. He shall strengthen thine heart.* She had precise, pretty handwriting, unlike Sam's. He had always gotten terrible marks for penmanship, no matter how hard he tried.

The teacher turned and smiled at him, and it felt like the sun rising in the east. His heart wasn't beating anymore. It was humming like a well-oiled engine. "Uh. Hi. Miss Stutzman."

She set down her chalk and took four steps toward him, as if she was happy to see him. "Please call me Elsie."

She wore a navy blue dress and a black apron covered with chalk dust. A spot of

153

chalk dotted her soft, creamy cheek, and Sam had to ball his hands into fists to keep from reaching out and brushing it off her face.

"Elsie." Sam stared at her until she gave him a tentative smile and made him remember why he had come. "How are you?"

"Wonderful-*gute.*"

"How did the leg work out?" he said. This morning without a word, Wally had shoved his fake leg into a bag and taken it to school.

Elsie seemed to burst. "*Ach,* Sam. I didn't even know he'd brought it until second recess when he put it on to play softball. You could have knocked me over with a feather."

He couldn't hold back a wide grin. The fake leg had given him some hope. "Me too. After last Friday, I didn't think he'd touch that thing again, even though I repaired it first thing Monday morning."

Elsie giggled. "I think he got sick of being a base."

Sam cocked an eyebrow. "You made him be a base?"

She was almost giddy. "On Monday and Tuesday he was first base, but then by Wednesday he must have gotten sick of it. He started playing on his crutches again. Then on Thursday he struck out three times. I think he'd had enough."

Sam pasted a mock scold on his lips. "You struck him out three times?"

"If you can't stand the heat, get out of the kitchen."

"I hope you were kinder to him today."

Miss Stutzman — Elsie — flashed a mischievous smile. "I might have gone a little easier on him. But if you ever tell him that, I'll pinch your ear."

He chuckled. "Pinch my ear? You can't even reach my ear. What kind of a threat is that?"

"A very serious one."

Sam lifted his hands in the air. "Okay, okay. I won't tell a soul. But did Wally hit the ball?"

"Oy, anyhow, Sam. He hit three into the outfield and got on base twice, even though he wasn't running. I've never seen him so satisfied with himself." Her eyes pooled with tears, but she was smiling, so Sam had to assume she was happy about it.

A thread of warmth traveled all the way up his spine. The teacher really did care about Wally, and she had all along. He had truly misjudged her. Sam cleared the lump from his throat. "*Denki,* Miss Stutzman. You're . . . I'm . . . I owe you . . ."

She shook her head. "Wally has it all

155

inside him. I'm just forcing it out."

Sam sighed. "It's very painful."

She studied his face. "Trouble at home?"

"He suspects something is up. I gave him two chores every day. He has to help with dinner dishes and make lunches for himself and his *bruders* before school. He was so mad on Tuesday, they went to school with a slice of bread and a pickle."

"*Jah.* Toby took pity on Danny and gave him half his sandwich," Elsie said.

"The food has gotten better. Wally suffers as much as anyone when the lunch is poor. But he throws quite a fit when it's time to do dishes. On Monday he said he had to go to the bathroom and didn't come back until the last dish was dried."

Elsie nodded. "It's one of his tricks. I won't let him go to the bathroom during class anymore."

Sam drew his brows together. "It seems harsh, but what else can I do? On Tuesday, when I made him wait to go to the bath-room, he dropped three plates, for sure and certain on purpose, probably hoping I'd throw up my hands and tell him to go play video games. He makes a wonderful fuss about it every night."

"But you've held your ground?"

"On Wednesday I almost gave in. Doing

the dishes makes him so unhappy, and it hurts his arms because he has to balance on his crutches in order to use both hands. I could tell he was in a lot of pain."

She tilted her head. "And how could you tell that?"

"He groaned and made all sorts of unpleasant faces."

Elsie raised an eyebrow. "He's a very *gute* actor."

Sam frowned. "Maybe, but I can't believe it doesn't hurt him."

"You could be right, but he also wants to be sure that you see his pain and feel guilty about it."

"Jah," Sam said. "I know. It's still hard for me to stay firm. I've given in for so many years."

"That's because you have a tender heart." She smirked. "Deep, deep, deep down there somewhere."

"Hah! Thanks a lot." He folded his arms and leaned his hip on her desk. "Maggie held her ground. She snapped a towel at him and scolded him for being lazy. He still whined about it, but he stayed until the dishes were done."

Elsie gave him an approving smile, which made him feel a lot better about himself. "Change is hard for everybody, but fighting through pain is what makes us grow. I'm proud of you. Remember that what you're trying to do for Wally is for his own good. Wally can't live like this anymore. He has nothing to show for his life but dozens of video games and a hefty sense of self-pity."

Sam slid his hand into his pocket and pulled out four twenty-dollar bills. "This is for you."

"What for?"

"You said you've been paying children back when Wally takes their money. I'm the one who should be making them whole. Is that enough?"

Elsie stared at the money in her hand with an unreadable expression on her face. "You don't have to do this."

"It's because I have a tender heart, some-where deep down."

She looked up and cracked a smile. "Deep, deep, deep down." She tried to give it back to him, and he slid his hands behind his back. "I can't take this," she said. "It's my decision to let Wally keep taking the money. I should pay for the consequences."

"It's my fault my *bruder* is a bully. I should pay."

Lines of reproach deepened around Elsie's mouth. "It's not your fault."

"It's not yours either."

Elsie stared at the money before sighing and stuffing it into her apron pocket. "If it makes you feel better, I haven't seen Wally take one cent this week."

"Maybe he's gotten better at hiding it."

"I hope not."

Sam pointed at Elsie. "Someday, Wally is going to pay those children back every penny of what he stole. Then you can pay me back if you want."

"Or I can buy toilet paper."

He pressed his lips to one side of his face. "You need toilet paper?"

She giggled. "Someone is stealing the toilet paper out of the porta-potty. The school board isn't happy about the extra expense."

Sam felt his face get hot. "Wally?"

"I don't know. But not everything bad that happens is Wally's fault."

"It just seems like it," Sam said, lowering his gaze to the floor.

She laid a hand on his arm. He wished she wouldn't do that. He couldn't think straight. "Wally is a *gute* boy. Don't ever forget that. He's the one who's organized the boys in digging up that rock on the softball diamond."

"I suppose."

Elsie tilted her head low enough that she

could look Sam in the eye. "Speaking of which, he volunteered your team tomorrow."

Sam managed a small smile. "I'm happy to help. It sounded like a *gute* project for Wally."

Elsie nodded. "The big boys brought their shovels on Tuesday, but after half an hour of digging, they could see that the rock was bigger than any of them had imagined. They reburied it so we could play softball the rest of the week and are hoping they can get it out tomorrow. I'm sure Wally volunteered your stable because he knows you won't just put him off and tell him it's too much trouble. He knows you'd do anything for him." She laced her fingers together. "Never underestimate the faith that boy has in you, Sam, and don't ever let yourself believe you've been a bad *bruder.*"

Sam couldn't have spoken a word if the school was on fire, so he did what any self-respecting boy would do to protect his dignity. He grunted.

"Do you want to see what you've got to dig out tomorrow?" Elsie said.

Still unable to speak, he raised his eyebrows into a question.

"Cum," she said. "I'll show you the rock."

She led the way outside to the softball

diamond, which was basically a diamond-shaped path worn into the grass by years of children's feet. The backstop was chain-link fencing nailed to a wooden frame. Not fancy, but functional. She showed him the place between home and first where a rock jutted out of the ground. It wasn't more than three inches above the ground, but Wally had said it had tripped several children on the way to first. It was the first unselfish thing Sam had heard from Wally in four years.

Sam stole a glance at Miss Stutzman — Elsie. This was all her doing. The softball, the leg, the chores, the unselfishness. He felt wide on the inside, as if he would burst with gratitude if he didn't hold it in. This puny, feisty, beautiful teacher had set Wally in motion again. Sam would never be able to thank her enough.

She bestowed a dazzling smile on him. "What do you think?"

What did he think? For sure and certain he couldn't tell her what he was thinking. He smiled back, if somewhat uncertainly. "What if we get in there and find out it's ten feet wide and twenty feet deep?"

"We might have to bring in a truckload of dirt and raise the entire diamond."

He twisted his lips. "That might be our

only choice." With the toe of his boot, he kicked up a dirt clod. "The real question is, are you as good a pitcher as my *bruders* say you are?"

She tipped her head and shrugged one shoulder. "I'm better."

He narrowed his eyes with teasing suspicion. "There's only one way to find out, but are you brave enough to face Sam Sensenig, the boy with more home runs than any eighth grader at Mapleview School?"

She folded her arms, puckered her lips, and looked him up and down like a horse for sale. "I'll strike you out so fast, you'll run home crying."

He gaped at her with mock indignation. "I accept that challenge."

She giggled. "You'll regret it."

"I'll go get a ball and bat and mitt. Don't run away while I'm gone."

"The balls are in a bucket in the coat closet. How long should I wait before I know you've chickened out?"

"Ha!" Sam jogged into the school and quickly found the equipment he needed. He'd go easy on the teacher. She'd been very *gute* to Wally. He ran back outside to where she stood on the pitcher's mound and handed her the mitt and two balls. He dropped the other two balls at her feet. "I brought four. You're going to be chasing a lot of balls."

Elsie's green eyes sparkled. "We'll see."

Sam stood at home plate and took a few easy swings. He wouldn't use his full power to hit. He'd rather not kill the teacher with a line drive.

On the mound, Elsie scooted the dirt around with her foot, as if just the right placement would make a difference. "Are you ready?" she called.

He nodded, lifted the bat, and eyed a spot of pasture three hundred feet away. The perfect spot to aim for.

It was almost as fast as a flash of lightning. Elsie brought her hands together in front of her then pulled the ball out of her mitt with her right hand. Taking a giant step forward, she whipped her arm in a circle. When her hand came to the bottom of the circle, she released the ball, and it hurtled toward Sam at probably forty miles an hour. He was so stunned that he instinctively jumped back, even though it was a perfect strike and wouldn't have hit him. But it would have hurt really bad if it had.

"Whoa!" he yelled, nearly losing his balance. "What was that?"

Elsie's smile couldn't have gotten any wider. "That was my fastball. Do you want to see my slider?"

"*Jah.* Of course I do." His heart did a flip. The teacher knew how to play ball. He might just have to kiss her.

But not really, because that would be completely inappropriate.

He lifted the bat, ready this time for whatever came his way. She wound up and released the ball. It came in fast, but he expected it this time. The bat made a whoosh as it sliced through the air, but he didn't come anywhere near to hitting the ball. It crashed into the backstop behind him.

"Whoa," he said again. "Where did you learn to pitch like that?"

She was still grinning from ear to ear as she picked up another ball. "I played in a softball league with some of my *Englisch* friends."

"You have a lot of power for someone so small."

She nodded. "The other teams underestimated me."

He stood at the ready, and she wound up again. He swung and missed for a third time. He'd never tried to hit a pitch that fast, and some of his friends in school had been pretty good. Sam made a big show of being upset. He groaned as if he were in pain and pounded the bat on the ground like a spoiled little boy. "I can't believe I missed again."

Elsie laughed. "Me either. You must look stronger than you really are."

Sam growled like a bear. "Pitch it to me again."

She picked up the last ball and her lips twitched with a private smile. This time, he was ready. Same windup, same release, but for some reason, the ball seemed to halt in midair. He swung the bat before the ball had even crossed the plate.

"That's my changeup."

He groaned in mock agony and made Elsie laugh. There wasn't a hint of smugness or superiority in her smile. She genuinely enjoyed playing softball, and she was genuinely pleased that Sam was impressed. How could he not be?

"Do you pitch this fast to Wally?"

"Of course not. He'd never forgive me."

Sam stooped and picked up the four balls behind him, then threw them one at a time to Elsie. "He'd probably show you a lot more respect if you showed him that fastball." Sam picked up the bat. Maybe it was his pride, but he wanted to show Elsie that he knew how to hit. "Okay. I'm warmed up now. Let's try this again."

He chased a ball low and outside, then another that curved into the dirt. The teacher was sly, and she didn't give an inch.

"Okay," she said. "I'm feeling sorry for you. This next one will be a fastball right down the middle."

Sam wasn't too proud to take her helpful hint. The ball came across the plate just as she promised, and he swung with all his might. The bat made a satisfying crack as it came in contact with the ball, but Sam gasped as the ball shot off the bat like a bullet and headed straight for Elsie's head. Reflexively, she lifted her mitt in front of her in time to block it. Unfortunately, its forward momentum shoved the mitt into her face, and her head snapped back as if she'd been slapped. Blood immediately began pouring from her nose.

It felt like a sharp blade pierced Sam's chest. He flung his bat to the ground and sprinted to the pitcher's mound. She swayed unsteadily as she put her hand to her forehead. He grabbed her wrist and pulled her to sit on the ground. "I'm so sorry. So sorry."

She gazed at him with a muddled expression and managed a smile. "If you can't take the heat, stay out of the kitchen."

"Is it broken?"

"I don't think so. I didn't hear anything crack. It hurts, but it doesn't feel like I-wish-I-were-dead kind of pain."

"Here," he said, nudging her head down so she faced the ground and her nose dripped onto the dirt. He placed his hand on her forehead to hold up her head. "Pinch the bridge of your nose. Do you feel dizzy?"

"*Nae,* but everything is spinning."

"You're not funny."

She put her hand over the top of his. "Do you think you could go into the school and get some tissues and a cold pack? The tissues are on my desk, and there is a small box of instant cold packs in my bottom drawer."

"I hate to leave you alone out here."

"I promise not to die while you're gone." She grabbed his arm before he pulled away. "If you hurry."

"Really, Elsie. You're not funny."

He heard her laughing softly as he ran for the school.

He went fast. When he came back out, Elsie hadn't moved a muscle.

With her head still down, she motioned to the cold pack. "Squeeze it until you hear a crack." While he did that, she took the handful of tissues he gave her and pressed them against her face. Blood immediately soaked the pile. It was a good thing he'd brought the whole box.

She held the cold pack against the bridge of her nose with one hand and dabbed at the blood with the tissues in her other hand. Only then did Sam notice her top lip had swollen to twice its size. "*Ach.* You have a fat lip."

She felt along her upper lip with her tongue. "Oh, *sis yuscht. Gute* thing it's Friday. The scholars would never be able to understand me with fish lips."

Sam felt sick about the whole thing. "What can I do? Do you need some Motrin? Can I rub your shoulders? Or your feet?"

Elsie slowly raised her head and gave him an encouraging smile. The movement made her wince. "Sam, it's okay. You do not need to rub my shoulders or my feet."

"I'm never playing softball again. First Wally, and now you."

She grabbed another handful of tissues from the box. "I've had worse. A ball knocked me out cold once. I couldn't play for a whole year. Did you see my fast reflexes? I could have lost my teeth."

"*Jah.* I'm impressed."

"That was a wonderful-*gute* hit."

"*Denki.* I'm never hitting again," he said.

She lifted her head again. "It would be a

168

shame to rob the world of your talent."

The look of pity on her face made him grin. "Maybe I'll just stand in the outfield the rest of my life."

She dabbed at her nose. "It stopped bleeding."

He couldn't resist. He traced his thumb along the fine line of her jaw and up her cheek. It felt heavenly. The world stopped turning for a moment as they stared at each other. He was close enough to catch the scent of lavender that floated around her. Lavender and blood. She definitely smelled like blood. "Your face is a mess," he said.

She cleared her throat and scooted back a few inches. "Is it my nose? I've always been too proud of my nose."

"*Vell,* it's swollen, but I don't think there's any permanent damage. But there's smeared blood everywhere." He pulled a white handkerchief from his pocket. Thank the good Lord Maggie liked to iron. She always stuck a clean handkerchief in his pants pocket when she folded laundry. "Just a minute."

He jogged to the water spigot and got his handkerchief wet, then brought it back to the softball diamond and knelt next to Elsie, who didn't seem inclined to go anywhere. Slowly, gently, he worked the handkerchief around her face, being careful of her nose and her swollen lip. She held perfectly still with her eyes glued to his as he wiped up the blood as best he could. She hissed only once, when he got too close to her lip, and then he was done. He stuffed the damp handkerchief in his pocket.

"*Denki,* Sam, that was very nice of you," she said, her voice shaking like a match in the wind. She looked down at her apron. The blood didn't really show, because the apron was black, but it was stiff where blood had fallen. "What I really need is a bath and the washing machine."

Sam stood and offered his hand. She hesitated only for a second and then let him pull her to her feet. She seemed a little unsteady, so he put a firm arm around her waist and led her to the school. "Let me take you home."

"*Ach,* Sam, you are wonderful kind, but I have to finish my tree. Each time someone gets a hundred points, they'll be able to tape a leaf to it. It's got to be on the wall by Monday."

"Can I help? I know about trees. I used to be a lumberjack."

She curled one side of her mouth. "*Jah,* I can see that you did." With his arm still around her, he helped her into the school and up the stairs. "I would love your help," she said, "but do you have time? Isn't there anywhere you need to be?"

It felt as if someone had dropped a brick on his head. Or hit him in the face with a softball. He *did* have somewhere he had to be tonight, and it was a secret.

Cobbler Pond was a beautiful spot for a picnic, except at this time of year when the mosquitoes were trying to bite everyone they could before first freeze. Sam pulled to the side of the road where there was ample space for the buggy. Three or four buggies were already parked there. Sam wouldn't have been surprised if everyone in Bonduel had been invited to the secret picnic.

"Did everybody get bug spray?" Sam said, turning to his brothers in the back.

"We got it," Perry said.

Danny made a face. "I got some in my mouth."

Sam shook his head. "It's okay. You won't die."

"But I can taste it."

"Eat a carrot," Maggie said. "I brought a whole bag of them."

"That won't help," Danny whined.

Anna Helmuth had invited his whole family, and probably every family within ten miles, but Mamm hadn't felt well enough to come, so it was just the five of them. Sam was already irritated that he even had to be here, but he had told Anna he would come. No matter how much he wanted to, he couldn't cancel on her twice. It would be rude.

He wasn't planning on having a *gute* time. He wanted to meet the Helmuths' granddaughter like he wanted a hole in the head.

The worst part was that if it hadn't been for this picnic, he could have spent at least another hour with Elsie Stutzman. He'd helped her hang her tree on the wall, and she'd been impressed that he hadn't even needed a ladder. Elsie had three step stools positioned around the classroom for the times when she needed to reach something on one of the higher shelves. She had told him twice in an hour how much she liked that he was tall.

She had pulled out her secret case of Diet Coke and given him one of her precious cans. They had laughed about softball and pitching and getting hit in the face and swapped scar and broken bone stories. Elsie had a scar on her ankle from sliding into second base. Sam had broken his collarbone at age eight when he fell out of a tree.

He'd had a wonderful-*gute* time with

172

Elsie, but he had been forced to pull himself away to make it to the secret picnic on time.

He sighed. He was going to have to tell Anna and her granddaughter that he wasn't interested. He wasn't looking forward to the conversation, especially since Anna was such a sweet little lady, but it had to be done.

Sam climbed out of the buggy and sprayed himself with repellent while Maggie and his brothers got out. It always took Wally a little longer with his crutches, but they were all used to it. Maggie cradled her giant bag of baby carrots in her arms. It was her version of a relish tray. It didn't matter. Nobody ever ate the celery anyway.

Sam and his family strolled the short distance to the pond from the road. Several families from the two districts had spread blankets on the ground and were pooling their food on a picnic table under one of the trees. Children ran everywhere as *fraas* arranged the food on the table and husbands put their heads together to hear the latest gossip.

Anna was sitting in the center of all the commotion with two knitting needles in her hands. She kept sending him pot holders. She probably had to knit twelve hours a day to keep up. She wore a startling neon green sweater over a plain black dress. Anna was known for wearing unconventional colors, but no one had the heart to tell her that she was flouting the *Ordnung.* A middle-aged woman sat next to her, also knitting. Was she the granddaughter? Sam expelled a long, weary breath. He hated to hurt Anna's feelings, but he refused to date anyone more than fifteen years older than he was.

Anna looked up, caught sight of Sam, and waved as if trying to stop a bus with her arm. She handed her knitting to her possible granddaughter and pushed herself to her feet. It was quite an achievement for an eighty-year-old woman. She tiptoed around all the people sitting on blankets, and Sam held his breath when she nearly toppled over into a plate of deviled eggs. He quickly walked toward her. He had younger legs, and he'd never forgive himself if Anna broke a hip on his account.

"Sam Sensenig," she said, clapping her hands and smiling as if he'd just agreed to marry her granddaughter. "You came. I told Felty you were a *gute* boy and that if you said you would come, you would come."

Sam had been sorely tempted to stay at the school with Elsie, but he'd always been as good as his word. His reputation was still intact. He took Anna's hand in both of his.

174

"Anna, I'm sorry. I have to tell you . . . I know you mean well, and I'm sure your granddaughter is a wonderful-*gute* girl, but —"

Anna squeezed his hand, then reached up and gave him a pat on the cheek. It was a long way up. She was as short as Elsie. "*Ach,* Sam. I have some very bad news. You went to all the trouble to come, and my granddaughter isn't here. There's something wrong with her nose."

Sam pressed his lips together. Something wrong with her nose like "she has a cold" or something wrong like "it's as big as a house"?

Sam didn't know if relief or disappointment was his greatest emotion. Anna's knitting partner was not her granddaughter. But Anna would insist that Sam meet her granddaughter sometime. He'd be forced to go to their house for dinner or attend another secret picnic, and he didn't think he could stand it.

"Anna, I appreciate that you want me to meet your granddaughter, but —"

Anna's eyes sparkled. "Now, Sam, I don't just want you to meet. I want you to fall in love."

Well, at least she wasn't one to beat around the bush. "I'm sorry, Anna. I'm sure

175

your granddaughter is a *gute* sort of girl, but I'm not going to fall in love with her, and to be honest, I don't want to meet her. I don't have the time or the temper for it."

To his consternation, Anna smiled a grandmotherly smile. "*Ach,* that is one of the things I most like about you. You're honest to a fault." She pulled her bright sweater tighter around her. "So tell me. Are you seeing a girl regularly? Do you have a girlfriend?"

He had no idea why Elsie Stutzman crossed his mind when Anna asked that question. Wally's teacher was not anyone he wanted to date. She was too — *ach,* he didn't know — too short and too . . . skinny. How could he date a girl with no meat on her bones? "I don't want a girlfriend, Anna. I don't have the time or the money."

Anna waved her hand as if swatting mosquitoes. "Stuff and nonsense. Boys only use that as an excuse. When you meet the right one, you suddenly have all the time in the world. I know Rose Mast has her eye on you" — Anna leaned in and lowered her voice — "she is a wonderful-*gute* girl but a bit of a whiner. She's not the one for you."

Sam agreed that Rose wasn't for him, but Anna was mistaken. Sam and Rose were friends. Rose didn't have her eye on him.

Anna leaned in even farther. "I didn't invite Rose to the secret picnic because I don't want her to be jealous of my grand-daughter."

Sam gave Anna a half smile. "I don't think there's any chance of that." Only Anna could concoct a scheme where Rose — who wasn't even interested in Sam — would be jealous of someone he hadn't even met yet. "Anna, what I'm trying to tell you is that I don't want to meet your granddaughter. Ever."

Anna lost her smile, and the lines around her eyes bunched in on each other. "But you're perfect for each other, and she wants to get married so badly."

Didn't Anna know that nothing made a boy less interested than a girl who was desperate to marry? "I'm sure there's some other boy better suited to your grand-daughter."

Something seemed to shift in Anna's expression — as if she'd made up her mind and wouldn't be moved. She patted his arm. "Sam, you're stubborn, no doubt about it. But I'm stubborn too, and I know a good match when I see one. I'm not giving up."

Sam slumped his shoulders. He had no doubt Anna meant what she said.

What else could he do? He'd been plain

with her. He'd just have to hope that the granddaughter would find another boy and get married soon.

Very soon.

Maybe he should move to Montana.

CHAPTER ELEVEN

Sam pulled onto the road with his mule team. Wally, Danny, and Perry were already at the school with some of the other boys, hopefully making progress on unearthing that rock. He feared the whole area might be one big rock shelf and that dislodging it would prove impossible. Not that it mattered. Besides softball, rock excavating was the first project Wally had shown any enthusiasm for in years, and Sam would go as far as humanly possible to get that rock out of the softball diamond.

He got the team moving just as he saw Rose strolling up the road toward him. She waved to him and called out in her high-pitched voice, "Yoo-hoo!"

He pulled back on the reins and stopped the wagon. "*Hallo,* Rose."

"Looks like you're going somewhere important this morning."

"Wally and some of the other boys are

smoothing out the softball field at the school. They've come across a rock they want me to pull out."

"Must be a big rock."

"I don't wonder that it is."

Rose rested her hand on the lip of the wagon. "What do they need to smooth out the diamond for? I thought you weren't going to make Wally play softball anymore. What did the teacher say when you talked to her at the singing? I hope you put her in her place."

Sam frowned. He shouldn't have been so vocal in his dislike for the new teacher. He'd been wrong about her, and Rose's ill feelings for Elsie were all his doing. "I . . . she . . . plain and simple, Rose, I was wrong. She is trying to help Wally. I just didn't understand her."

Rose's eyelid twitched. "So you understand her now?"

"Better than I did."

Rose looked around as if to make sure no one was listening in on their conversation. "I'm afraid you've been fooled, Sam. That teacher can't control her class, and the children are getting hurt because of it."

Sam furrowed his brow. "Who's getting hurt?"

Rose lowered her eyes and clasped her

hands together. "I would never want to hurt your feelings and I know you're nothing like your *bruder,* but Lizzy says that Wally has been bullying some of the little boys into giving him their money. She says the teacher doesn't even notice. What kind of a teacher can't even see when her students get picked on?" Rose gazed at Sam, her eyes full of sympathy. "I want you to know with all my heart that I don't blame Wally. He's just a little boy who needs some discipline and guidance. I blame that teacher for not protecting her students and for not teaching Wally the difference between right and wrong. You were right the first time. She is unfit to teach."

Sam secured the reins and slipped down from the wagon. Rose was a little too sure about the teacher, and he needed to make her understand, especially since Sam had been the one to set Rose against Elsie in the first place.

When he jumped down, Rose bloomed into a smile. Was it his imagination, or did she sidle closer? Sam swallowed a mouthful of dread. Anna had said that Rose had her eye on him, but that was when they were children. That crush had died over a decade ago.

"Rose, it's my fault that you don't like the

new teacher, and I need to apologize. The new teacher and I had a talk."

"I know. I saw you."

"She knows that Wally is taking money from the other kids."

Rose raised her eyebrows. "And she lets him get away with it?"

"She wants Wally to decide to quit on his own. If she forces him to stop, he'll never learn anything. That makes sense, doesn't it?"

"That doesn't make sense at all. She should give him the ruler." Rose seemed to remember who she was talking to and lowered her eyes. "I mean, you don't want your *bruder* to steal people's money, do you?"

"*Nae.* I want him to have a change of heart. Elsie thinks she can help him."

Rose narrowed her eyes. "It's not right to call the teacher by her first name."

"Okay. Miss Stutzman, then. She has a plan for Wally."

"Oh," Rose said, drawing out the word as if Sam had just said something very important. "She has a plan. I can't believe you trust her after all she's done to Wally."

Sam tried not to get irritated. Rose hadn't been there when Elsie and Sam had talked. She didn't understand what Elsie — Miss

Stutzman — was trying to do for Wally.

Rose shaped her lips into a pout. It was her least attractive look. "All the boys in the *gmay* are *ferhoodled.* They wouldn't be if they knew that she lets Wally bully the children at school."

Sam bit his tongue and gave Rose a brotherly smile. "You could *ferhoodle* all the boys if you paid attention to them. You're a wonderful pretty girl, Rose, but you don't give the boys any encouragement."

Rose smiled with her whole face. She had *gute* teeth. Surely her teeth alone would attract a husband. "You're just saying that because you're my best friend."

Best friend? Surely there were a dozen or so girls closer to her age that were better friends than Sam. A dozen or so at least. And even three or four boys that were closer to her than Sam was. Did she really consider them best friends? Sam frowned. He hadn't been that close of a friend for years.

He shrugged and smiled. "Give the boys some encouragement. Make more friends. Talk to a few boys at gatherings. They'll forget all about the new teacher."

Rose giggled. "I'm not a flirt. The new teacher is a flirt. Sadie Yoder says so."

Elsie was plainspoken and straightforward,

more inclined to lecture a boy than date him. She had a wonderful-*gute* fastball and lightning-fast reflexes, but Elsie was not a flirt. Sam wasn't going to argue. Sadie Yoder was the bishop's daughter, and most of *die youngie* believed everything that came out of her mouth. "I only know there's lots of boys out there who would be wonderful pleased if you would pay them some attention."

A blush rose on her cheeks. "You think so?"

He nodded.

She looked down at her hands. "I turn twenty in March, you know."

"*Jah.* I suppose I can't call you 'pipsqueak' anymore."

Her blush got deeper. "*Nae.* You can't. I'm all grown up. Finally."

"To me you'll always be the little girl who used to whine at the base of the tree until we let you into the hideout." He tugged on her bonnet string. "I'd better be going. Wally and the other boys should have that rock dug up by now." Unless it went all the way to China. He swung up into his seat. "See you later."

"I'll help."

"Huh?"

"I want to help at the school. It sounds

like a big rock."

"You don't need to do that."

She wasted no time bouncing into the seat next to him and making herself comfortable. "What kind of friend would I be if I didn't help?"

Didn't Rose have better things to do today? Shouldn't she stay home and start thinking of boys she wanted to date? Sam was sort of hoping Miss Stutzman would be at the school and he could check on her nose and maybe bask in one of her smiles. But basking would be awkward with Rose looking over his shoulder. "It isn't going to be much fun. I'm just going to pull the rock out of the ground and let the boys fill in the hole. Won't take but half an hour."

"It sounds like fun. I can help with the team, if you need me to."

Sam couldn't imagine what help with the team he'd need from Rose, but he probably couldn't wonder that out loud without offending her. He wracked his brain, trying to think of a *gute* reason to leave Rose behind, but *I want the new teacher to smile at me* didn't seem like an adequate excuse, especially when the new teacher might be home nursing a broken nose. "Okay," he said, trying hard not to sound disappointed. "It's very nice of you, but like as not, you'll be bored."

"It doesn't matter. A best friend is always there for you."

There was the best friend thing again. Not by any stretch of the imagination were they best friends, but did it really matter that Rose thought they were?

Rose talked about the quilt she was making and the new goat and the news that three Zook children had the chicken pox. Sam listened only well enough to nod in all the appropriate places when she paused to take a breath. It wasn't that he wasn't interested in quilts and chicken pox, it was just that he wasn't interested in Rose, so he didn't try real hard to be agreeable. It wasn't the way to treat a best friend, but Rose wasn't his best friend — at least, he didn't think so. That probably made him a terrible person. He sighed and threw insensitivity onto his pile of sins. It was wonderful high and grew every day, except for when he had laryngitis. It seemed when he opened his mouth he either said the wrong thing or said it the wrong way. Miss Stutzman would surely agree with that.

Sam's *bruders,* with Reuben Schmucker, Jethro Glick, and Tobias Raber, were hard at work around a wonderful big hole where the first base line used to be. Sam's heart did a little jig. Miss Stutzman was out there with them, working the dirt as if she had been born with a shovel in her hand. Something told Sam she'd be able to hold her own with a hammer and a pair of pliers as well.

"What's she doing here?" Rose said when she caught sight of Elsie, as if Rose had more right to set foot in the school yard than Elsie did.

Sam shrugged. "Looks like she's helping."

He pulled his wagon alongside the merry-go-round and jumped down. Rose quickly followed, bringing an air of authority with her, as if Rose and Sam were in charge of the rock and were here to supervise the excavation. Sam tried not to frown. If anybody was in charge of this project, it was Wally. Rose was just being Rose. She liked to feel important.

Miss Stutzman — was it inappropriate to call her Elsie? — flashed a smile that almost knocked him over. He might have thought the smile was just for him, but she gave the same one to Rose, even though it was completely wasted on her. Rose tried to look uninterested while giving Elsie a slight wave of her hand. Sam didn't know what she had expected. It was the teacher's ball field. Of

course she would be here to see that everything was done with care.

Elsie walked toward them, using her
shovel like a cane. "Sam, Rose, so nice of
you to bring the team." Her lip was still a
little swollen, but there was no sign that her
nose had been hit yesterday, except for a
little redness on the bridge.

He couldn't help the grin that spread over
his face. Elsie was just so cute. "Your nose
looks better."

She laughed and touched a finger to her
mouth. "No black eyes, and the lip is barely
noticeable. I'd say I got off easy." That smile
of hers was irresistible. His heart tumbled
over and over in his chest.

Sam almost forgot Rose was standing next
to him. "What happened to her lip?" she
said.

"*Ach.*" Sam stuffed his hands in his pockets
and pulled his gaze from Elsie's face. He
kicked at the dirt and stared faithfully at his
boots. "Elsie pitched a ball to me, and I hit
it at her face. She raised her mitt just in
time."

Rose's eyes darted from Sam to Elsie and
back again. "That's dangerous. Girls
shouldn't pitch to the boys."

Sam's gaze traveled to Elsie's face. He
smiled at her. She grinned back. "She kept

striking me out. I had to hit at least one to prove myself."

Elsie laughed. "You proved yourself, all right. And I've got the marks to show for it."

He didn't realize he was staring until Rose took a step forward and practically put herself between them. "When did you play softball together?"

"Yesterday. I wanted to see if she was as *gute* a pitcher as she said she was."

Rose pressed her lips together so tightly, they looked like they'd been ironed in place. "Girls shouldn't brag."

Elsie grinned and nodded. "It's my greatest weakness. I'm grateful that people here are so forgiving."

"I suppose we are, Miss Stutzman," Rose said.

"Please call me Elsie."

Rose shook her head. "I won't call you that. You're the teacher."

It was obvious Elsie sensed Rose's hostility, but she pretended that Rose was nothing but nice. "I hope we can be friends too."

Elsie probably had to smooth over many unpleasant situations when angry parents came to see her. Or rude brothers. Sam's mouth suddenly felt as dry as day-old toast.

She was especially patient with rude brothers.

Elsie looked over her shoulder. "These boys have been hard at work."

"Have they uncovered the rock?" Sam said.

"Almost enough to be able to move it. Come and see."

She led them to where the boys were digging. Wally sat on the ground, using a garden trowel and filling a plastic bucket with dirt. Tobias, Reuben, and Jethro were filling two more buckets with their shovels. Perry and Danny were the bucket movers, dragging the full buckets a few feet from the hole and dumping them out. They had quite a pile of dirt.

Wally glanced up and nearly knocked Sam over with that smile. He hadn't seen it in such a long time. "Sam, look how big it is! We'll need your team for sure and certain."

The boys really had been hard at work. The rock, or boulder — as it probably should have been called — jutted out of the hole like a tall pillar, nearly the size of a full-grown hog standing on its hind legs.

"How deep does it go?" Sam asked. He wasn't going to let them dig another ten feet.

"Jethro thinks he found the bottom another six inches down," Wally said. "Can the team pull it out or should we keep digging?"

Sam resisted the urge to ruffle Wally's hair. "Let's try it with the team. They should be able to get it."

Rose looked into the hole. "Why are you digging out this rock?"

Elsie drove her shovel into the dirt and wrapped her fingers around the handle. "Kids keep tripping on the edge of it when they run to first base. Wally had the *wunderbarr* idea to dig it out."

Rose wasn't impressed. "That's a lot of work for a little bump."

"We don't mind," Danny said. "Maizy Mischler tripped on it. We don't want anybody else to fall."

"That's right," Elsie said. "It is a very kind and Christian thing to do, thinking of others before yourself. I'm wonderful proud that these boys would give up their Saturday to do it."

Sam smiled at Elsie. "*Denki* for letting the boys dig up your softball field. I know how important this field is to you."

Rose shrugged. "I suppose a reward is waiting for them in heaven, but you shouldn't let Maizy play softball. She can't run real good. She's going to get hurt."

191

"She already did," Danny said. "She cut her leg."

Rose folded her arms. "That's what I mean."

"She didn't mind. She was having fun."

Rose frowned. "It's careless to put your students in danger like that."

Elsie didn't seem offended. "A little fun never hurt anybody."

"Get the team, Sam," Wally said. "Let's see if they can pull it out. Then we have a big job filling that hole back in."

Sam unhitched the team from the wagon and moved the mules into place. Reuben and Jethro helped him secure ropes around the boulder.

Rose glanced at Elsie and smiled at Sam. "I can help you drive the team. I don't know how to play softball, but I'm better than just about anybody with a mule team."

Sam shook his head. "Two drivers will confuse the team. They know my voice. I can do it."

Rose pursed her lips together but didn't argue. For sure and certain, she was regretting coming along. Elsie hooked her arm around Rose's elbow, and Rose stiffened as if she'd been slapped. Elsie didn't seem to notice. "Let's stand behind the backstop. *Cum,* Wally, Danny, everybody. Move back.

You want to be clear if a rope snaps or a chunk of rock flies out of the hole. We don't want anyone to lose an eye."

Wally stood and picked up his crutches. "I've already lost a leg. It's someone else's turn to lose a body part."

Sam almost fell over. Was Wally making a joke? And about his leg, no less?

Elsie giggled. "Let's not lose any body parts today, shall we? Wally has lost enough for the nine of us. We should all thank him for taking on our share."

Rose's mouth fell open, and she snapped her head around to look at Sam, her expression blazing with indignation. Two weeks ago, Sam would have felt the same way and probably yelled at the teacher for mocking his *bruder,* but Elsie wasn't being malicious. She was treating Wally like a normal child, teasing him as if he were in on the joke instead of the butt of it.

"*Denki* for giving my share, Wally," Jethro said, playfully punching Wally in the arm.

Wally grinned and punched back. It was the most ordinary, heartwarming thing Sam had ever seen — Wally laughing with his friends like a typical, healthy boy. Sam thought he might melt into a puddle right there in the school yard. He stood beside his team just staring at Elsie. How could he have wanted her in tears? How could he have yelled at her?

"You gonna stand there all day?" Reuben yelled.

Sam pulled himself out of his own head. He should probably see about getting this boulder out before Ascension Day. He grinned sheepishly at Elsie, trying to ignore the glare Rose was giving him. Elsie's arm was still hooked with Rose's elbow, but Rose might have been a statue.

He positioned himself partially behind and to the side of the team and snapped the reins. "Ho, haw, haw," he yelled. The mules dug in their heels and moved forward. The ropes grew taut as the mules strained against the boulder. Sam glanced behind him. The boulder slowly tilted toward him and then broke free from the soil altogether. He immediately pulled up on the reins. "Reuben, Wally, get another rope."

A week ago, Sam wouldn't have considered asking Wally to be the one to help him, but if Elsie could treat Wally like all the other boys, so could Sam.

Reuben sprinted to the wagon for another rope, then he and Wally helped Sam secure it around the bottom of the boulder. If Wally got his fingers briefly tangled in the knots, nobody said anything.

Sam turned to Elsie, who had finally released Rose and was standing with her fingers wrapped around the chinks in the backstop fence, intently studying what Sam and the boys were doing on the other side. "Where do you want this rock?"

Her smile couldn't have gotten any bigger. She pointed to the east side of the school. "Put it there a few feet from the wall. I'll work some other rocks around it and make a planter."

Sam gave her a nod. Wally and Reuben ran to the other side of the backstop, and Sam got his team moving again. The boys cheered when they pulled the boulder clear out of the hole. Sam guided the team to pull the boulder to the side of the school where Elsie wanted it. He untied the ropes and led his team to the water tub for a drink.

Elsie and the boys grabbed their buckets and shovels and started filling the hole. "Do you need me to haul in more dirt to fill up the hole?" Sam called.

Elsie pointed to the north side of the field. "*Nae.* There's a pile over there we can use."

Rose ambled toward Sam as if she'd had a very hard day. "I knew it was bad, Sam. I really did. But I had no idea it was this bad."

Sam patted Buck's neck while Jerry Boy took a drink. "What's bad?"

She wrapped her fingers around Sam's arm. "The way Miss Stutzman makes fun of Wally. No wonder you want her fired."

"I don't want her fired, Rose. I already told you. She wants to help Wally."

Rose shook her head. "She's a snob, and she thinks she's better than us. She talked to you as if you were her friend."

"Elsie is my friend. There's nothing wrong with that."

"Nae," Rose insisted. "A teacher should be humble and modest. Miss Stutzman doesn't know her place."

Sam furrowed his brow. Rose had some strange notions. "I don't see that a teacher's place is any different from yours or mine."

Rose's breathing became shallow, and beads of sweat appeared on her upper lip. Her hands trembled, and she clasped them together in front of her. "I'm talking sense, Sam. Why won't you believe me?"

Sam found himself wishing he was helping Elsie and the boys fill in that hole. What was he supposed to do with an agitated girl who thought she was his best friend? He was just trying to water his mules. "It's not a matter of believing. I have a different opinion, that's all."

"*Dat* agrees with me. He's not happy that she's been so mean to Wally."

Had Rose heard nothing he'd told her? How much plainer could he make himself? He tried to smile through gritted teeth. "Elsie is trying to help Wally stop feeling sorry for himself."

"By making fun of him?"

"By treating him like all the other children."

Rose narrowed her eyes. "She makes fun of all the children?"

Sam placed his hands on her shoulders and looked her squarely in the eye. "Rose, please will you trust me on this? Miss Stutzman is helping Wally. It would be terrible for our family if she got fired. Do you understand?"

Rose softened like butter in July. "Of course I understand. You're my best friend. All you have to do is ask, and I'll bake you a cake or drive your team or even help you dig up rocks. And if you ever have another problem with the teacher again, I will make sure my *dat* knows about it. I'll do whatever you need me to do."

Sam nodded. "Right now, I need you to hold your tongue and try to be nice to Elsie. She needs friends."

Rose pressed her lips together. "I don't think we should be her friend. And you shouldn't call her Elsie."

Sam stifled a growl. "Okay. That's okay. I just hope you'll believe me when I say that she is a wonderful-*gute* teacher, and she is taking very *gute* care of all the children."

"Are you her friend?"

Sam wasn't sure how to answer that. He liked Elsie, but he'd yelled at her and accused her of being cruel. Even if he wanted to be friends with her, she didn't necessarily want to be friends with him.

Rose sensed his hesitation. "She is Wally's teacher. You need to keep your distance. We all do."

Sam nodded and pasted an I'll-think-about-that look on his face, even though he wasn't going to give it one more thought.

Or was he?

Should he keep his distance from Elsie? Would it be better for Wally and his brothers? He glanced in the direction of the softball diamond, where Elsie and the boys were busy filling the hole. Elsie was a puny little thing with a personality like a firecracker. She made him mad, and she made him think. She wasn't afraid to stand up to him, and she did what she thought was right, no matter what. She had inspired Wally to practice hitting the ball — even if it was only because he wanted to hit it over her head.

Rose followed him while he hitched the team up to the wagon. "What is your favorite pie? I've never made you a pie before."

Sam winced. Rose shouldn't feel obligated to make him a pie. "Don't waste a pie on me. Find a boy you're interested in and make one for him."

Rose's ears turned bright red. "I want to make a pie for you, but I can't if you don't tell me your favorite kind."

"Okay, but make one for that boy you're interested in too."

She nodded enthusiastically. "Don't worry. I will."

"My favorite is pumpkin."

Her face fell. "Pumpkin? I don't like pumpkin. I'll make you a peanut butter chocolate pie. Everybody loves my recipe."

Sam didn't especially like peanut butter, but if that's what Rose wanted to make, his *bruders* would eat it. Sam finished hitching the mule team to the wagon and pulled his shovel and gloves from the wagon bed.

"What are you doing?" Rose said.

"I'm going to help fill up that hole. I brought another shovel if you want to help."

A line appeared between her brows. "I thought you were only going to take out that rock. They can fill it back up by themselves."

"I know, but I want to help." He flashed

her a smile. "It looks like they're having a *wunderbarr* time."

Rose's whole face sort of puckered. "You just said you had to help take out the rock. You didn't say anything about filling the hole. I was hoping you could take me home. We can spend more time together." She put her hands behind her back, leaned closer, and swayed back and forth. "I need to make a pie. You're going to love my peanut butter chocolate pie."

"I need to help fill that hole."

Rose cast a sour look in Elsie's direction. "Wally shouldn't be straining himself like that."

"That's why I need to stay."

Rose flounced to the wagon and retrieved the other shovel. "Okay then, but I won't have time to make a pie today."

Sam gave her a good-natured smile. "I don't mind. Save it for that boy you have your eye on."

Rose laughed. "You are so funny, Sam Sensenig."

He had no idea why she was so amused.

CHAPTER TWELVE

Elsie stood on the pitcher's mound and stared down Wally Sensenig. Prosthetic leg or no prosthetic leg, Wally had become a formidable hitter, and Elsie wasn't about to go easy on him.

Wally had started wearing his prosthetic leg to school every day. After second recess he always took it off and used his crutches. The leg couldn't have been comfortable, and Wally was still getting used to it.

From the first day, he had started hitting better with the prosthetic leg. Running was still slow and painful, but he hit farther and farther, and even for as awkwardly as he ran, he always made it to first base and sometimes to second.

They had spent an hour on Saturday filling in the hole on the first base line, and the diamond had never looked better. Sam had stayed the whole time, as had his friend Rose, who had taken a pointed dislike to

Elsie. Elsie didn't know why, except that Rose seemed the type of girl who needed a lot of attention, and Sam hadn't paid Rose a lot of attention that day. Rose knew that Elsie and Sam had played softball together. If Rose and Sam were dating, Rose might be jealous, but Elsie couldn't help that. If a girl didn't want to be jealous, she should pick an ugly boyfriend.

Wally lifted his bat and grinned in Elsie's direction. He was gaining confidence. Softball and his prosthetic leg were the reasons. Elsie nearly sighed out loud. Wally looked so much like his brother when he smiled. But it didn't matter. If Sam and Rose Mast were boyfriend and girlfriend, Elsie didn't care to get between them, no matter how handsome Sam Sensenig was.

"I'm going to hit it to the barn," Wally said, pointing at the Millers' barn at least a quarter mile behind the pitcher's mound.

Elsie raised an eyebrow. "Not with one of my pitches, you won't."

Two days before, on Tuesday, Ida Mae Burkholder finally voiced what should have been obvious to all of them. It was the second inning, and Wally had ambled to a section of the outfield where the ball never got hit. He didn't seem to mind. What he really wanted to do was hit. Ida Mae was pitching for Wally's team, and after a few warm-up pitches, she stepped off the mound and looked at Wally's section of the field. "Miss Stutzman," she said, "why doesn't Wally play first base?"

To Elsie, it was as if the clouds had parted and she was seeing the sun for the first time. Of course. She'd never thought of giving Wally the position of first baseman because until recently, he hadn't been that eager to actually be part of the game. The first baseman rarely had to go anywhere but to the bag. Wally could do that on his prosthetic leg. She had turned to Lizzy Jane Mast, who had been playing first base. First was her position. Elsie would switch only if Lizzy agreed to surrender her base. "What do you think about that, Lizzy Jane?"

Lizzy Jane had shrugged. "I don't care. Can I play third base?"

Reuben was playing third base, and he agreed to play catcher. The catcher traded for shortstop, and the shortstop, Tobias Raber, good-naturedly moved to the outfield.

Elsie nodded to Ida Mae. "Go ask Wally if he'd like to play first base."

Wally had been so far in the outfield, he hadn't heard a word they'd said. Ida Mae had hiked out to his spot and talked to him.

Elsie hadn't been able to hear what they were saying, but Wally's expression had traveled between surprise and doubt and finally excitement. As quickly as he had been able to come, he jogged to first base, smiling all the way, and stationed himself a foot or two from the bag.

It had been the best idea since softball had been invented. Wally was just as good at catching the ball as hitting, even with three fingers missing on his left hand. He had caught everything thrown to him and only dropped the ball when Maizy Mischler hit. He always let Maizy on base.

Wally had played first base for two days now, and he was already the best infielder in the school. Elsie couldn't have been more pleased if all her students had gotten 100 percent on their math papers.

Elsie decided to give Wally her fastest fast pitch. If he managed to hit it, it would go farther. She pitched it right down the middle, and Wally fanned up a stiff wind swinging at it.

"Strike one!" Reuben yelled, throwing the ball back to Elsie.

Elsie caught the ball and rolled it around with her fingers. "This one's coming in fast again, Wally. Keep your eye on it."

"You keep your eye on it," Wally said, with

more confidence than Elsie had ever seen from him. "I might hit you in the head."

Elsie narrowed her eyes in mock suspicion. "You'd like that, wouldn't you?"

She pitched it again, and this time, Wally was ready for the speed. His bat made contact with the ball, which soared over Elsie's head, whistling through the air like a firecracker. It went over everybody's head, including Titus Nelson's. He played far outfield because he couldn't catch anything and nobody thought he'd ever have a chance that far out. The children seemed to hold their breath as the ball landed somewhere in the cornfield. Children screamed and cheered and made an incredible ruckus as all five outfielders raced to get the ball.

Wally raised both fists in the air. "Home run!" he yelled.

Elsie came a hair's breadth away from jumping up and down and throwing her mitt in the air in exultation. Instead, she folded her arms and stared Wally down. It was time for one last challenge. "You still have to run the bases if you want it to count."

Wally glared at her, pressed his lips into a determined line, and tossed his bat to the side. With long, purposeful strides, he walked as fast as he could to first base.

Halfway there, his prosthetic leg slipped in the loose dirt, and he fell to the ground. He slapped his hand against the ground in frustration, and Elsie held her breath.

Dear Lord, please help him up. Please get him up.

Almost the instant he fell, Maizy Mischler was at his side. She patted both his cheeks, took his hand, and pulled him to his feet. Of course, she didn't really pull him — she was less than half his size — but she gave him the nudge and maybe the will he needed to stand again. Hand in hand, he and Maizy strode to first base. Elsie's gaze traveled to the outfield. The outfielders had reached the cornfield. It was only a matter of time before they found that ball, and Wally and Maizy weren't breaking any speed records.

She heard yelling from inside the cornfield. Someone had found Wally's ball, and he and Maizy had barely made it to second. Johnny Wengerd, who was playing shortstop, threw his mitt to the ground. "Come on, Reuben, Jethro. Come on, help me!"

Jethro ran to Wally, grabbed his arm, and slung it over his shoulder. Reuben Schmucker as catcher ran to help, along with Tobias and Johnny, Mark Hoover, and Perry Sensenig. Wally called out as the six boys lifted him into the air and started running for third base.

The outfielders emerged from the cornfield, and Titus had the ball firmly in his fist. He handed it to Susie Miller, who had the stronger arm, and she threw it to the second baseman, who had run halfway out to the cornfield to cut off the ball.

The boys, with Wally in tow and Maizy following close behind, rounded third base. Reuben looked over his shoulder as the second baseman threw the ball toward home. "Run, run!" Reuben screamed.

The boys grew wings on their feet. Elsie had never seen anything like it. She gasped as they dove for the plate. There was a fantastic crash of legs and arms and bodies as Wally reached out his hand and smacked home plate right before the ball got there.

"Safe!" Reuben yelled, from flat on his back.

Jethro and the other boys jumped to their feet and cheered as if they'd won a million dollars. Wally rolled onto his back and lifted his fists above his head in a victory salute. Maizy jumped on top of him, and he laughed and gave her a big hug. All the children from both teams sprinted to home plate, squealing and carrying on, jumping up and down and hugging each other. They had all hit a home run today, and they knew it.

Elsie stood alone on the pitcher's mound and sniffed back the threatening tears. It would do no good for her students to see a moment of vulnerability from their teacher. She still had a class to teach. Besides, Wally's triumph would be that much better if he thought he'd irritated his teacher instead of inspired her.

She wished Sam had been here to see it.

"Okay, class," Elsie said. She rang the large bell that sat on her desk. "It's time to go home. Please be sure your desks are clean and your rows are straight."

The last two hours of the day had been completely wasted. The children were too excited about their softball game to concentrate on anything, even singing time. Ringing the bell was like starting a race to escape from school. The classroom exploded, and children hurried out as fast as they could, as if they might get a prize for arriving home first.

The six boys who had carried Wally home had a few scabs and bruises for their trouble, and Elsie had exhausted her supply of ice packs after recess. Jethro had scraped his elbow. Tobias's eyebrow had met with

Johnny Wengerd's knee. The collision hadn't broken the skin, but he had a nice goose egg to prove that something important had happened at school today. Wally had scratched the side of his face diving for home plate, but he didn't seem to notice it. Elsie hoped it didn't keep him from sleeping tonight.

While the other children headed in the other direction, Wally limped to the front of the class to Elsie's desk. "You've never thrown it to me that fast before, Miss Stutzman. I didn't know if I could hit it."

Elsie shrugged. "I didn't want you to hit it. That was my fastest pitch."

Wally's eyes lit up like a pair of stars. "I guess I showed you."

"I guess you did," she said. She closed her notebook and pinned Wally with a significant look. "You have some wonderful-nice friends, you know."

Wally gave her a crooked smile and nodded. "I know."

"That's even better than a home run, don't you think?"

Wally swiped his hand across his eyes. "*Jah.* I guess it is."

CHAPTER THIRTEEN

Dear Sam,

I think we're going to have to go about this a different way. The first thing is, you need to break it off with Rose Mast. She is a very sweet girl, but if you are going to marry my granddaughter, you can't have a girlfriend. Secondly, I am sending Felty to your house with a pumpkin pie baked by my granddaughter. She thinks she made it for one of my *Englisch* neighbors, but I was secretly having her make it for you. I always say, the way to a man's heart is through his stomach. So, please enjoy the pie and think of my granddaughter while you're eating it, then remember that there is lots more where that came from. I will contact you in a few days to see how you liked the pie and then we can make plans from there.

Much love,
Anna Helmuth

P.S. One of my granddaughters had a baby and I have been knitting a blanket for her, so I have not had time to make more pot holders to send to you. Please don't hold this against my granddaughter. Most boys would take her without any pot holders whatsoever.

Sam's feet felt almost too heavy to lift as he trudged up the steps to the school. Despite his low mood, his heart did a little skip as he ascended the stairs into the classroom. It had been nearly a week since he'd seen Elsie. Being with her would be the only bright spot of another rotten day.

Sam didn't know how his life could get much worse. Not only was one of his cows sick, but Rose Mast had brought him a peanut butter chocolate pie, Mamm hadn't been out of bed for three days, and Anna Helmuth wasn't going to give up on her scheme to marry him to her granddaughter. And now this. He slipped his hand into his pocket and fingered the paper there. Just when he had hoped things were going well with Wally. The only bright spot of his week was the pumpkin pie from Anna Helmuth's mysterious granddaughter. Too bad he didn't want anything to do with her.

Elsie sat at her desk reading a textbook. Chalk dusted her hair, her face, her apron. She was an untidy, rumpled, beautiful sight. Sam felt better just breathing her in. He wasn't close enough, but he could almost smell the lavender on her skin and the lilac scent of her hair. It drove him crazy with anticipation.

She looked up and smiled, and it felt like spring again. "Sam." There was so much joy in her voice, he almost forgot why he was upset. Almost. Her smile faded. "Is everything okay?"

"Not really."

She stood and came to him, as if she could solve all his problems if he'd just let her. "What happened? Is Wally all right? What about Perry and Danny?" When he didn't respond, she took his arm, pulled him to a chair in the corner, and nudged him to sit. She pulled up the chair from her desk and sat next to him. She studied his face. "I'd really appreciate it if you said something." She tilted her head to meet his eye. "That is why you came, isn't it?"

He heaved a great sigh. "I'm the worst *bruder* in the world."

One side of her mouth curled up. "Oh, I wouldn't say that. What about Esau? What about Cain? What about Joseph's brothers? They sold him into slavery. I can think of at least a dozen *bruders* who are worse than you."

Sam cracked a smile. "I'd really appreciate it if you just let me wallow in my self-pity for a minute."

She leaned back and folded her arms. "Okay. Go ahead and wallow, but I'd like to be home for dinner by five. Do you want to lock up?"

Sam pulled the sheet of notebook paper from his pocket and handed it to Elsie. She read over it. "This is a grocery list," she said, a question alight in her eyes.

Sam nodded. "Maggie was washing dishes, so she asked Wally to write out a list for her. This is what he wrote."

Realization dawned on her face. It was just as he expected. Elsie wasn't surprised at all. "You're wondering why an eighth grader doesn't know how to spell *biscuit dough* or *oranges.*"

Sam motioned to the list. "He doesn't know how to spell anything."

Elsie folded the sheet of paper and gave it back to Sam. "*Nae,* he doesn't."

"How long have you known?"

"*Ach,* after the first week of school I have a *gute* idea of what my students can do. Wally is behind in all his subjects, but I didn't want to tell you yet. You have about a hundred things to worry about, and Wally's schoolwork isn't the most important thing right now. Wally has to want to learn. His teachers have let him get away with being lazy for so long, he doesn't even remember what hard work looks like."

"It isn't his teachers' fault, Elsie. It's me. It's all me."

Elsie propped her elbows on her knees. "This is why I didn't tell you. You take too much on yourself. Everyone has contributed to the way Wally is, but it's nobody's fault. It's hard not to feel sorry for him."

"But I let him get away with so much. If his teachers tried to push him, I pushed back. I wanted to make things easy on him, and now Danny can read better than Wally can."

"Danny is one of the best readers in his grade."

This should have made Sam feel better, but it didn't. He had no idea how Perry and Danny were doing in school or who their friends were or even whether they were happy or miserable. A growl came from deep in his throat. He had let Wally's problems overshadow his responsibility to the rest of the family. "I've been so worried about Wally that I've all but ignored Perry and Danny. And Maggie too."

"You take too much on yourself, Sam. Perry and Danny are doing fine yet. They're both wonderful nice boys and smart as tacks. Maggie has you for a *bruder.* I don't wonder but she's doing fine too."

Sam didn't feel much better. "I've neglected them."

She scrunched her lips to one side of her face. "The boys come to school in clean clothes every day. They say please and thank you, and it looks like somebody combs their hair in the morning before school. You're doing fine, Sam."

"Not with Wally."

"Wally too. As soon as you understood his problem, you were willing to do whatever you needed to do to help. It is the harder way, but it's obvious you'd do anything for your *bruder.*"

The look in her eyes made him feel all soft and mushy, like a slice of bread soaked in milk. Maybe she didn't think he was so bad. He heaved a sigh and asked the harder question. The question he was afraid he didn't want the answer to. "Is . . . is Wally *doppick?* Maybe he can't read any better than he does."

Elsie grunted. Even a grunt was adorable coming out of her mouth. "*Ach,* don't be silly. Wally isn't dumb. When he was nine, he talked you into electricity and an Xbox. That's not the work of a *dumkoff.* Wally is too smart for his own good. He knows how to manipulate any situation to his advantage." She sprouted a slight grin. "But now we are the ones doing the manipulating, and Wally has no idea what's happening to him. We're teaching him how to work. Wally used to be satisfied with his crutches because they were easier. He used to be satisfied with not playing softball. Do you know how much pain he's gone through to learn to hit? He got a home run yesterday. Did he tell you?"

"*Jah,* he told me first thing when he came home from school."

"He scraped the whole side of his face, but he didn't even care."

"You helped him with softball. Will you help him with his lessons?"

Elsie's lips twitched into a scold. "I already am. I have the four eighth graders read together every morning, and Ida Mae helps Wally especially. Jethro and Wally are math partners."

"Is he learning anything?"

216

She laced her fingers together. "*Jah,* but it's slow."

Sam couldn't stand the thought of his brother not knowing how to spell *buttermilk* or add fractions, even if Elsie said she was working on it. "He needs more help. You got him playing softball and wearing his leg. Can you give him more help with his lessons? Outside of school?"

She thought about it for a second. "He hit a home run. It's probably time to make him miserable again. Now is as good a time as any to start in on the schoolwork. That's going to be a lot less fun than softball, but if we can teach him to love learning and to see why it is *gute* for him, he'll quit fighting us on it."

"What about coming to our house after school? Maybe two days a week. Or probably three days would be better." The thought of seeing Elsie three times a week made his heart thump against his rib cage. Was it proper to have that sort of reaction to the teacher?

"My coming over would cut into Wally's video game time, wouldn't it?" Elsie said.

"*Jah.*"

"That will make him wonderful irritated." She nibbled on her bottom lip. "It's a *gute* plan, but Wally isn't going to like it. He

217

might become impossible to live with."

Sam exaggerated squaring his shoulders. "I can stand it. I lived through the softball nightmare. I can bear anything for Wally's sake."

She laughed. "Okay, then. I can *cum* on Monday."

Sam thought of the dairy he wanted to start. It would have to wait. Wally needed that money more than Sam did. "Is ten dollars an hour enough? I know it's not much."

Elsie nudged him on the shoulder with her pitching arm. He pretended to wince. "Don't be silly. I won't take any money."

"I can't ask you to do it for nothing."

"It's a chance to help one of my scholars. So many parents couldn't care less about how their children do in school."

Sam shook his head. "It's only right that I pay you something."

A light seemed to go on behind her eyes. "What about dinner?"

"What?"

Elsie seemed to grow more and more excited. "Who cooks dinner at your house?"

"Sometimes my *mamm.* Mostly my sister Maggie."

"I hope it doesn't sound rude, but is she a good cook?" she said.

"She makes the best Yankee bean soup I've

ever tasted."

"Hmm," she said, breathing deeply as if trying to catch a whiff of Maggie's soup. "Sounds *appeditlich*. Would Maggie mind feeding me?"

Sam wasn't quite sure he'd heard her right. "You want to eat dinner at my house?"

"Just on the afternoons I come to tutor Wally." She frowned. "Is that too much? I don't want to intrude on your family. Never mind. I shouldn't have asked."

She looked so concerned, Sam had to chuckle. "I think it's a wonderful-*gute* idea. If you are willing to tutor Wally for a meal, you're the one getting the short end of the stick."

"Are . . . are you sure?"

"Wally usually eats dinner in the basement. My *mamm* sometimes eats dinner in her room. It's often just me, Perry, Danny, and Maggie. You'd be the most excitement we've had since Maggie accidentally left a dish towel on top of the stove and almost burned down the kitchen."

She grinned from ear to ear. "I'll come on Monday. Be prepared for a little resistance from Wally."

Sam nodded thoughtfully. "Okay."

"You're strong, Sam. Just keep telling yourself that this is for Wally's own good —

especially when he tells you he hates you or when he cries like a *buplie.*"

"It's for his own good," Sam said.

"He's not going to like it, but I think you're going to have to work up the gumption to insist that he eat dinner with the family."

"Gumption? What kind of word is *gumption?"*

She curled one side of her mouth. "A good word. And you can do it."

"I can do it. I'd do anything for Wally."

"And I'd do just about anything for a *gute* meal, including put up with you."

Sam felt sorry for her for just a second. Elsie must live all alone in some cold little house. Who could blame her for not wanting to cook herself dinner when she got home from school?

Either that, or she wasn't a very *gute* cook.

Sam wasn't so much sneaking as he was ducking under the windows so Elsie couldn't see him. She was sitting right there in plain sight in the kitchen, but Sam didn't want her to see him — not yet, anyway. He was dripping with sweat, there was a smear of mud down his arm, and he probably smelled like an unpleasant mixture of manure and moldy cornstalks. He refused to let Elsie see him like this. Ducking below the kitchen windows, he sneaked around to the mudroom, saying a prayer of thanks that Dat had seen fit to put another entrance down the south hall and away from the kitchen. He could run upstairs and wash his hands, change his clothes, and clean his face all without Elsie being any the wiser. He wasn't vain, but he didn't want to scare her away from dinner with his foul smell.

Elsie had been coming to their house for two weeks. She'd spent six *wunderbarr* afternoons with his family — not that Sam was counting or anything. She always worked with Wally for an hour — which was probably more than either Wally or Elsie could stand — then visited with Maggie until dinner was ready.

Maggie cooked dinner while Wally and Elsie had their lessons in the kitchen. That way, Maggie could keep an eye on Wally and scold him for being lazy when she needed to. She hadn't needed to scold him often. Elsie was too smart to let Wally get away with anything, and Wally seemed to give her begrudging respect even while insisting he couldn't stand her.

Two weeks ago after he'd talked to Elsie, Sam had sat down with Wally and told him that the teacher was going to come after school three days a week to help him with his schoolwork. Wally had still been in a *gute* mood because of his home run, so he hadn't put up much of a fight. But when that first Monday had rolled around, Wally had come home from school with a terrible stomach-ache, telling Sam that he wouldn't be able to sit for a lesson. When Elsie had arrived, Sam had set a nice big bowl on the table and told Wally that if he needed to throw up while studying, he could throw up in that bowl. Wally had moaned and doubled over in pain — which almost made Sam cancel lessons for the day — but he had stood his ground until Elsie had arrived. She had taken one look at Wally and reassured Sam that his *bruder* was faking it, and that if he happened to throw up, the bowl was an excellent idea.

After a week, Wally could see that no one would budge, so he resigned himself to his fate and dragged himself to the kitchen table every day at four o'clock. He always com-plained loudly about having to work while not in school, but he didn't seem to mind the extra attention.

Sometimes when Sam finished his chores early, he'd sit in on part of Wally's lesson. Miss Stutzman always brought fun learning activities that even held Sam's interest.

Wally was sure to catch up on his reading and arithmetic with Elsie helping him. So far as Sam could see, she was the best teacher anyone had ever had.

Sam carefully opened and shut the back door so it didn't make any noise and tiptoed up the back stairs. He peeled off his filthy shirt, washed his face and hands, and shampooed his hair. Would Elsie notice it was wet? Would she think he was strange for washing his hair in the late afternoon? It was just that he wanted to smell as nice as possible for Elsie. She was kind enough to tutor his *bruder.* He should be thoughtful enough to smell *gute.* He scoured the towel over his wet hair to soak up as much water as possible, then smoothed it down as best he could. His curly hair never really behaved itself, but at least it wasn't sticking out all over his head, and it smelled like the ocean breeze. That's what it said right on the bottle.

Sam bounded halfway down the stairs before deciding that bounding seemed too eager. He held up and strolled the rest of the way, listening to Wally argue with Elsie in the kitchen.

"This is *dumm.* I'm never going to need to know how to use fractions."

Sam ambled into the kitchen as if he just

happened to find himself in this part of the house. Elsie looked up at him and smiled. He might as well have died and gone to heaven.

"You need fractions for cooking," Maggie said, stirring something boiling on the stove.

Wally grimaced. "Boys don't cook."

"You might need to learn to cook someday," Sam said, pulling out a chair next to his *bruder.* "What happens when Maggie gets married and moves away? One of us is going to have to cook for the family."

Wally set his pencil down. "Maybe Maggie won't get married."

Sam smirked in his little *bruder*'s direction. "Maggie is smart and sweet and knows how to make *yummasetti.* Besides, look how pretty she is. We'll be lucky to have three more years with her."

Maggie glanced up from the stove just long enough for Sam to catch her smile. "It smells wonderful-*gute* in here," Sam said, winking at his *schwester.*

"You need fractions when you work with money and time and crops," Elsie said. "If you can't do simple math, you'll never know if people are cheating you. You'll be suspicious of everybody or, worse, start to feel stupid. You don't want to go through your life feeling dumber than everyone else. You need to learn your fractions."

"I am dumber than everyone," Wally whined. "I'm dumb and crippled."

Elsie usually scolded Wally severely when he called himself a cripple. This time, she laughed. "You're not going to get off that easily, Wally Sensenig. You're as smart as anyone at that school, and you know it. Quit making excuses."

"But fractions are hard."

Elsie nodded. "The only things worth doing are the hard things." She motioned to a yellow circle cut from cardstock on the table in front of Wally. "Let's try it again. Write a fraction that represents this circle."

Wally's sigh was so deep, Sam thought Wally might pass out. He picked up his pencil and wrote "1/1" in his notebook.

"Gute," Elsie said. "Now take this ruler and draw a line right down the middle of the circle."

Wally did as he was told.

"Now," Elsie said, pointing to one side of the circle, "write a fraction that represents this part."

Wally thought about it for a second then wrote, "1/2."

It was as if he'd hit another home run. Elsie burst into a smile and patted him on the wrist. "Well done, Wally. You know more about fractions than you thought you did."

They kept dividing the circle, and Wally kept writing down fractions. Sam tried to temper his excitement. Wally had a long way to go. But at least for now, fractions seemed to make sense to him.

Maggie called Perry and Danny to dinner, and even Mamm joined them at the table. She seemed to enjoy Elsie's company. It was the fourth time she'd eaten with them since Elsie had started tutoring Wally.

On Elsie's request, Maggie had made chicken bacon ranch pizza, and they spent half the meal slicing pizza and talking about fractions. Danny and Perry enjoyed the lesson too, especially when Elsie praised them for their *gute* answers. Sam ate the last one-twelfth of the pizza, and then Wally cleared his own plate without being asked. He limped to the sink on his prosthetic leg. It was obvious the leg still hurt to walk on, but Wally was trying harder than he'd ever tried before.

It was almost too much to comprehend. How could one puny teacher with a stubborn streak and a blazing fastball have made so much difference in so short a time? The girl Sam had yelled at had somehow convinced Wally to wear his prosthetic leg. Sam had complained to the school board about the teacher who was willing to help Wally learn fractions on her own time.

Sam thought he might burst. He could never repay her for her kindness — not that she would accept payment anyway. While they did the dishes, he found himself longing for her to turn her gaze in his direction. What would he do to see her smile every day? To *make* her smile every day? She took a dish from Maggie and dried it with those graceful hands, and he ached to smooth his fingers against her soft cheeks.

He cleared his throat and shoved the clean silverware into the drawer. He should never let his gratitude get out of hand like that. The next thing he knew, he'd be imagining holding hands with her, or worse, snatching her in his arms and giving her a kiss.

Oy, anyhow.

He was grateful, but a kiss was out of the question.

Wasn't it?

He'd never kiss the teacher, and the girl who had told him he was arrogant wouldn't consider a kiss an expression of appreciation. She'd probably take it as an insult.

Sam swallowed hard. She didn't think he was that offensive, did she?

He had yelled at her. And accused her of being heartless and told her she was incapable of kindness. His heart sank. No kissing for him. He'd have to settle for sending a thank-you note.

After the dishes, Sam walked Elsie to her buggy. It was the least he could do after she'd spent the better part of the afternoon with Wally. And he certainly wasn't going to consider the kissing thing. But tonight was the first night that the thought of kissing her had sort of taken up residence in his head. He determined to say good night and sprint back into the house before he made a fool of himself and scared Miss Stutzman away for good.

"Wally is making *gute* progress," Elsie said. "He'll have fractions by Thanksgiving, Lord willing."

"Thanks to you," he said. His gaze involuntarily traveled to her mouth. *No kissing. No kissing.* He turned his face away and stared at nothing in particular while trying valiantly to get the thought of her lips out of his head.

"And to you. You were smart enough to ask me."

He cocked an eyebrow. "That surprises you, doesn't it?"

She giggled. "Not at all." She hesitated, stifling a grin. "Well, maybe a little. The first time we met, you came clomping into my classroom like an oaf, and then you started snarling. I wasn't sure you could talk in complete sentences."

He groaned. "I was trying to scare you. I didn't know it would never have worked."

"I had worse than you in Ohio. There was one *fraa* who would have had *you* running home with your tail between your legs."

He laughed. "I'm glad I'm not the worst parent you've had."

She shuddered, even though her smile stayed fixed in place. "I sometimes found myself thinking how much easier it would be if all the *kinner* were orphans. They always liked me better than the parents did."

Rose had said Elsie had been fired from her school in Ohio. Was that true, or had Rose made that up to have something to gossip about? If Elsie always refused to back down and made it a point to disagree with parents instead of try to get along for the sake of her job, she might have ruffled a few feathers in Ohio.

Someone with a chip on his shoulder could get a teacher fired, especially if the school board had been unwilling to give Elsie a chance to explain herself.

Like Sam had done.

He cringed when he thought of that first meeting. If the school board in Charm had reacted anywhere near the way he had, no wonder she had lost her job.

"Ach, vell," he said. "They lost a wonderful-*gute* teacher. I'm glad you decided to give our school a chance."

"I'm glad they decided to give me a chance." Her smile faded. "I speak my mind, which often gets me into trouble, but I've tried to hold my tongue, because I really do want this job. I love to teach, and I love the children."

"You've tried to hold your tongue? You called me a presumptuous busybody the first time we met. I had to go home and look up *presumptuous.* I don't even want to guess what it's like when you don't hold your tongue."

She lowered her eyes as an attractive blush traveled up her cheeks. He didn't think he'd upset her, but she was definitely embarrassed. "I shut down the school in Charm for a whole week in January last year."

He widened his eyes. "You closed the school?"

"Without permission. The school board and some of the parents were furious. In November I had requested a new woodstove because the school's stove was broken. It leaked in about seven different places, and the schoolroom would fill with smoke whenever we lit it. I asked for a new stove for weeks. I got some of the *maters* involved, pushing their husbands to press the school board for a new one, but they didn't want to spend the money. For ten days in December, the temperature inside the school was forty-five degrees. We wore coats and hats and the *kinner* brought blankets. I could see my breath during lessons. When January came, there was no stove in sight, so I sent a note home with all the children, telling their parents that school would be canceled until the school board saw fit to pay for a new stove."

Sam gasped. "You didn't."

"I was risking frostbite every time I went to school. One of *die kinner* was bound to catch pneumonia. There was a new stove in the school three days later."

Sam smiled. "It was the right thing to do for sure and certain, but school boards don't like pushy teachers."

She expelled a quick laugh. "Pushy? I was polite for two whole months."

"I don't wonder but that the children were grateful."

Elsie nibbled on her bottom lip. "The children had bright red cheeks and runny noses all winter. Most of the *maters* secretly thanked me, but no one defended me in

May when the school board told me I wasn't welcome back the next year." The memory seemed to give her some pain. He didn't like seeing the light fade from her eyes. "Don't tell anyone," she said with a hint of a smile on her face.

"I don't doubt but they are kicking themselves for letting you go. Who is going to whip their spoiled little boys into shape? Who will play softball with the children and teach fractions using pizza?"

"Mary Schlabach. She is a wonderful-shy girl who never raises her voice above a whisper and wouldn't dare squeak without permission. She would just as soon freeze to her chair as cross the school board in anything."

"It sounds as if she's better fitted to be a quilter."

Elsie lowered her head and giggled. "She's a very nice girl, but she shouldn't be teaching children. It isn't her fault that the school board was looking for someone completely different from me."

"Have you heard how she's doing?"

She waved her hand as if she didn't care. "My cousin Eliza has a son at the school, and she doesn't have much to say about Mary, but that is probably because she's my cousin and wants to make me feel better.

Amish children are easy to teach. Mary will do fine."

"Mary wouldn't do fine if Wally were in her class."

"*Ach, vell,* Wally is a special case."

"*Jah,*" Sam said. "He requires a very special kind of teacher. I thank the *gute* Lord the school board in Charm is so inflexible."

Elsie could have lit up a cave with her smile. "You've changed your mind since the first time we talked."

He pumped his eyebrows up and down. "I guess I have."

She giggled as if she couldn't hold it in. *"Denki."*

Rose Mast came strolling down the sidewalk with a bright pink cake in her hands. Sam groaned inwardly, but when Elsie snapped her head up to look at him, he wasn't altogether sure he hadn't groaned out loud. He immediately felt sorry. He and Rose were friends, but Rose's treatment of Elsie always bordered on rude, and Sam didn't like it. The *gute* Lord had sent Elsie to the Sensenig family, and nobody should treat Elsie with anything but kindness.

Rose pasted a smile on her lips and glued her gaze to Elsie's face. "*Vie gehts,* Sam?" she said, and it seemed as if she made a deliberate point of leaving Elsie out of her greeting.

Elsie smiled at Rose. Sam appreciated that Elsie was eager to like everybody, even when they did things that should have set her against them. That's why she was such a *gute* teacher. She loved her students no matter what, even when they were naughty.

"Look at that cake," Elsie said. "It's prettier than a picture."

Rose seemed to enjoy the praise, even if she didn't particularly like Elsie. "*Denki.* It's strawberry-vanilla. Sam's favorite."

Nae, it wasn't. He liked coconut and chocolate. Strawberry wasn't even one of his twenty-five most favorite.

"I make Sam and his family a cake every Friday night."

Sam smiled, even though the thought of strawberry cake made the roof of his mouth itch. "We're very grateful."

Rose kept her eyes on Elsie as the laughter tripped from her lips. Sam wasn't sure what was so funny, but if Rose was happy, he was happy. He wanted everybody to be happy, but he didn't really care about Rose's happiness in particular. Why was he so *ferhoodled* all of a sudden?

Elsie was still attempting to win Rose over with a smile. "Maggie says all the time that you are the kindest neighbor anyone could ask for."

Rose narrowed her eyes, as if trying to work out in her head why Elsie was standing in Sam's yard. "All the time?"

There was nothing to feel guilty about, but Sam felt uneasy all the same. Maybe it was because only moments earlier, he'd been thinking very seriously about Elsie Stutzman's lips. "Elsie comes three days a week to tutor Wally."

Rose's eyes narrowed to slits on her face. "A teacher shouldn't give the scholars homework. Learning stays at school. That's what my *dat* says."

Elsie kept smiling. "I agree. The *Englisch* schools give homework even to their first graders. But I haven't given Wally homework. I'm just helping him along with some of his lessons."

Rose looked sideways at Elsie while talking to Sam. "Lizzy says Wally is far behind in school."

Had everybody known that but Sam? He hated that other children talked about his brother behind his back. All the more reason for Elsie to tutor him. "That is why Miss Stutzman is helping Wally. So he can catch up."

Rose pursed her lips. "It doesn't seem fair

to the other students to give Wally extra lessons."

Sam clenched his teeth. It had always been hard to reason with Rose when she got an idea in her head. "Lizzy says he's behind. He needs the help."

"*Jah,* but it still doesn't seem fair," Rose said. "One student shouldn't get special treatment."

Elsie seemed as unruffled as ever. "I care about all my students. I'd be happy to help your *schwesteren* if they need it."

Rose frowned. "My *dat* doesn't like homework." The lines piled up on her forehead. "It isn't proper to spend so much time in a student's home, especially where a single man lives. It's in the *Ordnung,* I think."

Sam didn't follow her reasoning and didn't want to try. "Really, Rose, it's fine. Maggie cooks while Elsie and Wally sit at the kitchen table and do lessons, and then we have dinner together."

Of all the things Sam could have said, this seemed to upset Rose the most. She batted her eyes and sprouted a confused, disturbed look on her face. "I could cook dinner for you while the teacher and Wally do lessons. That would be better than making Maggie cook every night." She turned to Elsie. "What days do you come? I'll cook dinner for you."

That was completely unacceptable, but Sam didn't know how to say it without sounding as hostile as he felt. He pressed his lips together and swallowed the golf ball–sized lump in his throat. "Maggie doesn't mind cooking. She'd have nothing to do if you cooked for us. Besides, I don't want your family to go hungry."

Rose swatted his concern away and nearly dropped her cake. "*Ach,* they don't care. Mamm cooks dinner. She can spare me three days a week. What is your favorite food, Sam? I'll come over and make it Monday night."

Sam would have to put his foot down. Rose coming over to make dinner would cut into the time she should be looking for a husband, and it would cut into the time that Sam got to spend alone with Elsie. He was honest enough to admit that he enjoyed Elsie's company, and Rose would only be in the way, even if she was his fake best friend. "Rose," he said, making his tone hard and unyielding, "Maggie can make out just fine on her own."

Elsie was trying to be helpful. "I help her when I finish tutoring Wally."

That only made Rose more determined. "I won't hear of you helping Maggie, not when I am such a good cook. I like to cook for Sam. We're the best of friends."

The last thing Sam wanted was for Rose to feel obligated to him as a friend. It was too much. "We don't need help with meals, but *denki* for the offer. You are a kind neighbor, and we all appreciate your treats."

Rose smiled a condescending smile, as if Sam didn't know what was good for him and she was going to make him see. Elsie could probably hear his teeth grinding from where she stood.

"Let's go in and show everyone the cake," Rose said. She mustered a gracious, unpleasant smile for Elsie. "You were just leaving, weren't you?"

"Of course," Elsie said, with more grace than Rose had shown the entire conversation. "*Denki* again for dinner, Sam. Maggie makes wonderful-*gute* pizza. Be sure to tell her."

Rose set her gaze squarely on Sam. "I make *appeditlich* pizza. My *mamm* says I could win a prize."

"I *have* tried yours," Sam said, hoping to help Rose shed some of her hostility. "And it is delicious."

Rose was suddenly all smiles. "*Gute.* I'll bring some on Monday night."

How had she done that? Rose was almost

as persistent as Anna Helmuth.

Elsie practically tiptoed to her buggy and hopped into the seat without another word. She gave Sam a tiny wave before snapping the reins and turning her horse toward the road.

Rose watched Elsie's buggy all the way down the road. "I don't know, Sam. It doesn't feel right to me, her coming here like that."

"What's wrong with it? Wally needs help, and Elsie is willing to help him."

"She's the teacher. She shouldn't be eating dinner with your family. She's giving Wally special privileges that aren't fair to the other children."

Sam frowned. "Do you think so?"

"*Jah.* And it's not proper for her to be at your house, Sam. You're not married."

Sam didn't like the sound of that, but Rose might be right. The Amish could be touchy about nothing at all. Elsie was helping Wally. It had nothing to do with Sam. He growled silently and wrapped his fingers around the back of his neck. That's how it had started out, but it wasn't exactly true now. Milking cows and doing farm chores left his mind a lot of time for thinking, and Elsie seemed to wrap herself around his thoughts more and more often. Even if

239

Wally mastered fractions or got really good at spelling words like *presumptuous*, Sam would be very reluctant to tell Elsie not to come back. She was becoming a brighter and brighter spot to his days than he would have imagined she could. He liked being with her. Was that so bad?

Apparently it was.

"She isn't the modest, quiet type of girl who should be teaching. She's just too friendly. That's the long and short of it."

He wouldn't feel guilty about Elsie tutoring Wally if he didn't enjoy Elsie's company so much. Was Rose trying to steer him away from trouble?

Sam shook his head. He and Elsie were just friends, tied together in the common goal of helping Wally. "I don't think any of our neighbors would deny Wally the help he needs just because they're touchy about the teacher eating dinner at our house."

"Of course we want to do everything we can for Wally, but there's got to be a better way." Rose pressed her lips together. They turned white at the edges before she spoke. "I could tutor him."

"Rose, your last day of eighth grade, you told me you'd never set foot in a school again. In your last spelling bee, a fourth grader beat you with the word *munch*."

"Where did you hear that? That's just a rumor."

He chuckled. "Maggie was that fourth grader."

Rose gave him the stink eye. "I never liked school."

Sam shrugged. "Elsie is smart, and she knows how to handle Wally. You are a nice girl, Rose, but you were always better at hopscotch than arithmetic."

"That's a *hesslich* thing to say about your best friend."

Best friend again. Why in the world did she think they were best friends? Though he wanted to, it didn't seem right to set her straight, especially when she seemed to be so upset. Besides, she was holding a strawberry cake, and he didn't want to seem ungrateful. He shrugged off his annoyance. "Wally needs to learn his fractions."

And if the teacher was as pretty as a picture and wonderful pleasant to talk to, what was wrong with that? He couldn't see it in his heart to make a fuss about it. Surely his neighbors understood it was for Wally's own good.

"I'm not giving up," Rose said.

"Giving up what?"

She squared her shoulders. "We need to do what's best for Wally. And you, Sam.

241

That teacher has talked you into something that is not going to turn out well for either of you. Sometimes a best friend has to do what's right instead of what's wanted." She flashed him a smile. "Let's take this cake in and show Maggie. You're going to love it."

Do what's right instead of what's wanted? Surely Rose wasn't going to try to force herself into the house and teach Wally math. It would be painful for both of them, with or without the cake.

Anna Helmuth ushered Sam into her house and shut the door against the wind. "*Ach,* Sam Sensenig, on days like this I wish I had a phone! And a camera." She clutched at her chest, trying to catch her breath as if she'd just run all the way up Huckleberry Hill. "If I had a phone, I could have called you and told you not to come. My grand-daughter isn't here."

Sam tried to look puzzled, as if he didn't know what Anna was talking about. "Your granddaughter? I thought you needed me to look at your hay."

Anna smiled her twinkly grandmother smile. "*Ach,* Sam. I don't care about the hay."

Felty Helmuth sat in his recliner reading the newspaper. "I care."

Anna pulled Sam farther into the house. "I wanted you to meet my granddaughter, so I asked you to come check on our hay. I was being tricky, but it doesn't matter, because she's not here."

Sam didn't even have to try to look disappointed. Elsie had come to his house today because Wally had a doctor's appointment tomorrow, and Sam wouldn't get to see her — all because Anna was eager to get her granddaughter married off.

Anna had invited him up to her house because she had told him she was worried about not having enough hay for the winter. Sam had been fully aware the invitation had been a ploy to introduce him to her granddaughter. Amid his disappointment about Elsie, he was also relieved. Sam must have done something recently to please *Gotte*. His prayers weren't usually answered in such an obvious way.

"Annie-banannie," Felty said from his recliner, "even if you had a phone, Sam doesn't have a phone. You wouldn't have been able to call him."

Anna sighed and shook her head. "Oh, Sam, if only you had a phone."

Sam smiled sadly at Anna, as if he shared her frustration about not having a phone. "It's all right, Anna. I only came to look at your hay, and I'm sure it's still here." He handed Anna the beautiful chocolate cake he'd brought with him. "And I brought you a cake."

Anna cheered up immediately. She set the cake on the table and gazed at it like a baking trophy. "A cake? You truly do want to impress my granddaughter, don't you?"

He didn't want to impress anybody, and he certainly didn't want Anna to get the wrong idea. "*Nae,* not at all. We just had an extra cake sitting around, and I thought you might like it."

Anna's eyes sparkled as if she were in on the joke. "An extra cake sitting around? What a tease you are."

He was telling the truth. Nearly every day for two weeks, Rose had brought Sam's family some sort of dessert, be it cookies or a pie or glazed doughnuts. All homemade, all wonderful delicious, all unnecessary. Rose had been quite offended when Sam put his foot down and told her in no uncertain terms that she was *not* cooking dinner for his family on the nights Elsie came to tutor. Plump tears had rolled down her cheeks when she whined that she was just trying to be a *gute* friend. Being a *gute* friend was one thing — intruding on dinnertime three nights a week was another.

Rose was trying to be a true and loyal friend with all the desserts, but even Sam's sweet tooth was getting tired. The treats had been piling up, and Sam figured if he gave the cake to Anna and Felty, he wouldn't have to bury it in the backyard or force-feed it to his *bruders.*

"*Cum,* sit," Anna said, taking his elbow and pulling a chair out from under the table for him. "You're such a thoughtful boy. I didn't even know you could cook."

He shifted in his chair. "Rose Mast made it."

Anna gave him a kindly smile and shook her finger at him. "Now, Sam. I've already told you. You can't marry my granddaughter if you're dating Rose Mast. She is a lovely girl, but you are meant for my granddaughter. You young people have such a hard time following directions. I only wish I had a camera so I could take a picture of her and show you how pretty she is, though there was never a girl with so much beauty and so little vanity."

Sam gave Anna a half smile. He'd already tried being direct and blunt with Anna. He was just going to have to put her off until the granddaughter left town or found a boyfriend. The trouble was, if the granddaughter was as desperate as Anna hinted she was, she'd never find a boyfriend. "How long is your granddaughter going to be in town?"

Anna sat down and patted his hand. "Now don't you worry about that. She'll be here long enough."

Long enough to drive Sam crazy.

Long enough that he probably couldn't avoid her forever. He'd have to meet her. Even if the granddaughter was desperate, she could probably be made to see reason. He'd just tell her he wasn't interested, and then Anna would stop pestering him. He hated to hurt anyone's feelings, but he no longer had time for Anna's persistence.

"I would really like to talk to your granddaughter, Anna. The sooner the better."

This made Anna so happy, she would have exploded if she'd been a firecracker. "Even without seeing a picture? Why, Sam Sensenig, you are even more *wunderbarr* than I had hoped."

"What is her name?"

The wrinkles gathered around her mouth. "Well, her given name is Elizabeth."

Sam curled his lips upward. If he was going to have to meet the girl, he might as well be cheerful about it. "That's a very pretty name. I like it."

Anna nodded. "Then you should call her

Elizabeth — whatever you like the best."

"How old is she?" Sam said, not knowing if he wanted the answer.

Anna studied his face, as if wondering why he would ask such a question. This was not a good sign. "Well, she's not too young and not too old. The perfect age for you."

Sam swallowed hard and reconsidered his plan. Maybe it would be better to avoid a meeting altogether. If Anna didn't want to tell him how old the granddaughter was, it meant she was probably well into her thirties — at least. He squared his shoulders. All the more reason to get it over with. "There is a gathering for *die youngie* tomorrow night at Yutzys' house." He emphasized *die youngie,* just in case the granddaughter was too old to attend. "Do you think she would want to come?"

"For sure and certain, as long as she doesn't suspect anything."

"The Yutzys have a little footbridge out behind their house. Tell her to meet me there at seven o'clock sharp, and we can have a talk."

Sam could have read a book just by the light of Anna's smile. "That is a wonderful-*gute* idea." Her face suddenly fell and the light in her eyes went out. "But how will I ever convince her to meet you on the footbridge? She doesn't want a husband until January."

How picky was this girl that she even had a certain month in mind? He forced a smile. "You are the expert matchmaker, Anna. I know you will come up with a *gute* plan."

"He's right, Banannie," Felty said. "You are smart enough to outwit even our granddaughter."

Anna seemed satisfied with that answer. "I will do my best for Sam. His future happiness depends on it."

"Okay then," Sam said, standing up, "I'll look forward to meeting your granddaughter at seven o'clock tomorrow night." It wasn't really a lie. He looked forward to putting this whole nonsense behind him, even if it meant hurting Anna's plain, elderly granddaughter's feelings. It couldn't be helped.

Anna reached up and patted Sam on the cheek. "You're a *gute* boy, Sam. I've always thought so."

She wouldn't like him so well when he had dashed all her hopes and dreams, but for now, it was nice to be on her good side. Anna Helmuth was the *mammi* everyone wished they had, even if she did like to meddle.

Anna had to push extra hard to shut the

door behind Sam Sensenig. The wind was whipping up ferociously outside. She turned to Felty and clapped her hands together. "Well, dear, I knew he'd come around. Persistence is a matchmaker's most important quality."

"Why didn't you tell him how old Elsie is? There's no shame in being twenty-two or twenty-three or however old she is."

Anna waved a hand in his direction. "I didn't want to give Sam an excuse. Rose Mast is not yet twenty. Twenty-two might seem too old to him — or what if he likes older girls? He'd talk himself out of our Elsie before the lamb has a chance to shake its tail. Elsie is just the right age. He'll figure that out when he meets her."

"I suppose that makes sense," Felty said, "but why didn't you tell him she's the new schoolteacher?"

Anna pulled a knife from the cupboard and cut a generous slice of the cake Sam had brought. "It scares boys off when they think a girl is smarter than they are."

"But Banannie, Elsie doesn't want to date someone who's *dumm.*"

"Sam's not *dumm,* but I don't know how he feels about smart girls. It's best to let him fall in love with her first and let him find out how smart she is later." Anna pulled out two plates and two forks and served a slice of cake for Felty and one for herself.

Felty pointed to Anna. "A pretty face isn't the only thing Elsie inherited from you, Annie. You're both wonderful smart."

"Now, Felty dear," Anna said, handing her husband a thick piece of chocolate cake, and right before dinner, no less. "Elsie got my smarts, but she's much prettier than an eighty-five-year-old woman."

"Not to me she isn't."

CHAPTER FOURTEEN

There was only one way Elsie could see to put a stop to this nonsense, and it *wasn't* by putting her foot down with Mammi. If Mammi was so stubbornly determined that Elsie meet this mystery boy, Elsie would oblige her. She planned on marching up that footbridge and telling whoever he was that she was in no way interested in a boyfriend and to please never bother her again. She knew how to be blunt, and she knew how to be direct. She just didn't particularly want to embarrass him or hurt his feelings.

Ach, vell. It had to be done. She'd get no peace from Mammi until she did. As long as this boy didn't turn out to be like Wyman Wagler and follow her all over town like a puppy dog, everything would be put to rights by 7:05. Surely Mammi wouldn't try to match her with someone as desperate as Wyman Wagler. Surely he'd be a reasonable young man who would leave her alone for good.

There was no volleyball game in the Yutzys' front yard tonight. It was November first, and last night the wind had blown in an icy rain that had driven most activities inside. Though the children had gone outside to play today, Elsie hadn't organized a softball game. It was too wet and too cold. Wally had been one of the most disappointed, but even he could see that they couldn't play in weather like that.

Elsie walked into the Yutzys' house. Four young men were playing Ping-Pong at a portable table set up in the great room. Carolyn and Clara Yutzy were helping their *mater* with a batch of pretzels in the kitchen, and three or four other girls stood around the table mixing up bowls of honey butter and mustard sauce.

"Elsie!" Carolyn called as she dipped a twist of dough into a baking soda mixture.

"Hallo," Elsie called back.

Carolyn set her pretzel on the pan, wiped her hands, and came around the table. "*Ach, du lieva.* I haven't seen you for awhile."

Elsie smiled. She didn't know a lot of people in Bonduel yet, but it was nice that she had a few friends. Carolyn was one of the nicest girls she'd met — open and accepting and exceptionally kind. She didn't look at Elsie as if she were trying to find something wrong with her, and she had good sense and humor in her face that drew people to her as if they hoped some of her wisdom would rub off on them. "It's been over a month. The last time I saw you was at the Eichers' gathering."

Carolyn nodded. "Where Sam Sensenig ambushed you and gave you a lecture."

It *had* been a long time. That night, Elsie had wanted to run away at the very sight of Sam Sensenig. Now, not so much. Would Carolyn be shocked to know that Elsie would spend every day with Sam if she could find a *gute* excuse? Just the thought of him made her heart flip all over itself. Was it the way he smiled or the intensity in his eyes when he talked about his *bruder*? He was fiercely loyal to his family and yet so vulnerable because of them, unnecessarily hard on himself and unfailingly kind to everyone else.

And she really liked him.

Much as she would have preferred to spend the evening thinking of Sam, there were more pressing matters at hand. "Is there a window that looks out on the backyard?"

If she thought it was a strange request,

Carolyn didn't flinch. She hooked her elbow around Elsie's and led her down a long hall to the back door. The top half of the door held a nine-pane window.

"Where is the footbridge?" Elsie asked.

Carolyn pointed to the right. "Over there. Behind the tall aspens."

Elsie squinted into the light rain, and her stomach fell to the floor. There was indeed someone standing on the footbridge, for sure and certain waiting for her. He had his back turned to the house, so she couldn't see his face, but even from this distance, she could tell he was a hefty man with very bad posture.

Or maybe . . . she pressed her nose against the glass. He was hunched over with his elbows resting on the railing, and he was . . . fishing? Who fished in weather like this? Was the brook behind the Yutzys' house big enough to fish in?

Elsie turned around, pressed her back against the door, and blew air from between her lips. She had hoped against hope that he would have had the *gute* sense not to show up. "Oh, *sis yuscht,*" she whispered, as if whoever that was out there would hear her if she said it too loudly.

Carolyn cocked an eyebrow. She wasn't one for dramatics. Neither was Elsie, but this situation suddenly seemed very dire. "Something scary out there?" Carolyn said.

Elsie almost choked on her annoyance. "My *mammi* wants to marry me off to whoever is standing on your footbridge."

Carolyn's other eyebrow inched up to meet the first one. She turned her gaze out the window. "Are you sure that's who your *mammi* wants you to —"

"I love my *mammi,* but sometimes she makes me a little cross. She arranged a meeting on your footbridge with some boy she wants me to marry, and she's been so persistent and so eager that I finally agreed just to make her happy." Elsie wrapped her fingers around Carolyn's arm. "I really don't want to marry that boy standing on the bridge."

"Of course you don't," Carolyn said. "That's Vernon Schmucker."

Vernon Schmucker? The thirty-two-year-old bachelor who still came to gatherings in hopes of finding a bride? Elsie thought she might be sick. She'd already had an encounter with Vernon, and it hadn't been at all pleasant.

"At one time or another, Vernon has probably asked every girl in both Bonduel districts if he could drive them home from a *singeon,*" Carolyn said. "Poor Suvie

Newswenger said yes and then couldn't shake him for six months. He's very keen on finding a *fraa*."

Really, Mammi? Don't you think I could attract someone slightly younger and more interesting than Vernon Schmucker?

Was this what Mammi thought of her? Elsie did speak her mind and tended to ruffle feathers wherever she went, but she'd never be desperate enough for Vernon Schmucker. Never.

Never.

Elsie slumped her shoulders. "Mammi must think I'm hopeless."

"Stuff and nonsense," Carolyn said. "Your *mammi* can't help meddling. You came into town suddenly. Maybe she didn't have time to find another young man. Vernon is the most convenient, most willing bachelor in Bonduel."

"*Ach,* I wish she hadn't done this. Now I'm going to have to go out there and tell Vernon I'm not interested, and he's going to be embarrassed, especially if Mammi got his hopes up."

Carolyn shook her head. "Vernon doesn't get embarrassed, but he is persistent. If he thinks there is even the slightest interest on your part, he won't give up."

Elsie groaned. "My *mammi* has probably

planted all sorts of notions in his head."

Carolyn sighed in exasperation. "If she mentioned marriage to Vernon, he's probably drooling."

Elsie's groan turned into a growl. "Dear, dear Mammi. What has she gotten me into?"

Carolyn pulled on a heavy shawl that hung on a hook on the wall. "I'll go out and talk to him."

"I should do it myself."

"Vernon has already proposed to me twice. The last time was in November on my twenty-fifth birthday. He knows how obstinate I am. He won't argue with me."

Elsie tugged on one corner of Carolyn's shawl. "*Nae.* I'll go. It's my *mammi* who got me into this, and my mess to sort out."

Carolyn retrieved a black bonnet from the hook. "We'll go together. You don't know Vernon like I do. I can help if he gets pushy."

Elsie swallowed her objection. Carolyn shouldn't have to suffer aggravation just because Elsie's *mammi* liked to meddle. But Carolyn was right. Two plainspoken girls were better than one when it came to Vernon Schmucker.

Elsie zipped up the coat that she hadn't bothered to take off when she came into the house, heaved a long sigh, and stuffed her hands in her pockets. "We can make it short. It's too cold for long explanations."

Carolyn opened the door, and they trudged out into the freezing rain. Their shoes would get muddy and their bonnets would be soaked, but Mammi had chosen the footbridge, so the footbridge was where they would go.

Vernon turned at the sound of her footsteps on the bridge. He wore a straw hat with a scarf underneath tied around his ears. His cheeks were bright red, and rain dripped off the brim of his hat. If it got any colder, he'd have icicles for sure and certain.

"*Hallo,* Vernon," Elsie said. She winced at the tentative edge to her voice. She didn't want to hurt Vernon's feelings, but he was not one to take subtle hints. She'd have to be direct.

Vernon reeled in his line and smiled as if he'd been waiting his entire life for a girl to talk to him. "*Hallo,* Elsie Stutzman. *Hallo,* Carolyn. Did you come to watch me fish?"

Elsie squared her shoulders. It was better to rip a Band-Aid off than to pull it slowly. "Vernon," she said, this time adding forceful determination to her voice. "My *mammi* wants you and me to get married, but I do not want to marry you."

"Your *mammi* wants us to get married?"

Elsie forced a painful smile. "I hope you

understand, but I would ask that if my *mammi* suggests we meet again, you tell her no. My *mammi* has a *gute* heart, but I would appreciate it if you quit encouraging her. You and I will never suit, and we will never get married."

Vernon's smile got wider. Maybe he didn't want to date her as much as she didn't want to date him. "Your *mammi* wants us to get married?"

"And I don't," Elsie said through gritted teeth.

"Do you know how to cook? My *mamm* makes a pecan pie for me every Monday night."

"Vernon," Carolyn said, "aren't you listening? Elsie doesn't want to marry you or date you or cook for you."

Elsie nodded. "I just want to be friends."

Carolyn shot her a look that could have curdled milk. Elsie immediately understood. She shouldn't have left the door open for him like that. He was desperate for a wife and just aggravating enough to hope that friendship led to love.

"I'd like being your friend," Vernon said, pumping his eyebrows up and down as if she'd just spoken to him in a secret code that only he could understand. *Ach, du lieva.*

"What I mean," Elsie said, using the voice

she saved for unruly scholars, "is that I'm not interested and would be very grateful if you forgot the whole thing."

"Okay, I guess." Vernon's lips drooped in a slightly confused frown. "But I don't want to go against your *mammi.*"

Carolyn came to the rescue. "Maybe you should ask Anna Helmuth to match you with someone else, like Mary Zimmerman. She's only a few years older than you are."

Vernon furrowed his brow. "Is she a *gute* cook?"

"I hear she's very *gute,*" Carolyn said, nodding so hard that droplets of water flew off her bonnet.

Vernon glanced at Elsie, the regret evident on his face. "Okay. I suppose I can ask Anna."

Carolyn wrapped her fingers around the footbridge railing. "Why don't you come inside, Vernon? It's too cold for fishing, and there are pretzels fresh out of the oven."

Vernon brightened and shifted his focus squarely on Carolyn. "Did you make them? I know what a *gute* cook you are."

Carolyn practically glared at him. "None of us single girls made the pretzels, so you can just get that idea right out of your head."

"I was only asking," Vernon protested.

Carolyn kept glaring. "I know what you're

like, Vernon Schmucker."

Vernon pulled in his fishing line and removed the wriggling worm from the hook. He bent over and opened the tackle box at his feet. "I usually have good luck with fish on your bridge. But I suppose it's too early."

"I hope there are no hard feelings," Elsie said, wanting to smooth things over, even though Vernon might take her kindness the wrong way. In spite of everything, she felt sorry for him. It wasn't Vernon's fault that Mammi had gotten his hopes up.

Vernon picked up his tackle box and shook his head. "If you ever change your mind, let me know. I really like pork chops with apricot sauce." He turned his back on both of them and strolled off the bridge.

Elsie gave Carolyn a wry smile. "I'll keep that in mind."

Vernon tromped to the house. He moved faster than Elsie expected and made it to the back door several steps before Elsie and Carolyn. When he disappeared inside, Carolyn draped her wet arm over Elsie's wet shoulders. "I can't be sure he won't bother you again, but we did our best."

Elsie giggled. "*Jah,* we did. I can deal with Vernon. The best part is that Mammi will stop pestering me about it."

"Until she finds someone else for you to

love," Carolyn said, giving Elsie a comically hopeless look.

"Don't even think about that."

They went into the house. Vernon was long gone, but his tackle box and fishing pole sat against the wall. Both girls removed their bonnets and hung them to dry.

"At least Vernon didn't put up too much of a fight," Carolyn said. "I was afraid my lips would freeze to my teeth before we convinced him to come in."

"That's something to be grateful for."

Carolyn shrugged off her shawl and glanced out the window. Her eyes widened, and she inhaled a sharp breath. "Oh, *sis yuscht.*"

"Is something wrong?" Elsie tried to look out the window, but Carolyn stepped to the side and blocked her view.

"I left something on the bridge," Carolyn said, almost as if she was mad about it. She probably was. Who would want to go out in the cold again?

"What is it? I'll go fetch it."

"I'll go," Carolyn said, seemingly quite annoyed and obviously eager that Elsie not feel obligated to go outside with her. She put her hands on Elsie's shoulders, turned Elsie around, and pointed her in the direction of the kitchen. "You go get a pretzel and talk to my sister. I'll be right back."

"Okay," Elsie said, taking off her coat. "If you're sure."

"Of course. No reason for the both of us to go." Carolyn rewrapped her shawl around her shoulders. "Do your best to avoid Vernon. I'm afraid he won't be put off for very long."

Elsie shrugged. "I will, but don't worry about me. I can be very frightening when I have to be."

Carolyn smiled. "I don't think anyone wants to see that."

"Me either."

Sam had never tried so hard to get someplace he didn't want to go. Wally's physical therapy appointment had taken far longer than Sam had anticipated. They couldn't afford physical therapy at all, so the therapist had spent extra time explaining all the exercises to Wally so he could do them at home and not have to go back. Eventually, Wally wanted to learn how to run and do everything on his fake leg that other children could do on a real leg. Sam couldn't argue with that. Elsie had given Wally a new excitement for life, and Sam would have done just about anything to keep up his brother's enthusiasm.

Sam pulled the buggy far to the side of the road and unhitched the horse. Even though he was in a hurry, Rowdy deserved to be sheltered in the barn while Sam broke up with Anna Helmuth's granddaughter. Well, it wasn't a breakup, because they weren't together, but it felt like breaking up. Anna had her heart set on a match between Sam and her granddaughter, and she wasn't going to be happy about Sam nixing it before it even got off the ground. Sam couldn't begin to guess how the granddaughter would react. Like as not, she'd melt into a puddle of tears and sob like her heart was breaking. He couldn't help that girls liked him. The *gute* news was that it was rainy and cold. They wouldn't be able to stand out on that bridge all evening. He could make his rejection short and sweet and then go away and let the granddaughter cry into her lemonade if she wanted to. It wasn't his fault that Anna had picked the wrong boy to match with her granddaughter.

Sam pressed his straw hat onto his head as he ran out of the barn and around to the back of the house where Yutzys' footbridge stood. He slowed to a walk when he saw that no one was there to meet him. A low growl came from deep within his throat.

264

How late was he? Had the granddaughter already given up? If he had missed a chance to talk to her, he would kick himself into next Sunday. Oh, *sis yuscht,* he was irritated beyond belief.

With his gloved hands stuffed into his pockets, he strolled onto the bridge and stopped in the very center. How long should he wait? He would hate to give up. That would mean another forced meeting, another day spent dreading what he had to do. He glanced at the house. Maybe the granddaughter was watching for him inside. It was cold and wet, but he'd wait a few more minutes. Lord willing, the granddaughter would appear any minute.

The Yutzys' backdoor opened, and a girl stepped out of the house. Sam's heart thudded with dread and anticipation. Finally! This whole thing would be over once and for all. It was too far away to see her face, especially wrapped as she was in her shawl and bonnet, but she didn't look to be old or disabled in any way. Definitely not disabled. She marched across the lawn and through the trees as if she had a chip on her shoulder and she was planning on challenging Sam to a fight. She soon got close enough for Sam to see her face. Carolyn Yutzy? She was Anna's granddaughter?

Nae. That couldn't be. Sam had known Carolyn all his life. She and Anna weren't related. Carolyn was a wonderful nice girl, sensible and smart, but Sam had no interest in her. Certainly this couldn't be the match Anna was planning on.

Carolyn stomped onto the bridge and propped her hands on her hips. "Sam Sensenig, what are you doing here?"

Carolyn was usually much more friendly than this. Maybe she was still sore at him for bothering Elsie at that *singeon* at Eichers'. Her hostility put him in an even worse mood than he was in already. He felt humiliated enough without Carolyn knowing why he was standing on her footbridge. She wasn't a gossip, but he still didn't feel inclined to tell her his personal business.

Still, he wasn't going to lie to her. "I'm meeting someone, if you don't mind."

She narrowed her eyes and studied him as if she thought he might rob her if she wasn't on her guard. "You're the one, aren't you?"

"The one what?"

"You asked Anna Helmuth to match you up with her granddaughter, didn't you? You knew she wouldn't go willingly if she found out who you were."

Sam felt his frown cut into his face. "Don't blame me. I never asked Anna to

266

match me with anyone. It was her idea, and I only agreed to this meeting so Anna would quit pestering me." Only when he shut his mouth did he stop to consider that Carolyn knew an awful lot about it.

Carolyn didn't seem to mind prying. She took a step closer. "Do you know who Anna's granddaughter is?"

He rolled his eyes. "Probably some forty-year-old knitter who is desperate for a husband."

Carolyn folded her arms as a hint of a smile played at her lips. "You are incorrigible, Sam Sensenig, and I know firsthand that Anna's granddaughter does not want anything to do with you."

That was a little harsh. Sam wasn't that bad of a person. "Does she know who I am?" Because if she knew who he was, she probably would at least want to meet.

"She wants you to quit trying to meet her and leave well enough alone."

He gave her one of his most ferocious growls. He meant it to show her how irritated he was, but his pride was just the slightest bit wounded. Carolyn didn't seem the least bit impressed. "That's what I want too," he said. "I want Anna Helmuth and her homely granddaughter to leave me alone."

"*Gute.* I'll tell her she doesn't have to worry about you harassing her again."

If she was purposefully trying to annoy him, she was doing a *gute* job of it. "I'm not harassing her. Tell her *mammi* to stop knitting me pot holders and inviting me to dinner."

"You can be sure of it," Carolyn said. She turned her back on him, stepped off the bridge, and started across the lawn. "Some boys just can't get it through their heads to quit bothering people," she mumbled, but Sam heard her well enough. How could she even believe this was his fault? He gave her the stink eye, even though she had her back to him and couldn't see it. She turned suddenly as if she could feel his glare through the back of her head. "Just so you know, she's not old or homely, and you could be the bishop's son and a millionaire and you still wouldn't be good enough for her, so don't get on your high horse," Carolyn called, before she disappeared into the house.

Sam scowled. He was good enough for any girl. He just wasn't interested. It took all his energy to deal with Mamm and Wally, and even Rose sometimes. Elsie had finally set his family somewhat to rights. A girl would only complicate things.

Yesterday Elsie had helped Wally learn how to add fractions with a dozen cupcakes and a whole tub of frosting. And they weren't just any cupcakes. She called them her specialty, orange soda pop cupcakes, and they were *appeditlich.* Wally had learned how to add fractions in about ten minutes flat, because Elsie let him take a bite whenever he got the right answer. Sam smiled to himself. He'd never appreciated his teachers and had only found fault with Wally's, but Elsie was a genius. She probably could have taught a pig to whistle.

But smarts were only part of why Sam liked her so much. She was stubborn and determined and firm where she thought herself to be right — not to mention her smile made the hair on the back of his arms curl. He got all tingly just thinking about her, and Sam was not one to get tingly for anything.

Sam glanced over at the house. The lights were glowing inside, and he could hear the faint voices of *die youngie* visiting with each other and playing Ping-Pong. There was nothing there for him, except maybe a pretzel, and Rose had brought over a plate of cookies earlier today. He'd probably be fine if he didn't eat another thing for a month. He stepped off the bridge. Maybe

Elsie had decided to come tonight. Pretzels or no pretzels, he'd go in if Elsie were there. She'd smile at him, and he'd tell her a joke and make her laugh. He really liked the sound of her laugh and the glow of her smile. Maybe he'd go in for a minute, just to see if Elsie was there.

He turned in the direction of the house and just as quickly turned away again. Rose had told him that she was planning on being here tonight, and she had especially urged him to come, simpering and pouting that he never came to gatherings. Even though they were friends, Sam couldn't bear the thought of trying to put up with Rose tonight. It would be even worse if Elsie had come. Despite all his efforts, Rose seemed to dislike Elsie more than ever. She made herself very unpleasant when Elsie was around, and she had dropped in more than once to "sit in" on Elsie and Wally's lessons just to make sure Elsie was teaching Wally correctly. It was a little ironic, seeing as how Rose had always hated arithmetic. Sam would rather not deal with Rose's tantrums tonight, no matter how much he wanted to see Elsie.

He'd see her on Friday.

That thought warmed him clear through.

Sam trudged around the side of the house

to retrieve his horse from the barn and nearly ran into Elsie coming from the other direction. It was no wonder. She had her head down and walked as if escaping a burning house. "Elsie," he said, reaching out his arms and grabbing her shoulders before they had a collision. She had a folded napkin in one hand and her black bonnet in the other.

"Sam?" Elsie's smile bloomed like a patch of morning glory. "I'm surprised to see you here."

"I was just leaving."

"Before you even went in?"

He gave her a crooked smile. "I chickened out."

"I was just leaving too."

He glanced at the napkin in her hand. "Did you come just for the pretzels?"

Elsie laughed, but he sensed the irritation in her voice. "I thought taking three pretzels would make up for having a rotten time. There's a certain young man in there who can't leave well enough alone, and I'm not really in the mood to fend off would-be boyfriends."

"Somebody was bothering you?" Sam didn't know why, but his gut twisted around itself. Boys shouldn't bother girls who don't want to be bothered.

She grunted. "Somebody was *annoying* me."

"Why should that drive you away? I annoy you all the time."

She gazed at him, and her eyes sparkled with their own light. "You are wonderful annoying, but I put up with you because you feed me dinner and pull boulders from my ball field."

He chuckled. "Maggie feeds you dinner, and there was only one boulder. I'm afraid I may have used up all the goodwill you ever felt for me."

"Don't be silly. I never had any goodwill for you, Sam, ever since you came stomping up my stairs in those boots of yours."

A gust of wind nearly snatched the bonnet out of Elsie's hand.

"Cum," Sam said, cupping his hand around her elbow and leading her to the barn. "It's a little warmer and drier in here." Inside, he found some matches and a lantern hanging from a post. He struck a match and lit the mantle, and the lantern hissed to life. He hung it back on the peg, and he pulled out two milking stools for them to sit on.

She sat and offered him a pretzel. "There's no honey," she said. "I didn't want to get sticky."

He took the pretzel and bit into it. "Delicious. It doesn't need honey or mustard."

Elsie took a bite of one of her remaining pretzels and pure enjoyment spread over her face. It was the same when she came to eat at Sam's house. He loved that look. She was so appreciative and so feisty and so . . . adorable. He could look into her eyes for hours and never get bored.

"Mmm. I love *gute* food," she said.

He eyed her doubtfully. She must not be a very good cook. Every time she'd come to his house to eat, she ate as if it was her first or maybe last meal. "Hungry?" he said, winking at her.

She stopped chewing and cocked an eyebrow in his direction. "I worked up an appetite fending off a persistent boy."

Sam tried not to frown. Who was this persistent boy, and did Sam need to have a talk with him? *Quit bothering the teacher. She needs to keep up her strength.* Whoever he was, he wasn't good enough for Elsie. She was smart and feisty and . . . oh, just everything. There weren't enough words to describe how *wunderbarr* she was. Elsie needed a boy like Sam, who truly appreciated her intelligence and determination. She needed a boy who wasn't irritated that she liked to contradict people and speak her mind and do what she felt was right, no matter the consequences.

He kind of liked those things about her. He swallowed hard. She definitely needed someone like him.

"On Friday Wally and I are going to start subtracting fractions," Elsie said. "I'm going to bring my famous lasagna. It cuts nicely into twelve pieces."

Sam didn't want to say anything, but if Elsie was as bad a cook as he suspected, maybe Maggie should make the lasagna. "Okay," was all he could think to say.

She narrowed her eyes and smiled that mischievous smile of hers. "You don't believe me? I'll have you know, a boy fell in love with me after one taste of my lasagna."

That lump in his throat became a boulder. "Who?"

She pressed her lips together. "Someone in Charm. I won't embarrass him by telling you his name. He is another persistent one."

Who were these boys who wouldn't quit bothering Elsie? Sam had had just about enough of them. "Is he . . . is he your boyfriend?"

Elsie laughed, and Sam nearly sighed out loud with relief. "He wanted to be, and I tried to turn him down as gently as possible, but he wouldn't take no for an answer. It was probably a blessing in disguise that the school board didn't like me. He would still be trying too hard if I had stayed in Charm."

Sam wanted to march clear to Charm and give what's-his-name a talking to. "It sounds like it doesn't matter where you go. The boys won't leave you alone."

"Most of the boys in Bonduel are wonderful nice."

Sam did his best not to scowl. She'd only been here three months. How did she really know if the boys were nice or not?

Elsie licked some salt off her finger. "Of course, when I first came here, I didn't think the boys were nice. This one particular boy often came to the school and yelled at me."

He could tell she was joking, but his throat swelled up until he almost choked on his remorse. It was a sign of her *gute* heart that she didn't despise him. He lowered his eyes. "I was very rude. I'm sorry."

She studied his face. "You've already apologized, and I like to think we know each other better now."

"That should make it worse for me — now that you know me well. I'm not very good at being nice."

Elsie showed him her exasperated face. "Of course you are. You'd do anything for

Wally or anyone in your family. You pulled out that rock from the softball diamond, and you let me pitch to you."

"I smacked you in the face with a ball."

"That was my fault for giving you an easy pitch to hit." She popped the last bit of her pretzel in her mouth. "You actually improve with time, Sam — like a block of bleu cheese."

"You mean I get riper and stinkier?"

"I love that sharp, pungent smell. The more mold, the better."

That sounded like a compliment, sort of. "Well, I do like bleu cheese."

"Me too."

The way she said it sent a ribbon of warmth all the way down his spine. "Even though I was wonderful rude, I'm glad you don't try to avoid me like that boy in Charm."

She grinned. "You haven't driven me out of Bonduel yet. That should make you feel better."

He shook his head. "I'm ashamed to say I tried those first couple of weeks."

"You are nothing like Wyman," Elsie insisted. "Lord willing, he has found a girl who likes him just the way he is."

Sam made a mental note to be on guard for a boy named Wyman from Charm —

276

just in case Wyman decided to chase Elsie all the way to Wisconsin.

"Do you want to split the last pretzel?" Elsie said, tearing it in half before he had time to answer. She handed it to him. "This is half of a pretzel. The numerator is one, and the denominator is . . ." She glanced at him with that expectant expression on her face she used with Wally when she was trying to coax an answer out of him.

Sam chuckled. He wasn't too bad at fractions. "The denominator is two. We've eaten enough pizza and cake together that I'll forever be doing fractions in my head."

She nodded. "*Gute.* We all need more fractions in our lives."

"What I need is multiplication." He took a bite of the pretzel and chewed it slowly.

"You don't know your multiplication tables?"

"Of course I know my times tables. Nine times nine is eighty-one. Nine times eight is seventy-two. Nine times seven is sixty-three."

"Okay, okay," she protested. "I believe you."

"I need to convince Mamm that I can make a dairy successful. We have enough savings to buy more cows and some basic equipment, but she thinks I'm *deerich,* foolish to spend the money when she's sure I'll be a failure at it."

Elsie patted him on the wrist, and a zing of electricity traveled up his arm. "Maybe she doesn't think you'll be a failure. Maybe she's just frightened of taking a risk."

"Frightened of taking a risk on me."

Elsie laid her half pretzel in her lap. "Well, she's lost your *fater*. Without you, where would she be? You already run the farm and support the family. Your *mater* seems like someone who needs stability. It's not because she doesn't have faith in you."

Sam nodded. "You're right. I can see how you're exactly right." Sam was constantly amazed at Elsie's intelligence. "I should give up on the dairy for my *mamm*'s sake."

"Of course not. You just need to convince her that your plans won't upset her life. You need to show her how this will make her life better, and your life better, and Wally's. Those artificial legs can't be cheap."

He furrowed his brow. "I'm not wanting to start a dairy so I can get rich."

"I know. But more money would make it easier to support your family. There's no greed in that. You can give more to the church if you have more to give." Her face lit up with an idea. "Maybe some multiplication and fractions and addition will help convince your *mamm.* I can help you figure out how much it will cost to get a dairy up and running, and then we can compute how much money you can make every year selling your milk. We might be able to talk your *mamm* into it if we show her the numbers."

It was hard to talk with the lump in his throat. "You'd do that?"

"It sounds fun, and it would be a *gute* lesson for Wally that math isn't just for school."

"Okay," Sam whispered, unable to trust his voice. "I appreciate it."

In her excitement about all that math, she was leaning wonderful close — so close that he could smell the faint scent of lavender and autumn air. It was a *gute* smell. He breathed deep. And what was it about her eyes? They were lush forests of maple trees in midsummer. He wanted to get lost in those forests and feel the tingle of the brilliant green leaves on his skin. He held his breath. She held perfectly still. Their gazes locked, and he couldn't look away.

The barn door slid open, and a gust of icy wind took Sam's breath away. The noise and the cold severed the connection between them. Elsie pulled away from him, and he stood up, disappointed and a little relieved.

"And then she just left."

Sam felt guilty for the way his chest

tightened when Rose marched into the barn with three other girls in tow. He shouldn't feel put out about seeing her, especially when she had made him cakes and cookies and pies like a *mammi* at Christmastime. But was it too much to ask for a few more minutes in the forest with Elsie?

Rose stopped dead in her tracks when she saw Sam, and her face exploded into a smile. The smile withered when she spied Elsie, and she puckered her lips like she'd eaten some moldy bleu cheese.

"Move, Rose, move," Sadie Yoder said, nudging Rose farther into the barn so she could shut the door. The girls squeaked and fussed as they wrapped their arms around themselves and tried to get warm.

"My skin starts to peel off when it gets cold," Esther Shirk said, stomping her feet and brushing drops of water from her coat with her gloved hand. "Sadie has to take me home first."

"Lorene is the closest," said Sadie, "and your skin does not peel off. Don't be silly, Esther."

Esther and Sadie and Lorene Zook seemed to get their bearings. They quit trying to get warm and took turns staring at Sam and Elsie and then occasionally glancing in Rose's direction.

Elsie stood. "It's warmer in here, but not much. It looks like it's going to be a wonderful cold winter."

Rose's eyes flicked from Sam to Elsie and back again. He could tell she was trying not to glare at either of them. She finally settled on a small, miserly kind of smile that she bestowed on Sam. "You said you were coming to the gathering."

Sam twisted his lips sheepishly. "I only got as far as the barn."

"You told me you were going to try to come."

"Elsie had an extra pretzel, so I decided I didn't need to come in."

"Carolyn puts too much salt on her pretzels," Esther said.

Rose folded her arms and looked at Elsie. "You didn't have to be so rude to Vernon Schmucker."

Elsie frowned. "*Ach.* I'm sorry. I didn't mean to be. Vernon can be a little persistent."

Lorene Zook nodded. "We know. He's tried to date all of us."

Rose turned and gave Lorene the stink eye. "That's no excuse for being rude." She turned back to Elsie. "You're new here, so you don't know that we make allowances for Vernon because he's had a hard life."

Sam almost laughed out loud. Vernon had had a hard life? He lived with his parents, and his *mamm* did his washing and ironing and cooked him three square meals a day. A van picked him up at his house every weekday for his job at the RV factory. Vernon was harmless, a nice person who could talk your ear off if you liked to discuss fishing or food, but he didn't know when to leave well enough alone with a girl. If a girl wasn't interested in him, she had to be direct. It had always been that way. And Rose knew that even better than Sam did. She'd had to fend Vernon off a time or two.

Sam held out his hands. "Come, Rose. You know how difficult Vernon can be."

Rose barely acknowledged him. She was squarely focused on Elsie. "Did it even cross your mind that you should feel sorry for Vernon and try to be nice?"

"I did try to be nice," Elsie said. She used the curt tone Sam had often heard her use on Wally, when she was trying to be kind while making sure Wally knew who the teacher was.

Sam smiled to himself. Elsie would not be bullied. But that didn't mean he should just stand around and let Rose try. "I'm sure Elsie was as nice as she could be. You have to be firm with Vernon."

Elsie glanced his way and gave him a grateful smile. He could have flapped his arms and floated right off the ground.

"All he talks about is fishing," Lorene said, earning herself another dirty look from Rose.

Rose looked down her nose at Elsie. "You told him to go away and leave you alone."

Elsie sighed. Sam knew that sound. It was the one she used when she was barely putting up with someone — probably the one she'd used on the school board in Charm — completely unapologetic and utterly unimpressed. "I said *please.*"

Lorene nodded. "Dorothy Miller and Suvie Newswenger both had to tell him the same thing last year." She clamped her mouth shut at the look Rose gave her.

Rose's nose was so high in the air, she'd soon be able to catch rainwater in her nostrils. "Sam told me how mean you were to Wally. I didn't want to believe it until I saw how you treated Vernon." She turned to Sam as if she thought he were an ally in this. "Isn't that right, Sam? She was wonderful mean to Wally."

Elsie glanced at him, and for the first time since Rose had arrived, he saw real hurt flash in her eyes. Did she think he'd been gossiping about her? "As I've told you several times already, Rose, I was wrong about Elsie. Wally was stretching the truth for his own benefit."

For some reason, this made Rose even more indignant. "Are you calling your *bruder* a liar?"

Sam swallowed his irritation, and maybe a little bit of shame. The truth was the truth. He couldn't change it. "*Jah.* My brother lied."

Rose raised her eyebrows. He had surprised her. *"Ach, vell . . ."* She trailed off into oblivion. It was hard to defend Wally when even his own *bruder* wouldn't.

Esther wasn't known for her tact. "I don't know why you're so mad. If you like Vernon so much, go on a date with him."

Rose shuddered. "*Ach.* He's almost forty. I would never."

"Me either," Lorene said.

Sadie giggled. "I think she was very smart how Vernon handed her those pretzels, and she took them and walked right out the front door."

Esther glared at no one in particular. "Vernon almost proposed to me three times."

Sadie laughed. "He did not."

Esther grunted in Sadie's direction. "Well, I don't like him, and I don't blame Elsie for not liking him."

Rose glanced at Sam and pursed her lips. "I suppose I don't blame Elsie either."

At least they were all in agreement about that.

Esther stared at Elsie. "A boy and a girl shouldn't be alone in a barn together. Too many bad things can happen. That's what my *mamm* always says."

"We just ducked in here to get our horses," Sam said, feeling his face get warm despite the cold. Only a few minutes ago, he'd been gazing into Elsie Stutzman's shocking green eyes. Esther probably didn't need to know that.

Esther was almost as persistent as Vernon Schmucker, in her own way. "You said you were eating pretzels."

Elsie brushed some imaginary pretzel crumbs off her hands. "We had to eat the pretzels to free our hands for the horses." She reached into her pocket and pulled out her bonnet and some gloves. "Are you ready, Sam? We should get going before the roads get bad."

Sam let Elsie go first, then he tried to ignore the look Rose gave him as he led Rowdy from the stall. What was wrong with Rose? He'd already explained to her that he'd been wrong about Elsie. There was no reason for Rose to dislike her on his account.

Unless there was.

Oy, anyhow. It hit him like a load of bricks.

He was an idiot.

A girl didn't bake eight cakes in one month for a friend.

Jah. He was an idiot.

He and Elsie led their horses out of the barn. He sensed someone close to him and turned to see Rose just a pace or two behind. She seemed considerably more cheerful than she had a minute ago. "I told Sadie that you could take me home since we live just next door."

He inclined his head in agreement but didn't say anything. An idiot like him should speak as little as possible.

He stopped at his buggy and handed Rose the reins to his horse. "I need to help Elsie hitch up her horse. I'll be right back."

Rose opened her mouth, as if she wanted to protest, but she closed it again and nodded indulgently. She had finagled a ride home with him. She probably wasn't too concerned if he helped Elsie hitch up her horse.

Sam jogged through the rain, heavier and colder now, until he caught up with Elsie. He reached out his hand, and she smiled and let him take the reins. "Might as well get in," he said, motioning to her buggy. No sense for two of them to get rained on.

Her smile widened, and she climbed into her buggy and closed the door. He hitched up her horse in mere minutes, but he couldn't let Elsie go until he apologized for Rose's behavior. He knocked on her window, and she slid it open just a crack. *"Denki,"* she said. "That was wonderful nice of you."

"You're welcome," he said, and then his tongue tied itself into a very complicated knot.

How could he explain Rose to Elsie?

I'm sorry Rose was rude. I just now realized that she has a crush on me. Jah, *I am an idiot. She's just a little jealous, but all will be put to rights after I make her understand I'm not interested.*

The knot in his tongue pulled tighter. Rose was jealous of Elsie. Had he given her reason to be?

He thought of the way his heart sort of melted into a puddle like a chocolate ice cream cone on the hot pavement whenever Elsie smiled at him. Or the way he couldn't concentrate on his chores when he knew Elsie was coming over to tutor Wally. Had Rose noticed?

Surely she hadn't noticed anything of the sort. Sam's reaction to Elsie was nothing — just the nervousness he felt being around the teacher. She was the smart, take-charge sort, and naturally, he wanted to impress her for his *bruder*'s sake.

"I'm . . . I'm sorry about Rose," he said, reminding himself that her green eyes had no special power over him.

"You don't have to apologize, Sam."

"It's my fault she has a bad impression of you."

Elsie wiped away a trickle of water threatening to drip into her window. "I understand what Rose is feeling. Did you know she wanted the teaching job?"

Sam widened his eyes. "She did?" Rose could no more be a teacher than Sam could be a soldier.

Elsie's smile faded, and she turned her face away and gazed out the windshield. "I spend so much time at your house. Any girlfriend would get jealous."

Any *girlfriend*? Oh, *sis yuscht*. Anna Helmuth had told him he needed to break up with Rose. He had thought she was joking — or delusional. But in truth, if a sweet little *fraa* like Anna thought Rose was his girlfriend, how many others believed the same thing?

Elsie did.

Sam had dug himself a deep hole without even realizing it. Or, more appropriate, he was like that frog in the story who doesn't notice that the water in the pan is getting hotter and hotter until it's too late and he's been boiled to death.

Even though it was wet, he leaned his arm on the buggy and immediately soaked the sleeve of his coat. "Look, Elsie. It's not like that."

She leaned closer to the window and opened it a few inches more. "What . . . what's not like that?" Curiosity and some other emotion he couldn't name traveled across her features, and for a fraction of a second, she seemed to hold her breath.

"Rose and I are just friends," he said, keeping his voice low just in case someone overheard him.

"You . . . you are?" Elsie said. Doubt played at the edges of her mouth.

Sam caught a movement out of the corner of his eye and turned to see Rose trudging his way. She looked to be having a tug of war with the storm, her arms wrapped firmly around themselves, her bonnet flapping in the wind. She blinked the rain from her eyes but didn't lower her head, as if determined not to lose sight of him, even if she had to fight the forces of nature to do it.

Looking rather pleased with herself, she glanced at Elsie through the window. "I hitched up your horse, Sam," she said over the howl of the wind.

Sam forced a smile. "*Denki.* That was very kind."

"I'm not helpless like some girls."

Sam cringed. Had Rose always been so resentful? He made a mental note to apologize to Elsie for that too.

He glanced at Elsie, an unspoken apology in his eyes. She returned his gaze with a confused one of her own and picked up her reins. Had she not understood him? "Wait, Elsie," he said, suddenly struck with a wonderful-*gute* idea. It would be faster and easier to tell both of them at the same time that he and Rose were not dating. Surely Rose would appreciate his honesty.

He opened his mouth and just as quickly clamped it shut when he looked at Rose. He didn't know how she managed it, but her expression was a mixture of pure adoration and raw anger. The adoration was probably for him and the anger for Elsie, but it was just as likely the adoration and the anger were both for him. Sam was pretty thick sometimes, but it only took him about two seconds to see that it would probably be best to break up with Rose in private — not that he was breaking up with her. They had never been together. Surely Rose could see that.

Elsie nodded as if she understood — though he couldn't be sure exactly what it was she understood. She snapped the reins, and her horse took off. Sam stepped back before his foot got run over. It just hadn't been his day. Carolyn had lectured him but good for something that wasn't even his fault, Elsie had gotten her feelings hurt, and Rose Mast was in love with him. He was standing in the freezing rain with water filling his boots and Rose glaring after Elsie as if Elsie had pulled out a cigarette and started smoking it. Could things get any worse?

Rose brightened like a firefly when Elsie's buggy rolled out of sight. "You don't know how long I've waited for you to ask to drive me home. Mamm and Dat are going to be so happy."

Sam didn't say a word until they were halfway home, partly because Rose started chattering away the minute she got into his buggy but mostly because he was working out in his head what he wanted to say. He'd never had trouble being direct and plainspoken before. Elsie could attest to that. But he also tended to be too blunt and ended up hurting people's feelings, as Elsie could also attest.

He was too irritated to just blurt out what he wanted to say, so he spent the first fifteen minutes of the drive pretending to listen to Rose while trying to calm down enough to write a speech.

He had a feeling *Rose, you are wonderful nice, but irritating beyond belief* would not go over well. Rose's *fater* would probably come over and give Sam a stern talking-to if Sam treated his daughter that way.

"Sadie gave me her mom's recipe for apricot-cherry pie. I'm going to try it as soon as the apricots are on next spring. Do you like apricots, Sam?"

He cleared his throat. He needed to get this over with before they got home, but without being too harsh. Oy, anyhow, he would mess things up for sure and certain. "Rose, do you like me?" It was the best way to start. If he thought she liked him when she didn't, he wouldn't need to have this conversation at all.

She tilted her head to one side and smiled demurely, as if a modest Amish girl shouldn't talk about such things. "*Jah,* Sam.

I like you. I'm almost twenty, you know."

He swallowed hard. *Jah.* He knew. It was all she'd been talking about for weeks. Her excitement should have been his first clue that she had her eye on him. He was so dense when it came to girls. "Rose, you know I appreciate all the cakes and pies you've been bringing over."

That shy smile again. It made his teeth ache. "And don't forget the divinity. I made seven batches before I got it just right. I always try to give you the best of everything."

"And the divinity." He nodded, hoping she didn't ask him if he knew what divinity was. "You have always been a *gute* friend, Rose. You and Mark and Mos. We had a lot of fun playing when we were children."

"We did," she said, lowering her eyes and clasping her hands together.

Ach, du lieva. She was either going to burst into tears or throw something at him, but it had to be done. Either that or he'd get fat from all her desserts and never have a private moment with Elsie Stutzman again.

"Rose, even though I'm driving you home tonight, you need to know that I am not interested in dating you."

Her timid smile froze in place. "I don't understand."

"You need to forget me and find another boy. I'm too old."

Rose scrunched her lips into a pout. "You're not too old. I'll be twenty in a few months. My *onkel* is ten years older than my *aendi* Beth."

Sam grimaced. He shouldn't have said "too old." It was a reason she could argue with. "You're right. Age doesn't really matter."

Rose sniffed the air. "*Nae,* it doesn't."

"The truth is . . ." He cleared his throat again and shifted in his seat. "The truth is that I don't want to date you. I like you as a friend, but nothing else. I don't want to be your boyfriend."

She was silent for a full minute, and the rain slapping against the buggy became deafening. She had turned her face away, so he couldn't see her expression to know if she was getting ready to cry or yell at him. He hoped she didn't cry, though he deserved whatever reaction he got. Through his stupidity, he had led her to believe he was interested. No girl was going to take that cheerfully.

"It's because of the teacher, isn't it?"

Was it because of Elsie? He liked Elsie, and he enjoyed being with her a lot more than he liked being with Rose. A whole lot more. Rose was waiting for an answer, so he couldn't think too hard about how much he liked Elsie. "Why would you say it's about Elsie?"

"That's why. Because you call her Elsie."

"We're talking about you and me, and I don't want to be your boyfriend."

Rose suddenly seemed very concerned. "You put too much faith in her, Sam. Wally is going to end up getting hurt, and it's going to be your fault because you didn't listen to me. Miss Stutzman is just the teacher. She doesn't know Wally like you and I do."

"Wally is so much better than he used to be. He's started doing exercises to strengthen his legs. He's using his prosthetic. He's learning fractions and multiplication. I can't see how that's bad."

"All you care about is Wally," Rose said. "What about all the children Wally is stealing from? Does Miss Stutzman care about them?"

Sam didn't want to be reminded of Wally's sins, especially when Rose acted as if she cared about Wally one minute and then turned on him the next. "As far as I know, Wally hasn't taken money from anybody for weeks. Can't you see he's changing?" He stopped the buggy in front of her house. "I don't want to argue about Wally. I just don't want to date you."

"Ach," she grunted, as if he'd shoved her. "I'll have you know that I don't want to date a boy who is blind when it comes to Wally and Miss Stutzman. She is not *gute* for the children, even if you won't admit it." Rose retied the bonnet around her chin and slid the buggy door open. "Someone needs to save you from yourself, Sam, and since I'm your true friend, I've got to be the one to do it." She climbed out and shut the door hard. "No thanks for the ride home," she yelled through the window.

Sam drew in a breath. He was starting to wish she'd cried.

CHAPTER FIFTEEN

Elsie sat at her desk trying to concentrate on Ida Mae's essay on gratitude, but she wasn't getting much out of it. A smile tugged at her lips. Sam Sensenig had curly hair.

Not that she hadn't known that the first time they'd met, but last night a lock of his hair had been nudged askance by the wind and had dangled over his eyebrow like a bean plant over a trellis. It had taken all her willpower not to reach out, curl her fingers around it, and smooth it back into place. What would it feel like to bury her fingers in that hair? His curls were so tight, she'd probably never get her hands unstuck.

How *wunderbarr* that she had gone to the gathering with the unpleasant task of meeting the boy Mammi wanted her to marry, only to run into Sam. It had turned into a fine evening after all. Of course, Mammi was none too happy that Elsie had rejected

Vernon out of hand like that, but Elsie had held firm.

There is to be no more talk of boys or matches, Mammi. I met your boy and that is that.

Mammi hadn't been able to grasp why Elsie wouldn't want to date "that nice young man." Well, if Mammi thought Vernon was a nice young man, then Elsie would never trust her with a match again — of course, Elsie hadn't trusted her with a match to begin with, so she couldn't see how anything had changed.

Elsie didn't dwell on the Vernon unpleasantness — not when Sam crowded out every other thought. Beneath his arrogance and bluster, Sam was really quite unsure of himself, and Elsie thought it was the most adorable quality she'd ever seen.

And the best part was, he didn't have a girlfriend.

Rose was jealous. That was plain enough, but Elsie had misunderstood Sam and Rose's relationship. She'd never been so glad to be wrong. Rose was a very pretty girl, but she had a sour disposition and hadn't even tried to be nice. Elsie was kind of glad that Sam wasn't in love with Rose.

Ach, vell. In truth, she was very glad. He deserved better.

She glanced at the small clock on her desk and retrieved the bell from the bottom drawer. Raising it over her head, she waved it back and forth. It clanged loudly, startling at least three of her students from their independent reading. "Time to go, scholars," she said. "Please clean all books and papers off your desks and make sure you take home your coats and lunchboxes. We will see you tomorrow."

Wally limped to the back of the room and helped Maizy Mischler on with her coat, sitting on the floor to make sure her zipper got fastened correctly. Elsie smiled to herself. Wally was almost unrecognizable from the boy who had swaggered into her class more than two months ago. He wore his prosthetic leg every day, he was the most eager softball player, and he had a soft spot for Maizy Mischler. He zipped up Maizy's coat, stood up, and patted her on the head. "Put a blanket around you in the buggy so you don't catch cold."

Maizy nodded and clomped down the stairs, waving to Wally the whole way down.

Wally turned and lumbered up to Elsie's desk. "Do you think we'll be able to play softball tomorrow, Miss Stutzman?"

She smiled at his enthusiasm. She felt the same way herself about softball. "I don't know, Wally. It's getting wonderful cold out there."

"But if it's dry tomorrow, can we play? We haven't played all week."

Elsie nodded. "If it's dry, we'll play. We've got to get in all the games we can before it snows."

Wally pumped his fist in the air. "Can I be captain?"

"It's probably about your turn to be captain again," Elsie said. "I'll check my list."

"I went to the physical therapist yesterday. He gave me some more exercises and says if I keep growing, he'll have to fit me for another leg before spring."

Elsie grinned. "Just in time for softball season."

The children filed down the stairs and parted in two directions to avoid Sam and his *mamm,* who were coming up. Wally turned around. "Mamm? Sam? What are you doing here?"

Sam locked his gaze with Elsie and raised his eyebrows as if silently asking the same question.

Hannah Sensenig's face was drawn and weary, as if she'd lived a lifetime of heartache without a minute of happiness in between. "Menno Kiem asked us to meet him here after school."

Elsie's blood thickened like molasses. Menno was a member of the school board. Had the school board planned an impromptu meeting she wasn't told about? And why had they summoned the Sensenigs? A visit from the school board was seldom a *gute* thing.

Sam pulled a piece of paper from his pocket and handed it to Elsie. "Menno's son, Eli, dropped this note off to home this morning right after Wally and the boys left for school."

Elsie unfolded the note. *Hannah, would you please meet us at the school at three o'clock with Wally?*

Sam's lips twitched. "I wasn't invited."

His *mamm* frowned and patted him on the arm. "It is only right that you should be here. You and Miss Stutzman have been helping Wally with his schoolwork."

Sam had done more than his *mamm* would probably ever know, but she didn't feel well. Sam was truly the person who needed to be here if the school board had a concern about Wally.

Elsie's mind raced with a thousand possibilities. Maybe the school board had caught wind that Elsie was tutoring Wally after school. Would they oppose something like that? Had they heard about the boulder in the school yard? Surely such a thing wouldn't keep anyone up at night. Did they disapprove of so much softball? Had they found out Maizy Mischler had hurt her leg one day during a game? Maybe they thought Elsie was cruel to her students, just as Sam had. She was always doing something wrong. It could be any number of things. The thought left her with a slightly ill feeling, like the time when Mammi had made oyster kale salad with dandelion jelly sauce.

She looked up from the note and did her best to fake a genuine smile, hoping to reassure the Sensenigs that all would be well. It wasn't anywhere near true, but they didn't need to worry until the school board actually arrived. The bad news would emerge soon enough. "Maybe they heard how much Wally's arithmetic is improving and they want to congratulate him," she said weakly.

Nobody, not even Wally, believed her. He had turned a light shade of gray, and his hands shook slightly as he wiped the beads of sweat from his upper lip.

Sam's expression was especially heartbreaking. He needed her reassurance more than anyone did. When anything bad happened to Wally, Sam experienced the emotions ten times over. He took so much upon himself that Elsie feared he'd break from all the burdens he carried on his shoulders.

They fell silent as they heard the door open and footsteps on the stairs. Wally moved behind Sam so that his *bruder* would block the sight of him to anyone who came up the stairs. Elsie's heart tightened painfully. Despite what she'd told the Sensenigs, she couldn't begin to hope that this meeting was going to turn out well.

Menno Kiem, then Abe Yutzy and Andy Mast, came up the stairs. The entire school board. Elsie found it almost impossible to breathe. They were followed by Benjamin Hoover, Mark Hoover's *dat.* Mark was one of Elsie's fourth graders. He had twin sisters in the first grade. Benjamin was a slight man, with a short beard and deep, expressive eyes. Elsie had met Benjamin and his wife the first week of school. They were an unassuming, quiet couple who seemed content to leave the teaching to Elsie. They seemed a very nice family, especially Mark's *mamm,* who sent an extra sandwich with Mark every day just in case someone in the class forgot a lunch.

Menno Kiem was an older man who didn't have any children at the school anymore. His stomach hung over his waistband, much like a muffin top escapes its paper. Elsie liked Menno. He had a kind face with deep wrinkle lines around his mouth, as if he'd done a lot of smiling in his day. Abe Yutzy was younger, with fewer wrinkles than Menno and a slow blink that always made Elsie wonder if he was pondering or simply falling asleep. Andy Mast was Rose's *dat,* and that made Elsie more than a little nervous. Just how vindictive was Rose? Would she have told her *dat* something that wasn't true just to make trouble for Elsie? Surely she was too good of a friend with Sam to make trouble for him.

Menno, who was usually smiling, wore a frown any largemouth bass would have been proud of. "Why don't we all sit down?"

Elsie jumped as if someone had stuck her with a pin. She should have been doing something other than staring dumbly at her visitors. "*Ach,* of course. I have two folding chairs, or you could sit at the desks."

Menno scooted a couple of the desks around, signaling for the others to pull desks over. Abe pushed several desks out of the way so they could make a circle. Elsie cringed as desks scraped across the floor. Her room would be in chaos by the time they were finished. She only hoped Wally and Sam wouldn't be in shambles as well.

And herself. Would she even have a job by dinnertime?

Sam, not about to make a peep, folded himself into a desk, and Elsie had her doubts that he'd be able to pry himself out of there again. He looked very uncomfortable, and Elsie resisted the urge to put her arms around him and tell him it was going to be okay. Sam, for all his bluster, was sensitive and deep and harder on himself than even the sternest *fater* could have been.

Wally took a seat between Sam and his *mater*. Elsie wanted to give him a hug too. Did the school board even care that one thoughtless word could crush him?

No one looked comfortable, and it was only partly due to the fact that they had all tried to fit into children's desks.

Elsie glanced at Sam then slid into a desk in the circle. "I'm sorry. I didn't know you were coming, or I would have tidied the room a bit more."

Menno waved his hand. "School only just got out. We didn't expect it to be spotless." He clasped his hands together and rested his arms on the desk. "Now, to get to the point. We have some very serious concerns about Wally and you, Miss Stutzman, and we wanted to come and clear up any misunderstandings before things got out of hand at this school. We have heard from many parents that you are a *gute* teacher, and we would be wonderful sorry to lose you. Lord willing, we can solve this without taking any action."

Elsie's heart was a runaway train. *Ach, du lieva.* She was going to lose her job.

Menno motioned toward Benjamin. "Benjamin Hoover's son Mark says that Wally has been bullying the other children and demanding money from them."

Sam blanched, and Hannah formed her lips into an O.

Benjamin nodded. "Mark says Wally has taken ten dollars from him this year."

Wally gripped the edges of his desk as if it was the only solid thing left in the world. "I did not," he said softly. "I did not. Mark is a tattletale."

Benjamin's face darkened one shade of red. "Mark is not a tattletale. Someone told my *fraa* what had been happening, and we asked Mark if it was true. He confirmed it."

"Mark's a tattletale," Wally repeated, getting more agitated with every word.

Menno warned Wally with a silent, icy stare. "What is worse, Miss Stutzman, is that Rose Mast says you have known about this and haven't done anything to stop Wally from taking money from the other children.

Is that true?"

Rose Mast. Elsie had been expecting it, but the name still felt like a softball to the head. How could Rose have known unless Sam had told her? Elsie turned a troubled gaze to Sam. It felt like a betrayal of her trust, even though she hadn't specifically told him not to tell anyone.

"It's not true," Wally said, louder this time.

Elsie needed to do something before his lies got worse. "It is true that Wally took money from some of the children."

Wally slapped his hand on the desk. "How could you say that? You don't know anything."

"Try to calm down, Wally," his *mater* said. "We need to hear the whole story."

Elsie had never heard Hannah give Wally correction, and Sam never wanted to. It was up to her to keep Wally from crumbling like a pile of dirt. "Wally," she said, giving her voice both sternness and authority, "do not say anything you can't take back, and do not speak unless spoken to."

Wally clamped his mouth shut and glared at her as if she were the Angel of Death. She didn't care. She had to stay firm to save Wally from himself. Sam's arms were folded across his chest in stiff anxiety, and she could tell he was angry, even though he did a better job of hiding it than Wally.

Elsie swallowed hard and averted her eyes. Sam never was rational where Wally was concerned, and he jumped to so many conclusions, he should have been a rabbit. She pressed forward despite the looks she was getting from the other side of the circle. "Let me first tell you that Wally hasn't taken any money from anyone for weeks. He has been very kind with the younger children, and he is almost caught up with his fractions."

"No amount of good deeds can make up for stealing," Andy Mast said. It was already apparent that he was going to be the hardest one to convince of anything.

"I don't steal," Wally insisted.

Elsie silenced him with another stern look. "When I found out Wally was taking money from the other children, I wanted to do what was best for everyone."

"You should have told us immediately," Andy said.

Elsie nodded slowly and reminded herself that not one of these men was her enemy, and they all wanted what was best for the children. "Perhaps I should have told you, but as a teacher, I am responsible for my own class discipline, and I was determined to do the job you hired me to do in the manner that I saw fit." She took a deep breath to calm herself. "I am grateful for the trust you put in me, and I do my best to earn that trust every day. Each group of students I have taught is different. This group is exceptionally kind and sympathetic. You parents have done an excellent job of teaching them kindness."

"We don't need you to judge us one way or the other," Andy said.

Oh dear. The schoolhouse already felt about twenty degrees too warm. "One day when Wally was out of the classroom, I told the children that I knew Wally was taking money from them and if they would come to me whenever he stole their money, I would pay them back."

Wally's mouth fell open. Elsie felt terribly sorry for him. It must have shocked him to the core to know that everyone knew the truth but him. "That's not . . . she's lying," he protested, though nobody was paying him any attention but Sam. Wally fidgeted in his seat and breathed in and out like a snorting bull. He was a geyser about to erupt.

Indignation flared on Andy's face. "Why didn't you stop him?"

Menno held up his hand. "Now, Andy, give her a chance to explain."

Elsie cleared her throat. Her reasons seemed good to her, but maybe the school board wouldn't see it that way. "I knew that if I punished Wally, he would stop taking money, but he wouldn't learn anything. I wanted him to have a change of heart, and that change had to come from him, not from me, or it wouldn't have been sincere."

Menno's brows inched together, and the small movement gave Elsie some hope. He was thinking hard about what she said. "And did Wally have a change of heart?"

Elsie didn't look directly at Wally, but she could tell he didn't like them talking about him as if he wasn't there. His scowl could have burned a hole through the side of her head. "Like I said, he hasn't taken money in weeks, and his schoolwork is improving. Wally has made real progress."

Menno looked at Abe and then Andy, and both of them nodded their agreement. Menno turned his attention to Wally. "Very well, young man. We are satisfied with your teacher's reasons, but I want you to give us your solemn assurance that you will never take anything that doesn't belong to you again."

Everyone turned to Wally. Scrunching up his face, he pressed his fists to his eyes. "Stop it. Stop looking at me."

Sam reached over and placed a hand on his shoulder. "It's okay, Wally. We're not mad at you."

"Yes, you are," Wally said, his voice rising in pitch, his hands still covering his eyes. Something seemed to snap inside him like a rubber band, and he leaped to his feet. He grabbed the desk chair with both hands and shoved it forward, making a deafening scrape against the wood floor. "You hate me because I'm a cripple. Everybody hates me."

"You're not a cripple," Sam insisted, trying to stand up, but it was slow going disentangling himself from that desk.

"I didn't do anything wrong," Wally yelled, limping backward and overturning desks as he went. Everyone but Sam was on their feet as Wally swiped his arm across the top of the bookshelf and sent the stacks of books tumbling to the ground. "You think it's such a big joke," he wailed, pointing a shaking finger at Elsie. "Making fun of me behind my back. All the kids laugh at me. You told them to laugh at me."

Sam finally got himself out of his desk. "Wally, it's going to be okay."

Wally's face was wet with tears and as red as a beet. He glared at Sam, and his rage took Elsie's breath away. "You lied to me. You and Miss Stutzman pretended to help me when you were really laughing at me."

"Wally, stop," Elsie said, sidestepping four desks strewn across the floor to get to him. Before she could reach him, he hobbled down the stairs, snatching mitts from the stair railing as he went and hurling them in her direction.

She dodged them easily — she was a softball player, after all — and caught up with him at the bottom of the stairs. She wrapped her fingers around his forearm. "Wally, this behavior is beneath you. I will not stand for it."

"I hate you," Wally said, spitting the words from his mouth like venom.

Sam jogged down the stairs and wrapped his arms around Wally. Wally pounded on Sam's chest until Sam let go of him.

Wally gave Sam a shove for good measure. Sam barely budged. "I hate you. I hate all of you."

Wally might have slapped him for as wounded as Sam looked. "You don't mean that."

Wally shoved the door open. "Leave me alone. Everyone leave me alone."

He ran outside, and Sam followed him, but he soon returned looking as low as a worm, even though he was standing up.

"Where did he go?" Elsie said.

"Perry had the pony cart all hitched up. He got on and drove away."

Elsie laid a hand on Sam's arm. "It's all right. You know he's going to head straight home."

Sam wouldn't meet her eye as he pulled away from her touch. "You don't know that. How could you know that?"

Elsie felt a dull ache right in the center of her chest. How could things have gone so wrong?

Sam didn't spare her another look. He took the stairs two at a time. "Mamm," she heard him say, "I need to get you home and then make sure Wally is okay."

"Of course," Hannah said.

Elsie ascended the stairs slowly, then started righting the desks Wally had tipped over. Andy Mast and Abe Yutzy helped her as Benjamin Hoover and Menno picked up books. It all seemed so strange. Her heart was as heavy as an anvil, and she was straightening chairs.

Sam helped his *mamm* on with her coat. "We've got to go find Wally."

Benjamin stood up with a pile of books in his arms. "I'm wonderful sorry. I didn't think he'd be so upset."

The look on Sam's face stabbed Elsie right in the heart. "It's not your fault," he

313

said. "It's mine. All mine."

Of course he'd blame himself. He'd been blaming himself for years. Elsie shook her head. "That's not true, Sam."

Sam ignored her, took his *mater*'s arm, and led her down the stairs without another word.

Elsie watched out the window as Sam led Hannah to their buggy and they got in and drove away. She could barely breathe from the weight pressing on her chest. She could barely swallow with the icy hand of sorrow clamped around her throat. She could only pray that everything would be all right. Wally would be right as rain in a day or two. He was young, prone to imprudent outbursts, but also resilient and adaptable. Wally would be okay, Lord willing.

He had to be, or Sam would never forgive himself.

Elsie gripped her pan of lasagna and her basket of doughnuts as if they were the only things keeping her from falling over. Why was she so worried? Surely she could make everything all better with her famous lasagna made with both sausage and hamburger. And if that didn't work, her assortment of baker's specialty doughnuts would. Two old-fashioned, three jelly-filled, three apple fritters, and four chocolate with sprinkles. Everyone liked chocolate with sprinkles.

She shouldn't be feeling so nervous. Never mind that none of the Sensenig *bruders* had come to school today or that Rose Mast's sister Lizzy Jane had said that Sam refused to talk to anybody — today was Friday, and Elsie tutored Wally on Fridays. Nobody had sent her a note or anything, so she was determined to carry on as usual, with a dozen doughnuts and a lasagna as insurance.

She placed the pan and the basket on the bench that sat on the porch. She and Sam had sat on that bench several times after tutoring sessions and talked about Wally and the dairy Sam hoped to have someday and the lessons Elsie was teaching at school. She was very fond of that bench. She hoped there would be many more evenings spent sitting on it.

After freeing her hands, she knocked assertively on the Sensenigs' door as if she were certain they'd give her a warm welcome like they always did. Wally might even have gotten over his tantrum of the day before and be eager for a lesson, especially since he'd missed the introduction to geometry today.

It wasn't likely, but she held on to that

hope as if it were a basket filled with dough-nuts.

Maggie answered the door. "*Ach,* Elsie," she said, throwing herself into Elsie's arms.

"How are you, Maggie? How is Wally?"

Maggie pulled away and wiped her eyes. "It's like when *Fater* died, only worse. Wally won't say a word to anybody, and Sam paces around the kitchen like a tiger at the zoo. You know it's bad when Mamm has taken to trying to cheer everyone up."

"At least Wally's home. I was terrified he'd run away."

Maggie blinked, and a tear trickled down her face. "He came home and smashed our three kitchen windows with rocks. That was before Sam got here to stop him."

Elsie gasped. "He broke your windows?"

"I was in the kitchen when he did it. I thought someone was trying to rob us." Maggie lowered her eyes in embarrassment. "I got scared and crawled under the table."

Elsie slid an arm around Maggie's shoulders. "I would have done the same thing. Did you get hurt?"

Maggie pursed her lips in an attempt not to cry. "A couple of cuts on my hands when I got under the table."

"Oh, no. I'm sorry."

"I think he would have broken every

window in the house if Sam hadn't come when he did. He tackled Wally to the ground, then wrapped his arms around him so tight he couldn't breathe."

Elsie stopped breathing herself. Sam would hate himself for doing what had to be done. "He did?"

"Wally struggled something wonderful and whined that he couldn't breathe, so Sam finally let him up. You know how it says in the Bible that the wicked gnashed their teeth? Wally looked like that when Sam let him loose. He kept yelling over and over again that he hated Sam, then ran into the house and down to the basement. Me and Perry cleaned up the glass while Sam went downstairs to try to talk to Wally, but Wally won't budge. He won't talk to any of us. He doesn't even turn on his games. He just sits there and stares at the TV, like he's never going to move again."

Elsie motioned to her lasagna. "Will he eat?"

"*Ach,* he'll eat all right. Rose brought over a plate of cookies last night. He ate the whole thing."

Elsie bit her bottom lip and tried not to think bad thoughts about Rose. Rose had told Mark Hoover's *mamm* about the bullying. If it hadn't been for her, none of this ever would have happened. Her heart got that heavy feeling again. It wasn't Rose's fault that Wally had reacted badly. The school board had taken him by surprise.

Maggie frowned and turned her face away. "Wally likes to make everyone else uncomfortable, but he wouldn't dream of making himself uncomfortable. He's selfish that way, but Sam can't see it."

"Sam feels responsible for Wally. He's the big *bruder.*"

Pain flashed across Maggie's face. "He feels guilty."

Elsie nodded. Sam took too much on himself. He thought everything about Wally was his fault, as if he could make everything all better for Wally if he just tried hard enough.

"Wally has always been lazy." Maggie sighed. "I'm sorry to speak ill of my *bruder,* but it's true. The day of Wally's accident, Sam had insisted that Wally help with the corn. Wally would barely lift a finger after *Dat* died, and Sam thought it was time that Wally pulled his weight on the farm. Sam thinks it's his fault Wally lost his leg."

Elsie's throat tightened. It didn't surprise her that Sam blamed himself for Wally's accident, but it did make her very sad. No wonder he was afraid to demand anything of Wally. "I don't wonder that it's a nightmare he plays over and over in his head."

"Sam feels terrible about it. He thinks if he hadn't insisted Wally help, Wally never would have gotten in that accident."

"But Maggie, you don't believe it's Sam's fault, do you?"

Maggie widened her eyes. "Of course not, but the guilt eats at Sam all the same. It's why he quit demanding things of Wally the day Wally lost his leg." She gave Elsie a sad smile. "Then you came along, and they were both improving — until yesterday. Wally has gone back to pouting and playing the cripple to get his way, and Sam is like a machine. He won't listen to me or Mamm when we tell him that Wally needs a *gute* kick in the seat of his pants."

Elsie wasn't prone to cry, but she wanted to weep for Sam and Wally. They were both fighting hard battles in their heads, coping any way they knew how, making themselves more miserable than they had to be. "Do you think I could talk to Sam?"

Maggie shook her head. "I don't know. He's wonderful upset."

"I brought lasagna," she said.

Maggie's frown sank farther into her face. "He disappeared into his bedroom when Rose brought cookies last night."

Elsie pressed her lips together. A lasagna was more powerful than a plate of cookies, wasn't it? Mammi always said the way to a man's heart was through his stomach. Elsie caught her breath as she realized how badly she wanted to find a way to Sam's heart.

She really, really liked him.

Maybe she even loved him.

That thought sent her head reeling. How could she love Sam Sensenig? He was ill-tempered and rude and certainly didn't like her. Then again, he had made a point to tell her he didn't have a girlfriend, and he often sat in on tutoring sessions. Elsie got the feeling it wasn't just so he could supervise Elsie's teaching.

"Cum," Maggie said, picking up Elsie's basket. "There's no harm in trying."

Elsie retrieved her lasagna from the bench and followed Maggie into the house. It was cold and drafty in the living room and downright frigid when they got to the kitchen. Someone had boarded up the windows, which kept out critters and light, but it did nothing to stop the cold air. The room was dark and gloomy, even though two propane lanterns glowed on either side of the room.

"Sam ordered new windows today. They'll be here next week. I just hope the pipes don't freeze before then."

Elsie set the pan of lasagna on the table and surveyed the damage. The windows were gone, of course, but there were also scratches in the linoleum where the glass had hit. Three pieces of a red canister sat in the sink. "The cookie jar?"

Maggie nodded. "Hit by one of the rocks."

This was a setback for sure and certain. Sam was trying to save money for milking equipment, but he wouldn't get anywhere if he had to keep paying for broken windows and shattered cookie jars — not to mention the fact that Wally seemed to be back at square one, or maybe even worse than square one. She had to do something to help.

"What are you doing here?"

Elsie turned to see Sam come up from the basement and shut the door quickly behind him. He wore a day's growth of whiskers on his face and a scowl as threatening as a wolverine's.

It was all Elsie could do not to take a step back at the raw hostility on his face, but if she knew how to do anything, it was hold her ground. "Sam, I'm so sorry. How is Wally today? I missed him at school."

The muscles of Sam's jaw twitched. "You shouldn't be here. If Wally sees you, he'll get even more upset. You need to go."

Elsie's heart flipped over itself. "I . . . I just came to see how —"

Sam took two big steps that brought him close enough to loom over her, as he seemed so fond of doing. He wrapped his fingers around her upper arm and tugged her in the direction of the living room. She was so shocked, she didn't even try to resist as he pulled her past the sofa and out the front door. "I mean it, Miss Stutzman," he hissed. "If Wally sees you, he'll start throwing things."

Elsie couldn't have been more unnerved if he'd slapped her. "Okay, Sam. Okay. I'm not your enemy." She moved onto the porch and drew in a quick, horrified breath as Sam stepped back and tried to shut the door. She reached out her hand and pressed it against the door to keep it from closing. Sam had muscles, not to mention the fact that he weighed at least a hundred pounds more than she did, and it took all her strength to keep him from slamming it in her face. Sam stopped trying to close it when she resisted. No matter how mad he was, he didn't want to hurt her. Probably.

"You need to go," he said. "I just got Wally calmed down enough to play a video game."

"We need to talk."

He ran his fingers through his unkempt hair. "Why won't you go? Haven't you caused enough trouble?"

Elsie's pulse raced with a mixture of anger, hurt, and desperation. She tried to push away the thought that maybe she loved him so she wouldn't melt into a puddle on his porch. Her tears would not help him. He needed her strength if for no other reason than he was desperate for something solid to lean on. "Sam, listen to me. I am not here for a fight."

"Then let me close the door."

"Come out here and talk to me."

He glanced behind him, pressed his lips together, and stepped out onto the porch, closing the door behind him. He couldn't have looked stiffer if he were made out of wood.

"You need a coat."

He wouldn't look at her. "I won't be out here long."

She wished she'd had the presence of mind to bring the basket of doughnuts out with her. An apple fritter might have cheered him up a little. At the very least, he wouldn't have been able to scowl with a mouthful of doughnut. And he *was* scowling. At her. The thought sent a shard of glass right into her heart. "Sam," she said, unable to keep the plea out of her voice. "We're friends. Aren't we friends?"

"I trusted you," he said, folding his arms across his chest and looking anywhere but at her. "I trusted you when you said you wanted to help Wally."

"I do want to help Wally."

He snapped his head around to glare at her. Another shard of glass to the heart. Did she really want to torture herself with this conversation? "Do you? Or were you so impressed with your own cleverness you didn't stop to think how your actions would hurt my *bruder*? Rose warned me, but I wouldn't believe her."

"Sam, Wally is not a lost cause."

"Do you think if you say that enough times it will be true?"

Elsie almost wilted beneath his stare. Oy, anyhow, he was mad. "Give him a few days to calm down." Wiser words had never come out of her mouth. She should have given Sam a few days. She simply hadn't expected him to be this angry. "All this time he thought he'd gotten away with bullying the other children, and now it turns out that we knew about it. He's upset that he didn't fool us into believing he was a better kid than he was. In a strange way, Wally thinks we betrayed him. Like we were laughing at him behind his back."

"We were."

"*Nae,* we weren't."

Sam grunted. "Not laughing at him, but we tricked him. I let you talk me into tricking him."

"We didn't trick him, Sam. We did what we thought was best for him. Just because he's mad doesn't mean it wasn't a *gute* idea."

"It wasn't a *gute* idea, and I trusted you to know what was best for him."

"I'm not giving up," she said.

He narrowed his eyes. "*Jah,* you are giving up."

"*Nae,* I'm not."

"You will give up. I won't let you hurt Wally ever again."

Elsie's mouth felt as dry as a bale of hay. "I would never hurt him."

Sam hesitated, drawing his brows together and studying her face. "I should have stood firm the first day I met you. It's my own fault for letting you persuade me. What a fool I was to fall for a pretty face. I've hurt my *bruder.*"

He looked so miserable that she reached out to touch his arm. He pulled back as if she were a rattlesnake. Anger clawed at her throat and helplessness crept into her bones.

"This is not your fault, Sam."

"Of course it's my fault." He turned on her as if moving in for an attack. "For not protecting him from you."

This couldn't be happening. How had they gone from sitting in the barn sharing a pretzel and talking about his dairy to standing on his porch arguing about what was best for Wally? Did he even understand how deeply his words wounded her? "Please, Sam. I am not your enemy."

He seemed to sputter to a stop, as if he'd lost too much steam for a fight. "I'm sorry. You're right," he said softly. "You're right." He turned and opened the door. "You have meant a great deal to our family, and I am very grateful to you for tutoring my *bruder*. But from now on, Wally's well-being comes first. I know Wally better than a stranger like you does, and I see that you are not *gute* for him. Please don't come over again, and please leave my *bruder* alone. He's had enough trials for one lifetime."

She didn't try to stop him as he turned his back on her and went into the house.

Not even in Charm had she ever been called a trial. Elsie took a deep, shuddering breath and ambled to Dawdi's buggy as if she had just spent a pleasant evening at Sam's house. She would go on pretending she had skin as thick as a bear. Sam would never know how his words stung, especially after how hard she had tried with Wally, the nights she had paced the floor worrying about him and the days she had prayed for *Gotte*'s guiding hand. She'd never let on how deeply she cared for his family, how seriously she took her teaching, or how much she craved a kind word now and then from the parents. And he certainly would never know that her heart had crumbled like one of Mammi's chocolate and white bean cakes.

When they had first met, Sam had accused her of not having any human feelings. Well, she'd show him just how stoic she could be.

Because he'd never know how much she loved him.

CHAPTER SIXTEEN

Sam blew into his hands before putting on his gloves and picking up the bucket full of milk. Would this hollow feeling deep in his gut ever subside? Not likely, when his thoughts were a jumble of Elsie Stutzman, pizza fractions, Wally, and a dairy that would never be.

He dragged his feet out of the barn. His only two cows were producing well, but all dreams of starting a dairy had died after Wally's episode at the school almost three weeks ago. For sure and certain the new windows had set Sam back a bit, but it wasn't the money. He'd be selfish to start a dairy now when Wally and his other siblings needed so much of his attention. His most important priority was Wally — who seemed to be getting worse, despite all of Sam's efforts to the contrary.

When Wally had smashed their windows, Sam finally woke up and realized how much damage Miss Stutzman had done by trying to change his *bruder.* Sam had made the decision then and there that he wouldn't send Wally back to school at all. He was in eighth grade, nearly done anyway, and Wally didn't need the torture of seeing the other children every day, knowing that they had been tricking him all along — knowing that Miss Stutzman had been playing a game that Wally hadn't been included in.

Wally couldn't have been happier about staying home. Sam had let him play Xbox all day, every day, except the Sabbath. It was a blessing that Perry and Danny hadn't complained about having to go to school when Wally didn't. They liked school, and they liked Miss Stutzman. At least she hadn't done anything to damage his two youngest brothers. Sam was grateful for that.

Wally had only been home for a week when Menno Kiem told Sam they'd be in trouble with the state if Wally didn't go to school. Miss Stutzman must have told on him. Of course, he didn't blame her for that. She was walking on eggshells with the school board. For sure and certain she was trying to follow the rules with exactness so as not to lose her job. Something sharp stabbed into Sam's hollow innards. Miss

Stutzman shouldn't lose her job.

If truth be told, Sam was almost relieved when Wally had to go back to school. Wally drove Sam crazy when he was home all day.

Sam, will you fluff my pillow? I'd do it myself, but I have to finish this level.

Be sure to bring a sandwich down right at noon, or I get really hungry and start to shake. And a cookie, please.

Do you have milk chocolate chips? I don't like semisweet.

Sam pressed his lips together and shoved away the guilt. He shouldn't ever think of Wally as a nuisance. Wally was his *bruder.* He loved him like his own self.

None of his reasons mattered anyway. Two weeks ago, he had forced Wally to go back to school. Wally had been fit to be tied, but Sam had threatened a visit from the school board, and Wally's arguments died on his lips. Sam had sent Wally with a note to Miss Stutzman warning her that under no circumstances was Wally to play softball or even be forced to go outside for recess. He insisted there would be no cleaning of desks after school and that Wally be allowed to put his foot on the desk and go to the bathroom whenever he wanted for as long as he wanted.

If Miss Stutzman had had any doubts

before, Sam's note had made things very clear.

His lungs seized up, and he had to cough to loosen them, just like he always did when he thought of Elsie — Miss Stutzman. He couldn't understand it. He was so angry with her that he couldn't see straight, but he couldn't stop thinking about her, wondering what boys she was talking to at gatherings, wishing he could make her smile, wanting to see her eyes light up like springtime when he told her a joke. She had some sort of powerful hold over him, something he couldn't put a name to, but something he needed to stamp out like a grass fire. He would not let thoughts of her consume him in flames.

He hated her, didn't he?

He wished he hated her. His anger would have been so much easier to justify. His guilt would have been so much easier to swallow.

He hadn't been able to bring himself to ask the school board to fire her. The other children would suffer if Elsie left in the middle of the year. And he was honest enough with himself to admit that at least part of the fault was his. He held his breath as the pain washed over him. Elsie might have had the idea to help Wally, but Sam had gone along with it, despite his misgivings. He should have put his foot down with Elsie. He should have stayed away from those green eyes and that pretty smile. That was his fault. The responsibility sat squarely on his shoulders, and he thought he might break from the weight of it.

Wally had gone back to school, but he refused the pony cart, so Sam drove him every day in the buggy. Wally didn't do anything at school, just sat in his desk and said and did nothing — at least according to Perry. Danny said Wally went to the bathroom seven or eight times a day but didn't stay for long. It was too cold, and the porta-potty was too stinky as a hiding place. Most likely, Wally's goal was to irritate Miss Stutzman. Sam didn't wonder but that it worked.

Every day after school, Sam would bring Wally home, and Wally would play video games until bedtime. Sam had even bought him two new games. Wally probably got bored playing the same ones over and over.

Wally had slammed his prosthetic leg into the wall on the same night he had broken the kitchen windows, so now he used his crutches, and there was never any talk of physical therapy or softball. It was better that way.

On top of that, Sam was getting three or

four pot holders a week from Anna Helmuth with notes like, "My granddaughter didn't know what she was talking about on that bridge. Give her another chance, and I'll knit you more pot holders." Under no circumstances was he going to give this mystery granddaughter another chance, but Anna kept sending pot holders anyway. What had Carolyn said? He'd never be good enough for the granddaughter.

He had to agree with her there. He wasn't good enough for anybody.

Sam shut the barn door tight against the wind. November had turned out to be extra cold.

"Sam, wait!"

He lowered his head, clasped the edges of his collar around his throat, and marched with renewed purpose toward the house. His legs were longer than Rose's, but he also had to go slower than she did so he didn't spill the milk.

Rose jogged through the snow to catch up with him. "Sam, please let me talk to you. You've been avoiding me for three weeks."

"It's too cold."

"Then let's go in the house."

"I don't want you in my house." It was rude, but he meant it. As Rose would say, "best friends" always told each other the truth.

Rose grabbed his coat sleeve. He had to stop or spill the milk. "Please won't you listen? I'm not even going to say I told you so."

"You just did."

"Well, I was right, wasn't I? I told you Miss Stutzman would make things worse for Wally. You have to admit I tried to warn you."

Sam trudged up the porch steps. "It was also you who got Benjamin Hoover to go to the school board."

She followed close behind. "I did not. I just mentioned to his wife how concerned I was for the poor little children Wally was bullying."

"My *bruder*. Wally is my *bruder*. You wanted to hurt him, and when you hurt Wally, you hurt me." He opened the door and went into the house, with Rose hot on his heels. He didn't even protest. Rose was going to follow him whether he liked it or not, and it really was too cold to stand outside.

Rose pouted with her whole face. "I was trying to protect Wally, Sam. I warned you. Remember, I warned you about the teacher. I know you don't believe it, but I did what I thought was best for everyone."

He placed the milk on the floor next to the table. "It wasn't what was best for Wally."

She reached out and placed a hand on his arm. He flinched and drew away. "Sam, you care so much about Wally that sometimes you can't see your own hand in front of your face. The teacher wanted Wally to fail from the very beginning. It was clear she didn't like him. She wanted to prove what a bad kid he was by filling his head with all sorts of impossible dreams and then making him fall — and that's what happened."

Sam furrowed his brow. *Is* that what had happened? He had been rude to Elsie that first time they met. Had she held it against him all this time? Even Maggie was concerned that he'd gotten on the teacher's bad side on the first week of school.

He pressed his lips together. He couldn't see it. He just couldn't see it. Elsie was not about getting even. She cared about her scholars, even ones as troublesome as Wally. She'd simply gone about things the wrong way. She'd made mistakes, but Sam knew just as well as he knew that she had green eyes that she hadn't purposefully tried to hurt Wally.

That didn't mean he'd ever let her talk

him into anything again, but he knew Elsie wasn't as bad as Rose made her out to be. Of course, he wasn't about to defend Elsie to Rose. He'd done that once with disastrous consequences. Besides, they were Elsie's sins. Let Elsie defend herself if she was so clever.

Rose seemed to forget that they were having a serious conversation. She clasped her hands in front of her and flashed a shy smile. "Did you taste the pretzels I sent over last night?"

"Nae." He had refused to eat any of the cookies and cakes and goodies Rose had been bringing over for three weeks. Eating any of her treats felt as if he would be accepting her apology — which she still hadn't given him.

She stuck out her bottom lip like she was seven. "My pretzels are so much better than Carolyn Yutzy's. They'll make you forget every other pretzel you ever ate."

Sam turned away from her and slowly hung up his coat and hat. The only pretzels he remembered well were the ones he had shared with Elsie Stutzman in Yutzys' barn. They'd been warm and delicious and sweet as honey, and he could have eaten a whole plate of them. He loved those pretzels.

He washed his hands at the sink, then

turned to Rose and gave her a look that made it plain she had overstayed her welcome. She slumped her shoulders and shaped her lips into a troubled frown. She looked truly miserable. "Sam, I have accepted that you don't want to be my boyfriend, even though I'm almost twenty years old. But your *schwester* is married to my *bruder,* and we are next-door neighbors. We are spending Thanksgiving together tomorrow at Mark and Naomi's house. Can't we be friends?"

"I suppose," Sam said, not really meaning it. If he agreed to be friends, like as not she'd go away and leave him in peace. And they *were* spending the next day together at his sister's house. It would be easier to pretend he was her friend than to hear her whine about it. "I suppose I can still be your friend as long as you know that's as far as it goes."

She burst into a smile that could have broken a mirror. "Of course, Sam. I'm sorry I made you mad, but best friends always forgive each other in the end. I knew you'd come around."

Sam ground his teeth together.

He didn't like the sound of that.

Didn't like the sound of that at all.

CHAPTER SEVENTEEN

"I am a little star," Linda Sue recited. "I have a little light. And when I share my *schumerer,* my light is extra bright."

Elsie gave Linda Sue a big smile as she sat down next to the other children. Whenever Linda Sue forgot her part, she mumbled unintelligible words — like *schumerer* — to fill the silence. She'd never gotten it right in rehearsal. Why should the program be any different? Not that anybody cared. The parents were just pleased to see their children in a program. Nobody expected perfection. Not even Elsie.

Elsie sat in the center chair at the very front of the room with her script in hand, just in case one of the scholars needed help with his or her part. She nodded to children when it was their turn and started all their songs and prompted timid performers to give their parts.

The desks had been cleared out to make

room for benches to accommodate all the parents and siblings and grandparents who'd crowded into the classroom to see the annual Christmas program. Elsie and the children had spent a good portion of class time in December learning their parts and making decorations for their special evening.

Every child had a part — some of the older children had memorized long poems or passages of scriptures. Ida Mae had learned the entire Christmas story from Luke 2. For the grand finale, she was going to recite the scriptures while the rest of the children acted out the nativity as shepherds, sheep, wise men, and of course, Mary and Joseph. Elsie had chosen Ellen Zook to be Mary because Ellen's *mater* had let them borrow the new baby to be Jesus.

Elsie glanced out the corner of her eye at Wally Sensenig. Everybody had a part but Wally. He had refused to say one line, sing one song, or even be one of ten shepherds. And Elsie had no power to make him do anything. Wally's *bruder* had made that very clear.

Elsie breathed deeply to drive back the pain and led the children in singing "Silent Night."

Wally came to school every day, sat at his

desk, and glared at her for six hours until it was time to go home. He didn't speak — except to Reuben Schmucker — didn't associate with the other children, and certainly didn't do any work. He went to the bathroom over and over again, no doubt hoping to irritate Elsie beyond endurance. It was *gute* that he didn't know the truth. She'd rather he not be in her classroom. He was a constant reminder of her failure, and a constant reminder of his handsome older *bruder.*

The only person who seemed to affect him at all was Maizy Mischler. Every day after the bell, Maizy would stumble down Wally's row of desks, lay her hand on Wally's arm, and give him a kiss on the cheek. She never said anything, and neither did Wally, but he never pulled away from her touch and he always looked like he was thinking deep thoughts after Maizy left.

Sometimes Elsie would stand at the window after school and catch a glimpse of Sam in his buggy when he came to pick up Wally. Sam looked as miserable as his *bruder.* Would he ever open his eyes wide enough to see the truth of his own life? Her heart hurt, and not just because she was forced to watch Wally waste his life away. Sam Sensenig hated her, and that thought was a sharp sting to the heart. *Ach!* It would have been so much better if Wally and Sam had never come into her life.

She didn't wonder but Sam felt the same way, but maybe for different reasons.

Her eyes started to sting, and she pulled herself back to the school Christmas program. It wouldn't do for her to burst into tears during the carols. Of course, everyone would just assume her tears were because she'd been so moved by the performance. Crying wasn't the worst thing that could happen.

After the song, she pointed to Johnny Wengerd and Jethro Glick. Their job was to turn the wooden flats that Toby's *dat* had built for scenery. The flats were covered with cardboard, and Elsie and the children had decorated both sides for the Christmas program. Elsie had covered the first side with red butcher paper, and the children had painted a fireplace and hearth, complete with a roaring fire and a pile of wood. The back had been covered in midnight blue paper. They had glued cotton balls to the bottom to look like a field of snow, and each child had made a special star to hang in the paper sky. Elsie had even allowed for some glitter, even though glitter was a teacher's worst nightmare.

There was a collective gasp as Johnny and Jethro carefully turned the flats around to reveal the night sky full of sparkly Christmas stars. But the gasp wasn't for the stars. Written across the entire space in sharp, garish yellow letters were the words *"Miss Stutzman stinks."*

Elsie froze in place, and she thought she might be sick. She didn't care what names her students wanted to call her or whether one of them hated her or not, but to hurt the other children like this was more cruel than even she could have imagined. If she hadn't already guessed who had done such a thing, Wally would have given himself away in a heartbeat. He and Reuben sat in the back row with their heads together, hands covering their mouths, giggling as if they'd been sucking in laughing gas at the dentist. There was a tiny drop of yellow paint on Wally's shirt that she hadn't noticed earlier. No wonder it had smelled strange when she came into the classroom this evening to get ready for the program. Wally must have spray painted the flats right after she'd gone home.

By now, most of the children had looked behind them and seen what had happened to the beautiful sky and stars they had spent so many hours working on. Some of the younger children started to cry. Susie Miller screamed.

Martha Raber hugged her little sister. "Who did that, Miss Stutzman? Who did that?"

Almost in unison, the children turned to look at Wally. He folded his arms smugly across his chest, as if daring anyone to accuse him. It was obvious he wanted a big scene. He wanted to be known as the boy who had ruined the Christmas program, the boy who hurt so bad inside that he wanted everybody to hurt with him.

Elsie wouldn't stand for it.

Sam Sensenig jumped up from his bench on the back row, no doubt to drag Wally out and give him what for. Elsie's heart stopped. She didn't want to be bossy, but this was an emergency, and she would not let Sam ruin everything. She pointed to the space on the bench where he'd been sitting and forced a semisweet smile onto her lips. "Please don't trouble yourself, Sam."

Sam furrowed his brow and slowly sank to the bench, probably because he didn't want to make a fuss with his brother.

Elsie made her smile wider and looked around at the horrified faces of parents and neighbors who'd come for a nice Christmas program. At this point, its success depended solely on her. "Don't worry, everyone. Someone has decided to do his own artwork for our program, but I assure you that I took a shower just this morning."

One or two of the parents laughed uncomfortably. That was a start.

"The children are going to finish the program, because this last part is the most *wunderbarr* story of all. This is just a reminder to all of us that Jesus loves everyone, no matter our sins, no matter our mistakes. And we know that he loved the children best of all." Now some of the parents were smiling and nodding. She turned back to her scholars, who were in various stages of upset. Ida Mae held Maizy on her lap, and Ellen was comforting Mary and Lydia where they sat. "Children," Elsie said, "we all want to see the rest of your program. I know this will be hard, but the true lesson of Christmas is love and forgiveness. Can you do it?"

Toby Byler nodded, and it seemed that was the answer for the whole group. They all knew where to be next. The shepherds put on hats made out of towels, and Ellen went down into the audience to get her baby brother. There was a little sniffling as Ida Mae recited the scriptures, but everyone remembered her part, and the manger scene turned out to be quite lovely, even with "Miss Stutzman stinks" looming behind Mary and Joseph.

After the applause, some of the *faters* went to work setting up a table, and the *maters* arranged goodies, all the while whispering about who had done such a horrible thing, and was his *bruder* going to do anything about it.

Elsie tried not to look in Sam's direction, but she furtively watched as he marched up to the front, put his arm around Wally, and firmly but slowly weaved him through the crowd of people and down the steps on his crutches. They passed Maizy Mischler, who was holding her special star — now covered with yellow spray paint — and crying softly as she showed it to her *mamm* and *dat*. Wally paused as if he might say something to Maizy, as if he might apologize, and Elsie held her breath in anticipation. Instead, Wally quickly turned his face away and let Sam lead him down the stairs and out the door.

Perry, Danny, Maggie, and Sam's *mamm* followed close behind like mourners at a funeral. Their *bruder* had ruined the Christmas program, and they didn't even get to stay for eats. Elsie wanted to weep for all of them.

Serena Hoover sidled up to Elsie as she was getting some punch. "I'm so sorry, Miss Stutzman. It really was a *wunderbarr* program. If you ask me, Wally Sensenig should be kicked out of school. He's caused enough trouble."

Elsie wasn't going to participate in any gossip, especially where one of her students was concerned. "Mark did a fine job on his part. He is a *gute* memorizer and has a strong speaking voice."

Serena smiled and nodded. "For sure and certain he does. He calls the cows in from the far pasture every summer night."

Elsie spent the next half hour deflecting questions about Wally and his behavior and whether he should be allowed to come back to school. She couldn't, just couldn't be disloyal to Wally and Sam, not when the ache in her heart told her there was still hope for them — even if it was a vain and foolish wish.

Mammi and Dawdi had come to the program to support Elsie. "A teacher never gets the thanks she deserves," Mammi had said.

When the families started going home, Mammi handed Elsie a hard, round cookie on a napkin. "It's one of my ginger snaps. They are almost gone, and I wanted to make sure you got one."

Elsie pretended to be enthusiastic. "*Denki.* You are so thoughtful."

"So you are going to Greenwood for Christmas yet?" Mammi said.

"*Jah.* Dat says they miss me something wonderful, and it's only a two-hour drive. I'll be back on January second." She put her arm around her *mammi.* "I don't want to leave you alone, though."

Mammi made a face. "Nonsense. We will have plenty of family. Esther and her *kinner* on Christmas Day. Titus and Sally Mae and the family on Second Christmas. Three or four parties before Epiphany. Not to worry. I'll be so sick of family, I'll be glad to have them go back to their own homes." She took hold of Elsie's hand. "The best news is that on January first we can start looking for a husband. It's on my calendar. Only twelve days away."

"But Mammi, we already talked about this. You tried to match me up and it didn't work out. One match is enough."

Mammi scrunched her lips and studied Elsie's face with a twinkle in her eye. "I'm beginning to suspect your heart wasn't in it."

Elsie took her *mammi*'s hand and led her to one of the empty benches. "Mammi, I don't want to sound vain, but do you think I'm pretty?"

"Of course, dear. You are one of the prettiest girls in the state. Ohio and Wisconsin."

"But you don't think I'm the kind of girl most boys want to date?"

Mammi's mouth fell open. "Whatever gave you that idea?"

Elsie huffed out a breath. "Because you wanted to match me with Vernon Schmucker."

"Vernon Schmucker!" Mammi practically yelled and nearly lost her balance on the bench. Elsie grabbed her arm to keep her from falling backward. The dozen or so people left in the classroom all turned and eyed Elsie. Mammi cleared her throat, leaned close to Elsie, and whispered, "Elsie dear, I have never tried to match you with Vernon Schmucker. Vernon is a very nice young man, but he is quite persistent with the girls and" — she looked around to make sure no one was listening — "and a big baby. I don't mean to speak ill of him, but his *mater* still does his laundry. I could never approve of your marriage to him." She looked positively stricken. "Have you fallen in love with Vernon Schmucker?"

"*Nae,* Mammi," Elsie said. "But isn't he the one you wanted to match me up with? I

348

met him on the bridge and everything."

Mammi put her fingers to her mouth. "You met him on the bridge? At Yutzys'?"

Elsie nodded.

"Oh, dear. There has been a horrible mistake." She grabbed Elsie's hand and squeezed it tightly. "Vernon was not supposed to be on that bridge."

Elsie breathed a sigh of relief. "I'm wonderful glad to hear it."

Mammi brightened. "But this means that I can still set you up with the boy who was supposed to be on the bridge."

"*Nae,* Mammi. I don't want to be matched with anybody." Why did Sam's face come to mind just then? She'd certainly never convince him to love her.

Mammi seemed undeterred. "You said you'd be willing in January, remember?"

There was nothing Elsie could say. A calendar on the wall was counting down the days to January. She'd have to do what she had decided to do with Vernon — hold her nose and meet the boy and tell him she wasn't interested.

"Okay, Mammi," Elsie said, not even trying to sound enthusiastic. "Invite him over for dinner or something. I will meet him, but I won't promise to like him."

Mammi grinned. "Don't you worry. I

know you'll love him. It's too bad I didn't know this sooner. He was here earlier, but he seems to have disappeared."

That news made Elsie feel strangely better. If the boy Mammi had in mind was here tonight, she had nothing to worry about. What boy would be eager to date a teacher who couldn't even control her students — not to mention the fact that he might have gotten the impression that she had a body odor problem.

Nothing cooled a boy's passion like a bad smell.

CHAPTER EIGHTEEN

Elsie pulled the buggy in front of Sam's house, dread pulsing through her veins like sludge from the sewer. She hadn't been here since Friday, November 3, more than two months ago. Lord willing, he wouldn't even be here. She didn't need to be reminded of the heartache.

Even Mamm had noticed something was wrong when Elsie had gone home to Greenwood for Christmas. "You look sad, Bitty," Mamm had said after Elsie had been home a total of ten minutes.

Elsie hadn't been able to bring herself to tell Mamm and Dat anything about Wally or Sam. The wound was too fresh, and she didn't know how to make sense of everything yet. Her heart felt like a lump of coal. Maybe she never would make sense of it. Besides, Mamm tended to make a fuss about such things. Elsie did not want a fuss.

She took a deep breath and knocked on

Sam's door, praying with everything she had that Sam would not be home. She didn't think she could face him, and she was pretty sure she wouldn't be able to stand up to him if he resisted her. There was just too much pain, and she was done inflicting it on herself.

To her dismay, Sam opened the door, looking so handsome and miserable that it took her breath away. *Ach, du lieva.* Couldn't *Gotte* have said yes just this one time? Sam's eyes widened for a fraction of a second. He most certainly hadn't been expecting to see Elsie.

There wasn't any need for small talk. He didn't like her. She was trying not to like him. They understood each other. "I've come to take Wally to the hospital."

"What for?"

"Maizy Mischler has pneumonia. She's very sick, and the family has gathered to say goodbye."

His expression softened momentarily. "I'm sorry to hear that." He studied her face, and his look tied her tongue in a knot. She should have sent someone else to fetch Wally. She couldn't do this. "What does that have to do with Wally?"

"Maizy's been asking for him."

Sam pressed his lips into a hard line.

"Why Wally?"

"She still thinks of him as a friend." Even though he'd ruined her star. Even though he hardly said a word to her anymore. Maizy was an exceptional child. It was too bad everyone in the world wasn't more like her.

"Is she contagious? I don't want Wally to get sick."

"She wears an oxygen mask, and everybody else wears masks too."

Sam stood there for so long staring at her, she almost pushed past him into the house. "I'm sorry about what happened at the Christmas program," he said.

She knew exactly what he was thinking, and she felt compelled to scold him, even if it wouldn't do any good. "It wasn't your fault."

He leaned his arm on the doorjamb and gazed into the distance. "It was no one's but mine."

"Well," she snapped, "I'm not going to argue with you about it."

"It must be hard to admit you were wrong," he said.

How many times would he press a shard of glass into her heart before she learned her lesson? "I came to get Wally. That's all."

"I know what you're trying to do, but you

can't change Wally."

"I couldn't care less about Wally right now," Elsie hissed, and Sam narrowed his eyes in resentment. "Maizy is sick. She could die. She's asked to see Wally. Don't you have a shred of compassion?"

The muscles of Sam's jaw twitched rapidly. "He won't want to go."

"He's coming with me."

Sam shook his head. "He won't come."

Elsie pushed her way past him into the house. Trying to discuss anything with Sam was like trying to convince a brick wall to move. She walked through the kitchen, where Sam's *mamm* and Maggie were standing at the stove, each tending her own pot.

"Elsie?" Maggie said. "What are you doing here?"

Elsie raced down the stairs, just in case Sam was chasing her. Wally sat on the sofa, playing a game on his TV. There was noise and blood and mayhem, and Elsie resisted the urge to clap her hands over her ears. She would have turned everything off, but she didn't know how. Instead, she folded her arms and stood resolutely between Wally and his TV. Surprise registered on Wally's face before he leaned to his right to see past her and went right on playing.

She took a step to her left and blocked his view again. "Wally," she yelled.

"Get out of the way. I need to finish this level."

"Wally," Elsie said, moving again when Wally tried to crane his neck to see around her. "Maizy Mischler is very sick. She is in the hospital and wants to see you."

Wally seemed to lose interest in his game for a second. His hands froze on his controller, and he studied Elsie's face until something on the TV exploded behind her. Wally frowned. "Maizy doesn't want to see me. You're making that up."

"I think that seeing you would make her feel better. She likes you, Wally." Elsie tried to say it as if it was no big thing, even though it was a big thing that anybody liked Wally.

By this time, Sam had made it down the stairs. To her surprise, he walked over to the TV and turned it off.

"Hey!" Wally yelled, showing more emotion than Elsie had seen from him in two months. "My guy is going to die."

Sam folded his arms. "Do you hear what Miss Stutzman is asking you?"

"She's lying. Maizy hates me. Everyone hates me. I'm a cripple."

Elsie had never put up with his nonsense

before. She didn't plan to start now. "Nobody hates you, Wally, but it's true that nobody but Maizy likes you very much."

Sam scowled.

She ignored him. "Don't you want to come and see the one person who still likes you?"

Wally glared at her, the resentment so thick she could have sliced it. He clamped his arms around his chest, as if that would make him immovable. "Everybody hates me."

Elsie didn't even blink. She could be just as stubborn. "Enough pouting. Your feelings don't matter. I'm more concerned about Maizy."

Wally dug in his heels without moving a muscle. "I hate hospitals." His gaze flicked to Sam. "The last time I was in a hospital, they cut off my leg. Don't you even care about that?"

Elsie stifled a growl. It was aggravating how clever Wally could be when he wanted. It was brilliant to play off Sam's sympathies like that.

Just as she expected, Sam put his foot down. "Hospitals make Wally very upset. I won't put him through that. I'm sorry about Maizy, but Wally is staying put."

Wally's lips curled slightly, and his smug

grin made her want to give him a well-deserved spanking. "I really hate hospitals."

"*Nae,* Wally." Wally's *mamm,* Hannah, stood at the bottom of the stairs, clasping the railing with white knuckles. "Do as Miss Stutzman says."

Wally and Sam opened their mouths to protest, but in an amazing show of determination, Hannah hushed them both with a hiss and a severe look. "Put on your coat," she said, the danger in her voice as plain as the flash of righteous indignation in her eyes. "You are going to that hospital."

It was as if lightning had struck the floor at Wally's feet. He clamped his mouth shut and drew his brows together. Sam stuffed his hands into his pockets. Hannah had never said very much when Elsie had come to tutor Wally, but maybe her silence was more about sadness than a weak will. Well, there was no weak will today. She was a force of nature, like a stiff wind that blew all the doors shut with a loud bang.

"But he's frightened of hospitals, Mamm," Sam said weakly, as if even he knew the argument wasn't worth making.

Hannah descended the last step and marched to the sofa. Cupping her fingers around Wally's chin, she said, "You go to that hospital, and you apologize for ruining

Maizy's star and for upsetting Maizy the way you did. She has treated you with nothing but kindness, and you have repaid her with unkindness. You should be ashamed of yourself."

Wally couldn't withstand such a reproof. He burst into angry tears. "They all hate me, Mamm. They'll give me dirty looks. Maizy's *dat* will kick me out."

Hannah was unmoved. "You go, and you take your medicine like a man, because, Lord willing, you're going to be one someday, and you'll regret it your whole life if you don't go say goodbye to Maizy — especially if you don't say you're sorry."

Wally sniffled and swiped at the moisture on his face, but he didn't say another word. He reached for his crutches and slowly made his way up the stairs with Elsie, Hannah, then Sam following. Wally put on his coat and headed for the front door, not even glancing back to see if Elsie was coming. His *mater* had told him to go, and he obeyed.

Elsie was satisfied, but not happy. Maizy would be glad to see Wally, unless he did something to offend everybody at the hospital, but Elsie still had to spend an entire buggy ride with Wally. She had told him the truth. Right now, she didn't like him very much.

Wally spent the buggy ride the way he had spent the last two months of class — in complete silence — which suited Elsie just fine. When they got to the hospital, she led the way up the elevator and into Maizy's room, where the hospital bed seemed to dwarf such a small girl. She was sleeping with an oxygen mask over her face and a tube sticking out of her arm.

Wally stopped in his tracks in the doorway. "She looks so *strumpig,* little," he whispered.

Maizy's *mamm* sat in a chair next to the bed, one hand clasped around her embroidery hoop, the other holding a needle. She looked up, gave them a weary smile, and stuck her needle into the fabric. "*Vie geht,* Wally? Miss Stutzman?"

"How is she?" Elsie asked.

Maizy's *mamm* nodded. "About the same."

Elsie curled her fingers around Wally's shoulders and gave him a reassuring squeeze. "It's all right, Wally. Talk to her. She wants to hear your voice."

Wally shuffled to the bed and stuffed his hands into his coat pockets. "*Hallo,* Maizy."

Maizy opened her eyes, and even with her mask on, Elsie could tell she was smiling.

"Wally," she said. It was already hard to understand the words that Maizy said, but nearly impossible to understand her with that mask over her face. Still, they all knew what she said.

Wally paused as if he'd already run out of things to say and shifted his weight from one foot to the other. "Miss Stutzman said you were sick."

Maizy turned her head and motioned to her *mater* with her finger. Maizy's *mamm* bent down and searched through a small bag that sat next to her on the floor. She pulled a paper star from the bag and handed it to Maizy. It was the same size as the stars Elsie had cut out for the children to decorate for Christmas, the same as the ones Wally had sprayed with yellow paint. Maizy reached out her hand to Wally, and he took the star. It was cut out of white paper and had been colored with blue and purple crayon and decorated with heart and star stickers.

Maizy's *mamm* tucked her embroidery into her bag. "Maizy hoped you'd come because she wanted to give you a new star."

Wally shifted his weight again, and his face turned red. "*Ach. Denki.* It is really pretty."

"She felt so bad that all the stars got ruined that she spent the day after the

Christmas program making new stars for every one of the children."

Maizy mumbled something, and Wally leaned closer to hear her. Elsie took a step closer too. Maizy said it again, but neither of them could understand.

Her *mamm* smiled. "She says she loves you, Wally."

Wally seemed to stumble even though he wasn't walking. He leaned his crutches against the railing and knelt beside the bed on his one good knee. He leaned his elbow on the bed and buried his face in his hand as his shoulders began to shake. Maizy patted his head softly.

"I'm sorry, Maizy. I ruined your star. I ruined the Christmas program. I'm the one who spray painted the stars."

Maizy didn't lose her smile. She looked at her *mamm* again.

Her *mamm* nodded. "We know. That's why Maizy wanted to make everyone a star. She didn't want them to be mad at you."

Wally raised his head. "I . . . I wanted to make them mad. I was mad at them for hating me."

"Not me," Maizy said. The words came out thick and hard to understand.

Her *mamm* nodded. "Maizy doesn't hate you. She says you've been wonderful kind to her. You helped her play softball. Miss Stutzman says you dug up a boulder because Maizy tripped on it." She grabbed Maizy's hand like a lifeline. "We don't hate you." Her voice broke, and she pressed her lips together.

Wally stood up and wiped his nose with his sleeve. "*Denki*. And I don't hate them, really. I was embarrassed, I guess."

Maizy's eyes got heavy, as if she couldn't keep them open if she wanted to.

"We should probably go," Elsie said. "Let Maizy get some rest."

Wally sniffled and wiped his nose on his sleeve again for good measure. He awkwardly patted Maizy's hand. "I hope you feel better. I'll hang my star up next to my bed."

"Bye," she said.

"Bye." Wally picked up his crutches and backed out of the room, keeping his gaze squarely fixed on Maizy until he crossed the threshold.

Elsie nodded her silent thanks to Maizy's *mamm* and followed Wally out the door.

Wally practically sprinted down the hall to the elevator. Elsie had to jog to catch up with him. He could be very fast on those crutches. He pushed the elevator button four times, but it looked to be stuck on the first floor. Wally threw up his hands and ducked into a small waiting room just a few steps from the elevator. Elsie followed him as he plopped himself on one of the sofas. After leaning his crutches against the sofa, he pressed his palms against his thighs and rocked back and forth with his eyes closed and a stricken expression on his face.

The waiting room was enclosed in glass, and they were the only two inside. "Are you okay?" she said.

"Is Maizy going to die?"

"I don't know. She seemed better today than she did yesterday."

Wally looked down at his hands. The pain in his expression made Elsie's chest tighten. "Maybe it would be better if she died."

Elsie closed her mouth and swallowed her first reaction. It took her all of five seconds to know that Wally didn't wish Maizy dead. "Why . . . why do you say that, Wally?"

"Well, she's retarded. She can't hardly talk, and she's no good at school. She trips all over herself, and other people have to help her. She'll never get married."

Elsie kept her expression blank, choosing not to react to Wally's choice of words. "That's true, I suppose."

Wally stopped rubbing his hands back and forth and spread his fingers on top of his thighs. His mutilated hand stood in stark contrast to his whole one. Elsie's chest got all the tighter. "Maizy likes me because we're both damaged. She's a special child, and I'm a cripple."

Elsie didn't know whether to scold Wally soundly for using that word or to pull the poor kid into a warm embrace. She did neither. If ever there was a time to keep still and silent, it was now.

"I just turned fourteen, and my life is already over. I can't work or run or drive a plow. I'm useless, just like Maizy."

Elsie bit her bottom lip and blinked to keep her eyes from stinging. "So you think Maizy would be better off dead?"

Wally gazed out at the elevator which had just closed. "I don't know. Maybe. Maybe not."

"Would you be sad if she died?"

"*Jah,* but everyone else might be happier."

Elsie pulled a chair to face Wally and sat down. "You know what I like about Maizy? It's almost like she carries a handful of sunshine in her pocket wherever she goes. She's always smiling, even when she falls and scrapes her knee or when she can't understand the lesson. She laughs and makes other people laugh with her. She decorated dozens of stars just to make the other children happy. Do you think Maizy's *mamm* and *dat* are sad that Maizy was born? Do you think they wish she was dead?"

Wally frowned. "I guess not."

"Maizy makes so many people happy. All the children at the school adore her. They take care of her. You used to watch out for her when we played softball. That made you feel good, didn't it?"

"Jah."

"If Maizy makes that many people so happy, I can't see that her life is wasted."

"I guess I just feel sorry for her."

Elsie wrapped her fingers around Wally's crutches. "I don't feel sorry for Maizy. You're the one I feel sorry for."

Surprise flashed in Wally's eyes, and he lifted his chin. "Of course you feel sorry for me. I'm a cripple."

She shook her head. "That's not why I feel sorry for you, Wally. You're wasting your life. You could be making people happy, helping people like Maizy does, but instead you sit in that basement and play video games."

"I can't walk."

"Yes, you can. I've seen you run the bases and catch a fly ball. You can do fractions and write poems and spell 'buttermilk.'

You're the cleverest student I've ever had, Wally. You could do so much good if you wanted to."

Wally sat as still as a post. "I can't do anything."

"It's easier to believe that, isn't it?" Elsie pinned him with her stern teacher's gaze. "You were doing things. You learned how to hit. You even hit a home run."

Wally pressed his lips together. "That only made me worse. Sam even said so."

"But why? Why did it make things worse?" She laid a gentle hand on his shoulder. To her relief, he didn't pull away. "Why were you so angry that day with the school board?"

He thought about it for a minute. "You tricked me. Everybody was laughing at me behind my back. They all hate me."

Elsie wouldn't let him get away with that. "That's a weak excuse, and you know it. You've been telling yourself that lie for far too long."

He scowled. "I'm not lying."

"Yes, you are."

He fell silent for a minute, then seemed to explode with frustration. "It doesn't matter how hard I try, they all still hate me. I hit a home run, and the school board still looks at me like I'm nothing and I'll never be anything. It would have been better if I had died in that accident."

She squeezed his shoulder. "I don't believe that, not for one minute."

He leaned away from her grasp. "I'm a wonderful burden to Sam and my *mamm* — especially my *mamm.* She stays in bed all day, crying and praying, wishing I was dead." Tears flowed like heavy rain down his cheeks. "She likes it when I go to the basement because then she doesn't have to look at me. Sam used to be happy. Before the accident he gave me piggyback rides and took me and Perry camping. We used to wrestle on the living room floor, and he'd sometimes let me win. Now he can't hardly stand to touch me, like I have a disease." He pressed his fists into his eyes. "Maizy makes people happy. I only make them miserable."

"I know for a fact that Sam loves you better than he loves himself. He yelled at me plenty of times when he thought I hurt you."

This only seemed to make Wally more upset. His voice rose in pitch. "I made him yell at you. I told him things that weren't true."

Elsie shifted to the couch and put her arm around Wally. "Hush, hush," she whispered. "It's all right. All is well now."

"I'll never have a pure heart."

"What do you mean?"

"Blessed are the pure in heart. Like Sam. I'll never be good like Sam. I get frustrated and I lose my temper and I'm mad all the time."

What was it about the very mention of Sam's name that made it hard to breathe? She ruffled Wally's hair. "Whose idea was it to dig that boulder out of our baseball diamond? I don't wonder but you were wonderful sore the next day."

He huffed out a breath. "I could hardly get up for *gmay.*"

"But do you remember how Reuben and Jethro and Tobias smiled, even though they were working so hard? Do you remember how happy Sam was?"

Wally pressed his lips together to suppress a smile. "Sam bought us McDonald's that night."

"That happiness was all your fault, Wally. You wanted to do something nice for Maizy. That desire came from a pure heart."

He shrugged. "That wasn't really nothing, though."

"It was *wunderbarr.* Think how many skinned knees you saved us by getting rid of that rock."

Wally thought hard about that.

"You've been a *gute* friend to Reuben Schmucker too."

"He doesn't have any friends but me," Wally said.

Elsie nodded. She wouldn't in a million years point out that Wally had no friends but Reuben. At least they had each other. "You don't have to be Reuben's friend, but you are. Reuben needs people who care about him."

Wally met her gaze. They both knew how badly Reuben needed someone to care about him. "I guess I'm that person."

"How many people helped you that day you hit the home run?"

"Everybody."

She curled one side of her mouth. "If everyone hates you so much, why were they cheering?"

He thought long and hard about that one too. "I guess they were happy for me."

"They like you, Wally. You just have to give them a reason to want to be your friend." She gave him a lopsided grin. "You can't be all bad if Maizy likes you."

He wilted slightly. "They hate me now. I ruined the Christmas program."

"Well, you still have time to make it up to them. Maizy made everyone a star. Maybe you could muster an apology and bring some of Maggie's sugar doughnuts to school. No one can stay mad with a sugar doughnut."

"But I'm still crippled. That will never change."

She bristled at the word. Again. "Wally, when I think of you, I don't think of a boy who only has one leg. I think of a boy who can hit one of my fastballs. I think of someone who likes to laugh and think deep thoughts. The children will think of you as the boy who has one leg only if you think of yourself that way. Your accident is a part of you, to be sure, but it's not the only part or the most important part. You have it in you to be good, just like Sam."

Wally wiped the last of the tears from his face. "I'll try, for Maizy's sake."

"Try for your own sake. That will make Maizy happy."

"And maybe Sam will love me again."

Elsie's heart broke for more than one reason. "Sam loves you. He just doesn't know how to show it. Can you forgive him for being a little thick?"

Wally grinned. "And a little stubborn."

Elsie smiled sadly. Those were his best qualities. She'd never forgive him for that.

Wally wiped his face and stood up. "Will

you take me home? I need to ask Maggie about some sugar doughnuts."

CHAPTER NINETEEN

Elsie's heart raced like a runaway horse. There was no avoiding it. Sam Sensenig would for sure and certain come to the school today.

Ach, du lieva. She didn't know whether she was looking forward to it or dreading it more. She longed to see him again, talk to him, maybe coax a smile from those lips, but he was going to be angry, and he'd probably yell at her. She wasn't afraid of the yelling, but she certainly didn't enjoy it either.

Elsie stood at the stove to warm her hands with what heat was left from the dying fire. She couldn't justify putting more coal into the stove when she was going to close up the school in less than half an hour — unless Sam had saved up a whole hour's worth of yelling for her. Maybe she should get the coal bucket.

January had come in with a cold, hard

frost that took Elsie's breath away every time she went outside. The children had the option of going outside for recess or staying in, and they almost always chose the outdoors, no matter how cold it was. Elsie hated being cooped up indoors as much as her scholars, but she also hated being cold more than just about anything. It was the reason she had canceled school in Charm last year when it looked like the school board was going to refuse to get a new stove.

She couldn't pitch or catch a ball until it got a little warmer. Much to Wally's dismay, they wouldn't be playing softball until at least the end of February. Elsie sighed. Wally didn't know that he wouldn't be playing softball at all.

In November, Elsie had been given very strict orders from Sam that Wally was not to get within ten feet of the ball field. It didn't even matter that Wally had experienced a change of heart since then. Sam had sent Elsie another note on the day school started up in January, reminding her of his rules.

Wally is not to play ball. Wally can go to the bathroom whenever he wants. You will not make Wally do anything, including his lessons. Wally is not to be upset.

She had strangled that note in her hands

and thrown it into the stove, but it hadn't changed the fact that Sam made the rules for Wally, and if Elsie defied him, she'd risk losing her job. She thought of Wally's expression on the day he hit that home run. It might be worth getting fired if she could see that face again.

It might be worth getting fired if it woke Sam up.

Her chest tightened and her heart skipped a beat, and she was thoroughly disgusted with herself. Sam was resentful and stubborn and aggravating. Why did she still react like a lovesick schoolgirl when she thought of him?

Her fondest wish was to forget Sam ever existed and to be let alone to wallow in her self-pity for the rest of the school year. Of course, Mammi was having none of that. She was scheming to get Elsie together with her "perfect match." They were going to *gmay* in the other district next week in hopes of catching a glimpse of him. At this point, Elsie would let Mammi drag her anywhere if it meant she'd quit pestering Elsie about getting married.

It was a *gute* thing for Mammi that Elsie loved her so dearly.

She heard the muffled sound of horse hooves against gravel. Sam rode his horse when he was too mad and in too big of a hurry to hitch up the buggy. Elsie drew in a stiff breath. It shouldn't surprise her. Wally had gotten hurt. Sam was no doubt fit to be tied.

She decided to sit at her desk and look like she was busy doing fractions or something, like she really couldn't care less if Sam came storming into her classroom to vent his anger on the schoolteacher.

The door opened, and she heard his heavy footsteps on the stairs. He tried to intimidate her with those loud boots. Hadn't he learned his lesson by now? She would not be intimidated, and he would only have to apologize later.

Maybe.

She could always hope he would apologize later, but it wasn't likely.

Sam tromped up the stairs, and she had to concentrate on her breathing so she wouldn't hyperventilate. She hated that he was so good-looking. It wouldn't hurt to show him a smile. She'd done nothing wrong.

Instead of coming dangerously close and standing over her like a light post, he stopped at the top of the stairs and folded his arms across his chest. This was an improvement, or maybe just a change of

strategy. He frowned, and a hint of something deep and sad played at the corners of
his eyes. "Wally came home with a bruised
cheek today. I'd like to know why."

Hmm. No yelling. This was definitely an
improvement — maybe. She didn't like the
forlorn cast of his face or the sorrow that
lived in his expression. Elsie put down her
pencil, laced her fingers together, and gave
Sam a half smile. "Didn't he tell you?"

"Sometimes I don't get the whole story
from Wally."

Well. That was quite a concession. At least
he was humble enough not to jump to
conclusions as readily as he used to. "What
did Wally tell you?"

Sam studied her face and took a few steps
forward. "He said he fell and hit his face on
the merry-go-round." He lowered his eyes
and studied those big boots of his. "That
doesn't sound like Wally."

Nae, it didn't. But in the three weeks since
school had started up again, Wally had made
some drastic changes in his behavior.

Elsie stood up. "Would you like to sit
down?"

He shook his head. "He wasn't playing
softball, was he?"

"*Nae.* It's too cold."

"Then I'd like to know why my *bruder* has

a bruise the size of a fist on his face."

"Reuben Schmucker's fist." She walked around her desk and down the aisle toward Sam. Since he was behaving himself, she'd rather not try to have a conversation with him from across the room. He stiffened when she got closer. "Wally and Reuben have always been friends. Reuben needs *gute* friends."

Sam inclined his head slightly. He understood about Reuben.

"Something happened when Wally went to visit Maizy in the hospital. We were all so afraid she would die."

"Wally says she's going to be okay."

"*Jah.* We prayed hard for her, but that kind of fear does something to you. Wally realized that maybe he was wasting his life. He wants to be different."

"Wally doesn't need to change. Change only brings him pain."

Elsie wasn't going to argue. She knew how Sam felt, and he was stubborn enough to hold that opinion until he choked to death on it. "Reuben and Wally used to bully the *kinner.* As upsetting as it is, it was something they did together, something they shared as friends. Now Wally is trying to change that. He doesn't want to be a bully anymore. You should be proud of him."

"He won't do that again. He knows he'll get in trouble with the school board."

"That's not the only reason, Sam. He wants to be a better person. He wants to be more like you."

Sam caught her words with surprise and disbelief. "Why would he want to be like me?"

"He loves you. He looks up to you more than any other person in his life."

Sam turned his head and focused his gaze out one of the windows. "He shouldn't."

Elsie pursed her lips. Sam was so stubborn. "Wally is trying to bring Reuben along with him, to help Reuben be a better person too, but Reuben is afraid. He sees Wally changing, and he's terrified he'll lose the one friend he has."

"So Reuben hit my *bruder*?"

"Toby Byler brought a twenty-dollar bill he got for his birthday to school today because he wanted to show everyone the shiny stripe. Reuben tried to take it at recess. When Wally told him to stop, Reuben smacked him. Wally didn't even get mad. He's still determined to be Reuben's friend."

"Why didn't Wally tell me the truth?" Sam said.

"He doesn't want you going after Reuben

378

or telling Reuben's *dat.*"

If anything, Sam seemed to harden like ice on the lake. "Someone has to hold him responsible for hitting my *bruder.*"

Elsie's heart leaped into her throat, and she reached out and clamped her fingers around Sam's wrist. "Please, Sam. Promise me you won't go to Reuben's *dat.*"

He frowned. "I'm not that cruel. You should know that."

"Wally wants to fix things with Reuben by himself."

Sam's frown got deeper. "He can't, and you shouldn't let him. I will not stand for my *bruder* to get hurt again. Rose warned me not to get sucked into your schemes. I didn't listen the first time."

If Sam thought mentioning Rose would convince Elsie of anything, he didn't know her well. If Rose had minded her business in the first place, they wouldn't be having this conversation. "Reuben needs Wally. Wally can't just abandon the friendship because he might get hurt. We need to help Reuben. All of us."

"*Nae,* we don't. You will make sure Wally stays away from Reuben from now until the end of the school year. That's an order." He immediately averted his eyes.

How dare he try that bit of nonsense? "Go

home and tell your girlfriend that I do not take orders from her or you. So what if her *dat* is on the school board? He can come talk to me if he has a problem with how I run my classroom. I don't even care if they fire me."

"She's not my girlfriend."

Of all the things he could have said, *that* was all he had to say for himself? *Ach!* If she had been a hundred pounds heavier and twelve inches taller, she would have shoved Sam down the stairs, pushed him out the door, and hefted him onto his horse. Instead, she contained her rage and gave him her dirtiest look. "Go home, Sam. I'm sure your *girlfriend* will make a strawberry-vanilla cake to make Wally feel better. But don't let Wally cut it. He shouldn't be allowed to use a knife. He might get hurt."

Sam looked like lightning about to strike. His eyes grew wide, and his nostrils flared.

Elsie didn't even care. Nothing made her feel quite as powerful as righteous indignation. Let the school board fire her. She could marry the boy Mammi had picked out for her, or even go back to Charm and marry Wyman Wagler, and never have to worry about a job again. Or maybe not. She'd regret Wyman Wagler before she even made that decision.

"And one more thing," she said, marching to her desk like a runaway parade. She pulled a piece of paper from the bottom drawer, marched back to Sam, and shoved it into his hand. "Here are those numbers I put together for your dairy."

The anger fled from his face as he eyed the crinkled paper in his hand. "There's not going to be a dairy."

She didn't want to feel the profound sadness she felt at that declaration, but she did. Sam had given up on his dairy out of guilt or weariness or some other heavy emotion that pressed down on him, but he wasn't going to get her sympathy, at least none that she would show. She sighed as the anger seemed to seep from her pores like sweat. "Go home, Sam. I need to lock up the school."

"You'll promise me to keep Wally and Reuben away from each other?"

"I'll do what I feel is best for everyone. Go to the school board if you must. I'm done arguing." She walked past him and down the stairs. He followed. She opened the door for him, and he got close enough that she could smell leather and spring. "From now on, if you have something you want to say to me, please send a note. I'd rather not have to speak to you again."

Something desperate and pleading flashed in his eyes, as if he wanted to say he was sorry, as if he didn't like the idea of never speaking to her again. But it disappeared as fast as it had come. He squared his shoulders and put on his hat. "Okay. Fine with me. I don't have the time for this anyway."

The pain in her chest was almost unbearable. She tried to draw a breath. "Goodbye, Sam."

"Goodbye, Elsie."

Without looking back, he walked out, mounted his horse, and rode away. She watched the road until he was completely out of sight.

Oy, anyhow. She'd fallen in love with the only person who couldn't love her back.

She'd never be happy again.

CHAPTER TWENTY

The cold February sun beat down on Sam's neck as he kicked at the dirt clods and hard blocks of snow in his field. He squinted up at the sky. It was a rare sunny day. He should enjoy the warmth while he could. It was likely to cloud over and leave Wisconsin in shadow until March.

Another month and he could think about plowing. The thought of spring usually filled him with excitement and renewed energy for the hard work ahead. This year, he couldn't so much as muster a smile. Plowing and planting seemed as futile as getting Wally to obey him or asking Rose to stop making him a cake every week.

It had been easier when Wally was cooperative — when he sat in the basement and played his video games like a good boy. But after he'd gone to the hospital with Elsie, the video games hadn't been good enough. Miss Stutzman had gotten to Wally somehow, and now Wally wouldn't go quietly into the basement after school. He paced aimlessly around the house and ranted and raved about needing a new leg and wanting to play softball.

Since Sam hadn't been able to convince Miss Stutzman, he had ordered Wally to stay away from Reuben Schmucker at school, and Wally had out and out told him no. What was the world coming to when a boy wouldn't obey his older *bruder*? And short of going to school with Wally every day, there was nothing Sam could do about it. He couldn't talk to Reuben, because Reuben might decide to take his anger out on Wally, and Sam wouldn't go to Reuben's *fater,* because Reuben's *fater* might decide to take his anger out on Reuben.

Miss Stutzman would never be able to convince Sam that being friends with Reuben was good for Wally. Elsie might have the greenest eyes and the prettiest face he'd ever seen, but she couldn't begin to love Wally the way he did, and she most certainly didn't know what was best for his *bruder.*

He didn't regret anything he had said to her two weeks ago, except for maybe that part where he'd given her an order. He shouldn't have done that. He'd known it was wrong even as it slipped from between his lips. She had nearly knocked him over with the fire and ice in her eyes.

Ach, du lieva. She was beautiful and feisty and had the power to make him forget his own name. If he wasn't careful, she would wrap herself around his heart until he couldn't think straight. And if he needed anything right now, he needed his reason. He had to do what was best for Wally.

Rose always seemed to show up when he wasn't in the mood to talk to her. She showed up a lot. He wasn't in the mood very often. "It's a wonderful sunny day," Rose said, as she came up from behind him, shielding her eyes from the sun with one hand and carrying a covered plate in the other — no doubt some kind of cake to cheer him up or make him want a wife.

"You want to get me fat, don't you?" Sam said, trying for more cheerfulness than he felt. He shouldn't take his bad mood out on Rose. She'd been very kind to them, even though they were all a little sick of coconut and strawberry flavoring.

"The groundhog will for sure and certain see his shadow today," Rose said.

Maybe she'd made him rodent-shaped cookies to celebrate Groundhog Day. "I don't wonder that he will."

"Does that mean six more weeks of winter

or an early spring?"

Sam shrugged. "I don't know. It doesn't really matter one way or the other."

Rose puckered her lips and squinted in his direction. "Tsk, tsk, Sam. You've been so gloomy, it's like you take bad weather with you wherever you go."

"I'm sorry. I've got a lot of things on my mind, I guess." Why did he feel like he had to apologize to her — as if he had to ask her permission to be in a bad mood? It was none of her business what kind of mood he was in.

"You're still fretting about that Christmas program, aren't you?"

He gave her a slight nod. He had more serious concerns than the Christmas program, but he wasn't inclined to share his troubles with Rose. She had the bad habit of getting her nose bent out of shape. And she had the tendency to tattle to her *dat*.

"You can stop worrying about that. No one thinks less of you for what Wally did. If the teacher controlled her scholars better, it never would have happened. I've never seen such a lack of discipline in all my years."

Considering Rose was not yet twenty, Sam couldn't muster much indignation. From what he had seen, Miss Stutzman handled her students and her classroom with intelligence and kindness. Despite what she had done to Wally, she was a *gute* teacher. A *wunderbarr* teacher.

His gut twisted every which way, and he had to hold his breath to make it stop. Why couldn't he think of Elsie without breaking into a sweat?

Rose smoothed an imaginary piece of hair from her cheek. "People have been talking. They saw how the teacher ruined Wally. And then there was the paint and the Christmas program and the bullying that she didn't even try to stop."

Sam looked away and pretended to study a patch of ice in a depression in the ground. He should be agreeing wholeheartedly with everything Rose was saying, but he couldn't bring himself to do it. He should be mad at Elsie for Wally's sake, but at this moment, his anger felt forced and misplaced. Rose shouldn't be saying those things about Elsie. She didn't know what she was talking about.

Rose leaned in. "Mattie Byler says the teacher has been stealing toilet paper from the bathroom."

Stealing toilet paper? If he hadn't been so dumbfounded, Sam would have laughed out loud. Amish *fraas* loved nothing better than to gossip. Who had dreamed up the toilet paper rumor? It was absurd. "Why would

Miss Stutzman steal toilet paper?"

Her eyebrows rose as if she could not contain all her righteous indignation. "Why indeed?"

Sam huffed out a breath. "I don't think Elsie would steal the toilet paper."

Rose frowned. "Why are you defending her?"

Was he defending her? "I just . . . I don't like gossip."

"Gossip? Sam, she made Wally be a base — that children stepped on. Who knows what she won't do?"

Sam didn't want to argue. He knew from experience how touchy Rose could be about Elsie. He was touchy about Elsie himself. He nudged a clod of dirt with his boot.

Rose sighed. "We've got to cheer you up." She took the tin foil off her plate to reveal six cupcakes with urine-yellow frosting arranged in a circle with a dirt-brown cupcake in the middle. "It's a sunflower. Can you tell?"

Sam's smile was weak at best. At least it wasn't a whole cake. "Those are really something."

Rose bounced on her toes and let out a little squeak. "I know. I have an *Englisch* friend at the library who showed me this thing called 'Pinterest' on the computer.

You can make all sorts of designs with cupcakes and a little frosting."

Sam bit his tongue before he said something that would hurt Rose's feelings, like "Please don't bother" or "Do you know how many of your cupcakes we've secretly fed to your goat?"

"I'm going to make a special cake for my birthday party," Rose said. "I'm turning twenty in March. I can't decide if I should make one in the shape of a buggy or a heart. What do you think?"

"It doesn't matter to me."

Rose stuck out her bottom lip. "Doesn't matter to you? You're going to be one of my special guests at my party. You're going to get to eat it."

Sam pressed his fingers into the back of his neck to stave off the thundering headache that was surely seconds away. How many times did they have to go over this? "Rose," he groaned, "I just want to be friends. You need to find a boy your own age."

She pursed her lips as if he'd offended her. "Aren't I allowed to invite my best friend to my own party?"

He winced when he accidentally dug his nails into his skin. "We're just friends, Rose. Just friends."

She seemed to bounce without moving her feet. "Of course we're friends. Why do you think I made you these cupcakes?"

A movement to his right caught his eye, and he turned to see Wally storming across the field, dodging furrows and dirt clods as best he could with his crutches. Wally looked to be itching for a fight, and after fending off Rose, Sam didn't have the energy. It used to be so much easier when someone had hurt Wally's feelings at school. Then Sam could march off to Miss Stutzman, demand justice, and be Wally's hero. Now, in an effort to protect his *bruder* from himself, he was more Wally's adversary than anything else.

"Sam," Wally yelled when he was still a little ways off. "Miss Stutzman says I can't play softball."

Rose nodded. "Of course he can't," she whispered. "No good can come of it."

Sam glanced at Rose, willing her to be still. No need for Wally to feel picked on by both of them. "I wrote her a note in November and told her you wouldn't be playing anymore."

Wally planted himself squarely between Sam and Rose, turning his back on Rose as if she weren't even there. "That was November. It's February, and I want to play. We chose up teams today, and Miss Stutzman made me sit it out."

"You agreed that you shouldn't play anymore."

"That was wise," Rose said, earning herself a glare from Wally.

"I was wrong," Wally said. "I want to play, and so does Reuben. I think it would be good for him."

Sam clenched his jaw. "I told you to stay away from Reuben."

Wally lifted his chin slightly. "Reuben needs me."

Rose obviously couldn't bear to be left out of the conversation. She stepped around Wally to stand next to Sam. He wished she'd just go away. "Wally," Rose scolded, "Reuben punched you. You shouldn't be his friend."

Wally sent another glare in Rose's direction. "Miss Stutzman said he was frustrated, that's all."

Rose grunted her disapproval. "Miss Stutzman needs to quit defending her students' bad behavior."

"What else did Miss Stutzman say?" Sam said, before Rose could insert more of her opinions in a conversation she had no business being in.

"She talked to Reuben and then she asked

me to talk to him, even though he hit me. I got him to stop taking kids' money. He wouldn't be on a team today because Miss Stutzman wouldn't let me play. They need Reuben. He's a *gute* fielder."

Sam had a feeling the softball argument would be contentious enough without bringing Reuben into it. "Reuben can play softball if he wants. I'm not stopping him."

"As long as he doesn't hit the other players," Rose interjected.

Sam wanted to growl. He opted for a deep frown. "Rose, why don't you show Maggie the sunflower?"

Rose didn't seem to grasp his meaning, or didn't want to. She nodded earnestly and stayed put, gluing her gaze to Wally's face as if she cared deeply about him.

"It would be good for Reuben to be on my team," Wally said. "We make a good team, and Reuben helps the little kids when we play. Don't you see, it's *gute* for him."

Sam put his arm around Wally's shoulders. Wally shrugged it away. "Don't you remember how upset you were that night? You broke the kitchen windows."

"It's different now," Wally said. "I want the other kids to like me. I don't want them to think of me as someone with one leg. I want them to think of me as a friend."

"And if they don't," Sam said, "it will hurt worse than it did the first time. I'm doing this for your own good."

Wally twisted his face into a scowl. "You mean it's for your own good. You like it better when I sit in the basement and don't bother anybody."

It was like a blow to the shins, but Sam had to stand firm. He would never be able to make Wally see reason. He couldn't even make Elsie see reason, and she wasn't a fourteen-year-old boy. "Someone has to protect you, Wally, even if you don't want protection."

"Your *bruder* is right," Rose said. "He's only doing what's best for you. That teacher is no good."

Rose's support only made Sam doubt himself. Elsie may have been misguided, but she was more than good.

Wally balanced on his crutches and kicked at a snowdrift at his feet. "I want to be normal. I want to play softball, and you can't stop me."

Sam pressed his lips into a hard line. Wally would get the hard truth, whether he wanted it or not. "You can't hit on crutches, and you broke your prosthetic leg against the wall months ago."

"You could fix it, Sam. Won't you fix it?"

393

The doubt clamped around his chest like a vice. Was he doing the right thing?

Rose gave Sam a reassuring nod. "Sam is doing what is best."

Sam squared his shoulders. Rose was right. Wally was so eager, but in the end he'd find nothing but pain and heartache, just like before. Sam had to be strong for both of them. "I'm not going to fix your leg. You've grown out of it. It wouldn't fit even if I wanted it to — and I don't."

Wally's brows inched together. "Don't you want me to walk again? Or do you want me to stay a cripple all my life?"

"You are not a cripple, with or without crutches. You've been hurt enough, and I can't stand to see you in pain. And I won't. Miss Stutzman has been ordered not to allow you to play softball. That's all I'm going to say about that."

"She can't stop me, and neither can you."

Sam had never yelled at Wally, but he let him have it now. "You will do as I say or I will pull you out of school, and I won't even care what the school board has to say about it."

Surely Wally had never given such a nasty look to even his worst enemy. "I hate you. I hate you as much as you hate me."

That knocked the wind right out of him.

"I want what's best for you. That doesn't mean I hate you."

Wally shook his head. "That doesn't mean you love me either." He turned around and hobbled back the way he had come. "I'm not your problem anymore," Wally threw back over his shoulder. "I'm talking to Mamm."

"Don't bother Mamm. She's not feeling well today."

"I bother Mamm just by being alive, so it won't matter much."

Sam jogged to catch up with him, grabbed his sleeve, and pulled him to a stop. "Don't you ever say that about yourself again."

The muscles of Wally's jaw pulsed under his skin. "The truth hurts, Sam. It always has." He jerked away, and Sam didn't try to stop him.

"I brought cupcakes," Rose called after him.

Wally didn't turn back or even slow his steps. None of the Sensenigs were all that excited about Rose's cupcakes anymore.

Dear Sam,

I have gute news. My granddaughter thought you were Vernon Schmucker!

Well, that's not the gute news, and I apologize if being mistaken for Vernon hurts your feelings. The gute news is that we are coming to your district's gmay on Sunday. Keep a sharp eye out for us and I will introduce you to her after the fellowship supper.

And please break up with Rose Mast by then. It would not be right to have two girlfriends.

Much love,
Anna Helmuth

CHAPTER TWENTY-ONE

It was obvious Wally and Reuben were planning something. They'd had their heads together all day, whispering and scheming as if they were plotting a mutiny or something equally forbidden.

Elsie found it hard to swallow past the lump in her throat. They were going to force her to make a decision. She could see it in their eyes. But the only choice she felt good about would get her fired, as sure as rain fell in June in Wisconsin.

She rang the bell, and the children popped out of their seats like horseflies off an agitated horse, ready to go home as quickly as possible. Reuben and Wally stood at the back of the classroom and eyed Elsie as if preparing for an attack. It was so unfair. She wasn't the enemy, but up until now, she had been fighting Sam's battles.

The classroom finally cleared out as the children put on their coats and hats and filed down the stairs and out the door. Elsie straightened some papers on her desk, avoiding the inevitable. If the boys wanted her cooperation, they'd have to come to her.

After staring at her for a good minute, Wally cleared his throat. "Miss Stutzman?"

She looked up and flashed a smile. Wally had practically dragged Reuben back into his friendship by the scruff of the neck. Reuben craved acceptance, and he soaked up every bit of attention like a sponge. It had only been the work of two or three days for Wally to talk Reuben over to his way of thinking. Reuben stopped trying to take the other kids' money, and he and Wally had appointed themselves guardians of the playground. It hadn't hurt that Maizy had returned to school and had decided to make Reuben her project as well as Wally. Nobody could withstand Maizy's affection, not even Reuben. Wally had come so far since August, especially since Christmastime. She was proud of him, even if she was going to lose her job over this insecure, awkward, aggravatingly lovable boy. "Did you two have something you wanted to talk to me about?"

To her surprise, Reuben spoke first. "It's been a whole week, and we're tired of watching everyone else play softball. We want to play."

Elsie bit her bottom lip. "You can play anytime you want to, Reuben."

He frowned. "I'm Wally's best friend. If he can't play, I won't play."

"Wally's *bruder* has given me orders," she said, working hard to keep the bitterness out of her voice. Sam wasn't trying to be mean. He simply didn't understand, and she couldn't be mad at him for believing he was doing what was best for Wally.

Wally riveted his gaze to her face. "I want to play, Miss Stutzman."

She stood up and came from behind her desk. *"Cum,"* she said, directing them to the reading corner, where they sat on three chairs that made a little circle. The chairs were small, and Wally and Reuben sat with their knees tucked almost to their chins. Elsie propped her elbows on her knees and leaned her chin in her hand. "Wally, have you talked to Sam about playing softball?"

Wally pressed his lips together and looked away. "He says I can't play."

"*Denki* for telling me the truth."

Wally leaned back in his chair and balanced on two chair legs. "It wouldn't do any *gute* to lie. Rose's sisters tattle to Rose every day, and Rose tells Sam everything."

Elsie ignored the little catch in her heart.

"Getting caught isn't the only reason not to lie."

"I know, but it's a sore temptation." A grin played at the corners of his mouth, and Elsie's heart rebelled and did a flip. She'd seen that mischievous look before from his older *bruder.* On top of all the trouble Wally had caused her, he was a daily painful reminder of Sam. *Ach!* The school year couldn't end soon enough.

"Do you know what will happen if I let you play softball, Wally?"

"Sam will get mad." Wally glanced at Reuben. "But he'll just yell at me. He wouldn't never hit me. I don't care if he yells."

Elsie nodded. "He yells at me too."

Wally furrowed his brow. "I used to hate you. He yelled at you because of me. I'm sorry."

She waved away his concern even though her heart was heavy. "The yelling doesn't bother me. Let him yell all he wants."

"Jah," Wally said. "You're puny, but you're tough. Me and Reuben are the only ones who can hit your fastball." A smile crept onto his face. "So you'll let me play softball?"

"Yelling isn't the only thing Sam could do. He could pull you out of school."

Wally leaned forward so all four chair legs

were touching the floor. "He said he would, but he won't. He hates it when I'm home all day."

Wally still thought he was a burden. "You said Sam won't buy you a new leg. Will you play on your crutches?"

Wally sprouted a lopsided grin. "I've got the money to pay for a new leg, and Sam doesn't even know it."

Elsie didn't want to show a lack of faith, but she had to ask. "Where . . . where did you get the money, Wally?"

Wally caught her meaning, but the resentment on his face was soon replaced with a know-it-all smirk. "I sold my Xbox and all my games yesterday to an *Englischer.* And I made sure he gave me a *gute* price. It's enough to get a new leg, and Mamm says she'll take me to the doctor even if Sam won't."

Ach, du lieva. Elsie was momentarily speechless. Wally had sold his precious video games? They had been his constant companions for four years. How could he possibly bear to give them up? Warmth snaked up her spine. Because he wanted to be normal again. Because he trusted Elsie to help him, and because he had the courage to dream of something better.

Wally had experienced so many disappointments and trials in his life. So many people — teachers, neighbors, *mater, bruder* — had let him down. She could not, would not be one of them.

"*Ach,* Wally. I don't know what to say."

Wally smiled and nodded at Reuben, anticipating her answer. She'd never been very good at hiding her emotions. "Say yes, even though I know you're afraid I'll hit another home run."

She narrowed her eyes in mock indignation. "I'm not afraid of a pip-squeak like you."

"Look who's talking."

Wally had no idea what he was really asking her to do. He probably couldn't comprehend that she was in danger of losing her job if she let him play softball. But there was no need to tell him. He had made a huge sacrifice. She would make one too.

Elsie pushed aside the anxiety and gave the boys her brightest smile. "You have my permission to play."

You might have thought all the doughnuts were free at the bakery. Wally and Reuben leaped to their feet and jumped up and down, hugging each other and yelling like two first graders.

Elsie laughed, even though dread niggled in the pit of her stomach. "Before you get carried away," she said, "I am going to write Sam a note and tell him what we have decided to do. He's your *bruder,* and we must tell him the truth, even though he won't like it."

"He won't like it, but I don't mind if he yells at me."

If only that were the only consequence. "Since I'm being so generous, you boys can take down this bulletin board for me while I write the note."

Reuben groaned. "Aw, I don't want to be a teacher's helper. They'll make fun of me."

Elsie cocked an eyebrow. "No one will ever know." She armed each of them with a staple remover and set them to work. Surely they couldn't mess up removing pictures from the wall.

Elsie settled in to write a long note to Sam, but there really wasn't much to say. They'd discussed the subject so many times, she couldn't put much in a letter that he didn't know already.

Dear Sam,
　　Wally and I have talked it over, and I have decided to let him play softball dur-ing recess. I am sorry that this upsets you, but I cannot go on denying Wally a

chance to dream. His happiness is worth losing my job over.

Her heart hurt just writing the words. It was silly to think that Sam felt anything for her but irritation. The sooner she got him out of her thoughts, the better. Maybe going back to Charm wasn't the worst thing that could happen. She folded the paper in thirds, slipped it into an envelope, and sealed it. "Here, Wally. Please be sure to give it to Sam. We can't go behind his back."

Wally nodded and stuffed the envelope into his pocket. "I'll give it to him as soon as I get home. He doesn't know I sold my Xbox. He can yell at me for both things at the same time."

Elsie went back to her desk and straightened and restraightened some papers. If Sam was going to come over, he'd see that she had her classroom well under control.

The door at the bottom of the stairs opened and slammed shut, and Elsie's heart tripped all over itself with the thought that it might be Sam. She had to remind herself that he hadn't read the letter yet. If he was here, he wasn't here to yell at her about softball. But since there were about twenty other things he could yell at her about, that didn't give her much comfort.

Footsteps sounded up the stairs, and she saw the straw hat first. As he came into sight, her stomach crashed to the floor. In her agitation, she'd forgotten that Sam wasn't the last person she wanted to see in her classroom.

Reuben's *fater* ascended the stairs, and his face looked like a black-as-pitch storm looming on the horizon — the kind of storm that made mothers gather their children to their bosoms and fathers rush their families to the cellar. There was a gray and terrifying cast to his complexion, as if his cheeks were permanently frostbitten. Alvin Schmucker was the most frightening man Elsie had ever encountered, even though he'd never actually spoken a word to her. She'd seen him hovering around the fringes of the parents on the night they gathered at the school to meet the new teacher six months ago, and she'd had the misfortune of hearing him yell at Reuben one day out in front of Lark Country Store, where she and Mammi had been shopping.

Reuben and Wally fell silent and froze in place, Reuben with the staple remover behind his back as if he'd been caught stealing cookies.

Elsie swallowed hard and stood up, determined to show Alvin Schmucker nothing but strength and self-assurance. Except for the dangerous look in his eye, there was no reason to assume that Alvin was here to pick a fight. At least she could pretend. She gave him a welcome-to-my-classroom smile, which took a great deal of effort, and stepped around her desk to greet him. "Alvin," she said, pretending she was more than happy to have Reuben's *dat* lurking in her classroom.

"I'm sorry to bother you, Miss Stutzman," Alvin said, removing his hat.

Maybe this wouldn't be so bad after all. A man who was on the attack wasn't apt to start with an apology. "It's no bother at all. I hope you don't mind that I kept Reuben after school for a few minutes. He volunteered to help with my bulletin board."

The lines around Alvin's mouth hardened like cement. He raised a stiff arm and motioned at Reuben. "Get over here."

Reuben furtively stuffed the staple remover in his pocket, lowered his eyes, and shuffled to his *dat,* stopping before he got within an arm's length. He grasped his wrist with the other hand and stood with his shoulders slumped. He'd never looked so small before, even though he was still a good seven inches taller than Elsie.

Elsie's throat tightened until she could

barely swallow. "Reuben is a wonderful-*gute* helper in class, and he watches out for the little ones at recess." Well, not until recently, but Alvin Schmucker didn't need to know that. What else could she say? Alvin glared at his son as if Reuben had killed someone.

Wally didn't move a muscle as his gaze flicked from Reuben to Alvin to Elsie. The fear in his eyes gave Elsie more determination to stay calm, even though she thought her heart might claw its way out of her throat.

She took a deep breath to clear the tightness from her chest. "You will be happy to know that Reuben was one of the last children standing at the spelling bee on Monday. His spelling is improving all the time."

Alvin didn't acknowledge anything Elsie said, just glared at his son as if they were the only two in the room. She felt as if she were a schoolgirl prattling on and on about nothing of importance. Alvin reached out and set his hat on the nearest desk. It was then that Elsie noticed the roll of toilet paper in his other hand.

Toilet paper from the porta-potty.

Alvin ripped off a single square and waved it in front of Reuben's face. "I found ten rolls of this under your bed. Where did you get it?"

Reuben seemed to shrink even smaller. "I don't know," he mumbled.

"Don't lie to me," Alvin said, his voice threateningly soft.

Reuben lifted his head and glanced at Elsie, his eyes flashing with fear and dread and regret. The look took her breath away. He was sorry, truly sorry for stealing her toilet paper — and not sorry because he'd gotten caught. Sorry because he'd had a change of heart. Reuben shuffled his feet. "It was just a joke."

In a lightning-swift movement, Alvin raised his arm and smacked Reuben hard across the face with the back of his hand.

Elsie gasped as Reuben stumbled backward. Alvin might as well have hit her. The shock of his blow left her dizzy. "Mr. Schmucker," she said, trembling and stiffening at the same time as she stepped between Alvin and Reuben. "There is no need to hit your son. There is never a need to hit your son."

Alvin looked ready to hit Reuben again. Elsie raised her arms to stop him. "He's a thief," Alvin growled. "He'll go straight to hell."

Elsie was dazed and confused and frightened out of her mind, but she couldn't let Alvin hurt Reuben — but even if she convinced Alvin to calm down, there was nothing to stop him from taking it out on his son at home. "Reuben is not a thief," she burst out. "I asked him to take those rolls of toilet paper home because they were piling up in the bathroom and I didn't have any room to store them here. He was doing me a favor."

Alvin narrowed his eyes and studied Elsie's face. "Liars go to hell just as easy as thieves do."

Reuben laid his hand on Elsie's shoulder. Her heart was racing so fast, she jumped at his touch. She turned to look at him and willed him to stay silent and go along with her story. "I stole those rolls, Dat," he said, still with his eyes downcast, still with his shoulders slumped so low, he could have crawled under one of the floorboards. "I was trying to get the teacher in trouble." He'd changed more than she thought, or perhaps Reuben could see his *dat* didn't believe her. Maybe it was better for him to tell the truth.

Alvin stared at Reuben, silently absorbing his confession. Nothing in his expression softened, but he shoved the roll of toilet paper in Elsie's direction. "You'll bring it all back tomorrow. Is that clear?"

"*Jah.* Okay, Dat."

"And if I ever catch you stealing again, I'll whip you until you can't see straight. No boy of mine is going to hell."

"Okay, Dat."

Alvin picked up his hat. "Then let's go on home," he said, as if angry with Reuben for not being able to figure that out by himself.

Elsie was almost too stunned to speak. "Could . . . could Reuben stay a little longer and help with the bulletin board? It will help him make up for taking the toilet paper."

Alvin's scowl could have knocked her over. "He has chores." He tapped his hat onto his head. "He'll bring back the toilet paper, and I'll be the one to mete out punishment for his sins."

Elsie shuddered. She hated to think what that punishment looked like, but if she said something, anything, she might only make it worse for Reuben. She'd never felt so helpless in her life.

Reuben nodded, close to tears. He looked as if he felt more sorry for her than he did for himself. "I'll be all right, Miss Stutzman. We will see you tomorrow." He turned his face toward Wally but didn't look him in the eye. It was obvious that along with everything else, he was embarrassed, painfully embarrassed. "See you later, Wally."

"*Jah,* bye," Wally said, his voice as raspy as a gravel truck.

It was all Elsie could do not to grab onto Reuben's arm and insist that he stay. That boy needed a warm hug and a whole plate of pumpkin chocolate chip cookies. And a safe place. He for sure and certain wasn't going to find shelter at home.

Alvin marched down the stairs, with Reuben following. When he got to the bottom of the stairs, Reuben turned and gave Elsie a weak, reassuring smile, almost as if he was resigned to his fate and didn't want Elsie to worry.

She looked down at the toilet paper in her hand. She couldn't remember how it had gotten there. All this pain and upset over a few rolls of toilet paper! She had heard from a few of her friends that things were very bad at the Schmuckers' house. She simply hadn't known how bad. She set the toilet paper down and plopped herself into one of the desks before her knees gave out. Her hands trembled uncontrollably, and she laced her fingers together to try to stop the shaking.

Wally hadn't moved from his spot near the wall, as if he'd been glued into place. "Miss Stutzman," he said, almost as if he were afraid she'd hear him, "I told Reuben

411

to take the toilet paper. We thought it was a *gute* joke to play on you."

She attempted a smile. "It's all right, Wally."

"But it's my fault."

"It's nobody's fault. Reuben's *dat* . . ."

Wally looked positively stricken as he curled his fingers around the staple remover. "It's my fault. Reuben is going to get a whipping."

Elsie couldn't bear the thought of it. Though she felt too weak to stand and too helpless to stop it, she jumped to her feet. She couldn't sit idly by, knowing what Reuben's *fater* was going to do. Reuben was just a boy, and somebody needed to protect him.

Something inside her cried out in despair, and she sank into the desk again. She was five foot one on a *gute* day. Alvin stood at least a foot taller, with solid arms and a thick, tree-trunk neck. She couldn't use force on him, even if she wanted to.

She pulled the air into her lungs and forced it out again, over and over. There was only one person who could help her, and he hated the very sight of her.

CHAPTER TWENTY-TWO

Sam emerged from the barn with his full bucket of milk and almost ducked back inside when he saw who was standing on his porch.

"*Vie geht,* Sam?" Rose called. She smiled and raised a covered casserole dish in the air for his inspection. "I told Maggie I'd bring *yummasetti* for dinner tonight."

Sam forged ahead, even though it meant he'd meet Rose on the porch and feel obligated to invite her in because she'd been so nice to bring dinner. Rose appeared on his porch at least three days a week right after he milked the cows. Either he was going to have to change his schedule or stiffen his spine and hurt Rose's feelings. She was becoming a nuisance.

Ach, vell. She wasn't *becoming* a nuisance. She *was* a nuisance, and he didn't have time for her anymore.

He tried to swallow the resentment that

felt like a bigger and bigger lump in his throat. Nuisance or not, Rose had been a loyal friend, giving him good advice about Wally, baking things for his family, and supporting him whenever Wally threw a tantrum. But he couldn't stand her hovering around the house, poking her nose into his business, giving her opinion whether it was asked for or not. Despite all her protests, she was scheming to make Sam her boyfriend, and he wouldn't go along with it. He just wouldn't do it.

They'd have to have another talk.

The thought irritated him to no end. How many times did he have to break up with one girl whom he'd never dated in the first place?

"Maggie always works later on Fridays," Rose said, her smile getting wider with each step Sam took toward her. "I told her I'd be happy to bring dinner."

Sam trudged up the porch. "You didn't have to do that. You don't have to do any of it."

Rose giggled. "Nonsense. It's what friends do."

He opened the door for her, and she made a beeline for the kitchen. He followed. "Cook at 350 for half an hour." She bent over the oven and turned the knob. "I'll preheat right now."

Sam set the milk on the floor next to the back door. "*Denki,* Rose. I'll put it in the oven and be sure to set the timer." He took a couple of steps toward the front room. He needed to get her out before she settled in and invited herself to dinner. "*Denki* for coming."

Rose closed the oven door. "How is Wally doing? Lizzy says he hasn't played softball once this week and he's pretty mad about it."

This was the one *gute* reason to keep Rose around. She told him things that went on at school. "He still whines about it, but he can tell I'm not going to budge."

"I'm proud of you, Sam. It takes courage to stick to what you know is right."

He nodded, surprised to realize that Rose's approval meant almost nothing to him. Before he could usher her out of the house, he heard noises coming from downstairs, but not the usual noises of death and guns and mayhem. At least two of his *bruders* were down there talking to each other. They must have come home from school while he was milking, but Perry and Danny weren't allowed to watch Wally play games until their chores were done.

Without another word, he left Rose standing in the kitchen. He hadn't meant to be rude, but he was puzzled, and Rose knew her way to the front door. He jogged down the stairs, and for a second, he thought he was in the wrong house. Wally's sofa was in the same spot, along with the rug and two ratty throw pillows, but the television, the Xbox, and all of Wally's games were gone. Perry and Danny were standing with their backs to the sofa absorbed in what looked like a very serious conversation.

His *bruders* turned and looked at him as if they'd just been caught doing something naughty.

"We were going to tell you," Danny said.

Perry nudged him with an elbow. "We weren't hiding it. He would have found out."

Sam had never suspected that his younger *bruders* might be jealous of Wally, but maybe they were, and maybe they had finally had enough. He frowned. That didn't sound like Perry and Danny. They had always been so understanding. "What did you do?"

Rose clomped down the stairs behind him. *Ach!* Could that girl just one time take the hint and let herself out?

"We didn't do anything," Perry said. "It was Wally, last night while you were at the auction meeting."

Now they had Sam completely confused. "What about Wally?"

Danny nodded and pressed his lips together as if he was the authority on Wally and his TV. "An *Englischer* came over, and Wally sold everything to him for a thousand dollars."

Perry rolled his eyes. "It wasn't a thousand."

"Yes, it was," Danny whined. "He's got a whole wad of money in his pillowcase."

"Not a thousand. More like three hundred."

"He got cheated," Rose said, making Sam wish harder and harder that she would just go away.

Sam took the last step and walked around the room, stopping in the exact spot where the TV used to be. "He sold everything?"

"Jah," Danny said. "He wants a new leg."

A . . . new leg? Stunned beyond belief, Sam shuffled to the sofa and sank into its depths. It really was a soft sofa. No wonder Wally liked it so much. "He sold his Xbox to buy a new leg?"

Perry folded his arms, almost casually, but Sam could see the tension playing at the corners of his mouth. "He wants to play softball."

Anger flared inside him like a gasoline-dowsed flame. *Softball.* If he never heard that word again, it would be too soon.

Rose was making herself increasingly unwelcome. "Sam has already told Wally he can't play, no matter what."

Sam pressed his palm to his forehead and massaged his temples with his fingers. Why did Wally want to play softball when it had brought him so much pain? It was too much to comprehend that he would sell his precious Xbox for a game of softball. Those video games had been his best friends for more than four years. He took comfort in playing them. They made him forget he was a cripple. They gave him a little happiness in his wearisome life.

Sam's heart sank. He hadn't thought of Wally as a cripple for months yet. Until today.

Someone might as well have dumped Rose's pan of *yummasetti* on his head.

Wally was determined to be something other than the cripple everybody expected him to be, even though it was easier to sit in this dark, suffocating basement and waste his life away. Elsie knew it. Elsie had always known it. She'd done her best in spite of Sam and his misplaced sense of responsibility. He had tried to protect Wally and made them both miserable in the process.

If it had been up to Sam, Wally would be nothing but a cripple until the day he died. The self-reproach nearly smothered him. He had tried to spare Wally the pain of failure, the pain of shame and hard things. But it was the hard things that gave Wally a purpose, that made him try for happiness, even if the happiness was hard to come by and the purpose was impossible to see.

Softball was everything. Elsie knew. She had always known. Softball was a game that normal children played, something Wally could be good at, even though it was hard. Even though he fell and banged up his leg, or got blisters from trying to hit the ball. That home run had been Wally's first great accomplishment in Sam couldn't remember how long. No wonder Wally wanted to play. No wonder he was willing to sell everything and risk his *bruder*'s wrath. Softball was everything *and* the first thing. The first step.

And Elsie knew it.

The thought of Elsie drenched him like a warm summer rain. How had he lived without her for so many months? How had he taken breath after breath without her in his life? How could he sit here without her next to him?

How *deerich,* foolish, and blind could one

419

person be?

He had to make it right. With Wally, with his family, and especially with Elsie. It had taken him months to realize he loved her. He wasn't about to go one more minute without letting her know.

He stood so quickly his head started spinning. Or maybe it was his sudden, breathtaking realization that he loved Elsie Stutzman that made him so giddy. "I've got to go," he said, to no one in particular. Surely Elsie would still be at the school.

Danny chewed on his fingernail. "Are you mad?"

Sam answered by sliding his hands under Danny's arms, picking him up and swinging him around the room. Danny caught his breath and then laughed. Sam put him down. "I'm not mad. If Wally is happy, I'm happy." Danny made a face. His eight-year-old brain couldn't grasp the journey Sam had taken in just a few short minutes. Sam took the stairs two at a time and only remembered Rose when he got to the top. "I'll be back soon," he called from the top. "Rose, will you see that the *yummasetti* makes it into the oven?"

"Okay," she called back, and the uncertainty in her voice was unmistakable. He felt a little guilty that he didn't care, but he'd made his feelings very plain to Rose. If she was hurt, it was because she had chosen to ignore his warnings.

He was retrieving his hat from the hook when the realization punched him in the gut. He loved Elsie with all his heart, but she could never love him. He'd been petulant and rude and demanding, stubborn and proud. Right now she was probably thinking she'd be better off with that Wyman person in Charm, or even Vernon Schmucker — anybody but Sam Sensenig, the resentful *bruder* who never held his tongue and had insulted her in a hundred different ways.

The clock ticked as he stood there wallowing in regret. He loved Elsie. Did he have any hope of making her love him back?

Sounds from the basement got him moving. He didn't want to explain anything to Rose. He strode across the living room and opened the front door. *Ach, du lieva.* His lungs seized, and he wouldn't have been able to take a breath if his life depended on it — which it did. Elsie, looking like an angel from his dreams, was walking up his porch steps with Wally right behind her.

A few seconds ago, he had been aching to talk to Elsie. Now he struggled to speak, because her green eyes paralyzed his tongue.

She was so beautiful. He thought he'd have at least a few minutes to think of the words that would convince her to love him.

Wally tore up the steps on his crutches, looking like a tragedy had befallen him. "We need your help."

Elsie's red-rimmed eyes knocked him flat. She'd been crying. With his heart beating against his ribs, he wrapped his fingers around her arms and nudged her closer. She caught her breath as surprise and grief traveled across her face. "Elsie, what's wrong?"

"Sam," she managed to squeeze out before her voice faltered.

"What is it?"

She gazed at him with those exquisite green eyes. He'd never breathe again. "I'm sorry. I didn't know where else to go. My *dawdi* is eighty-seven. I couldn't ask him to . . ."

When she paused, he pulled her closer. "What's wrong, Elsie? I'll do anything."

"Reuben needs your help."

"His *dat* came to the school," Wally said, panting as if he'd run a race.

Sam clenched his jaw. Alvin at the school couldn't have been a *gute* thing.

Elsie blinked back fresh tears. "Reuben's been stealing toilet paper from the school, and Alvin found out."

Wally's knuckles were white around his crutches. "He hit Reuben right across the face. Both Miss Stutzman and me saw him."

Sam's anger flared. With one hand firmly holding on to Elsie, he reached out, wrapped his other hand around Wally's neck, and pulled him into an embrace. "Did he hurt you?"

Wally relaxed against Sam's warmth and disintegrated into a flood of tears. "I just stood there like a coward. I didn't know what to do."

Elsie smoothed her hand up and down Wally's arm. "Reuben knows you're his friend. Anything you did would have made it worse."

Sam was still having trouble breathing. "Did he hurt you, Elsie?" he whispered.

She looked away. "*Nae.* I am well." She didn't look *well.* Seeing something like that would have shaken almost anyone. She placed her hand over his hand — the one he still had wrapped around her arm. He felt the jolt of her touch all the way up his shoulder. "I know what you think of me, but I need your help." She didn't know anything of the sort, but now was not the time to tell her how much he loved her or beg her forgiveness. "I'm afraid of what Alvin might do to Reuben."

"He said he was going to punish him," Wally said, sobbing against Sam's chest.

"Are they still at the school?"

"They went home." Elsie shuddered. "Alvin was mad enough to strike Reuben in front of the two of us. What will he do in private with such a hot temper?"

There was no telling, not with a man like Alvin Schmucker.

"I should have helped him," Wally said. "I just . . . I was so scared. The toilet paper was my fault."

Sam resisted the urge to pull Elsie close and hold her until his heart slowed its breakneck pace. "What do you want me to do?"

"If you could go talk to him — give his temper time to cool — I just want Reuben to be all right."

"I'll go right now. I only need time to saddle my horse."

"Oh." She sighed as if she'd been holding all her sorrows in for a very long time. A tear rolled down her cheek. "*Denki,* Sam. *Denki,* a thousand times."

"I want to come," Wally said. "I want to help Reuben."

Sam couldn't let that happen, and up until a few minutes ago, he wouldn't have even given Wally a reason. He nudged Wally away

424

from him and placed a firm hand on his shoulder. "You have been a *gute* friend to Reuben, but Alvin is proud and bitter. He wouldn't like it if he thought a fourteen-year-old had come to chastise him. Do you understand?"

Wally sniffled and nodded. "I suppose."

Sam removed Wally's hat and ruffled his hair. "There was nothing you could have done but make it worse. It was better that you did what you did."

"Miss Stutzman wasn't afraid. She got right between Reuben and his *dat* and told him to stop. Reuben's *dat* looked like he was going to spit on her."

"I was wonderful afraid, Wally. Don't believe for one second that I wasn't."

Sam's heart hurt as if someone had ripped it into four pieces. He clamped his arms around his chest to keep from pulling Elsie into a hug and never letting go. How could he have ever yelled at this woman? How could he have ever not loved her?

Wally pressed his lips together as the line between his eyes deepened. "She lied, Sam. She bore false witness to protect Reuben. I could never be that brave."

Sam heard someone behind him and knew who it was without turning around. He should have left Rose on the porch with the casserole and never invited her into the house.

"What are you doing here?" Rose said, propping her hand on her hip and scowling at Elsie as if she were a door-to-door salesman.

"Sorry, Rose," Sam said. "I've got to go. You can let yourself out."

Rose turned her attention to Wally, who was still swiping at his nose and fighting the tears. "Danny told us everything. You sold your Xbox to buy a new leg so you can play softball. Sam isn't going to let you play softball, so you might as well forget it. Don't let Miss Stutzman get your hopes up."

"I'm sorry, Sam," Wally said.

Sam stretched his lips into an unyielding line. "We'll talk about that later. I've got to get to Reuben's." He glanced at Rose and then at Elsie. He couldn't ask Elsie to stay here with someone who disliked her so much. "Will you wait for me at the school, Elsie? Or do you want to go home?" He didn't even know where she lived.

"I'll wait at the school. *Denki,* Sam. I don't know how to tell you —"

If she said one more thing, he might have to kiss her. "I'll come to the school. Okay?"

She nodded, and he gave her a doubtful smile.

If he couldn't make her love him, he'd never smile again.

CHAPTER TWENTY-THREE

Hugging her knees to her chest and praying with all her might, Elsie sat on one of the steps about halfway down and stared out the window. She quietly thanked the person who'd had the *gute* sense to put a window in the schoolhouse door. It was useful when she wanted to look out on recess without being noticed and especially welcome tonight when she was eagerly awaiting news from Sam. She didn't even care if he yelled at her. She just needed to know that Reuben was all right.

It had started to snow lightly about half an hour ago, and then the wind had started to blow. First it sighed through the cracks in the schoolhouse, then it began to howl as it rattled the windows. She hated that Sam was out on a cold afternoon like this, but oh so grateful that he had agreed, without hesitation, to go.

That was one thing she loved about Sam.

He was a protector, with a heart for the weak and downtrodden. It was why he was so inflexible about Wally and so miserable when Wally was upset. It was why he yelled at her and why he was willing to give up his dream of a dairy for Wally's sake.

Oy, anyhow. She wished she didn't love him so much. It hurt that much more to know that he considered her his enemy.

Pressing her toes into the stair, she lifted her heels, and her feet started vibrating vigorously. She didn't want to leave her post, but she couldn't make herself be still either. When she had come back to the school, she had started and given up on about five projects before surrendering altogether and planting herself on the stairs to wait. It would soon be dark, and Mammi and Dawdi were going to worry if she didn't come home soon.

The blessed sound of a horse started quietly and got louder. Every nerve in her body pulsed with tension. She'd be okay as long as she knew Reuben was safe. She stood, tripped up the stairs, and paced the floor at the top where she could still see the door when Sam came in.

The wind blew a bushel of snow in with him. He forced the door shut, took off his hat, and shook the snow from it. He looked up and smiled at her, making her dizzy and light-headed and breathless all at the same time. Even if he hated her, she would always cherish that smile.

She was grateful when he practically ran up the stairs. She'd been in suspense for too long already. He took her hand in his and laid his other hand over the top of hers. She trembled, but she told herself it was only because his hands were so cold. "Elsie," he said, almost as if he liked her, almost as if he didn't think she had ruined Wally's life, "all is well. Reuben is safe."

She couldn't let herself breathe. Not yet. "What happened?"

"I talked with Alvin. You'll be happy to know that I didn't yell." He curled one side of his mouth before studying her face and losing any hint of a smile. "It's all right, Elsie. He calmed down and agreed to let Reuben spend the night at our house."

"Reuben's at your house?"

He squeezed her hand. "He and Wally are eating *yummasetti* and teasing Maggie mercilessly. He's going to be okay."

Elsie's relief was like a river overflowing its banks. She wrapped her arms around her waist as great, uncontrollable sobs wracked her body. "I . . . I . . . *denki. Denki,* Sam."

Concern darkened his features, and he

tugged her into his arms. She didn't try to resist him. His embrace felt so good, and she felt so unraveled. She buried her face against his chest and bawled, and he didn't seem to mind that she was soaking his shirt with her tears. "I — was — so — worried," she hiccupped, trying to explain herself even as she was helpless to pull away.

"Shh, shh, *heartzley.* You were so brave." His arms tightened around her. "Alvin should never have . . ."

Her heart did a somersault. Had he just called her *heartzley*? "I . . . I couldn't stand the thought of Reuben getting hurt."

"Wally said you lied to protect him."

He could yell at her if he wanted to. She would do the same again. "I told Alvin I gave Reuben the toilet paper. He didn't believe me."

Instead of releasing her like she expected he would after knowing her sin, he held on so tight, she thought she'd never feel adrift again. "Elsie, I'm sorry. So, so sorry," he said, his breathing shallow and fast. He kissed her forehead and made her head whirl like a snowflake in the wind.

Didn't he despise her? Hadn't he heard her confess to lying? And where were her wits? Shouldn't he let go of her so she could bend over and scoop them up off the floor?

She raised her gaze to his face. His eyes were hooded, and he looked at her as if she had something he wanted very badly. He lowered his head and kissed one eyebrow, and then the other. His touch was so gentle, his mouth like a feather against her skin. He smeared an errant tear from her face and kissed her eyelid. Cupping the side of her face with his hand, he traced his thumb along the edges of her bottom lip. The snowflake whirling inside her head turned into a blizzard — a wild, windy whiteout that left her breathless and shivering at his touch.

"I guess I shouldn't have lied," she murmured, because someone needed to wake Sam up from whatever strange dream he was in. She didn't want him to do something he'd regret later, even if she'd remember this for the rest of her life and *ach, du lieva* . . .

Without a word, he pulled her closer, squeezed the air right out of her, and brought his lips down on hers. Her heart banged against her chest at the absolutely *wunderbarr,* heavenly feel of his lips and heady smell of leather and soap on his skin. She should have pushed him away, because he couldn't possibly know what he was doing. He was kissing the girl he'd yelled at only weeks ago, the one who had injured Wally beyond repair. The one who lied about toilet paper and could strike him out without even trying. The one he hated.

A sigh came from deep within her throat as he slid both hands around her waist to bring her closer to him. *Ach, vell.* It was too late to talk him out of anything. Might as well enjoy it before he came to his senses. Rising to her tippy toes, she snaked her arms around his neck. He was too tall, but he was bending over to kiss her. She managed all right.

He broke off the kiss, but his lips hovered mere inches from her mouth. "Have I ruined my chances with you, Elsie?"

She gave him a lopsided, dreamy, discombobulated grin. "Apparently not."

His smile would have made her knees weak if they hadn't been jelly already. "Do you really mean that?"

"Jah." She didn't want to remind him how he felt about her, but for sure and certain he wasn't thinking straight. "But don't you hate me? I'm trying to ruin Wally's life."

He winced as if she'd slapped him, released her, and took a step back. The emptiness he left behind threatened to overtake her. "Elsie, I've been wrong about so many things, I don't even know where to begin to apologize to you."

"You can start by saying you're sorry for almost breaking my nose."

Despite his distress, he chuckled. "You insisted on challenging my manhood. I had to do it." His smile faded. "Wally sold his Xbox. Did you know that?"

She nodded.

"I thought I was protecting him, but all I did was hurt him. Badly."

Elsie couldn't bear that look on his face. She took his hand and led him to sit on the edge of her desk. Then she wrapped her arms around his neck and gave him a kiss on the lips. It was very nice, very short, and set her heart running madly around the bases. His eyes lit up as hope played at the corners of his mouth. *Ach!* He was too lovable for words. "You did your best by Wally. No one can fault you for that, even though you were wrong and stubborn about it."

He hung his head. "I'm sorry."

She cupped her fingers around his chin and lifted it so he'd look her in the eye. "Everything you've done is because you love Wally, but he's even more stubborn than you are. You never would have been able to smother him, no matter how hard you tried. You can take comfort in that."

"I can't take comfort in anything."

She took his hand and laced her fingers with his. It felt so good, she might never let go. "Because you were so obstinate, you forced him to find the strength to defy you. You held him down, and he resisted until he grew strong enough to break free — not because he doesn't love you, but because he's finally finding his own way."

"It's worse than I imagined."

"*Nae,* it isn't. At the first of the year, I was the one he fought. He started playing softball because he wanted to irritate me."

"That's true." Sam curled one corner of his mouth. "You were the enemy."

"You thought so too. I made Wally's life miserable, and you both hated me for it."

"I never hated you." He expelled a quick puff of air and smiled. "*Vell,* I disliked you a lot."

"Wally needed someone to push him hard enough so that he would push back. Eventually he realized he wasn't a good-for-nothing cripple. He saw that he could be normal and whole."

Sam's expression got all mushy, and he wrapped his hands around her waist and pulled her close. She'd never get tired of the warmth that enveloped her. "What would we have done without you?"

"*Vell,* you never would have learned how

to cut your pizza into twelve equal slices."

Sam's eyebrows shot up. "I almost forgot. I have something for you." He reached into his pocket and pulled out an envelope. It was the one she'd given Wally to give to Sam. "Oh," he said. "This isn't it."

"Did you read it?"

"I read it. Wally gave it to me when I brought Reuben home." He pulled her note from the envelope and unfolded it. "*Dear Sam, Wally and I have talked it over, and I have decided to let him play softball during recess.* You were very brave to send this. You had to know how mad it would make me."

Elsie's lips twitched with a smile. "I can't believe you kissed me after that."

He shrugged in mock resignation. "I'd been resisting for a wonderful long time. I couldn't help myself." He knocked her over with a smile and squeezed her hand. "You were right about everything. I realized how *deerich* I'd been when I went down to the basement and saw what Wally had done." He reached into his other pocket and pulled out a piece of crumpled and misused notebook paper. "Here is what I brought for you."

With great curiosity, she reached for it, but he pulled it away. "*Nae,* teacher. I will read this to you." He tucked her arm under his elbow and led her to sit at her desk. He went back around to the other side, got down on his knees across from her, and rested his elbows on her desk. "The last time I came to the school, you told me you didn't want to talk to me ever again. Do you remember?"

She scrunched her lips to one side of her face. "I remember you gave me an order."

He grimaced. "*Jah, vell.* Try to forget that." He laid the paper on the desk and smoothed it with his fingers. "You told me that if I had something to say to you I should send a note, because you didn't want to talk to me."

It was her turn to make a face. "I remember something like that."

"It hurt me like an ache in the gut, even though I was mad at you."

Elsie felt the ache as if it were her own. "I thought you hated me. I couldn't bear your sharp looks."

He crumpled the paper in his fist. "*Ach,* Elsie. I've been so foolish."

She wrapped her fingers around his wrist. "So what does your note say?"

He studied the paper in his hand and smoothed it out again. "I wrote this right before I came, so I've probably misspelled half the words and left out all the commas."

"I don't care about commas."

He cleared his throat. *"Dear Elsie, I fell in love with you months ago. I hope you'll forgive me and try to love me back. Love, Sam."* He looked up, folded the paper, and put it back in his pocket. "That's all," he said, his face a bright and attractive shade of red.

Elsie stifled a smile. She had definitely not fallen in love with a poet, but he had so many other *gute* qualities, how could she complain? "You love me?"

"With all my heart."

She thought she might burst. "And I love you too, Sam Sensenig."

The warmth in his eyes could have set the forest on fire. He leaned across the desk and laid a perfect kiss on her mouth. She'd never been kissed by a boy in her life, and three in one night was quite intoxicating. "There's no *gute* reason for you to love me, but I'm glad all the same," he said.

She tapped her finger to her forehead and looked at the ceiling. "Let's see. You're wonderful handsome, but that doesn't make up for your bad temper. You're the most stubborn person I know, and you tend to yell at people you've only just met. You're fiercely loyal to the ones you love, but you're too hard on yourself."

He caressed the back of her hand with his thumb. "Like I said. There's no *gute* reason for you to love me."

She stared at their hands until she felt his gaze on her. She slowly looked up and into his eyes. They were so full of hope and happiness that she had to blink back the tears. Could anyone in the world be as happy as she was at this moment?

He stood up so fast he bumped his knee on her desk. "I have to go before you change your mind about loving me."

"I'm not going to change my mind."

"Then before I lose all sanity and kiss you again. The bishop would never approve."

Elsie smiled. "What the bishop doesn't know won't hurt him."

Sam stopped rubbing his knee and eyed her as if he liked the idea, then he seemed to think better of it. "Wanting to kiss you this bad must be a sin. I'd better go home."

He looked so earnest that Elsie had to giggle. Sam was right. Kissing made her altogether too giddy and too head-over-heels to think rationally. "Okay. If you say so."

"But can I see you tomorrow?"

"I'd like that. But it's Saturday. There's no *gute* excuse."

"The *gute* excuse is that I love you."

Her pulse raced just hearing him say it.

"You can come tutor Wally tomorrow," Sam said. "He's farther behind than ever."

"I'd like that."

"Maybe I will hire you to tutor everyone in my family. Then you can come every day."

Sam helped her on with her coat, and she extinguished the propane floor lantern. There was still a little light outside, but it was almost full dark in the schoolhouse. He gave her his arm as they walked down the stairs together. Before he opened the door, he surprised her by tugging her into an embrace and kissing her senseless. When he drew away, she couldn't for the life of her remember her own name.

"I love you, Elsie Stutzman," he whispered.

Elsie Stutzman. That was her name.

"I love you too." She tied her bonnet into place and put on her gloves. It would be a cold ride home.

"I should follow you home," he said. "It's almost dark."

"I'll be all right. It's not that far."

Even in the dimness, she could see his bright smile. "I don't even know where you live."

"Do you know Anna and Felty Helmuth? They're my grandparents."

"Umm . . ."

Elsie gasped as a face appeared at the window and someone rapped on the door with thundering determination. "Sam?" Rose's muffled voice was loud enough to hear in the next schoolhouse over. "Sam? Is everything all right?"

Sam stiffened and stepped away while Elsie opened the door and Rose barreled her way into the school. There wasn't much room between the door and the steps up to the classroom, but since Rose insisted on coming in, the three of them squeezed awkwardly into what little space they had.

Rose looked both of them up and down and sniffed her displeasure. A flurry of snow drifted from her bonnet. "I was worried when you didn't come back. Wally and Reuben would have eaten all the *yummasetti* if I hadn't made them save you some."

Elsie bit her bottom lip. Sam said he loved her, but where did Rose fit in? She cooked for the Sensenigs so often, she might as well have lived there. And it was as plain as Wally's missing leg that Rose was in love with Sam. Where did that leave Elsie? The thought stole some of her happiness, even though Sam had just kissed her like he'd meant it. Her breathing still hadn't slowed to normal.

Sam's mouth twitched into an awkward,

painful smile. "*Denki* for making sure the boys got fed."

"You've got to come now or you won't get your share," Rose said, sticking out her bottom lip as if she were the one who wasn't going to get any.

"I'm going to make sure Elsie gets home first." Sam opened the door and ushered Rose out into the cold.

Elsie followed and locked the door behind them.

Rose narrowed her eyes in Elsie's direction. "Miss Stutzman knows how to get to her own house, and you need to take me home. I walked."

Sam's forehead creased with irritation. "You walked?"

She nodded. "It's wonderful cold out here."

Sam frowned, and his eyes flashed with anger. Elsie had seen that look when she had accused him of being unreasonable and short-tempered. "You'll have to wait here while I see Elsie home. I'll come back and get you."

Rose stuck her lip out even farther and glanced at Elsie with barely disguised hostility. "But Sam, it's too cold to wait. Do you want your best friend to get frostbite?"

Elsie was not going to play a game of

"Let's See Who Sam Likes Best" with Rose Mast. "It's okay, Sam. My grandparents' house isn't far, and it's not even dark yet."

"Jah," Rose said, a smug smile tugging at her mouth. "Miss Stutzman goes home by herself every day. You don't have to coddle her."

Sam clenched his jaw and closed his eyes. His breath hung in the cold air as the world waited for him to say something. "You shouldn't have walked."

"I wanted you to take me home on your horse," she said, lowering her eyes and tracing her shoe around in the snow. She probably hadn't meant to say that out loud, but at least she was honest.

Sam looked as if he might explode, and Elsie had to put a stop to it. She started walking toward the little shelter where she stabled her horse during the school day. "I'll be fine," she called over her shoulder. "It's too cold for any of us to be out."

"But Elsie . . ." Sam said.

She turned and gave him a dazzling smile. She *had* just confessed her love. He *had* just given her the most exciting, most exhilarating experience of her entire life. Who knew how much happiness one kiss could create? Well, four kisses. Oy, anyhow! "I will see you . . ." She almost tripped up and said "tomorrow," but for sure and certain, Rose would show up at Sam's house if she knew Elsie was going to be there. "I will see you *soon.*"

His face relaxed, and he smiled at her and made her tingle all over, even if there was a little irritation in the lines around his eyes. "See you soon, Elsie."

Rose's voice was clear enough, even the farther away Elsie got. "Why will you see her soon? There's no reason to see her soon."

Tomorrow couldn't come soon enough. "Long division is next," she called.

"Long division? I thought you weren't going to allow her to tutor anymore." Elsie smiled to herself. Rose's voice was carried away on the wind.

Sam was so angry that he refused to speak the entire ride home — not because he didn't want to give Rose a good talking-to, but because he tended to regret things he said in anger. Although if he waited to set Rose straight when he wasn't angry, he might never do it. She'd gone too far this time, and he intended to put a stop to it. He grunted his displeasure. She'd gone too far more than once, and he should have put a stop to it long ago. It was no one's fault but his own that Rose was still baking him cakes and butting into his family's business.

Rose was comfortably settled against his chest with both hands clutching the saddle horn, cooing and humming and smiling to herself as if she were the happiest girl in the world. *Vell,* of course she was. She'd gotten her way *again,* and Sam hadn't done anything to stop her. She was just another Wally, manipulating Sam's feelings so he'd feel sorry for her and give in to whatever she wanted.

In spite of the fact that Rose was on his horse and he was ferociously mad at her, his heart swelled at the thought of Elsie Stutzman, the prettiest teacher in the whole state. He had fought the urge to kiss her until it had overpowered him, but he certainly didn't regret it. That kiss was the best thing that had ever happened to him. No other experience even came close.

And she was Anna and Felty Helmuth's granddaughter. Sam shook his head and stifled a chuckle. In his imagination, Anna's granddaughter was a thirty-five-year-old spinster with bad teeth and eyes squinty from knitting too much. He shouldn't have resisted Anna so adamantly. She really did have a gift as a matchmaker.

"It's wonderful cold, ain't not?" Rose said,

turning and smiling up at him as if he were enjoying the ride as much as she was. He didn't reply. *If you can't say something nice, don't say anything at all.*

Sam frowned to himself. He'd tried to meet Anna's granddaughter on Yutzys' bridge months ago and Carolyn had scolded him. What had she told him? That Anna's granddaughter didn't want anything to do with him? *You could be the bishop's son, and you still wouldn't be good enough for her.*

He pressed his lips together. He'd made a mess of things with Wally, and he'd said more than a few mean things to Elsie. But then again, she'd told him she loved him.

Maybe she hadn't been thinking straight.

He would have to prove himself before she had time to reconsider. He loved her. He would be devastated if she decided she didn't love him back. Hopelessness wrapped an icy hand around his throat. He should have left Rose at the school and seen Elsie home. What must she think of him?

She could do so much better.

His elbow brushed against his coat pocket, and he heard the crinkling of paper inside. Anna had written him another letter. At least Anna thought he was good enough for her granddaughter. That was something. He needed all the help he could get.

446

Because of the snow and the cloud cover, it was dark when they reached Rose's house. It was easy enough to find, though, because several lanterns glowed inside.

He stopped the horse on the road. Surely she could make it up the driveway herself.

"Ach," she said, furrowing her brow. "I thought I might come to your house and get you settled in."

"No need. We're already well settled in." Whatever that meant.

She stuck out her bottom lip. "I need to get my *yummasetti* pan."

"I'll wash it and send it over with Danny tomorrow."

She didn't move. "But maybe we can play Scrabble."

He'd have to be more direct if he wanted to get rid of her. He just hadn't figured out a way to be nice about it. As long as he was still on the horse, he'd never get her down without prying her off. Heaving a sigh, he slid off his horse and turned to her. With a secret smile, she laid her hands on his shoulders and let him help her down.

"Do you want to come in?" she said. "I'll make cocoa."

It was his own fault that Rose still held out hope that he was interested. "Rose, you've been a wonderful-*gute* friend, but I

447

don't want you coming over anymore."

She scrunched her lips together. "Why not?"

"You want to be my girlfriend, but you need to find another boy."

"You don't mean that."

"I do."

Her bottom lip stuck out so far, she could have used it as a shelf for acorns. "Everybody knows we're boyfriend and girlfriend. You've been courting me for months. Even my *dat* thinks so."

He shouldn't have been so willing to take Rose's cakes and casseroles. "We're not courting, no matter what your *dat* thinks."

Rose whimpered as if she'd been deeply hurt, but in truth she seemed more angry than wounded. "People will say you used me, and you were sneaking around with that teacher behind my back."

"Rose, I don't want to be your boyfriend, and I wouldn't be your boyfriend even if Elsie had never come to Bonduel."

"You admit you like her."

He expelled a mighty puff of air, enough to make its own cumulous cloud in front of his face. "*Jah.* I like her." He loved her, but Rose was not going to be the first to hear it.

Rose sniffed precisely once. "You kissed her. I saw it through the window. I was so shocked I froze like an icicle."

Oh, *sis yuscht.* Her breath came out in little spurts, like a leaky bicycle tire. Sam cupped his hands around her shoulders to keep her from falling over — or smacking him in the face. "Rose, I don't want to be your boyfriend. It's time to find someone else."

"You like me. You wouldn't touch my shoulders like that if you didn't like me."

Sam dropped his hands to his sides. "It's cold. I've got to go."

"Don't you even care that I made you all those pies and cakes? And divinity. You have to make like seven batches before you get it right. I made you *divinity.*"

Sam slumped his shoulders. "I never asked you to."

"That teacher tricked you. Nobody likes fractions that much."

Sam couldn't help but smile. "Elsie does."

Rose was practically spitting now. "That's what you think."

Sam nudged Rose aside and climbed back on his horse. "Can you see your way in?" She was wonderful upset. He didn't want her to fall, even if he was thoroughly annoyed with her.

She kicked a small block of ice at her feet. "I'm almost twenty. Not a child anymore."

He had to be sure she knew, had to be sure she didn't hold out any hope. He struck the final blow. "Rose," he said, turning his horse around. "I'm not coming to your birthday party."

Dear Anna,

I am sorry I have been so stubborn. I really, really, really want to meet your granddaughter. When can I come to dinner?

Sam

CHAPTER TWENTY-FOUR

"Miss Stutzman?"

Elsie looked up from Toby's penmanship assignment, which she hadn't really been reading. She'd lose her job for sure and certain if she didn't start paying attention. How long had Jethro been standing there? "Yes, Jethro?"

"Miss Stutzman, it was time for recess five minutes ago."

Recess was as important to *die kinner* as breathing. They watched the clock faithfully when it came to recess. Jethro was one of her most enthusiastic softball players, and he was probably quite frustrated that Elsie had been seriously distracted for the last two weeks. "Very well. Go back to your seat and I'll ring the bell."

Elsie glanced out the window. The sky was unusually dark for ten o'clock in the morning. Ominous clouds rolled in from the west, and it looked like it might come down hard. The children always went out to recess unless it was bitterly cold or pouring rain or lightning was a danger, and even the bad weather didn't discourage some of the stalwarts.

Especially not Wally and Reuben. If it was raining too hard to play softball, they went outside anyway and practiced swinging the bat or organized *die kinner* into playing tag. Now that Wally had his new leg, he could run just as fast as anybody and faster than most. Elsie had never seen Wally so happy, even though his new leg was surely causing him a great deal of pain and even though they had resumed math lessons three nights a week. He didn't seem to miss his Xbox, even though he and Reuben sometimes played *FIFA* during recess.

Reuben was doing better too. Having a loyal friend like Wally tended to make a kid feel at least a little secure. Sam had gone to the bishop, and the bishop had talked Alvin Schmucker into letting Reuben spend a few weeks at Wally's house. Reuben's *mater* and sister had also been temporarily removed from the home and had gone to live with the bishop and his family. The change had made a lot of difference in Reuben's demeanor. Who wouldn't walk with more spring in his step when he wasn't living in constant fear?

Elsie had gotten all her toilet paper back, and Reuben's punishment had been to clean the porta-potty every day for a whole week. He hadn't liked it, but he hadn't complained either. Elsie had stood up to his *fater*. Reuben wasn't going to forget that anytime soon.

Of course, none of this was the distraction that Sam Sensenig proved to be. Just thinking about him made her heart trip all over itself and her body tingle with warmth. After tutoring and dinner three nights a week at Sam's house, she and Sam would sit in the kitchen and talk or play Scrabble with Wally and Maggie or, if it was warm enough, stroll around his farm and talk about his dreams for the dairy.

After Wally sold his Xbox, Sam was more open to the possibility of a dairy. Within a few short weeks, he had started talking about it more, and his eyes always lit up at the mention of it. Elsie loved how practical Sam was about his future. He didn't want to start a dairy until he had the funds and the plans in place. He needed a little bit more money, but hoped to have it after harvest time.

On the days when she didn't tutor, he came after school and helped her tidy up the classroom or put up displays, even though he didn't have a lick of artistic ability and she usually had to rearrange things when he left. They talked and laughed, and she was sure that no girl had ever been happier.

She should probably invite Sam to Mammi and Dawdi's house so he could court her like a normal Amish boy with a normal Amish girl, but Mammi's feelings would be hurt if she knew that Elsie was in love with someone Mammi hadn't picked out. So even when Sam had asked, she'd put him off. It would be better if Elsie broke the news to Mammi first, maybe sometime after the school year was over.

Every time Elsie thought of Sam, it was like a thousand fireworks going off in her head or a thrilling buggy ride up and down the roads of Bonduel. Nobody had ever loved anyone as much as she loved Sam Sensenig. Who wouldn't be distracted?

Elsie stood up to ring the bell just as a clap of thunder rattled the schoolhouse. Several children jumped out of their skins, and some ducked their heads as if to avoid getting hit by lightning. Three or four of the smallest children whimpered or called out. Thunder could be a terrifying thing. "It's all right, everyone. We're safe in here." She went to little Titus Nelson, who was curled into a ball at his desk with his hands clamped over his ears. She picked him up and cradled him in her arms. "*Cum,* Titus," she said. "Let's see if we can catch a look at some of that lightning."

Another flash of light and an immediate roar of thunder. The twins, Lily and Lois, screamed. Maizy Mischler jumped from her desk and ran into Wally's arms. Wally set her on his lap and wrapped his arms around her shoulders.

Linda Sue Glick's eyes were as round as saucers. "Are we going to get hit by lightning, Miss Stutzman?"

"My great uncle got struck by lightning," Mark Hoover said. "He went deaf in one ear."

"I don't want to go deaf," Mary Zook wailed.

Bouncing Titus on her hip, Elsie walked to one of the many windows. "Do you know what causes that loud noise?" she said, acting as if this were the most thrilling thing to happen since Wally hit his home run last fall. "The lightning is electricity and it heats up the sky, and the sky gets so hot, it makes a big bang." If she made it sound exciting instead of terrifying, the children might not disintegrate into a panic.

And it *was* exciting. Lightning was one of Elsie's favorite things. Even though Amish schools taught very little science, it had always fascinated her.

"But are we going to get hit?"

"*Cum,* everyone," she said, motioning to the windows around the room. "*Cum* and see."

The children congregated around the windows. Wally lifted Maizy so she could see outside. Some of the smaller ones dragged desks to stand on. On Elsie's side, a bolt of lightning traveled from one cloud to another, and the noise rattled the floorboards.

"Did you see that?" Toby said.

Elsie put her forehead against Titus's and pointed to the clouds. "Lightning always finds the easiest place to land, usually in a field or a lake. But even if it hit our school, we might get shaken up a bit, but we would be okay. Then you could tell all your friends you were hit by lightning." Elsie sincerely hoped it didn't come to that — especially if the lightning started a fire. She didn't even want to think about that possibility. No use starting an evacuation unless she had to.

The children on the other side of the room squealed, and at least half of them jumped away from the windows as light flashed and a crack of thunder split the air.

"It hit right out in left field," Wally yelled.

Jethro laughed nervously. "It's *gute* we weren't playing a game, or Ida Mae would be dead."

"I would not," Ida Mae protested.

The loud roar was followed by the clatter of a million pebbles. Penny-sized balls of hail fell from the sky as if a dump truck had scattered its gravel, making a terrific racket on the roof. The hail fell in the school yard, hitting the ground and bouncing like popping popcorn. Elsie had always been fascinated with hail. For sure and certain, the children would get a science lesson about the wonder of thunderstorms next week.

"It's popping!" Lydia Ruth squeaked.

Squeals of distress turned to squeals of delight as little balls of hail covered the ground like snow. No wonder it could be so devastating to crops.

The hail couldn't have lasted more than three minutes. Just enough time to give everyone a thrill. The thunder faded to a low rumble and the sky turned a dark shade of greenish-blue as the storm moved on across the plain.

Elsie set Titus on his feet, saying a silent prayer of thanks that only left field had been hit by lightning. "Well, that was exciting for a minute, wasn't it? Time to go back to arithmetic."

"Miss Stutzman, we can still go out." It was Jethro again, not about to be robbed of his recess time on account of a little thunderstorm.

Wally lit up like the Fourth of July. "We should check where the lightning hit. Make sure we can still play ball."

Elsie slowly curled her lips. "All right. Fifteen minutes, but wear your gloves, coats, and hats." Most of them didn't hear her last instructions — too much shuffling of feet and too many shouts for joy.

Ida Mae helped Maizy and a couple of the other first graders on with their coats before shepherding them down the stairs and out the door. Elsie peeked out the window. Wally and the other boys were already halfway to left field to inspect the damage, kicking up little balls of hail as they went.

Elsie put on her coat and bonnet and ambled down the stairs and outside. Might as well be part of the excitement. It wasn't every day that lightning struck the school yard and hail covered the ground like a blanket of dandelions.

Most of the older children had hiked to left field to look at the place where the lightning had landed. Others were swinging on the swings or playing on the merry-go-round. A group of second and third graders had organized a game of freeze tag, appropriate for the cold temperature.

Elsie drew her brows together. The air was calm, but the sky was unusually dark. Something wasn't right. She snapped her head to the left as a low, ominous shriek, like the wheels of a freight train against a track, caught her attention. Her heart skipped a beat. A cloud of dirt and debris crawled along the ground half a mile to the west, heading straight for the playground. Behind it in the air, a black funnel cloud swirled like a dust devil — times one hundred.

She'd never seen one, but if that wasn't a tornado, she'd be glad to eat her bonnet. "Children, children!" she screamed to the ones nearest to her. She yanked Toby and Max by the shoulders and pulled them to a stop. "Hold hands and go to the cellar now!"

The wind suddenly whipped up as if it had lost its temper, blowing Elsie's bonnet right off her head and hurling ice and dirt into the sky. Grasping at children right and left, she shoved them toward the school. "Go to the cellar. Run to the cellar." Oh, how she wished she'd brought the bell with her. She could barely hear herself.

As soon as the wind started howling, the children realized something was wrong. They screamed and cried, grabbing on to each other and running for the school. Elsie braced herself against the wind and did her best to shield her eyes from flying debris as she grabbed the nearest child and dragged him to the school. Just to the side of the cement stairs were two heavy doors that led to the cellar. They were locked with a combination lock, because Elsie didn't want anyone going down there and getting into mischief. She quickly entered the right combination and tore the lock from the doors.

Jethro helped her open the doors, and she ushered the terrified children down the steps. The wind tore the *kapp* off her head as she looked in the direction of the ball field. A dozen or so boys and girls were still out there, but they had seen the whirlwind and were running back toward the school. Wally had fallen behind the group, limping badly and waving his arms above his head. She couldn't hear anything but the wind, but she could tell that Wally was calling to Reuben, who was at the front of the group. Whether Reuben heard him was anybody's guess. Wally was wearing his Cheetah foot today. He could run faster than Elsie with that thing on. Elsie caught her breath as Lizzy Jane Mast tripped and fell. Wally hooked his elbow around hers and dragged her to her feet, then pushed her forward toward the others.

Wally hadn't fallen behind. Reuben was leading the children to safety, and Wally was taking up the rear, making sure no one got left behind. Elsie's eyes stung like fire, but she couldn't look away. "Come on, Wally. Come on," she whispered.

Clinging fiercely to each other, Prissy and Lydia Ruth struggled toward Elsie. She grabbed Lydia Ruth's shoulders and nudged the sisters into the cellar. Danny and Perry, with a first grader, between them, fought their way forward. Elsie and Jethro pulled them the rest of the way.

It sounded like a speeding freight train was heading right for them as Reuben and Wally and the others made it to the cellar. Covering their eyes, the older children ducked into the cellar, with Wally taking up the rear. "Everyone in," Elsie yelled, pushing Ida Mae down the stairs.

"Miss Stutzman," Jethro screamed, pointing to the merry-go-round.

Elsie's stomach lurched. Maizy Mischler sat on the merry-go-round with her arms and legs clamped around one of the bars. Her eyes were closed, and her mouth gaped open in a terrified, silent wail. "Maizy!"

Before she could take a step toward Maizy, Wally shoved Elsie aside with such force she stumbled backward and fell to the ground. "Wally!" Elsie yelled, but it was too late. He was going out for Maizy, and there was nothing she could do to stop him.

"Wally!" She was furiously angry. Saving Maizy was her job. She was the teacher. She should be risking herself, not Wally. She was terrified to the point of being sick. Would Wally or Maizy survive this? And would she ever be able to live with herself if they didn't?

"Jethro, Ida Mae," she screamed. "Get inside now!"

"I need to help you close the doors," Jethro said. She should have shoved him down the steps, but she could see the determination on his face, and she had no strength left for a fight. The only strength left to her was prayer.

Fighting with all his might against the beastly wind, Wally made it to the merry-go-round in mere seconds. Elsie had never seen him move so fast. How could he even see which direction he was going?

Wally tried to tug Maizy from the bar, but

Maizy wouldn't budge, holding on like her life depended on it. Elsie held her breath. *Dear Heavenly Father . . .*

Wally leaned down and said something in Maizy's ear. In a swift movement, Maizy let go of the bar and wrapped her arms around Wally's neck. With his arms clamped around her, he turned and tried to outrun the storm. His limp was achingly profound, and pain overspread his face with each step, but he kept moving, doing battle with the wind and his own agony.

Holding fast to the door handle so she wouldn't be swept away, Elsie reached out her hand and grabbed onto the sleeve of Wally's coat and pulled with all her might. With Maizy in his arms, Wally stumbled into the cellar, where waiting arms pulled him and Maizy in. Each holding one side of the door, Jethro and Elsie jumped into the cellar together and slammed the doors shut.

Everything went dark.

CHAPTER TWENTY-FIVE

Sam's heart hammered so hard, he could feel it over the thump of Rowdy's hooves against the road. Once the storm had passed over them, he hadn't even waited to help Mamm hitch up the buggy. She would come as soon as she could, but Sam had to get there immediately. Some of the people he loved the most were in that schoolhouse.

They'd all seen and heard it. The violent thunder brought all the neighbors to their windows to see the funnel cloud that had hovered over their pastures and farms and headed straight for the school. The sight had all but ripped Sam's heart out. Lord willing the tornado had hopped right over them or changed course or died out before it got there. Nobody ever heard of a tornado touching down in Wisconsin in March, had they?

Sam's gut clenched until the pain doubled him over. Danny, Perry, Wally. And Elsie.

They had to be okay.

He pushed the horse hard, but it still took too much time to get there. He passed Benjamin Hoover in his wagon headed in the same direction, and Rose Mast and her parents on foot. Maybe it was rude, but he didn't offer to give any of the Masts a ride.

Every minute was too precious to delay.

The school yard was as quiet as summer vacation. A gentle breeze nudged the swings back and forth, and hail dotted the softball field like so many wildflowers. Not a soul to be seen anywhere. His hand relaxed around his saddle horn. They were probably all inside without a scratch, doing long division or writing poetry. His gaze scanned the ball field. It had missed them. Praise the Lord, the tornado had missed them.

Unless . . .

He sucked in his breath. Where was the merry-go-round?

He jumped off his horse and ran into the schoolhouse and up the stairs. No one here. Panic pressed into his chest like a vice. Every window on the right side of the room was shattered, and papers and glass were scattered all over the floor, as if the tornado had forced its way into the room and blown everything about.

There was only one place they could have

gone. With dread filling every space inside him, Sam tore back down the stairs and slammed the door behind him. He leaped off the small cement porch and grabbed the handle of the cellar door. It wouldn't budge. They'd secured it from the inside. *Gute* girl, Elsie.

He rapped on the door with all the force of his blistering emotions. "Elsie, are you in there?"

Wood slid against wood, and the doors bounced up and down before two hands pushed at them. Sam finished the job, practically tearing them off their hinges to open them. His knees buckled. Elsie gazed up at him, squinting at the bright light, whole and alive. Her hair was loose, falling like a waterfall around her shoulders, and blood crusted just above her eyebrow.

His heart started thumping. "You're hurt."

"We are all as right as rain." Her smile was like a thousand soothing embraces. "But we are wonderful glad to see you."

A dozen other faces peered out at him from the cellar.

He reached out his hand. "Is everybody okay? Danny, Perry, Wally? Are you in there?"

"We're here," Perry called from deep within the cellar. "We're alive."

Sam thought he might faint with relief.

Several of the children were crying. Most were shivering with cold and fear.

"We need to get everyone in by the stove." Elsie took off her coat, wrapped it around the little girl standing next to her, then picked up the girl and handed her out to Sam.

"It's not much warmer in the school," Sam said. As soon as they got everyone out, he'd cover the broken windows and stoke up the fire.

Jethro, with unruly hair and a rip in his sleeve, heaved himself out of the cellar and started helping other children out with him.

The little girl in Sam's arms clamped on to him like a barnacle.

"I'll take her into the school," Ida Mae said, prying the girl from him and grabbing the hand of another little one. Ida Mae's *kapp* dangled from her head like the pendulum of a clock, held suspended by a single pin. "Mary, take Max's hand," she said to the girl at her side. Mary grabbed onto the boy next to her, who in turn took the hand of the boy next to him. Ida Mae walked her little train into the school.

Danny appeared at the bottom of the steps. Sam caught his breath, reached into the cellar, and yanked his *bruder* out by the armpits. "Danny!"

"Sam!"

Sam fell to his knees and squeezed the air out of his *bruder.* "You're okay. I'm so glad you're okay."

"We almost died," Danny said. "Especially Wally."

Before Sam could ask, Elsie ascended the steps with another young scholar in her arms. "I'm going to pinch Wally's ear, and then I'm going to make that boy clean desks for the rest of the school year. For the rest of his life."

Sam raised his eyebrows. "What did he do?"

Two identical girls climbed from the cellar together, and their faces bloomed into smiles. "Dat!" they yelled at the same time.

Benjamin Hoover scooped them into his arms. "Where's Mark? Have you seen Mark?"

"I'm here," Mark called, stepping out of the cellar on shaky legs.

Benjamin knelt down. "Are you hurt?"

"I scraped both knees."

Other parents arrived, and the scene in the school yard was both heartwarming and sobering. *Faters* hugged their children as if there was no tomorrow. *Maters* fussed and fretted. "Are you sure you're all right?"

"Where does it hurt the worst?"

"It was the loudest noise you ever heard, Dat. The little kids were bawling."

"We'll put a bandage on that when we get home."

"It's okay. We can buy you another hat."

"Wally and Maizy almost died," Jethro told his *mamm.*

Sam's mouth went dry. What had happened with Wally?

Perry emerged holding hands with Rose's *schwester* Prissy. Did they like each other? More likely a scare like this drove the most unlike pairs together. Perry let go of Prissy's hand, and Sam pulled Perry's head to his chest. "You okay, bud?"

Perry nodded as best he could with Sam's palm pressing against the side of his face. "My hat blew away."

"It's okay."

"And my gloves."

Prissy ran to Rose and her parents, who hugged her in pure relief. Rose caught Sam looking at her, and she puckered her lips in that coy, flirtatious thing she did. She came closer. "Are your *bruders* all right?"

Sam nodded. "And your *schwesteren*?"

"They're shaken up, and Lizzy Jane has some scratches, but they're not hurt bad." She leaned even closer, and Sam felt compelled to lean away. "It wonders me why the children were allowed outside in such weather," she whispered, her gaze darting to Elsie and back again.

Sam shook his head. "She shouldn't have let them go outside."

"One of them could have been hit by lightning."

Sam turned from Rose as Wally, with Maizy Mischler hanging on to his neck like a tie, shuffled to the bottom of the cellar stairs. Sam clenched his jaw. Wally's eyelids were so puffy, his eyes were tiny slits on his face. Three long red scratches traveled down his right cheek, and a spot of blood trickled from his nose. From the bottom step, Wally looked up at Sam and grinned so wide, Sam could count his molars.

"Hey, kid," Sam said.

"Hey, Sam." His voice was raspy, his breathing labored.

Wally tried to climb the stairs, but when he put weight on his artificial leg, he winced in pain. Sam and Elsie each grabbed on to one of his arms and pulled him up.

Maizy's *mamm* was there before Sam even thought to look for her. "Oh, my darling," she said. Maizy reluctantly let go of Wally, heaved a great sob, and buried her face in her *mater*'s neck.

Wally smoothed his hand down Maizy's back. "It's okay, Maizy. The big wind is all gone."

Sam shot out his arm and pulled Wally to him. Wally resisted for a second, then seemed to lose all strength as he sagged against Sam's chest. "It's okay," Sam said, not really knowing if it was. Danny said they had almost died, "especially Wally." The thought was a knife straight into Sam's chest.

Wally raised his head and nudged himself away from Sam. "I'm okay," he said, sniffing his tears away as if they didn't exist. Elsie pulled a handkerchief that had somehow survived the wind from her apron pocket and handed it to him. "Your nose is bleeding."

Wally dabbed at his nose and examined the handkerchief. "Totally rad."

He often said strange phrases he picked up from his video games. Sam seldom knew what they meant.

Wally took a deep breath and wiped the rest of the moisture from his face. He was fourteen years old, and apparently fourteen-year-old boys didn't cry. "Where's Reuben? A tin can conked him in the head while we were standing in left field."

Sam pointed to the porch steps. "Over

there with his *dat.* I don't see any blood."
He lightly touched Wally's cheek. "But
you've got some nasty scratches."

Wally hissed, and his eyes pooled with
tears. "*Jah.* I know."

Elsie's expression flooded with concern.
She glanced at Sam and shook her head
slightly. Then she propped her hands on her
hips and pursed her lips in annoyance. "*Ach,
vell,* young man, you might not see any
blood, but" — she pointed to a spot just
above her collarbone — "I'm going to have
a big bruise right here. A very big bruise,
and if I have my way, you're going to be
cleaning a lot of porta-potties before the
year is out."

Wally regained his composure and grinned
like a mischievous cat. "That tornado would
have blown you away before you ever got to
the merry-go-round, and there wasn't time
to explain. You would have just argued anyway."

Elsie was doing her best not to smile. "For
sure and certain, I would have argued." She
brushed her hands briskly down her apron.
"You pushed me!"

Sam couldn't help but chuckle at the
positively outraged, positively adorable look
on Elsie's face. "What happened out there?"

Elsie grunted in indignation. "I was herding everyone to the cellar as fast as I could when we saw Maizy all by herself on the merry-go-round. I was just about to run out and fetch her when Wally knocked me down and got her himself. I'll probably be black and blue in places I'd rather not mention, Wally Sensenig. I hope you're sorry."

His smile got wider, and he shook his head. "Not sorry at all."

Elsie lost her bluster as she bit her bottom lip. "You almost didn't make it."

Sam couldn't breathe at the thought of Wally's courage or of what might have been. Six months ago, Wally wouldn't have lifted a finger to help anyone, let alone risk his life. Sam wrapped his hand around Wally's neck and pulled him so their foreheads were touching. "*Gute* job."

"I had to get Maizy. She's my friend," Wally said, his voice cracking in about a dozen different places.

"Look!" Maizy's mom inclined her head toward the playground even as she burst into tears. "The merry-go-round is gone."

In awed silence, they stared at the post where the merry-go-round had once been.

"*Ach, du lieva,*" Elsie murmured under her breath.

It was too much for Wally. His knees collapsed, and Sam lowered him to the ground before he fell. Wally propped his forearms on his knees and buried his face in his hands. Sometimes a fourteen-year-old boy had to cry. No one could blame him, and there certainly wasn't a kid at that school who would dare poke fun of him. Not after what he'd done to save Maizy. Nobody had more courage than that.

CHAPTER TWENTY-SIX

Sam put his arms around Elsie's waist and helped her from the buggy. Clinging to Sam's strong arms to hold herself up, she tried to stand on her quivering legs. After supporting her through a thunderstorm, a tornado, a blow to the head, and a dark and terrifying time in the cellar, her legs had finally given out. "You okay?" he said, bracing his arm around her and practically dragging her to Mammi's front door.

She nodded. "You okay?"

He nodded but didn't look at her. He was just as shaken up as she was, though his legs seemed to be having an easier time moving than hers. He'd very nearly lost a *bruder* today, and that wasn't something he was going to just get over.

Elsie closed her eyes to try to shut out the memories.

Two police cars, an ambulance, and someone calling herself a reporter had come to the school as parents were gathering up their children. Nobody had been hurt badly enough to want to pay for a ride to the hospital, so one of the policemen had talked to Andy Mast and gone away. Reuben Schmucker and Maizy's *mamm* had talked to the reporter.

Sam's *mamm* had taken Danny, Perry, and Wally home in the buggy, while Sam had stayed for Elsie. They had walked all around the school yard as far as the pasture and found four hats and a *kapp* too dirty to salvage. In the pasture, they had found the backstop tangled with what was left of the merry-go-round. Wally and Maizy never would have survived that collision.

Elsie opened the door, and Sam helped her to one of the chairs at the table. Mammi and Dawdi weren't home, and Elsie was grateful they'd been spared the anxiety of the storm. They had hired a driver to take them to Green Bay to "see the sights." At least that was what they told Elsie, though she didn't know that there were many sights in Green Bay to be seen. She could only be glad that her grandparents were gone. She needed to explain Sam, but she'd rather do it when he wasn't here. There was no telling how upset her grandparents would be that Elsie wasn't going to marry the boy Mammi had chosen for her, whoever he was.

Sam pulled out a chair and sat next to her at the table.

"*Denki* for driving me home. I couldn't have made it by myself."

Sam had tethered his horse to the back of Elsie's buggy so he'd have a way back after bringing her home. "I'm worried about you." He stood up, walked around to the other side of the counter, and started pulling drawers open. He came back with a dampened dish towel, a bottle of hand soap, and some sort of first aid ointment. "Let me fix your head."

He sat next to her, and she leaned her face closer. His touch was gentle and unnerving at the same time as he sponged off the blood with the towel. She loved his strong hands. His strong hands and his *gute* heart.

"How does it look?" she said.

"Not deep. Do you know what hit you?"

"I didn't even notice I was bleeding until you said something."

After cleaning the cut, he applied some ointment to it. Taking her chin in his hand, he nudged her head to the side. "I don't think you'll even have a scar." He fell silent and studied her face as several undefined emotions glowed in his eyes. "I'd feel better about leaving if your grandparents were here, but I'm worried about my *bruders*. I need to be with them."

"Of course."

He frowned. "But I need to be with you too."

She laid her hand over the top of his. "Your *bruders* need you. Go."

"I've always tried to do what was right by my family." He stood up, looked out the window, and ran his hand down the side of his face. "Wally could have died. They all could have died." He had repeated it over and over on their way home. *My* bruders *could be dead. Wally risked his life.* In his own reserved way, Sam was inconsolable. Protecting his family was everything to him.

"They were all so brave."

He cupped his fingers around the back of his neck and glanced at her. "After a hailstorm like that, you should have kept them inside."

"The children wanted to go out. I saw no harm —"

"Don't you know how to recognize tornado weather?" It was an accusation, not a question.

Stunned as she was that Sam had said it, she also felt a sinking dread. It was her fault the children had been caught in the storm. She'd put them in danger with her ignorance. "I've . . . I've never seen a tornado."

He closed his eyes and huffed out a breath. "I'm sorry. I'm doing it again. Blaming you for something that wasn't your fault."

"Maybe it was."

"*Nae,* Elsie. I'm sorry. I speak before I think."

She didn't have the energy or the will to argue with him. Maybe it was her fault. Maybe she would see it in her nightmares until she grew old.

Sam hadn't meant to hurt her feelings, but now she was doubting herself, and the pain of it made her head ache something wonderful. She wanted nothing more than to have Sam gone. She couldn't stand to guess what he really thought of her. She cradled her head in her hand. "Go be with your *bruders,* Sam. My grandparents will be home soon."

"My *bruders* and I will be at the school in the morning to clean up. Abe Yutzy said he would order new windows, but we'll probably have to cover them with something better than plastic until they come in."

"*Jah.* That will be fine."

He rocked back and forth on his heels as if he didn't know what to do. "I'll unhitch the buggy and water the horse before I leave."

"Denki," she said. Sam was watching out for her, even if he blamed her for the storm.

He left without another word, and a tear trickled down her cheek.

He loved her. Wasn't it true that he loved her?

Elsie couldn't even remember how she'd gotten to the couch, but she was resting on it when Mammi shook her awake. "Elsie? Elsie, are you all right?"

Elsie opened one eye halfway. Mammi and Dawdi were staring down at her as if she were a museum exhibit. She groaned, tried to sit up, and laid her head back onto the armrest that served as her pillow. "I think I fell asleep on the train tracks and got run over."

Mammi wrung her hands. "We came back as soon as we heard. Our driver got word on her cell phone that there had been a funnel cloud at the school."

Dawdi nodded. "We left our groceries sitting in the cart at Walmart."

Well, Walmart was one thing to do in Green Bay.

"We heard on the radio that no one was hurt but that one boy had saved a girl's life.

480

Is that true?"

"Wally Sensenig saved Maizy Mischler from the merry-go-round just before the tornado got there. We all got into the cellar, but we lost the merry-go-round."

Mammi nodded thoughtfully. "I don't like merry-go-rounds. They make me dizzy."

"I like that dizzy feeling," Dawdi said. "Even if it makes me throw up."

Mammi sat on the armrest right next to Elsie's head. "You have a cut."

Elsie touched her finger to her eyebrow. "Something hit me, but I don't remember what."

Mammi's eyes grew wide. "You have amnesia?"

Elsie giggled. "*Nae,* Mammi. I remember it all very well."

"Oh, dear," Mammi said. "I wish we hadn't left those groceries at Walmart. I could have made you rice-cranberry pudding. It's my famous recipe, and it cures headaches."

"I'll settle for a piece of toast." Store-bought bread, slathered in butter.

"I've got Wonder or cheesy jalapeño bread."

"Wonder bread," Elsie said, even at the risk of hurting Mammi's feelings. She was too weak to gag her way through cheesy

481

jalapeño bread.

Mammi sighed. "It's probably better on the stomach."

Mammi made Elsie some toast, and when Elsie felt well enough, she got up and helped Mammi make dinner. Things always went better when Elsie secretly supervised the recipes. Fried chicken was hard to mess up, even for Mammi, and if Elsie forgot to put in as many red pepper flakes as Mammi's recipe called for, Mammi didn't seem to notice.

Dawdi set the table, and they were just about to bow their heads for silent prayer when a knock came at the door.

"Stuff and nonsense," Mammi said, scooting her chair out from under the table. "Has everyone forgotten their manners to be coming at dinnertime?"

Probably not everyone, but definitely the person at the door.

Or people.

The school board, to be exact.

Elsie's breath caught in her throat. She hated it when the school board came to visit. It usually meant she was in trouble. Mammi invited them into the house, and Andy Mast led the way, looking as solemn as if he were conducting a funeral. Abe Yutzy and Menno Kiem didn't look any more cheerful than Andy. Andy clutched a thick notebook to his chest.

"*Hallo,* Felty," Menno said, shaking hands with Dawdi, who'd decided he'd better get up and greet the men at his door.

Menno glanced at Elsie. Any spark of hope she might have felt died with the look on Menno's face. She'd seen that look before. It was the look they'd given her in Charm just before they'd told her she was not going to be invited back to teach. "I see we're interrupting dinner," Menno said. "I'm sorry, but it can't be helped."

Mammi frowned and raised her eyebrows. "Of course it can be helped, Menno. Just go away and come back tomorrow. Elsie made fried chicken. It'll get soggy if we wait."

Elsie held up her hand. "It's okay, Mammi." She'd rather get it over with — ripping off the bandage was always less painful in the long run. Probably.

"Can we sit?" Menno said.

Mammi harrumphed. "You interrupt dinner, and you want to sit. This is quite an imposition."

Mammi was usually hospitable with guests, but for sure and certain she realized why the school board was here. Elsie wanted to give her a big kiss. There was no one more loyal than Mammi, especially when it came to one of her grandchildren. Elsie loved her all the more for it.

"Now, Banannie," Dawdi said. "Let's hear what they have to say yet. The longer they stand here, the soggier the fried chicken will get." He motioned for Andy to sit in the recliner, which was definitely a great sacrifice. Dawdi loved his recliner.

Andy sat down, but the recliner didn't suit him. He looked like a fence post trying to get comfortable on a pillow. Menno and Abe went to the sofa, while Mammi sat in her rocker. Dawdi told Elsie to take the soft chair, and Dawdi pulled a chair from the table.

"Now," Dawdi said, leaning forward on his elbows. "Tell us what this is all about so we can all go home to dinner."

"We're already home, Felty," Mammi said, "and I'd like my dinner now."

Menno glanced at Andy, the one with the notebook. Whatever was to be said, he was the one to do the talking. Elsie tried for a calm expression on her face, even though she was in turns seething and crying on the inside. It wasn't Andy's fault that he reminded Elsie so much of his daughter Rose, with her pouty lips and devious eyes, but she couldn't help but wonder if Rose had something to do with this.

Andy cleared his throat and opened his notebook. "Is it true, Miss Stutzman, that you were fired from your school in Charm before you came to Bonduel?"

Elsie's throat constricted. "They told me they wanted to hire someone else for the new school year. I don't consider it being fired."

"Why didn't you tell us this when we hired you?" Menno said.

"I didn't think it was important." *Nae,* that wasn't exactly true. She hadn't wanted it to be important, but that's not the reason she'd failed to mention it to the school board. She had always been plainspoken. Why should she back down just because the school board had gotten their noses out of joint? She squared her shoulders. "I didn't want you to know because I was afraid you wouldn't hire me."

Andy seemed to take this as a personal insult. "Of course we wouldn't have hired you."

Elsie took a deep breath. The men of the school board weren't too old to learn a lesson, and she wasn't afraid to deliver it. She was a teacher, after all. "But you *should* have hired me, in the spirit of forgiveness."

Andy flared his nostrils, as if Elsie had a bad smell hanging about her. "We don't have to forgive anyone."

Menno and Abe glanced at each other, as if each was wondering if the other was going to correct Andy for saying such a thing.

Andy returned to his notes. "We understand that you lied to a parent and have been stealing school toilet paper for your own use. This is very troubling."

"I can answer that," Mammi said. "Elsie has never stolen a thing in her life, and no lie has ever crossed her lips."

Elsie winced for Mammi's sake, but she didn't regret for one minute lying to Alvin Schmucker. "I never stole the toilet paper, but I did lie to Alvin Schmucker. I was afraid he was going to beat his son, and I wanted to stop it."

Abe nodded to Menno.

Mammi gave Menno a pointed look. "You of all people should know what Alvin Schmucker is like."

Elsie smiled at her *mammi,* who didn't seem the least bit troubled that her granddaughter had told a lie. But how did the school board find out? Only Sam, Wally, Reuben, and Elsie knew about it.

"You turned your back when Wally Sensenig stole money from the other children."

Menno narrowed his eyes in Andy's direction. "Now, Andy, we already resolved that. No use bringing it up again."

Andy pursed his lips, more than a little put out that he wouldn't be allowed to beat Elsie over the head with that one again. He fingered the paper in his notebook. "I have a troubling report that you would not allow Wally Sensenig to go to the bathroom at school. Children should never be tortured like that."

Andy, Menno, and Abe stared at her with wide eyes, no doubt waiting for an explanation for such cruel behavior.

Mammi sighed. "Wally Sensenig can be a pill, but his *bruder* Sam is a wonderful-*gute* boy."

Dear Mammi. Didn't she know it was useless to argue? The school board was bent on firing her. She could see the conviction in their eyes. This little exercise of listing her shortcomings was only to make themselves feel better.

Elsie lifted her chin. It was plain that nothing she said or didn't say would change their minds. They hadn't come to discuss how school was working out or to make sure she was okay after the tornado. A tornado! — the single most traumatic event to happen at school in who-knew-how-many years, and they hadn't mentioned it. Not once.

She wished Sam were here. He wouldn't have even had to say anything. It simply would have been nice to have him sitting by her, lending her his strength, giving his support against the men who had set themselves up as her adversaries. Elsie didn't want to grovel, and she didn't need to defend herself. They were just wasting her time. She might as well stroll into her room and start packing.

She sat up straighter. "I don't need to explain myself every time I make a decision in my classroom."

That got their attention, if it hadn't been riveted to her before. She wasn't going to play their game. She'd rather be a base.

Andy hadn't finished. She hadn't expected him to be. "We heard reports that you were giving a certain boy special tutoring that none of the other children got, and you spent an inappropriate amount of time with a single young man as part of that tutoring, and that you spent some time alone in a barn with him."

Even if she'd wanted to reply, Elsie couldn't have. She was speechless. Rose Mast had been busy. Her *dat* probably had writer's cramp from all the information he'd had to write down in his notebook.

"Maizy Mischler got hurt playing softball," Menno said. "It's your responsibility to see that your students are safe, especially Maizy."

When Elsie didn't say anything, Andy searched his notes again. "The Christmas program was ruined because you can't control your students. What do you have to say to that?"

Elsie sat up straighter, even though she felt the weight of their condemnation pressing down on her. Their accusations were so unfair.

When she didn't reply, Andy pointed to something in his notebook highlighted in yellow marker. "Maybe you would be willing to explain your wanton behavior. We are troubled by reports we have heard that you have been kissing boys after school hours *in* the classroom."

"That can't be true," Mammi interjected. "Elsie won't even agree to let me match her with the right boy."

Elsie's blood turned to ice. There were only two people in the world who knew about the kissing. Elsie and Sam Sensenig, and *she* hadn't told anybody. What . . . what had Sam done? She clasped her hands together so no one would notice they were shaking and pasted a pleasant smile in her face, which was a small miracle, considering the big crack down the center of her heart. "Anything else?"

Andy seemed taken aback, as if he was expecting more from her on that subject. "*Vell,* there are many things. But we don't want to wear out our welcome."

Mammi rocked her chair back and forth and gave Andy a fake smile. He had worn out his welcome with her about three days ago. She glanced at Elsie and pressed her lips together. She had obviously decided that if Elsie was going to remain silent, then Mammi would do the same. She was always so supportive that way.

Andy closed his notebook and propped it lengthwise across his knees. "We were very troubled about what happened at school today."

The poor school board. They were very troubled about a great many things.

Menno leaned forward. "The children should not have been playing outside."

"You put them in danger," Andy said. "Some of the boys asked to go out, and you let them, even though a tornado was coming."

Was it her fault? How could she have known? She swallowed hard and reminded herself they were going to fire her anyway. She kept her mouth shut even as her heart plummeted to the floor.

Dawdi must have decided that since neither Elsie nor Mammi was making a peep, he'd have to speak up. "No one was hurt. And Wally Sensenig saved the little Mischler girl."

Andy pointed a finger in Dawdi's direction. "He wouldn't have had to save her if they'd all been inside. Wally's *bruder* Sam even said so. He told my Rose that the children should never have been outside."

The mention of Sam's name was like a blow to the head that left Elsie dizzy and disoriented. She wanted to adamantly insist that Sam would have never said such a thing. Unfortunately, he'd stood in this very kitchen and questioned why she let the children go out.

"Miss Stutzman should have protected the children. We discussed it earlier with some of the families."

Elsie's heart broke in two.

When they first met, Sam had threatened to get her fired. She simply hadn't realized to what lengths he would go to do it. Had he and Rose planned this from the beginning? Had everything he'd done, everything they'd ever shared, been a ruse?

She trembled at the thought. Could she really have been so blind?

She balled her hands into fists. *Nae.* She couldn't, she wouldn't believe that. She knew Sam. She loved Sam. He wouldn't behave so despicably, no matter how mad he was at her. He had loved her. Surely he had loved her once. *Ach,* she wanted to believe it so badly.

But maybe the tornado had been the last straw. Maybe he thought Elsie put his *bruders* in danger just by being around them. Maybe he thought she made Wally take unnecessary risks. Maybe he feared he couldn't protect his *bruders* from Elsie, that he had to choose between Elsie and safety. If that was true, he'd choose his family every time.

So. The tornado had made up Sam's mind for him. He'd given Rose the ammunition she needed, and she'd given it to her *fater.*

She wanted to run to her room, throw herself on her bed, and cry until she couldn't cry anymore — not because she was about to lose her job, but because she had just lost her heart. She didn't know anything could hurt this much. "Anything else?" Elsie said. The words choked her, but she forced herself to sound indifferent.

Andy gripped the edge of his notebook. "We have been repeatedly shocked and troubled by the disrespectful way you have been known to treat parents, students, and

492

the school board. A teacher should know when to keep silent in front of her elders."

It was more than Elsie could endure. "I know *gute* Amish girls are supposed to keep quiet, but I will not cower to anyone — not when I know I'm right and you're wrong. You require a teacher to discipline *die kinner,* teach arithmetic and English, monitor the well-being of two dozen children for eight hours a day, and yet be as timid and meek as a mouse. Why do you want a weakling teaching your children?"

Andy caught her words as if she'd been throwing rocks at him. "We do not want a weakling. We want someone compliant and dutiful. That is why we are replacing you immediately with my daughter Rose. She knows how a teacher should behave."

Rose Mast teaching school? The poor girl couldn't even do fractions.

Elsie held her breath. If she started laughing, she'd end up crying, and she refused to do either in front of Andy Mast. If Rose wanted to be the teacher that badly, Elsie would gladly step aside, and if Rose thought this would make Sam fall at her feet, she was welcome to try. He was more likely to come storming up the stairs to yell at her, and she was welcome to it. Elsie was through with Sam and his out-of-control temper.

She almost lost her composure when she thought of the children, but what did it matter? They'd barely remember her in a few weeks. They never needed to know how much she cared.

Mammi and Dawdi rose to their feet at the same time. *"Vell,"* Mammi said, "you can go now. I'm wonderful sorry you came."

Elsie cracked a smile at the look on Menno Kiem's face. No one expected such feistiness from Mammi.

The school board didn't need to be told twice. They stood in unison and marched to the door as if the house was on fire.

Mammi followed them. "Menno, tell Freeman I am working on a girl for him, but I have to find a granddaughter who will like his cleft chin. I'll let you know. And Abe, how is Edna doing after surgery?"

"Uh, fine," Abe stammered, obviously unsure of what to make of Mammi's sudden friendliness.

"I'll bring some soup next week."

"Okay."

Menno leaned his head back into the house. "I hope your head feels better, Miss Stutzman."

Elsie had absolutely nothing to say to that.

Mammi shut the door a little too forcefully. "Well," she said. "Well. Well. Andy Mast has a chip on his shoulder as big as a tree stump. I'm so angry, I could spit. But I'm not very *gute* at it."

Dawdi reached out and squeezed Elsie's hand. "I'm wonderful proud of how you told them what was what. Andy Mast got so mad he turned yellow."

Mammi huffed out a breath. "Abe was just embarrassed. He's never been able to stand up to Andy. They know there's no better teacher than you, Elsie. It's plain jealousy. That's what it is. Andy has wanted Rose to have that job for three years, but everybody knows she's as thick as a pile of manure."

This time Elsie did laugh. She laughed until her head throbbed and her back ached. Then she sank into a kitchen chair, covered her face, and sobbed.

She would never laugh again.

And the fried chicken was definitely soggy.

CHAPTER TWENTY-SEVEN

Sam was thoroughly ashamed of himself, and Elsie had to know immediately. Why did it take him so long to learn a lesson? How many times had he lost his temper and said something to Elsie that he didn't mean? How many times had he jumped to conclusions and stomped to the school, only to be put in his place by Elsie's *gute* sense?

He'd been wonderful shaken up last night, but there was no justification for what he'd said to her, even if he'd been so scared he hadn't been able to think straight. He'd been wrong. Again. When it came to Elsie, Sam had been wrong more than he'd been right, and he wouldn't blame her for refusing to speak to him ever again.

You should have kept them inside, he'd said, as if he was smart enough to know — as if he had been there. He didn't know anything, and he'd been a fool to say something so *hesslich,* ugly. He'd gone home to be with his *bruders* because he'd been frightened and angry and confused. Wally had nearly been killed. Sam had needed someone to blame, and Elsie was the easy target.

He was a *dumkoff,* pure and simple.

At about three this morning, he'd realized that if the children had been inside when the tornado hit, many of them would have been injured by the broken glass and other flying objects. It would have been worse had they stayed inside. Elsie probably hadn't realized it, but letting the children go outside probably saved them from many severe injuries.

And he had chastised her because she didn't know what tornado weather looked like.

She was never going to speak to him again.

Sam snapped the reins to get the horse to go a little faster. His three *bruders* and Reuben were in the back seat of the buggy, and Maggie and Mamm sat alongside him in the front. They had all volunteered to help clean up the classroom so it would be ready for school on Monday. Sam pulled into the school yard. Another buggy was already here, but it wasn't the open-air buggy Elsie usually drove. Maybe she'd brought her *mammi* and *dawdi* with her.

Sam parked the buggy next to Elsie's and set the brake. "Wally, take care of the horse, would you? Perry, can you bring in the cardboard?" He had to get in there and apologize to Elsie first thing. He wouldn't feel right until she knew what an idiot he was. *Vell,* she already knew what an idiot he was. He just hoped she wouldn't change her mind about loving him, because he loved her something wonderful and he'd never forgive himself if something he'd said made her question that for a minute.

He opened the door and bounded up the stairs, his heart aching like a taut rubber band. Rose, bundled in a knitted shawl, sat at Elsie's desk stacking papers into nice, neat piles. "What are you doing here?" he said. It sounded like an accusation, when it should have been a compliment. It was wonderful nice of Rose to come and help clean up the school, especially since she didn't like Elsie all that much.

She jumped to her feet and gave him a glowing, gushing, all-is-forgiven smile. "You came."

"Of course I came. I brought my whole family."

Her smile stretched all the way across her face. "*Ach,* Sam! I knew you would come. I just knew it. Miss Stutzman did her best to pit us against each other, but I knew you'd come around in the end."

Sam clenched his teeth. "I don't want to talk about Elsie."

To his surprise, she smiled even wider. "Neither do I, ever, ever again." She skipped from behind Elsie's desk and weaved between two rows of desks that had been shifted and upended in the wind. "I'm wonderful glad to see you. My *dat* is coming soon to measure the windows. I wanted to get a head start on things." She bent over and picked up two pieces of paper at her feet.

"It wonders me when Elsie will be here," Sam said. She should be the one to organize the papers and such. She knew where everything went, where Rose could only guess.

Rose made a sour face. "She won't come. She's petty like that."

Sam's *bruders,* Maggie, his *mamm,* and Reuben trudged up the stairs. Perry and Reuben each carried several collapsed cardboard boxes. Yesterday, Ben Hoover had covered the windows with garbage bags in case it rained, but the cardboard would be a better window covering until new windows came. They would make the classroom extra dark but would do better than plastic in

499

keeping out the cold. Sam righted one of the desks and directed Reuben and Perry to stack the cardboard on it.

Wally was still limping, but Sam hadn't heard one word of complaint from him since the tornado, so Sam didn't bring it up. Wally had done something truly amazing yesterday. The pain in his leg probably paled in comparison to the satisfaction he must be feeling for saving Maizy's life.

It was wrong to set oneself above others, but Sam had never been more proud in his whole life.

"The Hoovers are here," Danny said. "And Jethro Glick and the Bylers."

"I don't wonder but the whole school will turn out to help," Sam said. It was a testament to the love they had for Elsie and the sense of belonging they had to the school. They had been through something traumatic together. An experience like that tended to bond people to one another.

Rose beamed. "I'm humbled that they would do this for me. And honored. It's wonderful nice."

Rose thought the world rotated around her. Just because she had been the first to arrive didn't mean anyone was coming specifically to help her.

Sam built a fire in the stove, then set to

work measuring the windows. Rose had said her *dat* was going to do it, but he wanted to finish measuring so the windows could be covered as soon as possible. The room was freezing cold. Simon Mischler soon arrived, and he and Wally covered each window after Sam measured it.

Mamm was usually withdrawn in a group, but Sam was pleased to see that she set to work assigning people to tasks in the school and outside. To keep them from stepping on the broken glass, younger children were sent to the playground to pick up trash and other debris. Toby Byler and his crew found four mitts, two more straw hats, and an unbroken chicken egg. They also picked up seven bags of trash and a pair of trousers that must have blown off someone's clothesline.

Rose announced that she was in charge of rehanging all the leaves on the paper tree, though Serena Hoover had to completely reconstruct the tree before Rose could hang anything. Other parents and children picked up papers and books, straightened pictures, cleaned the chalkboard, and swept and swept and swept. Five *fraas* had brought their brooms and mops. They pushed the desks out from the center of the room, swept up the glass and dirt, and mopped.

Arie Burkholder insisted they mop three times. Glass had a way of slipping into crevices and cracks, and she wanted to be triple sure they got it all.

"You're all so very nice to come and help me," Rose said more than once. Sam did his best not to roll his eyes.

Sam finished measuring and Wally and Simon Mischler covered the rest of the windows, and still Elsie hadn't come. Sam frowned. It wasn't like Elsie to leave the work for others to do, especially at her own school. Where was she? His heart twisted at the possibility that she had been hurt worse than Sam had realized last night. Maybe she was in the hospital with a concussion or something.

He slid the measuring tape into his small toolbox and picked the toolbox off the floor so Serena Hoover could mop under it. "Has anybody seen Miss Stutzman yet?" he said, loud enough so everyone in the classroom could hear him.

There was a lot of head shaking and a few *"naes."* Sam's concern grew. He should go find her.

"I told you, Sam. She's not coming," Rose said, as she casually rolled a piece of tape in her fingers.

She was so sure of herself. "How do you know?"

Rose glanced from one face to another. "Well, you know." She paused as a shadow of doubt passed over her features. "Doesn't everybody know? I . . . thought everybody knew."

"What don't we know?" Benjamin Hoover asked.

Rose pulled some tape from the dispenser, but she pulled too hard and got a foot-long piece. She wadded it up into a ball as she forced the corners of her mouth into an uncomfortable smile. "It had to be done, didn't it, Sam?"

Sam went mute. What was she trying to pull him into?

The entire room seemed to freeze, half of the eyes turned to Rose, half turned to Sam.

It was obvious Rose hadn't been expecting this reaction. She sort of smiled and whimpered at the same time. "We were all so upset yesterday. Sam and I agreed that Miss Stutzman should not have let *die kinner* out to recess when a tornado was coming. She was *negligee* in her duties."

Did she mean *negligent*?

Sam's head started pounding right at the base of his skull. Had Rose said something cruel to Elsie? Had she used Sam's name to justify herself?

"How could she know a storm was coming?" Benjamin Hoover asked. There was a murmur of assent around the room.

Arie thudded her mop against the floor. "She saved everybody."

"Did you see the big cut on her head?" another *mater* said. "She wasn't negligent. I think she was very brave."

"Me too."

Rose's smile drooped as she realized that not everyone agreed with her. In fact, she'd be hard-pressed to find anyone who did. "Well . . . me and Sam . . . my *dat* . . . the school board met yesterday and decided that Miss Stutzman will no longer be teaching at Mapleview School."

It felt as if someone had punched Sam in the gut.

More murmuring from the parents. Wally gaped at Sam as if Sam had pulled Wally's other leg off. Sam shook his head at Wally. No matter what he had said to Rose yesterday, this was not his fault. At least he hoped it wasn't. Could one careless word really have set such a disaster in motion? He was going to be sick.

"They fired Miss Stutzman?" Reuben said, not bothering to keep his voice down around his elders.

"They should have consulted with the parents first," Simon Mischler said. "My Maizy won't go to school if Miss Stutzman isn't the teacher."

"Good news!" Rose spread her arms wide and tried to pretend her announcement hadn't gone horribly wrong. "I am going to be the new teacher." She had the nerve to reach out and tousle Wally's hair. Wally yanked away from her.

Sam wasn't sure how Rose had expected people to react, but she probably hadn't expected what she got. Freeman Zook and Adam Byler started yelling at no one in particular, and the *fraas* put their heads together and whispered.

Wally strode to Sam. Even with his limp, he looked as if he were on the attack. "What did you do?"

"I didn't do anything."

"You never liked Miss Stutzman. You got her fired."

Sam couldn't swallow. He could barely breathe. "I didn't. You have to believe me."

Rose's eyes flashed like a wildcat cornered in a barn. "She kissed someone in this classroom," she shrieked. "Sam knows. We had to tell the school board."

Sam wanted to shrink into a little ball. He'd been the one who'd kissed Elsie. Had he been the one to get her fired because of it?

"You're making that up," Benjamin Hoover said, and his eyes were on Sam, not Rose.

Simon Mischler folded his arms across his chest. "It's a sin to gossip."

The noise in the classroom rose to a dull roar. No one was happy about this, and they were all looking at Sam as if he'd betrayed them.

Wally especially. "You told the school board that Miss Stutzman kissed somebody?"

"*Nae,* Wally."

Wally leaned close and lowered his voice. "You're the one who kissed her. You wanted her to get in trouble."

Sam hesitated a second too long. He *had* been the one to kiss her. This whole thing was his fault. "Let me explain."

Wally scowled. "You always hated her. You always hated me, never wanted me to do anything but play video games." He threw the trash in his hand to the floor. "I hate you. I'll hate you forever."

He turned and hobbled quickly down the stairs. Sam had no choice but to follow him. "Wally, wait." Wally ran out the door and started for home on foot. It took about three seconds for Sam to catch up with him. "Wally, stop and let me explain."

Wally was having none of it, so Sam grabbed his collar and wrenched him backward. Wally toppled to the ground. Sam hadn't meant to pull that hard, but now that his *bruder* was in a position to listen, he saw no need to let him up. He pressed his palm to Wally's chest and held him fast. Wally struggled and carried on, kicking his legs, both fake and real, and waving his hands like a drowning man, but Sam was too strong. "Listen to me," he yelled, putting more pressure on Wally's chest. "Stop it, and listen to me."

Wally finally gave up, probably because he could see he was getting nowhere and the longer he laid there, the wetter his coat got. "Let go of me," he said weakly. Tears rolled out of his eyes and into his ears.

"Wally," Sam said. "I am the one who kissed Elsie, but if I had known that it was going to get her in trouble, I never would have done it." At least he wouldn't have done it at the school.

"Then why did you tell Rose?"

"I didn't. Remember that day Reuben's *dat* hit him? Rose brought *yummasetti* and then she walked over to the school to check on me. She saw us kissing. I didn't tell her anything."

Wally wiped a tear from the corner of his eye. "She told us she was going to the school."

"I'm not lying to you."

"What about that other thing you said about Elsie? That she shouldn't have let us go outside yesterday?"

Sam heaved out a breath to try to get rid of the ache in his chest. "I was scared, and I said it without really thinking. I shouldn't have said it."

"She was just being nice. We wanted to play softball." He let out a shuddering breath. "I wanted to play softball. She was trying to make me happy."

Sam's heart just about broke. "It wasn't your fault, Wally."

"We just wanted to go outside. I used to hate her, but I didn't want her to get fired."

Sam lifted his hand from Wally's chest and pulled him to his feet. "If you had stayed in the classroom, what do you think would have happened?"

Wally thought about that for a minute. "Glass blew everywhere. Somebody could have lost an eye or something."

"*Jah.* It was better you were outside, even though you and Maizy almost blew away." Sam stifled a shudder. *Gotte* had been watching out for them.

Wally gave Sam a hard shove. "You've got to go get her, Sam. You've got to make her come back."

"She didn't leave. The school board fired her. She can't come back without their permission."

"She's the best teacher I ever had," Wally said. "You've got to make them. Go talk to the school board and make them bring her back."

"It'll take more than me to get Elsie back." Sam frowned. He'd already done so much damage already. "Are you willing to help?"

"What do you want me to do?"

"Go back in there and tell everyone that I'm calling a meeting with the school board at the school tonight at six o'clock. Then you and Reuben go to all the families who aren't here and tell them what's happened and invite them to the meeting."

Wally shook his head. "You can't call a meeting. You're too young. They don't respect you." Sometimes, Wally was smarter than Sam.

"Then ask Simon Mischler to call a meeting. You saved his daughter's life."

"*Gute* idea," Wally said. "What are you going to do?"

"I'm going to find Elsie."

A grin formed on Wally's lips. "Do you love her?"

Sam grabbed a handful of Wally's collar and pulled him close. "Even more than I love you, and I do love you, with all my heart."

Tears pooled in Wally's eyes, but he quickly sniffed them away. "*Vell, gute.* She deserves it." Wally stuffed his hands into his pockets and turned to go back into the school. "Sam and Elsie sitting in a tree. K-I-S-S-I-N-G," he recited in a high-pitched voice.

Elsie deserved every *gute* thing. Sam, on the other hand, didn't even deserve Elsie, but Lord willing, she'd take him anyway.

And maybe she'd agree to do some K-I-S-S-I-N-G.

CHAPTER TWENTY-EIGHT

Elsie sat in the haymow, playing with the puppies and feeling sorry for herself. In a single day she'd lost her composure, her job, and Sam Sensenig. Her heart had broken into so many pieces, she didn't think she'd ever be able to put it back together again.

A tear rolled down her cheek and plopped onto one of the wood slats. She swiped at the moisture on her face. She wasn't going to wallow in self-pity any longer. She couldn't abide wallowing. Of course, such a resolution was easier made than done, especially since Sam Sensenig was too *wunderbarr* for words, and she had lost him because she hadn't known what tornado weather looked like.

On Saturday morning, before the rooster was even awake, a driver had picked up Elsie and taken her to Greenwood. Mammi was beside herself because Elsie wouldn't stay long enough to meet the nice young man who was her perfect match, but Elsie couldn't stand to be in Bonduel one more minute. They had chosen Rose Mast over Elsie Stutzman, and the humiliation stung like a wasp.

Elsie had considered going back to Charm, but there was nothing for her there but Wyman Wagler and Onkel Peter's spare bedroom. She couldn't impose on her relatives that way, especially when she didn't even have a job. Besides, Greenwood was only a two-hour drive from Huckleberry Hill. She had arrived before breakfast.

After the dust had settled and she had told her family the whole pitiful story, her *bruder* Aaron had agreed to let her stay at his house. Aaron was a twenty-nine-year-old bachelor who grew soybeans and feed corn on a hundred acres. Aaron didn't put up with nonsense from anyone, and he wasn't inclined to get sentimental about anything, not even newborn *buplies* or weddings. That was why Elsie had chosen to stay with him instead of her parents. Mamm had clucked and fussed over Elsie something wonderful, and Elsie couldn't stand the fussing. To Aaron, a broken heart was like a blister — just stab a needle in it, drain the pus, and get on with your life. Aaron didn't care that she had a broken heart and didn't treat her like an invalid because of it. She wouldn't be allowed to wallow at Aaron's house. His was just the unsympathetic shoulder she needed.

Elsie picked up a fuzzy black puppy and snuggled it against her cheek. How could anything be so soft? It wriggled and whined in her hands until she set it down into the safety of its mother's warmth.

"How many puppies?" Aaron asked from the floor below. She couldn't see him from where she sat, but she could hear him putting down fresh straw in the stalls.

"*Cum* and see."

"Not interested. How many?"

Elsie smiled to herself. Aaron did not have a tender bone in his whole body. "Four. All black as coal."

"*Gute.* Eight puppies are hard to give away. Four won't take but an hour."

"Don't you want to keep one for yourself, Aaron? They are the most adorable things you have ever seen."

"Nah. Puppies grow up to be dogs, and I already have two fine dogs."

Elsie couldn't resist teasing him. "Three dogs is that much more love to spread around."

"Why would I want that?"

She giggled and ran her fingers down one

of the puppies' silky backs. Maybe she'd keep one of Aaron's puppies. She needed all the love she could get.

Someone clomped loudly into the barn. Elsie couldn't see him, but she could tell he wore a sturdy pair of boots. "Are you Aaron Stutzman?"

Elsie caught her breath, wrapped her arms around her knees, and tried to make herself smaller. She'd know that petulant, I'm-so-mad-I-could-spit tone anywhere. What was Sam doing here, and why did she care so much? Her heart was likely to bounce out of her chest, it was beating so hard.

She clamped her eyes shut. It didn't matter how mad he was or what he wanted to lecture her about. She would not let Sam intimidate her.

"*Jah.* I'm Aaron."

"I'm looking for your sister Elsie."

"Why?" Aaron said, sounding more than a little suspicious. *Gute.* He was right to be wary of Sam Sensenig. Sam wasn't one to keep his temper.

"Because I need to talk to her."

"Who are you?"

"My name is Sam Sensenig. I need to talk to your sister immediately."

Elsie heard Aaron stab his pitchfork into a bale of hay. "Maybe she doesn't want to talk to you."

Denki, Aaron! What a *gute bruder* he was, keeping pests and ornery boys away from his baby sister.

She heard a shuffling of feet. "Just tell me where she is, and I'll leave you to your chores. I need to see her."

"Elsie says you yelled at her."

Jah, he had, and she wouldn't be yelled at again. She wasn't the teacher anymore. He had no power over her. Her throat got tight. *Ach.* He had too much power over her. She would love him and no one else until the day she died.

"Look, Aaron, I've been through the wringer these past three days. I stormed up Huckleberry Hill only to find out Elsie had left town, but I couldn't follow her because I had to go to the school board meeting on Saturday night. All I could do on the Sabbath was worry about her. I didn't sleep but three hours last night. And then the minute I could manage it, I found a driver to bring me here this morning. Do you know how hard it is to find a driver on Monday morning?"

"I really don't care." Elsie smiled smugly to herself. Sam deserved every bit of frustration he got.

"We drove around for an hour trying to

find your house because all the direction your *mamm* could give was that you live in a white house three miles south. Do you think I'm in any kind of mood to be lectured by you?"

"I don't care what kind of mood you're in," Aaron said. "You made my sister cry, and if you think I'm going to let you get within a mile of her, you're wrong."

Elsie's heart swelled. Aaron cared more than he let on. Oh, how she loved her *bruder*.

Sam's voice dropped to almost a whisper. "I made her cry?"

"You kissed her and then told the school board. No boy should treat a girl that way."

"Angry Sam" was back. "She told you that?"

"She told me everything. How you blamed her for the storm. How you yelled at her when she was only trying to help your *bruder*."

Sam was breathing heavily. For sure and certain he'd start throwing hay bales any minute now. "I was angry, *deerich* and angry. She was so brave during the tornado. She saved those children. I didn't mean what I said about the storm."

"Then why did you say it?"

"Because I was frightened out of my mind," Sam yelled. "Haven't you ever said

516

something you didn't mean?"

"*Nae.* I always say exactly what I mean."

"Well, I did. I was mean and *doppick,* and that's why I need to talk to her. I have to tell her I'm sorry." Sam never had learned that lesson about catching more flies with honey than vinegar. He shouldn't yell at Aaron if he actually wanted to win her brother's cooperation. "Let me talk to her."

Aaron, on the other hand, remained so calm, he could have tied up a hammock and taken a nap. "She didn't deserve to be fired. Elsie is the best teacher those children will ever have."

"I know it. Don't you think I know it?" She could hear more movement from Sam. Maybe he was running his fingers through that beautiful curly hair of his, or putting her *bruder* in a choke hold.

"If you feel so bad, why did you tell the school board to fire her?"

"I didn't," Sam shouted, proving that he truly was fearless, to dare provoke a protective brother with a handy pitchfork. "Rose saw me kiss Elsie. Rose told her *dat.* It wasn't me."

Elsie swallowed the sob that nearly escaped her throat. Sam hadn't told? Sam hadn't told! Of course he hadn't. She knew him better than that. She should have had more faith in him.

"I don't approve of you kissing my sister."

"I don't care if you approve or not."

"She still lost her job over it," Aaron said.

"That's why I've got to talk to her. The parents called a meeting. The school was packed clear down the stairs. Even some *fraas* spoke up, though Andy Mast didn't like it. He said women had to keep silent, and Simon stood right up and said that rule was only for church. There was a big argument, and they threatened to vote out the whole school board unless they brought Elsie back. That's what I have to tell her. We want her back. *Die kinner* need her. Wally will never talk to me again if I don't come home with her. I don't even care if she thinks she's in love with Wyman Wagler and Wagman Wyler or whatever his name is. I need her." His voice faltered. "I'm nothing without her."

How could she possibly hold this much happiness in? The dam broke, and tears flowed down Elsie's face. They wanted her back. More importantly, Sam wanted her back. It was almost too good to be true.

"You love my sister?"

"Of course I love her," Sam snapped. "More than anything, and if you don't let me talk to her, I'll camp out on your front lawn until your grass dies."

The straw rustled as Aaron picked up his pitchfork. "Have you heard enough, Elsie?" he called.

"I suppose I have." Elsie stood up so she could see Aaron and Sam down below.

Sam's mouth fell open — so wide she could have driven a buggy down his throat. His surprise turned into a smile, a bright, fresh-as-springtime, I-love-Elsie smile. Not wasting another minute, he climbed the steep steps to the haymow in his clunky boots, took Elsie in his arms, and kissed her like a starving man.

Trembling with happiness, Elsie slid her arms around his neck and kissed him back. "I love you, Sam."

"I love you right back," he said between kisses.

"Sam Sensenig," Aaron called. "I don't approve of you kissing my *schwester.* Stop it this minute."

CHAPTER TWENTY-NINE

Elsie made her bed, giving her sheets hospital corners like her *mater* had taught her. Elsie loved Saturdays. She didn't have to rush around to get ready for school, and she had a chance to help Mammi around the house. Elsie mopped the floor on Saturdays, and cleaned the bathrooms. A woman Mammi's age shouldn't be mopping.

Elsie ran the dust rag over the top of her dresser and the windowsills. It was making down hard out there. If the rain let up, she'd wash the windows this afternoon.

She'd been back in Bonduel for two weeks, and spring had finally made an entrance. The forsythia bushes seemed afire, with their magnificent yellow blooms, and the red tulips that lined Mammi's flower beds were just beginning to open their heads.

The children had missed only one day of school while Elsie had been away, but they welcomed her back that next Tuesday as if she'd been gone for a whole year. Wally had brought a basket of apples on her first day back, and Maizy Mischler had given Elsie a picture she'd painted with watercolors. It was a picture of Maizy, Elsie, and Wally holding hands and smiling. It didn't take an artist to see that the three of them were very happy.

The weather had warmed up enough for them to play softball every day, except when it rained. Wally hit a home run almost every time. She was going to have to start really pitching to him.

Even though Rose had never tried to be her friend, Elsie felt awful sorry for her. Rose had been completely humiliated by what had happened with the school board. Prissy had told Danny that Rose had stayed in her room for a whole week and had only come out for her birthday party, to which Elsie and Sam had not been invited.

The *gute* news was that Freeman Kiem, Menno's son, had taken an interest in Rose very soon after all the embarrassment, and Rose was attending gatherings and *singeons* again, telling anyone who would listen how badly she'd been used by Elsie and Sam. Elsie didn't mind if Rose spread gossip. The people who knew Elsie and Sam never thought much of it.

Elsie had started tutoring Wally again, which meant she got to see Sam at least three days a week. She would eat dinner with the family and then play games or visit with Sam for hours before going home. She found herself wishing she could tutor Wally every day just for the thrill of being with his handsome *bruder.*

There was no getting around it. She loved Sam Sensenig to the moon and back. She wasn't a scientist, but she knew it was a really long way.

Mammi opened Elsie's door and stuck her head into the room. Her eyes sparkled like a thousand stars on a clear night. She was up to something, no doubt about it. "Elsie, dear. The day has finally come. The boy I want to match you with has agreed to meet you. He seems very excited about it."

Elsie gave Mammi a half-hearted smile. She should have told her about Sam weeks ago. "Mammi, I appreciate it very much, but there's something I need to tell you."

"Can it wait, dear? It's taken me so long to get you two together that I'm afraid we'll lose him if we make him wait."

Elsie swallowed hard. "Make him wait?"

"*Jah.* He's at the front door, very eager to meet you. He wants to take you for a buggy ride. Doesn't that sound fun, in the rain?"

Oh, *sis yuscht!* The day she'd been dreading had finally arrived. Elsie considered closing the door on her *mammi* and climbing out the window, but it would only hurt Mammi's feelings and make everything worse in the end. All she could do was go on that buggy ride and tell Mammi's boy that she wasn't interested. It would be the shortest buggy ride ever. She hated to hurt anyone's feelings, but it had to be done. Mammi had backed her into a corner, and she was stuck.

Mammi misunderstood her hesitation. "Now, Elsie, don't worry about the dress. You look beautiful."

Elsie looked down at what she was wearing — a gray smock that had seen many laundry days. It was her ugliest dress, the one she did chores in. Perfect. If this boy didn't like the dress, maybe he wouldn't like her. Being plain had its advantages.

She smoothed her hand down the dress. "Okay, Mammi. If you say so." She feigned a little disappointment, as if she was sorry she wasn't wearing a better dress. Mammi had to believe that she was at least trying.

"*Cum,* dear," Mammi said. "He's waiting."

Mustn't keep him waiting. Elsie slipped

into her shoes and trudged into the great room as if she had a meeting with the school board. Dawdi sat in his recliner reading the paper. A tall figure filled the doorway. Elsie gasped as her heart flipped over itself.

Sam Sensenig stood on the porch holding a fistful of wildflowers and smiling with his whole face. How long had he known, and why hadn't he told her? He had no business grinning like that. To think of the months and the grief she'd spent avoiding him!

Mammi clasped her hands together in front of her, probably saying a silent prayer that Elsie wouldn't back out at the last minute. "Elsie, this is Sam Sensenig. The school board sent Sam up here to our house to find you the day after the tornado."

"That's nice," Elsie said.

"Sam, this is my granddaughter Elsie."

"*Hallo,* Elsie," Sam said, a private joke tugging at his lips. "I'm glad you agreed to meet me, even though you didn't want to."

Mammi laughed nervously. "Now what makes you think that Elsie didn't want to meet you? She's thrilled. Aren't you, Elsie?"

Elsie stepped in front of Mammi and gave Sam the stinkiest of stink eyes that had ever been. He lowered his gaze, but she could still hear the soft chuckle coming from his throat. She had half a mind to stick her nose in the air and tell Sam he was too homely to date, but she was going to burst into laughter herself at any moment, so she kept her mouth shut, took his flowers, and gave his arm a pinch. She would have pinched his ear, but Mammi would have noticed.

"Ouch," he said, rubbing his arm and taking a few steps away from her.

A giggle tripped from her lips. She loved him too much to be mad.

Mammi was not just a *gute* matchmaker. She was the master. Elsie shouldn't have questioned her judgment. As soon as she got home, she was going to apologize for doubting.

Elsie handed Mammi the flowers. "Would you mind putting these in some water?"

It was plain that Mammi would have done anything to help Elsie get in that buggy sooner. "Of course not, dear. You go enjoy yourself."

Sam cleared his throat — probably to keep from laughing out loud. "Before we go on our exciting buggy ride, I have something to say." He reached out and took Elsie's hand, then slowly got down on one knee.

Mammi gasped.

Elsie couldn't catch her breath. She thought she might possibly, probably faint.

Sam flashed that beautiful, irritating, irresistible smile she loved so much. "I don't have a lot to offer you, Elsie, but I'm a hard worker, and there's no one who will ever love you more than I do. I know we just met, but will you marry me?"

Elsie giggled even as the tears ran down her face. "Yes, Sam. Nothing would make me happier."

Dawdi slowly lowered the paper he was reading as if he wasn't quite sure he'd just heard what he thought he heard.

With the most adorable look of shock on her face, Mammi clutched her bosom and swayed back and forth as if she might topple over. Elsie yanked away from Sam's grasp and led Mammi to the nearest kitchen chair. Dawdi got up from his recliner as fast as he could and took one of Mammi's arms. "Are you all right?"

"That's the fastest match I ever made," she said breathlessly. "I never knew I had it in me."

Sam smiled at Elsie as if she was both his heaven and his earth. Her heart skipped about five beats. "I'd really like to take you on that buggy ride now," he said.

Elsie put on her jacket, grabbed an umbrella from the hook, and gave Mammi a peck on the cheek. "I love you, Mammi."

"I love you, dear," Mammi said, still a

little dazed.

"Will you be okay if I go for a ride with Sam?"

Mammi nodded. "Of course. Of course. You should get to know each other before the wedding."

Elsie turned and smiled at Sam. He had no idea how happy he'd just made her.

As soon as she got in that buggy, she was going to kiss him.

And then pinch his ear.

ABOUT THE AUTHOR

Jennifer Beckstrand is the RITA nominated and award-winning author of the Matchmakers of Huckleberry Hill series. She loves writing about the plain Amish life and the antics of Anna and Felty Helmuth. She and her husband have been married for thirty-one years, and she has four daughters, two sons, and four adorable grandchildren, whom she spoils rotten. Readers can visit her website at www.jenniferbeckstrand.com.